ON THE TRAIL OF A KILLER

"So what do we have?" Adam walked into the conference room M.K. had commandeered as her own the day after Tiffany Faulk's murder.

"What have we got? Nothing. That's why I thought we needed to talk."

"That isn't true. You've worked hard for days and we've got a list of possible suspects now, right? So let's go over them."

"We've got Patrick Purnell, the security guy. He found Peter Wright's body."

"Who else?"

"Buddy Caruso.  , pro-fessor of biology. re all either presently tak ne of his classes in the la n on the table. "I feel like ws here, with no physical evidence to go on. No witnesses, no forensics that will help us . . ."

"It's how we do it in these situations, M.K. You heard Crackhow yesterday morning. He warned you these serial killer cases can take years."

"We haven't got years!" She slapped down the pen and leaned forward, pressing her hands to the table to move closer to him. "Adam, this guy's on a hot streak. He's going to kill again and you know it . . ."

Books by Hunter Morgan

THE OTHER TWIN

SHE'LL NEVER TELL

SHE'LL NEVER KNOW

SHE'LL NEVER LIVE

WHAT SHE CAN'T SEE

Published by Kensington Publishing Corporation

WHAT SHE CAN'T SEE

Hunter Morgan

ZEBRA BOOKS
KENSINGTON PUBLISHING CORP.
http://www.kensingtonbooks.com

ZEBRA BOOKS are published by

Kensington Publishing Corp.
850 Third Avenue
New York, NY 10022

All Kensington titles, imprints and distributed lines are available at special quantity discounts for bulk purchases for sales promotion, premiums, fund-raising, educational or institutional use.

Special book excerpts or customized printing can also be created to fit specific needs. For details, write or phone the office of the Kensington Special Sales Manager: Kensington Publishing Corp., 850 Third Avenue, New York, NY 10022. Attn. Special Sales Department. Phone: 1-800-221-2647.

Zebra and the Z logo Reg. U.S. Pat. & TM Off.

First Printing: May 2005
10 9 8 7 6 5 4 3 2 1

Printed in the United States of America

Prologue

Drew ripped into the China Garden parking lot, hit his brakes hard, and slid into a parking space marked HANDI-CAPPED PARKING ONLY. "Okay, cough it up if you're eating." He threw his arm over the seat and opened his hand. "I bought the case."

His best buddy and a fellow frat brother, Pete, was sitting next to him and slapped an empty beer bottle into his hand. The two other guys from the Delta Chi house in the backseat broke up laughing.

Drew glanced in the rearview mirror, tossing the empty at Pete's sneakers. "Come on, you guys. I'm serious. I'm not paying. You want to eat, you flash the cash."

All three guys pushed warm bills into his hand, and Drew climbed out of the car, breathing in the hot, humid night air. "Whoa." He leaned against the Jeep, catching himself as the pavement beneath him tilted. He had a seriously decent beer buzz going.

"Easy there," one of the stooges in the backseat called. Someone laughed.

Drew adjusted the brim of his green Chesapeake Bay College ballcap and slammed the front driver's-side door of the Jeep as he slipped the money into the front pocket of his cargo shorts. The fresh air sobered him up a little, and he headed across the parking lot toward the blinking neon chopsticks in the window.

The place was mad crazy inside; most of the tables were occupied by students returning for the fall semester at Chesapeake Bay. Classes started in two days, so students were out, getting a head start on their mega-partying before reading assignments, research papers, and labs got in the way. There were people from the town, too. Just regular types: a campus security guy, a couple of bluehairs, a motorcycle dude and this tongue-pierced, big-titty biker chick.

"Drew." A frat brother sitting at one of the tables offered a hand.

"Kyle." Drew pumped it, turning around to talk to him, backing up toward the take-out counter. "We're headed over to Fedder Park to have a few brewskies. You in?"

Kyle lifted a dark eyebrow, taking the eyebrow ring with it. "Looks like you already had a few." He laughed. "Nah, can't." He eyed the fifty-something couple across the table from him.

Rent's still in town. What a drag, Drew thought. Good thing the senator and his lovely new wife were too busy to bring him to school. He'd just thrown his shit in the back of the Jeep, taken the three hundred dollars his father had left on the dining room table and another sixty-two-fifty he'd found in the housekeeper's petty-cash cookie jar, and headed out. "Catch you back at the house later, maybe," he said, still backing up. His stomach rumbled. He didn't feel quite as good as he had, but f-o-o-d-o would fix that.

Kyle turned away just as Drew backed into some pimple-faced jerk carrying a tray of egg-drop soup and tea. The bowls and teapot clattered to the stained green-carpeted floor, throwing hot broth and egg slime across Drew's bare arm and down his t-shirt. "Hey, faggot," he said, giving the gook waiter a push. He recognized the four-eyed jerk from his biology class last semester.

"So solly. My apology," the waiter groaned, falling to one knee to scoop up the bowls. Yellow egg goop ran in rivulets down his white apron.

Drew guessed this wasn't the first time the fairy had had egg-drop soup down the front of him. One of the waitresses started hollering in Chinese and came out from behind the counter, waving handfuls of paper towels.

"Watch where you're going next time, will you?" Drew spun around, looking at his arm and the egg shit running down it. "Excuse me," he said, pushing through the line of people waiting for their takeout. They were mostly business people from town—a guy in khakis and a flowered shirt, a woman in a suit, another guy in khakis, a professor from the college, and a mother with a whining kid in her arms. "Excuse me. I'm not trying to butt, just get some napkins." Someone stepped back to let him pass. He grabbed a handful of white napkins adorned with red chopsticks and wiped off his arm, stepping back into his place in line.

At the counter a few minutes later, Drew tossed the dirty napkins in the wastebasket and picked up the order. "Tell your boss they ought to get rid of that moron waiting on tables."

The slanty-eyed woman at the cash register just smiled, bobbing her head, and handed him his change. Tweedle Dee and Tweedle Dum in the backseat of the Jeep had given him too much money. Drew pocketed the extra five.

In the parking lot, he jumped into the Jeep, handing the bags back. "Don't open it until we get there," he ordered, starting the engine and throwing the shift into reverse. "I don't want that shit smelling up the car."

Out of the corner of his eye, Drew caught Pete wrinkling his nose and pulling back. "Smells like you've already been sampling."

Drew popped the Jeep into drive and squealed out of the parking lot, pulling a nice fishtail under the street lamp. "This fag waiter spilled soup all over me. Should sue. Make a fortune so I don't have to *get an education*." He mimicked the senator, laughing because he did it so well.

"Maybe he likes you, Drew," Tweedle Dum said.

Tweedle Dee cackled.

They sped out of town, making a left onto Old Marlboro Road, a back way into the state park that officially closed at dusk. It was one of the Kappa Gamma guys' favorite hangouts. On weekends they played on the Frisbee golf course there, nights it was a secluded place to party. Not that they couldn't party at the frat house, but a change of scenery was always nice.

Drew clicked on his high beams. Old Marlboro was a county road that twisted along the bay, through the pine trees and big soybean and cornfields. It had a couple of seriously sharp curves. Last year a bunch of girls from the campus had run off the same road; one had been in a coma for like a week or something. The road made a sharp bend to the right and the back tires squealed as he maneuvered through it.

"Hey, man, you got to change that CD," one of the guys in the back called. "I'm sick of this old Pink Floyd crap."

Drew punched the "eject" button and when the CD didn't immediately pop out, he slammed the CD player with his fist. "Piece of shit," he muttered, hitting the interior light switch overhead.

"I thought the senator was going to get you a new stereo."

"You want to walk home?" Drew glanced at Pete in the dim light, giving the CD player another smack. "Because if you—"

"Look out!"

Drew heard one of the guys in the backseat call out. He looked up in time to see that he was traveling too fast to negotiate the turn. He didn't even have time to get his other hand on the wheel. The tires screeched beneath them and the smell of rubber and shrimp chow mein filled his nostrils. The red Jeep his father had given him for high-school graduation seemed almost to be flying. It happened so fast, and yet time seemed to drag . . . snag. It took forever for the car to careen off the road and there wasn't a damned thing Drew was going to be able to do to stop it.

There was a slight bump as one of the front tires hit a drainage ditch, and at the same time he heard a big pop and something white flew up in front of him, slamming him backward into the seat. Suddenly shit was flying all over: beer bottles, the Chinese takeout bags and cartons, CDs. The next thing he knew, he was upside down. But the car was still rolling. He was upright, then upside down, and then upright again before the car finally slammed down on all four wheels.

For a second Drew couldn't move. Pete moaned in the seat beside him, and he turned his head slowly to look at him. For some reason the interior light was on. Drew could see Pete was leaning forward, caught in the seat belt, a big gash across his forehead and down his ear. His earlobe was hanging funny. Drew didn't remember hearing glass shatter but it was everywhere, all crackly and sticky.

He leaned back in his seat, feeling like he was going to be sick. His chest hurt like hell where he had made contact with the seat belt when he'd been thrown forward; he stared at the white fabric draped over the wheel. It took a minute for it to register that it was the airbag.

Something smelled awful, something vaguely familiar. "Jud? Derrick?" he called. He tried to turn his head to look into the backseat but his neck hurt like hell. He was surprised to find that his ballcap was still on his head and he adjusted the brim, pulling it down farther on his head.

There was no answer from the back.

"Shit," Drew whispered. "Shit." He lowered his right arm that hurt, too, and pressed his thumb on the seat belt release. It wouldn't give.

He looked up to see smoke pouring from under the hood. One headlight was still on, illuminating the soybean field they'd plowed through. Somehow the car had ended up facing the way they'd come. Shit, had they somehow flipped over sideways, then end to end, or had the car spun? He vaguely remembered a pole coming at them. Had they hit that, too?

Pete moaned again, and Drew looked over at his friend. The head cut was really bleeding . . . and that smell. He *knew* that smell.

For some reason he thought about mowing the lawn. He'd always hated doing it and had been glad when the senator had finally started hiring someone. It wasn't the smell of fresh grass in the car, though. It was . . . gasoline.

"Shit," Drew muttered again, his chest fluttering with fear. He clicked the seat belt latch over and over again. "Pete, Jud, Derrick. Come on guys, you got to wake up. We got to get out of here."

There was a flash of headlights in the darkness. Drew stared at the bloody dashboard Pete must have slammed into; no airbag on his side. "It . . . it's okay, man." He squeezed his buddy's arm and wiped at his eyes that were watering. "Someone's coming, Pete. Guys. We'll get some help."

Drew turned his head to look out through his door. The glass was gone from it, too. He watched as a figure came toward him through the darkness from the car parked up on the road. A beam of light appeared. A flashlight. "Man, thank God," he hollered out. "My buddies are unconscious, and I can't get out of my seat belt." He clicked it again frantically.

As the figure walked up to the car, Drew thought he recognized the person from somewhere. "Can you help us get out of here?"

The stranger shined the beam inside the car, and Drew squinted. He couldn't see shit now. "I smell gas. I think the tank must have ruptured." He took a whiff of his damp shoulder and jerked back. "It's all over us. I don't know how it got inside the car, but—"

"You say you can't get out?" The stranger leaned closer, shining the flashlight right in Drew's face.

"Yeah, man. I have no idea where my cell is." He used his arm to block the bright bream. "Can you call 911? I think my buddies here might be hurt."

"I heard what you said at the restaurant."

"What?" Drew squinted.

"I heard what you called that boy. That wasn't very nice."

"What the hell—"

"You called him a faggot," the voice said, snatching his ballcap off his head.

Drew suddenly felt weird, like maybe he was dreaming. The voice was so bizarre that he wondered if he was dead. Was this, like, God, or something in the bright light, come to take him to heaven?

The stranger leaned into the car and plucked something from Drew's pocket. Drew stared at it for a second, confused. It was his lighter. What did—

The stranger flicked the Bic and a little blue flame shot up.

Drew stared at the flame, then into the flashlight beam. "Hey, that isn't funny!"

"You shouldn't have called that boy a faggot," the voice repeated in the same eerie tone. "You have no idea how harmful such actions can be, the length and breadth of the ramifications."

Drew watched the flame move toward him and he was in such shock, such disbelief, that he didn't even scream, not until the sleeve of his t-shirt burst into flames . . .

Then he screamed.

I can't catch my breath. The sounds of the young man screaming, the roar of the flames. It is such a shot of adrenaline.

I slide into the front seat of my car and grip the steering wheel, the green ballcap still in my hand, my fingers trembling. I hear him scream again. I can smell the heady scent of ignited gasoline and heavy smoke mingling with more subtle perfumes of burning leather, clothing, flesh . . .

"What have I done?" I whisper aloud. I am shocked by what I have done. I have many faults, but impulsiveness has never been one of them. To kill unplanned—it is so unlike me. In the past I have always been so careful, so protective of the life I've built for myself out of the ashes.

But the obnoxious college student, what he said, pushed me over the edge. I lean forward, pressing my forehead to the steering wheel, fighting the tightness in my chest. I realize now this had been building for days . . . weeks, maybe. It is that damned reality TV show the college is allowing to be broadcast from their local access cable channel. *Fraternity Row*. Everyone loves it, not just on campus but the locals, too. They are all talking about it at the quaint coffee shops, in the bars and pubs, in line at the Wawa minimart, even on the local talk radio station. Everyone loves it—that is, except me.

The sound of an emergency vehicle siren makes me lift my head from the steering wheel, my chest suddenly fluttering with panic. I can't be found here, of course.

I take a deep, cleansing breath, exhaling and opening my eyes. I stare at the ballcap in my hand for a moment. I know that I should not take it. I should throw it out the window. Instead, I lay it carefully on the seat beside me. I start the engine, buckle my seat belt, and pull away from the burning car, leaving the dead and dying young men to their just desserts.

Chapter One

Adam rapped his knuckles on the glass door of his supervisor's office and walked in. "You rang, *Cap-i-tan*?" In the two weeks he'd been in the new field office, he'd learned that the captain didn't appreciate humor of any sort, but it never hurt to give it a whirl. Over the years, humor had gotten him out of some pretty tight places.

When Crackhow didn't respond, Adam glanced at the petite woman in the dark suit seated stiffly in front of the desk. He'd caught a couple of glimpses of her in the bullpen where most of the field agents worked. She had that freshly scrubbed, slightly spooked look of a new academy graduate, but she was older than most.

She was maybe thirty, hard to tell for sure. She wore no makeup, and her brown hair was cut short. No jewelry except for a watch, and a tiny gold crucifix and medallion around her neck. The whole look screamed *dyke,* but Adam didn't think she was. His guess was an overachiever, a firstborn just like himself. She was a smart, petite woman with a chip on her shoulder the size of Montana, trying to make her way in the macho man's FBI world.

Crackhow frowned from the other side of his desk that

was piled high with manila file folders that all appeared to be identical. "We talked last week about office attire, Special Agent Thomas."

So it was the polo shirt creating the crow's feet at the corners of the boss's eyes, not a lack of bran muffins on the coffee cart this morning.

"I had an interview." Adam took the other chair in front of the desk, running his hand over his pressed khakis—he thought he *had* dressed for the office. He'd left the Hawaiian shirt, his typical workday uniform in California, in the drawer. "Dockworkers. Suits scare these guys, Captain."

Marvin Crackhow continued to frown, looking over the rims of his frameless reading glasses. The poor balding guy looked like he was about to be engulfed by the files heaped on his desk. "Special Agent M.K. Shaughnessy." He lifted his pointed chin in the direction of the woman. It was his idea of an introduction. "Special Agent Adam Thomas."

Adam leaned forward, offering his hand, but didn't rise. He was a tall guy and didn't want to tower over her and make that chip any bigger. He imagined Montana was already difficult enough to shoulder. "Nice to meet you." He smiled, easing back into the crackly fake-leather chair. "I'm new, too. To this office, not the Bureau."

He took note that she had a decent handshake for a woman with such small hands—firm, but not overly so, like she was trying to arm wrestle him. And she smelled good, despite her obvious attempts to appear unfeminine to the untrained eye. Fortunately, his was well trained.

"Nice to meet you, Special Agent Thomas."

Her voice was surprisingly pleasant, a little husky for such a small woman. She didn't sound any happier to be in this office than he did. Crackhow calling them in together could only mean one thing: he was partnering them up for an assignment.

As if on cue, the captain slid a manila file across the desk at them; it was up for grabs. Adam and Shaughnessy reached for it at the same time. He withdrew his hand. After almost twenty years on the job, he was never that anxious to pick up the next file, anyway. It was definitely a love-hate relationship he and the Bureau shared. Kind of like the rest of the relationships in his life.

Shaughnessy flipped open the file, glanced inside and then up. "An automobile accident, Captain?" There was an edge to her voice.

Another surprise. Newbies, especially females, didn't usually have the cojones to stand up to Crackhow. He had a history of transferring the agents he found difficult to remote locations and crappy jobs. He'd been in the Baltimore field office years ago when Adam had worked here in his previous life, before undercover and the aggressive takeover of his marriage by his best buddy. As far as Adam knew, the office had been built around Crackhow.

"A car wreck? What the hell?" Adam had been warned by more than one supervisor over the years that he had to be more respectful, but he just couldn't help himself.

Shaughnessy flinched at the sound of his expletive.

Perfect—a female partner who didn't swear.

Crackhow again looked over the rim of his glasses. He was painfully thin and had a penchant for yellow suits that hung on his runner's thin frame like a scarecrow's tattered clothes. "Assistant SAC Godowsky asked me to look into it personally. Senator Palmer's son was the driver killed."

Adam leaned back, the chair crackling under him. "*The* Senator Palmer of the Foreign Relations Committee?"

"His twenty-year-old son was one of the fatalities in an automobile accident outside of Ashview in Anne Arundel County three days ago," Shaughnessy read from the file.

"I'm sorry for his loss, but what's it have to do with the FBI?"

It came out sounding glib, which hadn't been Adam's intention.

Crackhow reached for another file from one of the mountains, signaling that the powwow was just about over. "Three other boys from the local college were killed, too. Vehicle went up in flames before anyone could get out. The senator is making noises about the vehicle manufacturer being responsible for the deaths, and Senator Joseph out of Michigan is threatening to change his vote on some economic bill." The captain shrugged; the jacket never moved. "I don't know all the particulars, but somebody upstairs owes somebody a favor—"

"And now it's our problem." Adam put out his hand for the file, and Shaughnessy hesitated for a second, then surrendered it with obvious reluctance. *Damn, he hated women partners.*

"Just make sure the causes of death were accurate, especially on the Palmer boy. Take a quick look at the local police's accident report."

"Get you a cup of coffee, too, Captain?" Adam said under his breath as he rose.

"What's that?" Crackhow didn't look up from the report in front of him.

'We'll get right on it, sir." Adam opened the door and stepped back to let Shaughnessy pass. "You want me to put a hold on this union dockworkers thing, Captain?"

"Think you can handle both?"

Adam was tempted to come back with a snappy reply, but he squelched the urge. He had asked to be assigned to this office so he could be closer to Liza Jane. He didn't need to find a transfer slip to Tulsa in his in-box. "Yes, sir." He followed Shaughnessy out of the glass-walled office.

"You don't have to do things like that," she said, the instant the door swung shut.

"What's that. Annoy the captain?" He flipped open the file. Crackhow had been giving him these kind of crappy assignments ever since he transferred. Even the dockworkers' union was garbage, but at least it got him out of the bullpen and into the field.

"Hold doors open for me." She crossed her arms over her chest.

Adam hoped that wasn't her tough-guy look because it wasn't working for him. "Because you're a woman?" He glanced at her, then down at the file again. The details of the accident were pretty gruesome. Burning to death was not the way to go.

"I'm just an agent like you, Special Agent Thomas." There was that edge again to her voice; this time it had a touch of women's lib thrown in.

"Look, let's get two things straight. First, it's Adam. Second, I hold doors open for everyone—male, female, aging astronauts, and biker chicks, so don't take offense." He started for his cubicle. "I guess we're working on this together. What should I call you?"

"M.K. will be fine, unless we're on a case. Among civilians, I prefer Special Agent Shaughnessy."

He gave her his best *you've got to be kidding* look. "What's M.K. stand for?"

"You've never known someone who goes by his or her initials?" The tone was there again.

He sighed, wishing for the one-hundredth time in the last six weeks that he was back in Malibu, catching a wave. Maybe his ex was right, maybe he was getting too old for this. He returned his attention to the file Crackhow had handed them. "This case looks simple enough. I'll give the county coroner a call and see if we can stop by. We confirm the causes of death, we swing by the Ashview police station with a box of donuts, and we'll have this file back on Crackhow's desk by morning."

M.K. leaned her arm on the half wall of Special Agent Thomas's—*Adam's*—cubicle, feeling uncomfortable, trying not to look like it. She'd been in the Baltimore field office seven weeks, but every day still felt like her first. And now she was being pawned off with yet another male agent. This morning, her great-aunt's offer to get her in at Mt. St. Joseph's convent was looking pretty good. *Like there was a waiting list* . . . "Is this typical? Requests out of Washington?"

Adam shrugged, punching the buttons on his phone.

M.K. was usually good with first impressions, but she couldn't get a read on this guy. He looked like one of the boys—no, *better* than any of the boys she'd seen in this office. His slightly tousled hair was a natural, sun-bleached blond and he had a nice tan. As he reached for a pen, then a second when the first had no ink, she saw a flex of bicep at the hem of his short-sleeved orange polo shirt.

"I guess it happens occasionally," he said. "It's been a long time since I worked this office, though. Ten years under-cover on the West Coast."

Against her will, she was impressed. At some point, every agent in training lay on his or her back on a lumpy mattress at Quantico dreaming of working undercover. That was *real* FBI work. M.K. was realistic enough to know it wasn't for her, but hairdressers never gave up dreaming of being princesses, either.

"Dr. Wood, Special Agent Thomas, FBI. Glad I caught you." Adam stood at his desk, phone cradled to his ear, and reached for a coffee mug. He paused, listening, then chuck-led.

It hadn't occurred to M.K. that the coroner might be a woman, but even if she hadn't been able to catch the sound of her voice, her new partner's grin and body language con-firmed it. She glanced at his left hand. No wedding ring, just long, tanned, masculine fingers. She speculated that Special Agent Surfer Boy was single, divorced, with likely more than one ex. She was good at evaluating men and rarely missed the mark. As a whole, they were a pretty useless species, save for their reproductive purposes.

"I've got a case I'd like to run through with you," Adam was saying into the phone. He sipped his coffee. "Multiple fatality vehicular three days ago in Ashview." He paused.

"Yeah, I know, we don't usually handle this kind of thing. Long story. Anyway, would you have a second for me"—he eyed M.K.—"and my partner?" He glanced at his wrist-watch, steel with a black face. Expensive.

M.K. wondered if it had been a gift from some woman.

"Great. See you then."

He hung up and looked at M.K. She lifted her arm off the half wall, meeting his gaze. He had kind eyes, dark, and just a little sad behind the Type B, laid-back attitude it was obvi-ous he worked hard at presenting.

"Dr. Wood can meet with us at one. It's her lunch break, but I figure we'll be in and out in ten minutes." He gave the manila file a push and it glided forward on his desk until it bumped into a picture frame of a teenage girl with white-blond hair that mousy brunettes like M.K. only dreamed of. Same hair as Adam. Same smile.

"Your daughter?" She reached for the file. Whether they were just going through the motions to make some senator happy or not, she wanted to read it before they met with the coroner.

He grinned again, but this was different from the good-looking-and-he knows-it smile. This was that of a proud father. "Liza Jane. She's a freshman at Chesapeake Bay College."

"Same college the boys who were killed attended." For a moment, M.K. admired the photo of the young woman taken on the deck of a sailboat. She was as pretty as her father was handsome. The Shaughnessy girls, all eight of them, were many things, but *pretty* wasn't one of them.

"Liza Jane didn't know any of them. Upper classmen." He eased into his chair, identical to the one she occupied in a row of cubicles near the watercooler. "The county coro-ner's office isn't far, Annapolis, but traffic . . ." He shrugged, reaching for a file on his desk marked with a dockworker's union number. "We'll leave about twelve-fifteen."

"I'll get the car, meet you downstairs."

He eyed her. "I usually drive."

She was tempted to grin at the challenge. She kept a straight face. "I usually drive."

He rolled his eyes. "Whatever."

And just when she was beginning to think the guy was okay . . . "Downstairs, twelve-fifteen." She walked away before he had a chance to answer.

Now she just had to figure out how the heck to go about procuring a vehicle . . .

M.K.'s first thought was that Dr. Wood had the longest, most beautiful legs she'd ever seen on a woman. Her second thought was that she had a face to go with the legs. How unfair was that? It was at times like this that M.K. wished she was Buddist instead of Roman Catholic. She could have swallowed the whole idea of accepting the face and body she'd been given, had she the hope of returning to this earth reincarnated as a beauty pageant queen, or even a gorgeous county coroner, at some later date.

"Special Agent Thomas." Adam thrust out his hand.

Dr. Wood was almost as tall as he was. She had to be close to six feet, without the stylish heels. "Nice to meet you, Special Agent Thomas."

"Special Agent Shaughnessy," M.K. said, trying not to feel like the ugly stepsister, cousin, whatever the heck the phrase was. She put on her FBI-agent face, tucking a manila envelope under her arm and shaking the doctor's hand. "We appreciate you seeing us, Dr. Wood. I know these are slightly unusual circumstances."

She smiled, leading them down a hallway to a door marked STAIRS. "I have to admit I'm curious. I've been here almost two years, and the FBI has never darkened my doorstep. Our Chief Medical Examiner in Baltimore always gets the good cases. The murders, the unidentified victims, the partial remains." Her pleasant voice echoed in the stairwell. At the bottom of the steps they turned right and took the first door, marked MORGUE in caps. "Welcome to my lair."

The coroner's creepy tone was meant to be amusing. M.K. wasn't. She'd been in a morgue only once in all her years of being with the FBI. Statisticians didn't have much need for them, and her field-agent training had only included one day of morgue basics. The day they had visited one in a hospital there had not even been any deceased in residence.

An antiseptic smell assaulted M.K.'s nostrils as they entered a large room, its tiled floor and ceiling a pale, soothing green. A stainless steel autopsy table stood to one side with a cart beside it. One wall was lined with oak cabinets and a nice counter. It looked like someone's kitchen.

"Come on into my office." Dr. Wood gave a wave, inviting them through a door.

Her office had a glass wall that separated it from the tiled autopsy room. As M.K. stepped in, she glanced up at the rows of shelving that lined three walls with jars containing pieces of human anatomy. She halted in the doorway, letting Adam walk past her and flop into the only chair in front of the desk. She stared at the gallon-sized specimen jars, her mouth suddenly going dry. She couldn't identify all the body parts, but she knew the biggies: a brain, a diseased liver, a healthy lung, the other one blackened by some ailment that had obviously been fatal. When she saw the eyes staring out at her, her stomach gave a tumble.

"Here you go, Agent Shaughnessy. I knew I had another chair somewhere." Dr. Wood walked up behind M.K., giving her no choice but to step into the office. If Adam noticed one blue and one brown eye watching him from the jar directly behind the doctor's chair, he gave no indication.

Dr. Wood set the chair down beside Adam's and started around her desk, her white lab coat fluttering. She looked at M.K., who was still standing, then at the jars. "Shrinks display Picassos, lawyers Monets." She shrugged her shoulders. "You'd have to expect medical examiners to be a little bizarre."

M.K. slid into the chair, still staring at the jars. "They . . . they don't creep you out?" she asked, sounding completely unprofessional, but unable to help herself.

"Nah, it can be lonely down here in the basement of the county offices. They keep me company."

Adam chuckled. "Beats some of the guys in our office in the cubicles next to us."

Dr. Wood flashed a smile in appreciation of his humor, then looked to M.K. "If they make you uncomfortable, we can grab my files and go up to the break room."

"No, no. That's fine." M.K. tore her gaze from a shattered spleen.

"She's the new girl in school," Adam explained.

Dr. Wood flashed another grin, and M.K. cut her eyes at Adam. She didn't need him taking up for her; he wasn't her big brother.

"We're just here to confirm what took the lives of the four young men in the vehicular accident," M.K. said in her best agent tone.

"No surprise there." Dr. Wood opened a pale blue file folder and removed an official-looking sheet of paper. "Smoke inhalation, your basic asphyxiation."

"But the bodies burned." M.K. reached for the autopsy report and scanned it.

"This one post mortem." Dr. Wood leaned back in her leather executive chair and crossed her lovely legs. The hem of her skirt couldn't be seen beneath her lab coat so it had to be fairly short. "Burn victims are always gruesome." She wrinkled her pert nose. "All these years, and I never get used to the smell of incinerated flesh."

M.K. slid the preliminary autopsy report in front of Adam. He didn't look at it; he was too busy smiling at the coroner.

"This report is for Peter Rivera. Are the others identical?"

"All but Drew Palmer's." Dr. Wood sighed, slipping another sheet of paper from the file. "The fire guys said the actual ignition point was the driver's seat."

M.K. knew the blood drained from her face, but she kept it emotionless. Maybe her father was right. Maybe she wasn't cut out for being a field agent. Maybe she did belong back in Quantico, buried under her clean, nameless statistics. "He burned to death."

Dr. Wood's face was respectfully void of her sexy smile. "I'm afraid so."

"He was a senator's son," Adam offered. "We're not questioning your conclusions. Just dotting our i's, crossing our t's."

Dr. Wood raised her palm. "No explanation is necessary. I know how bureaucracy works on a county level—I can only imagine what it's like for you guys."

"Could we get copies of these?" M.K. asked, rising. Now that their business was completed, she was anxious to get out of the morgue and back into the warm September sunshine.

"I can fax them." Dr. Wood hesitated. "Is that your file on the boys?" She nodded to the manila envelope tucked under M.K.'s arm.

"Yes."

"Have you photos of the young men?" She hesitated. "I was just curious . . . what they had looked like before."

M.K. looked to Adam, unsure of protocol. FBI files weren't readily shared with anyone, even those who worked in conjunction with them. Leftover from the J. Edgar Hoover days, no doubt.

Adam grabbed the envelope and opened it, fishing out four eight-by-ten photos. The coroner took the stack and studied each one for a moment. "I look at dead people every day—you'd think I'd become immune," she mused.

"Let's hope we never do." Adam grimly accepted the photos back.

"Thank you for your time, Dr. Wood." M.K. strode across the tiled floor, her sensible loafers making a hollow echo off cool, ceramic walls. "We can see ourselves out."

"Thanks, Doc." Adam tipped an imaginary hat and followed M.K. across the green-tiled floor and out into the hallway. "You know," he said, when they reached the stairs, "your interview skills could use a little work."

She glared at him over her shoulder. "What? I'm not flirting enough with my interviewee?"

"I wasn't flirting."

She took the steps quickly, as anxious to get away from Adam as the eyeballs. "You most certainly were."

"I'm a friendly guy."

M.K. grabbed the door at the top of the stairs and jerked it open. "Let's just see how much flirtation goes on with you and the Ashview police chief, Buck Seipp."

"Hey, Dad. Sorry I'm late." Liza Jane walked up behind where he was seated at one of the tables and wrapped her arms around him, giving him a kiss on the cheek.

"That's okay. I needed a wind-down beer anyway." He watched her drop her backpack on the floor and slide into a chair.

"I didn't know you knew this bar." She leaned back in her chair so the waitress in jean shorts and sneakers could add a place setting in front of her.

"You kidding?" Adam glanced around at the classic pub with its subdued lighting, dark oak paneling, and bar that stretched the length of the room. "I used to come here all the time when your mother was pissed at me." He grinned.

She grinned back. Liza Jane was pretty well adjusted, for the child of a divorce. She liked her stepfather, whom she had known since birth, and they got along well. Mark was as proud of Liza Jane as Adam was.

"You order?" She reached for the menu the waitress had left.

"Just wings, hot, and dune fries."

She dropped the menu. "Perfect. So, what's up with you?"

She lifted her chin. "Why you looking so depressed? Missing your surfboard?"

He raised the stein of ale and took a sip. "Got a new partner. She's okay." He shrugged, trying to think how to explain it. "I'm just not sure how we're going to get along. We had one assignment last week, and today the boss paired us up again."

"She?" Liza Jane lifted a pale eyebrow. She had classic Norwegian good looks—suntanned with a clear complexion and bright blue eyes. Today she was wearing her shoulder-length blond hair tucked beneath a hot pink bandana. Despite her entrance into college life, so far, she was still looking pretty normal: only two holes per ear, no additional body piercing, and no tattoos. The color of her hair did change from time to time; she liked it a strawberry blond, but today it was the color she had been born with. "She hot?" Liza Jane asked.

He set the mug on the heavily varnished, square wooden table and grimaced. "She's unusual for a fed chick. Doesn't fit the classic profile." She wasn't his type. He liked his women long-legged and sassy, but there was something about M.K. . . .

Liza Jane leaned back in her chair, crossing her arms over her chest and smiling. "Oh, yeah?"

"All tough and bitchy on the outside, which is typical." Adam thought for a moment, searching for the best way to describe M.K. "But there's something about her that makes her different. I just haven't figured out what it is. I don't know—a vulnerability, maybe."

"That makes you want to sweep her into your arms and protect her from the big, bad world?"

He laughed. "She carries a gun, and I don't think she'd be afraid to use it on the bad guys—or me, for that matter."

"Aha, I see. So she *is* hot. She just doesn't think you are."

He frowned and reached for his beer. "You didn't say how classes were today."

The waitress stopped back at the table.

"Just a Coke," Liza Jane said. "I'll eat my dad's food."

The college-age waitress bobbed her head. "Be right back."

Liza Jane looked back at her dad. "They were fine. Biology is going to be a pain in the ass."

It was Adam's turn to lift an eyebrow. Liza Jane was a special combination of her mother's creativity and the cynic in him he tried so hard to disguise.

"But what's great is the newspaper staff." She leaned on the table. "Everyone was so nice to me. They didn't even care that I was a freshman. I met with the student editor, Tawny—showed her some of the stuff I did in high school, and I'm in."

"That's great!"

Liza Jane leaned back to let the waitress set her soda in front of her.

"Food will be right up."

"Thanks." Liza Jane ripped the paper off her straw. "At first, Tawny wanted me to, like, do this goofy column about what classes to take and what classes to avoid, but I told her I really like the *on the beat* kind of thing, and she said I could go with it. Just check in with her before I write the whole article." She dropped her straw into the glass and took a sip. "You know, so I don't waste time on something they would never print."

"And how often is the paper published?"

"Well, just twice a week now, Wednesdays and Fridays, but they're thinking about adding Mondays if the circulation goes up."

"Think you could get me a subscription?"

"Dad." She wrinkled her lightly freckled nose. She'd spent the summer teaching surfing to kids for a surf shop at the beach in southern Delaware and she was still nicely tanned. "It's just a campus newspaper. You know, what frats are about to lose their charter for partying too hard, how the football and lacrosse teams are playing. They've got this robot competition going for the mid-Atlantic states. Boring stuff like that."

"I doubt anything you write would be boring. I want a subscription and another beer." Adam lifted his mug, glancing around the busy pub in search of the waitress. "And then I want to hear about your love life, preferably the lack thereof."

"*Dad* . . ."

Chapter Two

"Hey." M.K. leaned over the half wall of Adam's cubicle. "Crackhow wants to see us."

Adam took his time sipping his coffee. "You're looking entirely too serious, M.K." He studied her intently, hoping to get her to at least crack a smile. In the week since they'd investigated the senator's son's accident, he'd made a point to speak to her every day. Even offered to get her a cup of coffee the morning before. So far, she wasn't warming up to his charm. "My number one pick is Mary Katherine. You know—what the M.K. stands for."

She turned away. "He said *now*."

Adam groaned as he set down his coffee cup and got out of his chair carefully; one of the wheels was wobbly and it was making him crazy. He'd have to pull a switcheroo with someone else's chair after hours one night this week. "He say what he wanted?" He had to almost run to catch up. The woman had long legs for being so short.

"No, but he didn't look happy." She glanced over her shoulder at him, looking him up and down.

Adam ran his hand over his new button-up oxford shirt; the saleswoman in the department store had called it *butter-*

cup yellow. He found the practice of naming colors of men's shirts after genera of flowers a little bizarre, but what did he know about fashion? "What. I spill coffee?" He looked down, searching for a stain. This was precisely why he liked brightly colored Hawaiian shirts; no one could see coffee or lunch down the front.

"You own a tie?" she asked over one small, squared shoulder. She was wearing another dark, nondescript suit like the one she'd worn every day for the last week. Or was it the same suit?

"Of course I have a tie. Sponge Bob, I think. My daughter gave it to me a few years ago for Christmas."

"Probably a good thing you left it home." She tapped on Crackhow's door and walked in; she did not hold it open for Adam.

"You wanted to see us, sir?"

M.K. was a woman without preamble. Definite cojones beneath the dark suit.

Adam just waited in the doorway. Part of the job of a senior agent was to break new agents in, offering guidance when it was necessary, but letting them go on their own whenever possible.

"I left the report on the automobile accident that killed the senator's kid on your desk two days ago," M.K. rattled on when Crackhow didn't speak at once. "We talked to the Ashview chief of police and everything in the report is accurate. Special Agent Thomas and I—"

"Have you seen this?" Crackhow jerked a newspaper off one of the stacks of files and slid it across his desk.

If M.K. hadn't shot her arm out, it would have landed on the floor. She scanned the front page of the paper that was only half the length and width of a local daily paper. "I can't say that I have, sir. I don't usually read college campus newspapers."

Her last words caught Adam's attention. He took a step into the office, letting the glass door close behind him.

"Have a look at the front-page story byline, Special

Agent Thomas." Crackhow gave him the same once-over he'd already gotten from his partner. Apparently neither of them liked *buttercup yellow*.

M.K. handed the paper off to Adam. The headline bullet across the front page read MURDER OR MISHAP? Beneath it in small black letters was the name *Liza Thomas*. Adam scanned the first paragraph quickly. Liza Jane was questioning the safety of the county owned-and-maintained road, citing several major accidents that had occurred in the last three years on the same stretch of Old Marlboro where the senator's kid had died. Apparently, there had been two previous fatal accidents.

Adam didn't finish the article. He glanced up. "What's the problem, Chief?"

"That your daughter?"

Adam tucked the paper under his arm, intending to read the entire article once he was safely in his cubicle. He couldn't resist a burst of pride. Liza Jane had been on the newspaper staff all of one week, and she had the front-page headline. "Yes, sir. What's the problem?"

"The *problem*, Special Agent *Thomas* and Special Agent *Shaughnessy*,"—he looked over the rims of his glasses at one and then the other—"is that the senator's office saw it, too. Apparently Senator Palmer has a subscription sent to his offices in Washington." He set his cheap Bic pen down on his desk. "I thought the two of you looked into this and concluded that the accident was due to high speed and a minor drinking alcohol while driving."

"Yes, sir, we did." M.K. stood stiffly in front of the desk, as if at attention.

"Then why the hell did this article get written and why the hell was it your daughter who wrote it?" Crackhow's eyes bulged, his Adam's apple bobbing.

M.K. winced with each *hell*.

"I knew nothing about the article, sir, or the possibility that there could be a problem with the road." Adam did not avert his gaze. In truth, he was a little annoyed with Liza Jane for not coming to him before she allowed the article to be printed, but he certainly wasn't going to tell Crackhow that. "It's a country road that leads by a back way into the state park on the bay. College kids use it all the time."

"Now Senator Palmer is meeting with the governor. That's bad for me," Crackhow said, "which means it's bad for you."

"We'll take another look, sir." M.K. started to back up. "We'll gather the stats on the county road, double-check the blood alcohol on all four boys, and get a rundown on where they went that night, what led them down that road."

"I want the two of you to make this go away." Crackhow picked up his pen. "I don't have time for this crap."

Again, M.K. flinched.

Crap? She thought *crap* was a curse word? Adam almost groaned out loud. This was not going to work out, he and Special Agent whatever-her-first-name-was Shaughnessy. Their styles obviously didn't mesh. He couldn't deal with this kind of uptight broad; he shouldn't have to. Not after twenty years with the Bureau.

"Give us a day or two." Adam walked out the door. "We'll get back to you."

"See that you do," Crackhow called as the door swung shut behind them.

"Don't do that." Adam strode down the hall, taking long, powerful steps.

"Don't do what?" This time Shaughnessy was the one running to catch up to him.

"Speak for me."

"I wasn't—"

"This is my daughter, my problem." He kept his gaze fixed on the gray carpet in front of him.

"No, actually, it's my problem now." M.K. halted, hands on hips, raising her voice a notch. A couple of agents in the bullpen glanced their way. "Looks like you made it my problem."

He turned around, swiping the newspaper out from under his arm. "She's nineteen years old. I have no control over what she submits to a school newspaper." He kept his tone even. He wasn't the kind of guy who lost his temper often, but his new partner was certainly challenging his self-control.

If she knew she'd pissed him off, she gave no indication. The few female agents he had worked with in the past had always been worried about who might be angry with them, and Adam didn't have any use for women like that. Not on the job. If he hadn't been so angry, he would have been impressed that M.K. wasn't backpedaling.

"I'll get the stats on the county road for the last five years," she said. "You want to call the medical examiner's office to get those detailed autopsy reports or shall I?"

He hesitated, glancing at the American and Maryland flags flanking the far door to the offices. He didn't like feeling this way. It was counterproductive. If he was stuck with M.K. Shaughnessy on this case, he was stuck with her. He'd make the best of it. In his career he'd had a lot of partners, some good, some bad, most just average. He could certainly deal with one small Roman Catholic female for a couple of days more. "I'll call Dr. Wood's office."

"We should probably speak with Ashview police again and pay a visit to the frat house. Trace the boys' steps that night."

"Fine." He looked back at her. "I just have one question. Are you going to flinch every time someone utters a curse word, because if you are—"

Her brows knitted. "I don't flinch."

"You flinch." He started down the hallway again. "Anything else you need me to do?"

"You might want to call your daughter."

Adam tapped his hand with the rolled-up newspaper. "Yeah, I'm thinking I might want to do that."

* * *

I had no intention of turning the TV on. I hadn't even thought about the fact that it was Tuesday night and that damned show would be on. I carry a glass of iced tea and a deli sandwich to my favorite chair and sit down to go over some files. The TV is just on for white noise.

I'm not even sure how the TV got on that station. The public access channel is not something I watch. I prefer news programs, documentaries, and old movies.

I hear the music intro and look up, my mouth full of lean roast beef and Swiss on rye.

"Hey, welcome to another week on *Fraternity Row*," says the young man in the cool wraparound sunglasses from the front step of one of the sorority houses on campus.

The rare roast beef suddenly tastes like wallpaper in my mouth. It is all I can do to swallow it and wash it down with a gulp of iced tea.

"I know you want to find out what's up with Casey and Ty back at Sigma Pi." The young man, Axel from Phi Kappa Alpha, is good-looking and he knows it. Shaggy blond hair, blue eyes; a younger version of Brad Pitt. He talks easily into the camera as if he'd been born in front of it, as if the viewer is his best friend. "I mean, the whole argument over Katie was mad crazy, but hey,"—he raises both hands—"you know how these guys can be over their girls." He poses and smiles.

It is all I can do not to throw my iced tea glass at the TV screen.

"Don't worry, we'll get back to them next week. Tonight, we're going to take you to the other side of campus, to Sugar Maple Street." Axel rises, hooking his thumbs into the pockets of his khaki cargo shorts. "Come on inside."

I know I should turn it off. I know it is silly to watch something that disturbs me so greatly, but I can't help myself. I watch the TV screen as Axel knocks on the door of the big Victorian house and it is answered at once by a cute blonde with the longest, darkest lashes. She reminds me of that Hilton girl.

"Hey, Axel." She looks at the camera coyly, then back at him. "Come on in, we've been expecting you."

Axel turns to the camera and motions with a lift of his slightly cleft chin. "Come on in to the Delta Zeta house and meet the girls."

I reach for my iced tea glass again, my hand trembling. "This shouldn't be allowed on TV. It shouldn't." I take a sip and set the glass down again, focusing on the cool liquid that runs down my throat.

Where is the remote? I have to shut the TV off. I have to avoid the things that agitate me. That upset the balance.

I look on the table beside me for it, on the floor at my feet. I pick up the stack of files on the footstool, but it isn't there. It is nowhere.

I lift my head, shifting my gaze to the TV again. There it is, on top of the TV. What good did a remote control do on top of the TV?

I will myself up and out of the chair. Axel is still talking. Jeannie, the blonde, is giggling, thrusting her small, pert breasts at the camera. She is introducing her sisters, Sam and Katie, whom we've met the previous week at a Phi Kappa Alpha party. There are others, and their young women's faces are a blur across the Sony flat-screen.

I haven't had a panic attack in years and yet I can feel the familiar buzz in my head, the increase in my heart rate, the tightness in my chest. I take a step toward the TV, the floor seeming to tilt slightly. I will myself another step closer, then another. I can hardly catch my breath by the time I reach the TV and punch the "power" button.

Axel and Jeannie and the other girls in tight, spaghetti-strap shirts are sucked into the vortex of light and then the black screen. Leaning on the TV, I close my eyes and take a couple of deep breaths. After a moment, the dizziness passes.

I walk back to the chair and reach for my sandwich with one hand, the closest file with the other. I need to get to work if I am going to get through all this reading and still get to bed at a decent time.

M.K. climbed into the passenger side of the red, mud-spattered Jeep Wrangler and drew the seat belt across her waist. "I appreciate you giving me a lift to my car but I really don't need to go with you. You can just drop me off at the repair shop."

Adam pushed the convertible roof back to secure it. "It's in the same direction. Besides, I want you to come. You can work on your interview skills." He chuckled at his own joke.

She took a deep breath and exhaled, her hands on her thighs. Her new partner had her totally off-kilter. He was nothing like the other males she'd worked with so far in the Baltimore field office, or even the male agents she'd known in Quantico. Adam certainly had a masculine air about him but none of that macho nonsense. And he didn't treat her like she was stupid. This week he'd allowed her to do most of the investigation on the accident and even run the interview with the deceaseds' fraternity brothers. And now he was being nice to her. Technically, they were off duty, so this "road trip," as he was calling it, could have been classified as on *personal time*. M.K. didn't do so well in the *personal time* department.

Adam jumped into the driver's seat and pulled on his seat belt. The Jeep was small, the quarters close. He brushed his arm against hers as he grabbed a ballcap off the dash and pulled it down on his head, brim backwards. "Don't look so scared. I don't bite."

She tried to relax. Was she really that easy to read?

"You want to take off your jacket?"

"I'm fine." She crossed her arms over her chest, and then, feeling awkward, dropped her hands to her lap.

"Suit yourself." Adam threw the Jeep into reverse and they careened out of the parking lot and onto the street, going quite a bit faster than she did at the day's end in her Honda.

"So I'm thinking it must be Margaret," Adam said, turning at the corner. "I'm still sticking with Katherine for the middle name. Am I right?"

She dared a glance at him. "It would be easy enough to check my personnel file if you want to know so badly."

"I know." He gave a wave. "But that's no fun."

M.K. was unable to resist a quick smile, then she looked away. This really wasn't a good idea, going with him. She should, at the very least, have taken her own vehicle. But he'd insisted it wasn't necessary; he'd take her back to her car later. He apparently also lived in Ashview where M.K. had rented an apartment. A lot of the agents lived in the town that served as a bedroom community for D.C. and Baltimore.

"Aha, so I see it is possible." He eased into the heavy traffic on the 695 beltway headed east.

"What's that?"

"To make you smile."

"It's not your job to make me smile, Special Agent Thomas." She didn't say it unkindly. "Now tell me exactly how a family barbeque constitutes work."

Thirty minutes later, on a trip that should have taken forty-five if the person at the wheel didn't drive like a maniac, they turned into a quaint neighborhood just outside of Ashview. Adam pulled up in front of a white Cape Cod complete with dormers, green shutters, and a picket fence and cut the engine. "Ex's name is Sophie." He climbed out and waited for her. "Her husband is Mark. He's with the Bureau, too. Headquarters now, downtown D.C. We were once partners in anti-crime."

M.K. stepped down out of the Jeep. Now that there wasn't wind whipping her in the face, she was hot. She slipped out of her jacket and left it on the seat, hoping her cream-colored silk blouse wasn't too transparent. Thank heavens she'd worn the beige bra. Usually it didn't matter because no one saw her without her jacket.

Of course, removing her jacket presented another problem—her firearm. It was now in full view; obviously she couldn't take it off and leave it in the car. "This okay?" she asked over the hood of the vehicle, indicating the Glock in her shoulder holster.

He winked. "I think they already know we're the feds. Come on."

She walked around the front of the red Jeep. The air smelled of freshly mowed lawn and barbeque smoke. It was a nice neighborhood—dogs barking, kids on bikes riding down the sidewalk. "Wait a minute," she said, stopping as she shifted gears, focusing on what Adam had said a minute ago. "Your ex-wife married your partner?"

"Are you *trying* to make me feel bad?"

M.K. winced inwardly. She was so not good at this kind of thing. The guy was trying to be nice, trying to make her feel more comfortable in their work relationship by letting her see a little of his personal life, and here she was, pointing out his failings. That was so like her father, it wasn't funny. "I'm sorry," she said, catching up with him. "I didn't mean to—"

"M.K.,"—Adam turned around, a silly grin on his face— "I was kidding. It's okay."

She halted again. "Oh. Okay, well—" She had no idea what she was going to say, so she shut her mouth while she was still ahead.

"It happened a long time ago," Adam explained, leading her up the front brick walk.

There were flower beds on each side filled with yellow and purple pansies. M.K. loved flowers; she had a lot of houseplants that she fed and watered and pruned religiously.

"It was mostly my fault," he continued. "I got what I deserved and Mark and Sophie got what they deserved. A little happiness and the picket fence." At the front step he opened the door without even ringing the doorbell. "Honey, I'm home."

"Out back," a woman called.

"Sophie," he explained over his shoulder, leading her through an entryway and into a big country kitchen. "She's a sweetheart, but she's a little hormonal right now." He cut through the kitchen, grabbing a bowl of potato salad covered with plastic wrap off the counter.

She stared at him, not sure what he meant.

He grinned. "You are warming up to me, aren't you?"

With a frown, she followed him through the open doors that led into a deck in the backyard. "Against my better judgment."

"Hey, hon, I brought potato salad." Adam walked over to a beautiful blonde—a very pregnant, beautiful blonde—and kissed her on the mouth.

So that was what he had meant when he said Sophie was a little hormonal. She had to be at least six months pregnant.

"Hey," the blonde said. "Glad you could come, and *I* made the potato salad, thank you very much." She pointed to a picnic table already laden with food. "Put it there." The woman turned to M.K. and smiled warmly. "Hi, I'm Sophie." She offered her slender hand.

M.K. took a step toward her, feeling completely awkward. "It's nice to meet you. Thank you for having me."

Sophie shook her hand. "Adam has never been one for manners. Your name is?"

"I'm sorry." M.K. stepped back, feeling the warmth of embarrassment spread across her cheeks. "I'm M.K. Shaughnessy." She pointed lamely. "I work with Adam. Didn't he tell you I was coming? He said he told you."

Sophie gave a casual wave of dismissal. "I'm sure he did. Soda and beer are in the cooler down there. My husband, Mark, at the grill, should have hamburgers and chicken boobs ready anytime now. Our daughter, Savannah, blond hair, dirty face, is on the swings. I'm not going to walk around and introduce you to everyone, because my back is killing me and we're all family, so please make yourself comfortable."

M.K. looked out into the fenced-in yard. There were several adults standing around the food table and four more under a tree near the smoking barbeque. There were children on a swing set against the fence, more children running through the yard with badminton rackets, and two toddlers playing on the deck steps. It reminded her of a late-summer barbeque at one of her cousins' houses. As a kid, she had loved those family get-togethers.

"Beer?" Adam appeared at her side, a frosty bottle in each hand.

"No, thank you, I—"

"M.K., have a beer. You can relax—work's over for the day."

She lowered her voice to be sure no one else would hear her. "I thought we came here to interview your daughter about the article."

He pushed the beer into her hand. "We did, sort of. Well, I did. I just brought you along because I know very well you were just going to go back to your apartment and eat something out of a take-out container while you did paperwork."

M.K. took a sip of the beer. It was icy cold and delicious. "Are you suggesting, Special Agent Thomas, that I have no personal life? That I have nothing better to do on a Friday night than freeload off your ex-wife for a meal and a bottle of beer?"

He tipped the beer bottle back to take a drink. "Do you, *Marguerite Kathryn*?"

She had several snappy retorts on the end of her tongue. Instead she just took another drink of her beer. "Is Liza Jane here? I'd like to meet her."

"Not yet, but she will be. She's always late. I think she does it to drive her mother crazy. Now, come on." He tilted his head in the direction of the barbeque and the cluster of men standing around it. "I want you meet Mark. He's a great guy. Was a great partner." Adam turned away. "And you say another word about the fact he stole my wife, I'm not getting you another beer."

Chapter Three

"Okay, so what is it, Dad? You've been circling the wagons since I got here." Liza Jane leaned against the deck railing and tipped a soda can to her mouth. Tonight she was wearing her hair parted down the middle in two short, fat, blond braids, with one loose blond lock dangling over her eye.

Darkness had settled over the backyard, leaving it cloaked only in the pale yellow light of tiki torches strategically placed around the deck. Through the open doors, Adam could see M.K. standing in front of the sink, washing dishes, talking to Sophie. He found it intriguing that the two had hit it off so well, because they seemed so different. Sophie owned a little health food store in downtown Ashview. She wore her hair long and straight and liked funky floral skirts and dangling earrings. Tonight she was wearing a pink skirt with a very tight t-shirt, leaving nothing of her growing abdomen to the imagination. M.K., with her short, sensible haircut, her gold crucifix, the conservative navy trousers, and plain, short-sleeved silk shirt, seemed like a foreigner in Sophie's kitchen, and yet he could hear the two of them laughing, chatting. He hoped they weren't talking about him.

"Dad, are you, like, just going to totally ignore me?" Liza Jane bumped her hip against his. "Quit gawking at the lady cop. You see the size of that gun she's carrying? She's liable to take you out."

Adam looked down at Liza Jane. "I wasn't gawking."

"Dad, your nose is growing. Now tell me what you want. I can already guess what it is."

"All right, look into your magic eight ball and tell me what I wanted to talk to you about." He gave her his full attention.

"The calculus class I dropped. And before you start talking about how much my tuition is and how hard you've worked to—"

"You dropped calculus?"

She closed her eyes and groaned.

"No, that wasn't what I wanted to talk to you about." He pointed a parental finger. "But I want to talk to you about that, too. *Next*."

She set the can on the deck rail and crossed her arms over her chest. Like all the other college girls, she wore a tight t-shirt that bared her flat belly above her jean shorts. "What else have I done wrong?"

"The front-page article in the campus newspaper."

"You read it?" She looked at him, grinning with perfect teeth that had only required three years of braces and enough cash to have bought a nice used car.

"Yup. And so did Senator Palmer and so did my boss's boss."

She made a face at him, her pert nose wrinkling. "The FBI is looking into Marlboro Road? I didn't know you guys did anything with safety issues. I thought you were too busy with the mafia and bank robbers and shit."

He blinked, ala M.K. Shaughnessy. He saw nothing wrong with him cursing on the job; it was almost expected with the men he worked with, but somehow hearing the same words come out of his daughter's mouth bothered him. He didn't say anything, though, because it would give her an opportunity to go off on one of her tangents. She was very good at steering him away from the conversation at hand as it was, especially if it was a conversation she really didn't want to have.

"I can't say why we're investigating the incident, but the assistant SAC—special agent in charge—my boss, was really pissed about some of the things you had to say."

She slipped her hands into the front pockets of her shorts. "Sorry you got into trouble."

"Not a big deal. I just need you to back off on the whole incident." Adam slipped his arm around her shoulders. "Leave the matter to the police, legislators, whoever else wants to get into it, okay?"

She pulled away, looking at him as if he'd grown horns from his forehead. "Okay? No, it's not okay." She turned to face him. "Dad, as a reporter, I have a moral obligation to inform the public of any information I uncover. Now, I'm sorry if your boss is pms-ing over my article, but maybe—"

"Moral obligation?" Adam interrupted. "*Please*. You're talking about a campus rag—"

"Campus rag?" Liza Jane flared, lowering her hands to her hips just the way her mother used to do with him. "Is that what you think of me? Of my journalistic—"

"Liza Jane, that headline was a cheap shot and you know it." He pointed an accusing finger. "I know for a fact you can do a better job than that."

"I don't write the headlines, Dad. Now, I'm sorry if you didn't like what I had to say but it was all true, and I'm not backing down on this issue. I plan to continue my investigation." She stood backbone-straight, all five-foot-four of her. "In fact, I've been asked to do a five-minute news spot on our local access channel, and I think I'm going to take them up on the offer."

"Liza Jane, listen to me—"

"Hey, hey, hey, what's going on here?" Mark walked up the deck steps. "You two getting into it again?"

"He's being an ass. I'm going inside." Liza Jane looked at her father with disgust and walked away.

Adam watched her go, unsure whether he should follow her or not. He glanced at Mark.

"I'd let her go," he said, backing up against the railing beside Adam. "You know how she is. Half the time she agrees with us when we get into an argument. She just hates to say so."

Adam shook his head. "I didn't come to fight with her, but my assistant SAC is pretty pissed about an article she wrote."

"The one about the road the boys were killed on?"

Adam nodded.

"It wasn't bad. And why are we getting into it?"

"It smacked of sensationalism. She was just trying to see who she could rile. And we're getting into it because the senator's office is getting into it. Somebody owes somebody a favor somewhere upstairs."

"Or knows where a body is." Mark shrugged. "Anyway, I'm sure Liza Jane didn't know you were involved. She's just trying to find her way on this new newspaper staff. You remember what it was like starting college. Knowing nothing and no one."

Adam watched through the open French doors as his daughter kissed her mother's cheek and then walked out of the kitchen, to return to her dorm, probably. He'd call her tomorrow or the day after.

"So what's up with you?" Adam turned to Mark. They didn't talk as much as they used to. Not even now that he had moved back to the East Coast.

"Not much."

"You doing all right?" Adam searched Mark's face in the semidarkness. Sophie had told him Mark had been having some problems sleeping, some anxiety. He looked pale and drawn and he'd lost weight.

"I don't know. You know," he said, noncommittal.

Adam waited quietly in the darkness, listening to the

croak of frogs in the woods behind the house. "Yeah, I know. The nightmares back?"

He nodded. "You'd think after all these years . . ." Mark grew quiet, letting his sentence go unfinished.

Adam understood. In December it would be ten years since the Lombardo shoot-out and the subsequent circumstances that had changed their lives forever. "I know, man." He wanted to reach out to him, give his arm a squeeze, hug him, something, but knew how hard these episodes in Mark's life could be. He didn't want anyone making a fuss. "It'll pass. Always does."

"I know, but with the baby coming, it's such shitty timing." Mark slapped a mosquito on his arm.

"You thought about some more counseling?"

"Thought about it."

The two were silent again for a couple of minutes. Adam checked his watch. "Guess I better get going. I need to take M.K. back to her car."

"Listen, thanks for coming." Mark offered his hand.

Adam pumped it. "You mean, thanks for chasing Liza Jane off."

Mark grinned. "A week's just not a week unless she stomps out of the house about something."

"Take it easy." Adam slapped Mark on the back and walked away. "And you call me if you need to talk. Remember, I was there, too." Mark didn't say anything and Adam walked into Sophie's bright yellow kitchen. "M.K., you ready to hit the road?"

When M.K. heard the phone ring, she was tempted not to answer it. She checked her wristwatch. It was ten-thirty. Her father was watching the evening news to find out if she'd been killed in a shoot-out today. Her mother, having washed the dishes, swept the kitchen floor, tucked in the two children remaining at home, and said her evening prayers, was making the call at his request; Margaret always acted on James's requests.

The phone rang again and M.K. picked up the TV remote and hit "mute." She wasn't really watching it anyway. As Adam the soothsayer had predicted, she was going over some case files.

The phone rang again. The answering machine would pick up in a minute. Then her father would begin calling the local hospitals in preparation for claiming her body.

M.K. picked up the cordless phone and pressed the "talk" button. "Hello, Mama."

"How did you know it was me, dear?"

"Caller ID, Mama. Remember?" M.K. stared at the silent TV screen turned to CNN. The film clip was enough to see what was happening in the Middle East. She didn't need the sound to know that with the passing of another day it was a step closer to the apocalyptic ending laid out in the Book of Revelation. "You should have caller ID, too, so you and Da aren't bothered with the telemarketers."

"I don't need such fancy things. How was your week? Meet anyone new? A nice young man, maybe."

"Mama, it's not high school, and it's not a dating service—it's my job." M.K. drew her feet up under her. She was wearing a nightgown her mother had made her fifteen years ago that was hopelessly faded and obscenely thin. Fortunately . . . or unfortunately, depending on how she looked at it, no one ever saw her in it. "My week was fine. How was yours?"

"Last night's fish fry went good. The auxiliary made almost two hundred dollars. Oh, and Father Houlihan is retiring. I've been waiting to tell you all week—it was announced last Sunday at Mass. We'll be having a going-away supper, of course. I hope you can come—you know how he always liked you."

M.K. closed her eyes. She didn't know if it was the birth and care of eight children or the unending housework, or the lack of a life beyond the Philadelphia stone row house and the neighborhood church, but her mother sounded old beyond her fifty-two years. "Mama, you don't have to wait until Saturday night to call me. I told you, you can call me any night. We'll have to see about the church supper. I'm just getting settled in the office. I never know when I'll have to work."

"Sundays? Surely you don't have to work on the Lord's Day," her mother exclaimed in appropriate shock.

"Sometimes I do, Mama. The bad guys don't shut down on Sundays."

"But you go to Mass?"

"Of course, Mama, and I almost always make it before the homily."

She chuckled on the other end of the phone. "You were always such a kidder, dear. Well, your father says hello."

M.K. knew that wasn't true. Her father never said anything so pleasant. But she wasn't going to get into that tonight. Besides, the phone call was almost over. It always lasted six minutes. Never five, but never seven, either. "Give the girls a hug for me. How is everyone?"

"Come home and see. Theresa is expecting again. Patricia and Patrick settled on their new house. Everyone misses you, dear, especially Anna."

M.K. smiled. Her youngest sister, Anna, who was now fourteen, had Down's syndrome and always held a special place in her heart. "Give her a hug for me, will you?"

"Come home and give her a hug yourself. You could come tomorrow for supper—we could eat early. I could make a nice pot roast."

"Mama, I can't." *I can't, because your house is toxic and your husband, my father, is toxic to my life, to all our lives*, M.K. thought. But she didn't say it. She never did. "Maybe next Sunday, Ma."

"Talk to you next week, dear. God rest you and keep you."

M.K. knew her mother was crossing herself. "Good night, Mama. I love you."

She hung up the phone and set it gently on the table beside her easy chair, staring at the TV screen. As the oldest daughter of the Shaughnessy clan, M.K. always somehow felt responsible for her mother's plight. When she had lived at home, she had worked relentlessly to try to ease some of the daily burden of caring for such a large family. She'd even attended a local community college so as not to have to move away from home. She had been twenty-three the first time she had slept alone in a house.

M.K. shifted her gaze to the pile of folders at her feet. She was tired but she wanted to go through one more before she went to bed. She might as well; she didn't sleep well. Going to bed late after a long day, getting up early, made the nights seem shorter.

"You're not disturbing me at all, sugar." Cradling the phone on his shoulder, Jerome pushed back in his leather chair behind his massive mahogany desk, giving his full attention to his wife. It was difficult for him to be separated from her all day, worrying about her. The last round of chemo had wiped her out, and she didn't seem to be springing back the way she had last time. The prognosis was not good, but he wasn't ready to think about that, not yet.

"You eat the lunch I left for you?" He glanced at the eight-by-ten photograph of her in a sapphire gown on the corner of his desk. It had been taken a year ago at the hospital benefit ball that she had coordinated. In the photo she was laughing, her head tipped back, her glossy black hair pulled up in an elegant twist, the diamond-and-platinum necklace he had given her for their twenty-fifth anniversary around her slender neck. That had been before the cancer and successive treatments had left her bald and spotted her exquisite ebony skin with patches of red rashes.

"Now, Sela, it was only half a sandwich and a cup of my minestrone soup. That certainly does not qualify as a feast." He straightened her photo, thinking how amazing it was that at fifty-two she'd not had a single gray hair, unlike his head that had seemed to turn white overnight at forty-five. "You've got to try and eat." He paused, letting her speak. He knew how important it was to allow cancer patients to talk. They had so little control over so much of their lives that the little things like what they ate for lunch could become very important.

"Just a couple of bites—that's all I'm asking."

There was a tap on the door and Jerome looked up to see his receptionist, Mrs. Elright, stick her tightly permed head through the doorway. "Dr. Fisher, your new patient has arrived."

He smiled, indicating with a wave of his hand to send the patient in. "Listen, hon, I've got an intake patient so I need to go, but I'm calling back in half an hour and you had better have eaten a bite or two of that sandwich."

He smiled bittersweetly. He would never tire of her melodic voice. "I love you, too."

Jerome hung up the phone, swallowing the lump in his throat as he rose.

The door to his office swung open as Mrs. Elright showed the patient in the door. Jerome picked up his leather notebook he used to take notes during sessions and came around his desk. "Good afternoon, welcome." He opened his hand toward two comfy leather chairs separated by a coffee table. "Thank you, Mrs. Elright," he called as she discreetly stepped out and closed the door behind her.

"Thank you for seeing me on my lunch break," the patient said, settling in the chair. "My job is such that I can't easily slip out."

Jerome nodded, flipping open his notebook to look at his initial notes. "I see, M—"

"*Blue*, please," the patient interrupted.

Jerome glanced up. "Excuse me?"

The patient maintained eye contact with him. "Blue. I would prefer that you call me Blue here inside this office."

"I see." Jerome scribbled *Blue* across the heading of the page. Later he would meticulously enter his notes in a new file, but he liked to jot down impressions during sessions, which he would later consider more thoroughly. "May I ask why?"

"A way of keeping my personal life separate from my professional life." The patient managed a wry smile. "Surely you must have other patients who do the same. As my history unfolds, you'll see that I've been battling many issues for years. But somehow, I have managed to establish a well-respected career, one that gives me a great deal of pleasure, which can rarely be said of life in general."

Jerome scribbled in shorthand. The patient was nicely dressed, well spoken, obviously educated. He quickly flipped back a page to check the preliminary information provided, noting the patient's occupation, then flipped forward again.

"Attaching a different name to the person inside this office . . . the person who struggles," the patient continued, "it helps me keep my life in balance." There was a pause. "Is that a problem, Dr. Fisher?"

Jerome looked up. "Not at all. It's not unusual for patients in treatment to refer to themselves by different names than those the world knows them as. Not uncommon to hear different speech patterns inside this office. I even have patients who I swear look different in here than they do beyond that door."

"So this doesn't make me crazy."

Jerome chuckled. "It's been my experience that patients who inquire as to whether or not they are crazy usually aren't."

The patient smiled with relief. "Good. I think you and I will get along well, Dr. Fisher."

Jerome leaned back, studying the patient in the chair

across from him. "I have here in my notes your initial concern, but I'd like to hear it in your own words. Often, simply stating the problem is the best way to start tackling it."

The patient looked down, avoiding eye contact for the first time since entering the office, and Jerome watched carefully, focusing not just on the words, but the body language as well.

"I . . ." The patient hesitated, and then started again. "I'm afraid I might be bisexual." The words came out in a rush. "There, I've said it."

Jerome waited. When it was obvious the patient was done, he spoke gently. "I take it that in the past you've had heterosexual relationships?"

The patient nodded.

Again, Jerome allowed for silence before speaking again. "And what has made you question your sexuality now?"

"I . . ." There was a twisting of hands. A crossing and uncrossing of legs. "I've been going to bars. Not here, of course, never here where I could be seen by someone who knows me."

Jerome nodded sympathetically. "Go on."

"I've been going to bars in D.C., sometimes over on the Delaware shore, and picking up . . . picking up strangers of my own sex. Having—" The patient seemed unable or unwilling to finish the sentence.

"Have you been having sex with these strangers, Blue?"

The patient nodded.

"And you find this disturbing?"

The patient met Jerome's gaze. "The most important thing to me in my life, the only *real* thing in my life, is my work. If something like this were to get out—" A pause. "Dr. Fisher, if someone I knew found out about this, I would lose respect among my colleagues. As you know, in my line of work, respect can mean everything."

"So what do you hope to accomplish in our sessions, Blue?"

"I want to stop." There was a tremble in the patient's voice. A flexing of hands, gritting of teeth. "I find this behavior abhorrent and I want it to stop. I was told you specialized in sexual behavior. That you and your wife were the best."

Jerome took his time to respond. "I cannot promise you I can help you make that happen."

"I *have* to try."

Jerome studied the patient's face for a moment and then nodded. "Fair enough. My plan would be to help you explore your feelings, ascertain why, at this stage in your life, these urges have begun to surface, and then, if you still want to put an end to your behavior, we can build a strategy that will help you accomplish that."

"Thank you so much, Doctor." The patient rose. "As I told your receptionist, I couldn't make a full appointment today, but I did want to come see you." There was a hint of a smile. "Plead my case."

Jerome stood, offering his hand, and the patient shook it with a firm grip. "Mrs. Elright will see that you're put on my schedule. To begin with, I'd like to see you once a week, then we'll see how it goes."

"Thank you again, Dr. Fisher."

Jerome waited until the patient closed the door and then returned to his desk and punched his home number into the phone. His wife picked up on the second ring and he eased into his chair. "And you thought you were going to have some peace and quiet today with me out of the house, didn't you?" he teased.

"I did have a new patient. Just a quick chat." He glanced at his open notes on his desk. "Very interesting person. Well controlled, well spoken, but, I sense, close to desperation. I may need a consult from the best psychiatrist I know." He pushed the notes aside. "Now, did you eat that sandwich or not?"

Chapter Four

Jessica swirled her margarita glass and, glancing over the salt-encrusted rim, took another sip. She couldn't believe her roommate had stood her up. They were supposed to meet at O'Shea's before happy hour was over—two-for-one *grande* frozen margaritas. She watched as a couple more college kids came in the door. The pub was busy; most of the dark, heavy tables were already occupied, and people were standing three deep at the bar and congregating in the hallway that led to the pay phones and bathrooms.

She liked O'Shea's because it wasn't just a college-kids hangout—she could go to the student center if she wanted that. But older guys came, too, guys already out of school—lawyers, teachers, cops. Last week she'd met this guy who was a resident at the local hospital. She wouldn't mind dating a doctor, and her parents certainly wouldn't complain.

Jessica drained her glass and pushed it across the smooth, polished wooden bar. She'd already had two. If Leanne wasn't coming, she didn't know that she should order two more. She'd be stumbling back to the dorm with four margaritas on a stomach of bar popcorn and the pop tart she'd eaten when she got up at noon.

"Come on, Leanne," she muttered, glancing at the door again. Her roommate said she had to stop by her biology professor's office to schedule a lab she'd missed, but how long could that take? Unless, of course, Leanne was flirting with him. Jessica liked her roommate, but she wasn't crazy about the way she manipulated professors by using sex. Leanne claimed she rarely had to sleep with a guy or girl, that usually flirting with them was enough to get a passing grade, but Jessica didn't care. It wasn't her style. She did, however, have to admire Leanne for how open she was about being bi. It took a lot of guts to be like that at twenty-one years old.

"Ready for two more?" the bartender asked.

"I don't know." Jessica spun around on the bar stool. Jay was cute. Once in a while he even gave her a free drink. "I don't really need two more." She laughed, already half drunk.

"Neither do I," said the person on the next bar stool over. "You want to order two more together and we'll split the tab?"

I don't know what made me go into O'Shea's, a bar so close to home where I could potentially be recognized in my present emotional condition. Not that it would matter if I was recognized; after all, I am a part of the community. I just have to be careful. Think before I act. With that nagging investigation into the accident still going on, I can't take chances. It's something I probably need to talk with Dr. Fisher about without giving details. Why *am* I taking this risk?

I look up over the rim of my glass. I don't really like margaritas, but the coed on the stool beside me is so cute. Her face is so fresh, so alive with all the possibilities a college girl has before her. Before I can catch myself, I am offering to have a drink with her. No, it is more intimate than that. I know it the moment her green eyes meet my gaze.

"It's just margaritas that are two for one," the girl says, glancing at my beer.

I shrug, smiling. Someone reaches over me, throwing money on the bar. "Bar dude, another four margaritas over here when you get a chance."

My new friend and I look up at the drunk between us and our gazes meet. We are on the same wavelength. I don't have to say a word. We both smile.

"Jay, two more when you get to it," the young woman beside me calls to one of the three bartenders.

"You got it, Jessica."

The drunk wanders away and I lean closer so I can be heard. Happy hour is almost over and the bar is now packed, smoky, loud. There is no live music because it's a weeknight, but Dave Matthews's voice comes from the round speakers strategically placed on the dark beams overhead. People are starting to get lit on the twofers. Names and faces are beginning to blur, which is what I realize I am counting on.

"You're a student at Chesapeake Bay, right?" I ask.

She smiles. She doesn't seem to care that I am older than she is. Maybe she is even a little flattered.

She nods, leaning closer so I can hear. "Psych major."

"Thinking about going into counseling?"

"Maybe troubled teens." She folds the damp napkin in front of her one way, then another, as if it is a piece of origami paper. "A safe house for battered kids, maybe pregnant teenagers." She shrugs. "I don't know yet."

She certainly does not. Sitting here beside her, looking at her adorable WASP face, I can guess not only her religious background and ethnicity, but I can probably guess her socioeconomic status, even what kind of car her parents gave her on her sixteenth birthday. Young women like this have no idea what troubled teens are faced with. Her biggest agony in the last three or four years has probably been whether to give up her virginity on prom night.

I have known girls like Jessica. I still have the scars to prove it.

"Wow," I hear myself say. "Giving back to the community. That's awesome."

The bartender delivers two frozen margaritas.

Jessica and I put our money on the counter at the same time and laugh. It is silly, I know, inane. But isn't the whole human mating dance inane? And that is what is going on in O'Shea's tonight. Of course these college kids, the young professionals, don't see it as mating per se. Most of them are looking for a one-night stand. Hot sex with a stranger, hopefully a stranger who won't remember you in the morning. But I know it is that innate desire in all humans to continue to reproduce that brings them to bars, to parties, even to Mass on Sunday mornings. Every place, every situation is a potential hunting ground. Life is all about sex. Procreation. The other hours are just filled with anger, pain, ugliness, to make the day go by.

Jessica lifts her glass and giggles. "Well, cheers."

I listen to the *tink* of the glasses as the two collide. Salt falls to the bar top and she presses her finger to the tiny granules and then touches her finger to her lips.

I watch, mesmerized. I set my glass down without partaking. She doesn't seem to notice.

"So what about you? You're not a student." Again, the giggle.

I smile, making myself what she wants me to be. I have learned that technique well over the years. I can be almost anything to anyone, at least for a short time. Self-preservation. "It's a dull tale. You here with someone?"

She rolls her green eyes, tucking a lock of brown hair behind one ear. She has the prettiest hair that falls past her shoulders, all glossy like a silk curtain. I find myself wanting to touch her hair as she tells me about her roommate standing her up. I pretend to listen, pretend to be interested, but it is her hair that fascinates me, not her inane conversation. It is such perfect hair for such an obviously imperfect person.

We talk for another twenty minutes, about what, I'm not even sure. Then she slides off the bar stool. "Hey, you leaving me?" I ask, ducking as a waitress lifts a tray over my head to get past me.

"I should be."

"But you haven't finished your margarita," I tease.

"You mean, yours." Someone bumps into Jessica and she grabs my shoulder, pressing her right breast against my arm. "I gotta pee," she says.

I just smile. "Then come back and finish my drink. No sense letting it go to waste."

She lifts her lashes, looking into my eyes. I know that look. And I know that we will walk out of O'Shea's together.

"Be right back. Watch my purse?" She lays the small black leather bag on her bar stool to keep someone from snatching up her seat.

"Sure." I smile. Watch her weave her way through the crowd. She is very drunk.

Here is where my evening takes an unexpected turn. Without any preconceived plan, from the pocket of my jacket I remove a bubble pack of tablets I have used before in other bars, though not so near to home. I pop one into my hand, hesitate, then pop another, for a reason I cannot fathom. My heart is pounding in my chest as I draw my hand over the glass that is mine and drop in the tablets. Slipping one hand back into my pocket, I raise the glass, swirl it, lift it to my lips to pretend I am drinking.

As I lower it to the bar, I glance around. The guy sitting on Jessica's other side left his bar stool at the same time she got up to go to the bathroom. Someone slides into it a moment later. Jay the bartender has disappeared into the back. A young woman seems to have taken his place. Shift change, perhaps, or maybe Jay is one of those young men who doesn't believe the surgeon general's warnings on cigarette packages. Maybe he is taking a smoke break outside the back kitchen door.

A moment later, Jessica returns. As she walks toward me I take in the tight blue jeans and t-shirt, her youthful stride. Again, she lays her hand on my shoulder as she squeezes past several guys doing shots, to take her seat again. She smiles and raises the margarita glass to me and then to her lips.

I watch her drink, imagining the dissolved rohypnol gliding down her throat. She said she was hungry; her stomach was empty. The drug will reach her bloodstream even faster.

"You want another?" I ask as she tips the glass back and licks the rim.

She shakes her head and reaches into the half-empty bowl of popcorn one of the bartenders has put out. "I'm already going to have a headache tomorrow." She crams the popcorn into her mouth.

I finish off my second beer. Chat. Within ten minutes, her forehead begins to break out in beads of sweat. Her speech becomes noticeably slurred.

"I . . . I don't feel so well," she says, wiping her forehead. "Hot."

"Maybe you just need something to eat."

She shakes her head. "Nah, I better go." She slips off the bar stool and sways. "Whoa."

I press my hand to her back to steady her. "You going to be all right? You want me to walk you back to your dorm?"

She walks away, bumping into a girl, splashing a drink down her t-shirt. "I'm . . . fr . . . fine," Jessica slurs, disappearing into the crowd.

I make myself remain on the bar stool, giving her time to weave her way out the door, allowing plenty of witnesses to see her leave alone. I have already paid the bar bill. I get off my stool, which is immediately claimed by a young man with dreadlocks. I go down the hallway toward the bathrooms, then, checking over my shoulder to see that no one is looking, I slip out the emergency exit door, which has been propped open by someone.

The door opens to the alley that runs along the side of the bar. There is a tall fence overgrown by shrubs and vines. As if staged by a world-renowned director, Jessica comes stumbling toward me.

The alley is empty and cast in heavy shadows. It is meant to be.

"Jessica," I say softly, my heart pounding. *She believes she is going to counsel abused teens, unwed mothers*, I think with scorn.

She looks up, disoriented. I don't even think she recognizes me. Her breathing is labored and she is sweating profusely, both side effects of the drug. "Head hurts," she mumbles.

I reach out to catch her and she is in my arms. Her life is mine. She sways and falls back and I feel her full weight against me. "Here," I hear myself say. "Take some aspirin for that headache."

"Don't want . . ." Her head falls against my arm. I pop another roofie from the package in my pocket and press it to her lips. She swallows it and there is no turning back for me.

In a moment of brilliance, I tuck the bubble pack into her purse. Just the other day I read in the *Baltimore Sun* how teen girls were using the so-called date-rape drug to lower their sexual inhibitions. How tragic.

"F . . . feel . . . sh . . . sick," Jessica pants, pressing her face into my chest.

"Shhh," I soothe, stroking her silky hair. "It's all right."

Faces in the bar swirled around Jessica. She caught herself on the edge of the bathroom sink.

Dizzy. Disoriented.

Time skipped, a stone on a pond's surface.

She could feel the cool air of the evening on her bare

arms. Saw the security light overhead. She was in someone's arms. A gentle voice. Leanne? Had she finally shown up just in time to drag Jessica home and put her in bed?

She'd had too much to drink. Too many margaritas. Not enough popcorn . . .

"Feeling better, Jessica?" the voice asked.

She opened her eyes and realized she was having a hard time catching her breath. She was breathing—she could feel her chest moving, but she felt like she was holding her breath under water. Something wasn't right. She wasn't in a pool. Wasn't in her dorm room. Wasn't in the bar. Outside. A dog barking. The sound of nearby street traffic. She gazed up into the eyes of the person who held her.

A stranger? She had to be dreaming. A nightmare.

She saw the knife.

Jessica felt herself falling, saw the stranger's face looming overhead. She heard herself scream . . . or was that just in her dream, too?

Adam was typing in the last bit of the information on the Palmer file before he submitted it to Crackhow when his cell phone rang. He glanced at the little screen; it read Liza Jane. "Hey," he said picking up.

He continued to peck on the keyboard. "What's up?" He glanced at his watch. "Only ten-thirty—you're up early."

"I have a nine A.M. class on Wednesdays, Dad. Look, the reason I'm calling is that something's going on down here that you might want to know about." She hesitated. "This girl, a student here, was found dead behind O'Shea's this morning."

"You're kidding." He stopped typing. Despite its proximity to Baltimore and D.C., Ashview was a quiet place with a hometown feeling. There was very little crime, mostly break-ins, a shoplifting, no more than a mugging a year, and then it usually involved college students and some kind of payback. It was part of the reason why Adam had wanted Liza Jane to go to Chesapeake, instead of Temple in Philadelphia.

"What happened?"

"I don't know. I'm on my way over now."

He heard the sound of a car horn and pictured his only child darting through traffic to make a newspaper headline. "Liza Jane, you don't belong at a crime scene."

"So you think a crime has taken place?" she inquired. "You don't think the girl just died?" It was her reporter's voice, the same he'd heard on her first four-minute spot on the college's TV station the other night—she'd come on right after *Fraternity Row*.

"Liza, this isn't the kind of thing you play games—"

"I'm not playing games, Dad. Look, I got to go. They've got the street blocked off, but I know a way around through the alley."

"Liza Jane, wait. You—"

"I'll talk to you later, Dad."

She hung up, leaving Adam to stare at the cell phone in his hand. Should he call her back? She probably wouldn't answer if he did.

A dead girl behind O'Shea's. How bizarre was that? The community would be reeling; first the four frat boys, now this young woman.

Grabbing his cell phone, he got out of his chair and walked down the aisle of cubicles, past the water fountain. He leaned over M.K.'s half wall. "Hey, you want to take a ride to Ashview?" he asked quietly, looking around to see who else was there. It was pretty quiet; most of the field agents were out of the office.

"What's up?" She was already out of her chair, reaching for her black jacket.

"I don't know. Nothing, probably." He halted, then went on. "I just got a call from Liza Jane. She says there's a dead girl behind O'Shea's—a little pub just off the Chesapeake Bay College campus."

"Some connection with the dead boys?"

"I can't see how," he said slowly. "Just bizarre coincidence."

"How'd she die?"

"I don't know. My sleuth hadn't reached the crime scene yet. I was thinking maybe I would head that way. She gets arrested, you know, I can bail her out."

"I'll go with you. Sure." She walked past him. "Just let me tell Crackhow what's up."

"M.K., I don't think that's necessary." He followed her down the hall. "Sometimes it's just better if you go fishing on your own. Come back to the boss if you find something."

"Just to cover ourselves."

"Yeah, but—" He put out his hand. "What excuse do we use?"

"No excuse." She halted at the assistant SAC's door, knocked, and walked in.

"Something interesting going on in Ashview, Captain," she said. "Special Agent Thomas and I are going to have a look."

He peered up from the unrelenting piles of records on his desk. "Something to do with the auto accident? The senator's office is still calling every day."

"Report's about done, concluding there's nothing to report. Kids driving drunk. Tragic accident."

"So what's going on in Ashview that would concern the Bureau?"

M.K. hesitated for a moment, and Adam considered coming to her rescue, but this was her idea to begin with.

"A dead girl behind a bar. No connection to the Palmer boy at all, sir, but I think when you send that report over to the senator's office, it would be a good idea for us to be knowledgeable enough to be able to say so."

In spite of himself, Adam almost smiled. The woman had an entirely different approach than he did, but he couldn't help but be impressed.

"You say Thomas's going with you?" Crackhow looked down at the form in front of him.

"Yes, sir."

"Report back to me. And I want the Palmer file on my desk in the morning."

"Yes, sir." M.K. walked out.

"Pretty slick," Adam said.

She lifted a shoulder. She seemed taller to him than she had the first week they had worked together. At the very least, not so helpless.

"My turn to get the car," Adam said, walking past her. "Meet you downstairs."

"Get one with lights and a siren," she called after him as she walked around the corner.

"Yes, ma'am."

Chapter Five

M.K. was nervous about attending her first crime scene, but a part of her was excited, too. Exhilarated. She'd worked hard to earn the right to walk in on a crime investigation and flash her ID card. Worked hard with no support from those she loved.

Adam parked the car half a block from O'Shea's pub and they walked up the brick sidewalk. He pointed in the direction of the campus, then where the police station they'd visited last week was located. The bar was in the downtown area of Ashview, easily accessible to college students, but it also had a large parking lot in the rear—for men like her partner, she supposed. He told her he came here all the time, had met Liza Jane here just last week.

Adam ducked under the yellow tape marking the crime scene area, and a middle-aged Ashview police officer approached them. "You'll have to step back behind the tape, sir, ma'am."

"FBI," Adam said.

M.K. reached inside her coat for her ID and clipped it on her lapel. Adam dug his out of the front pocket of his khaki slacks and the officer was so startled that he barely looked at it. He mumbled something and stepped back to let them pass.

"We're supposed to wear our badges in plain sight," M.K. said. "It's in the regs."

"Maybe once upon a time, but these days, you have to be more careful." He strode across the parking lot that was filled with navy Ashview police cars with their large, old-fashioned gold shields painted on the side. There were also two emergency vehicles: an EMT truck and an ambulance, and a dark blue minivan marked with the seal of Maryland and the word *Coroner* across the side.

"I don't know about you," Adam continued, pointing to his badge when a freshly-scrubbed-faced police officer approached them. "But I feel no great desire to get gunned down in a Wawa minimart while stopping for a cup of coffee. I show it when I need to."

"Your captain here?" M.K. asked the young officer standing next to one of the marked cars. He looked a little bewildered. There were camera flashes going off behind him, reporters shouting questions, and a Baltimore news channel truck with a satellite dish on the roof was trying to inch its way into the parking lot. The press.

The officer pointed around the end of the brick building. "In the alley." He hurried away, waving his arms. "Sir! Sir, you can't park that there."

M.K. walked around the corner, stepping on a tuft of dandelions that had grown up from a crack in the blacktop. She understood how the officer was feeling; she was a little overwhelmed herself. She'd been trained to deal with a crime scene and the processes to follow, but somehow the real thing was different. She hadn't expected the dandelions, the stale smell of fries coming from the kitchen door left open, the bright, whirling lights of the emergency vehicles, the expressions on the faces of the people around her.

"Captain Seipp." Adam approached the Ashview police chief they'd met with the previous week. He was leaning against the wall of the brick building near an emergency exit door that had been propped open.

He turned at the sound of his name, his pudgy face bright red. He looked more out of place than M.K. felt.

"Special Agent Thomas. Shaughnessy. Ma'am." He tipped his hat, coming off the wall, hitching up his navy uniform pants and his holstered sidearm with it.

M.K. nodded.

"What brings you here?" Sweat gleamed across Seipp's broad forehead.

"Heard you lost another student. We were in the area so we stopped by. Wanted to see if we could be of any use."

Adam was smooth. Of course, M.K had known that since day one. She listened to the men's conversation as she surveyed the crime scene. The alley that ran along the side of the pub was wide, wide enough for two cars to pass. One side was the building, on the other, was a tall white wooden fence overgrown with vines. Her gaze shifted to the large green Dumpster beneath a security light high on an electric pole. At the foot of the pole lay a young woman in a pair of jeans and a yellow t-shirt. There was one sandal on her foot, one on the pavement. A bare foot revealed blue nail polish.

Somehow the nail polish made the grim scene all the more real.

"A Jessica Lawson, twenty-one years of age, junior at Chesapeake. Found this morning around ten after ten, city garbage men. No blood, no sign of any physical trauma." Seipp wiped his forehead with an already-damp handkerchief.

M.K. allowed her gaze to linger over the young woman's face. Her eyes were closed. She looked away as a lump rose in her throat. Jessica Lawson was pretty the way twenty-one-year-olds are . . . at least she had been.

"Cause of death?" Adam was speaking to the captain, but he was searching the crowd. Looking for Liza Jane, M.K. guessed.

"Hard to say."

"An educated guess?"

"Two-for-one margarita night. Alcohol poisoning." The police chief lifted his double chin in the direction of the body. "Looks like she vomited at some point. There were some kind of pills in her purse, too. Don't know what they are yet. Then maybe it's something else. Heart attack. Aneurysm. Had a cousin, only twenty-three—threw a blood clot one day while he was carrying out the trash. Killed him before he hit the ground."

M.K. spotted a thirty-something man in a navy blue jumpsuit with the word CORONER written across the back of it. He had to be Dr. Wood's assistant. She shifted her gaze, checking out one person and then the next—the inner circle, those permitted beyond the yellow tape: EMTs, more Ashview police, an ambulance driver. Some stood near the Dumpster, others against the fence. Only a few feet from the trash receptacle was a break in the fence. At least two boards were missing; it was wide enough to walk through if you turned sideways.

M.K. imagined herself walking out of the bar, stumbling, going down the alley, maybe hoping to take a shortcut home? She caught movement out of the corner of her eye and looked at the fence again. This time she spotted a splash of color against the overgrowth she could see between the missing boards—a hot pink bandana. A blonde wearing a pink bandana.

"Back in a sec," M.K. said. Adam was still talking to Seipp. The body would be transported to Annapolis for autopsy, he was saying.

M.K. circumnavigated the crowd of people standing around the body; no one seemed to notice her. She walked along the fence, still taking in the scene. Loose trash around the Dumpster. A crushed pen on the pavement. An empty soda can. She wondered if the street lamp worked. It probably had a sensor that turned it on at dusk. She would check into it.

At the hole in the fence, she halted. Liza Jane must have spotted her because M.K. couldn't see her now.

M.K. presented her back to the fence, crossing her arms over her chest. She was hot in her suit, wishing she had the guts to wear a polo and khakis like Adam and not care what Crackhow thought. "You shouldn't be here. Shouldn't have to see this," she said quietly.

There was silence for a moment. "It isn't like I expected," Liza Jane said in a small voice from behind the fence. "She doesn't look dead. She looks asleep."

"She's not asleep."

"What killed her? There's no blood."

"I don't know, Liza Jane."

"So, what? It's a secret?" She immediately took on a conspiratorial tone. "Someone trying to hide something?"

M.K. closed her fingers around the splintered boards of the fence and looked through the hole. Liza Jane stood there in jeans and a tee, a notebook and pen in hand; she looked so much like the dead girl—except for her hair color—that it startled her. "You should go now before the police see you and escort you from the premises."

"I have a right to know what's happened." Now she was combative, full of youthful righteousness. "The students at Chesapeake have a right to know, Agent Shaughnessy."

"So go stand with the rest of the press behind the yellow tape." M.K. walked away.

"Listen, I appreciate you putting a rush on this autopsy and getting the report worked up right away," Adam said, sitting back in his chair and propping one ankle on his knee. He wore boat moccasins without socks and M.K. could see his suntanned ankle.

They sat in Dr. Wood's office off the examining room of the morgue. As they spoke, M.K. tried to keep her gaze and her mind off the human organs in the jars. That left her with

the dead body of Jessica Lawson on the autopsy table to concentrate on.

Dr. Wood sat relaxed in her chair behind her desk, unaf-
fected by the organs in the jars or the dead college student
fifteen feet away. "Not a problem, Special Agent Thomas. I
know how upset the community is—I saw the piece on the
evening news last night."

"Please, call me Adam."

M.K. didn't look up to see Adam flirting with the doctor.
Didn't have to. She was learning quickly that he pretty much
flirted with every female between the ages of four and a hundred and four. He definitely had a special thing for Dr. Wood,
though. Maybe it was the long, shapely legs that went on forever. Maybe it was the beautiful face. Her warm personality.
M.K. didn't have time to think about all the reasons why a
single, good-looking, heterosexual man like Adam would
want to go out with a woman like Dr. Valerie Wood.

She glanced down at the preliminary autopsy report in
her hand that the doctor had just produced. On the desk in
front of her was a manila envelope with autopsy photos. "So
it was an overdose of rohypnol and not some kind of alcohol-
related thing?"

"She did have a blood alcohol level of .12, over the legal
limit to drive in the state of Maryland, but not enough alcohol in her system to kill her. The alcohol could very well,
however, have contributed to the effects of the rohypnol."

M.K. studied the words typed across the form. "I spoke
with her father yesterday. He was very upset, obviously."
She tried not to acknowledge how greatly her first interview
with a decedent's family member had upset her. "He said she
didn't do drugs, not pot, pills, not coke. He couldn't believe
a drug overdose had killed her."

"The accidental death rate of Americans ages fifteen to
twenty-two is alarming, Special Agent Shaughnessy. I have
no children myself, but I can imagine how disconcerting it

would be for a parent." She looked across the desk at M.K.'s partner. "You said you have a daughter, didn't you, Adam?"

"I do. Nineteen years old. She attends Chesapeake." He stroked his chin. "And you're right, pretty scary stuff. I try not to think about it, especially with what I see on the job."

"Okay, I understand kids doing drugs and sometimes it kills them, but why a date-rape drug?" M.K. wondered aloud, glancing up at the medical examiner. "I thought that was something guys put in girls' drinks so they could have their way with them."

Dr. Wood shrugged her lovely shoulders beneath her spotless white lab coat. She was wearing a cute pale peach summer sweater under the coat that lent a casual, though still professional air to her appearance. "I wondered the same," she admitted, leaning forward on her desk. "So, I did a little Internet research last night and I discovered that while it's not common, it's not unheard of for young people to take the drug for the high it produces. It's very cheap, a couple of bucks a pop, and some think it enhances sexual pleasure."

M.K. glanced at Adam. "According to witnesses, she left the bar alone. Think she was meeting someone?"

"Possibly, but I don't know that it matters. Dr. Wood's provided our cause of death. I think that's really all Crackhow wanted." He looked to the medical examiner. "Our boss. The Bureau was getting some pressure from Senator Palmer's office. With this accidental death falling so close after the auto accident."

"I understand." Dr. Wood folded her arms in front of her. "Not a good year for Chesapeake Bay College."

"I'd say not," Adam mused.

M.K. passed the report to Adam and opened the envelope. Graphic autopsy photos slid into her hand. She flipped through them. As the doctor reported, there were no cuts or bruises on her nude body. M.K. found the color photographs chilling; for some reason, she had always thought autopsy photos were in black and white. They were always in black and white on TV.

Jessica Lawson still looked so beautiful, even dead on the medical examiner's table.

M.K. flipped to the last photo, a head shot. "That's odd," she said aloud after staring at it for a moment.

"What's that?" Dr. Wood reached for the photo.

M.K. offered the eight-by-ten, pointing to the splash of hair beside the dead girl's face. "There. Isn't there hair missing?"

"What do you mean, *missing*?" Adam rose, walking around the desk so he could look at the photograph the doctor held. He didn't seem to worry about getting into someone else's *space* the way M.K. did.

"Look." M.K. pointed with her finger. "Doesn't it look to you like a piece of hair has been cut off? A pretty big piece."

Adam studied the photo of the dead girl's face for a moment. Frowned. "Yeah, I guess it's been cut or something." He looked up, walking back around to sit in the chair again. "But, so? Rohypnol killed her. What's that got to do with her death?"

M.K. glanced up at the medical examiner. "Did you notice this during your exam, Dr. Wood?"

She gave the photo a final look and then offered it back to M.K. "Not really. I did note on the report, though, that there was a small contusion on the back of her head that probably occurred when she fell in the alley."

"Do you think I could have a look at the body?" M.K. didn't really want another up-close look at the dead girl, but the cut hair just seemed so odd to her. Out of place.

"By all means." The doctor rose and walked around her desk, out into the tiled autopsy room. M.K. followed and Adam reluctantly got out of his chair.

"I've already stitched her up, prepared her to be taken to the funeral home," Dr. Wood explained, crossing the distance to the chrome table in long strides. "The body's being released this afternoon."

M.K. halted at the head of the table and studied the pale face that no longer looked quite real. "So she just stays here until then?"

"We have a storage unit." The doctor pointed to an open doorway to the right of her office. "We're a small morgue, so I can only store up to eight bodies at a time. Not that we would ever need that many." She smiled grimly. "An accident like the one with the boys a few weeks ago was a full house for here."

M.K. walked to the other side of the head of the table, comparing the photo in her hand to Jessica's face. Her naked body was covered discreetly with a pale blue disposable drape, leaving nothing bared but her shoulders and head. M.K. studied the pale brown hair that fell on the shiny chrome table. Sure enough, as in the photo, the hair looked cut. She reached out tentatively. "May I?"

"Certainly," Dr. Wood said. "My exam is complete—you can't contaminate the evidence. Let me get you some disposable gloves." She stepped away, her high heels clicking on the tile floor.

"No, that'll be all right." M.K. hoped her hand didn't tremble as she touched the silky hair. It didn't feel like that of a dead girl's. "That look like a jagged cut to you?" She turned to Adam, handing him the photo.

He looked at the photo, then at the dead girl. "I suppose. I don't know."

"It looks as if it was sawed off rather than cut with shears."

Adam lowered the photo to his side. "Kids do crazy things with their hair. My Liza Jane is always dyeing hers a different color. I never know when I go to meet her if I'm looking for a redhead or a blonde. She once dyed it shoe-polish black for Halloween."

The doctor, standing on the other side of the autopsy

table, chuckled. "I had a Farrah Fawcett *do* when I was in junior high." She looked at M.K. "You're probably too young to remember that look but—"

"Oh, I remember it," Adam chimed in. "Every girl in the eighth grade had that feathered hair, with the wings. Everyone wanted to be one of *Charlie's Angels*."

"I suppose you're right," M.K. agreed. "It just seems so—" She cut herself off, looking up at the doctor. "Would you mind having a look at this?"

"Certainly." Dr. Wood walked to the blue counter along the wall and pulled a pair of exam gloves from a box that looked like it dispensed Kleenex. "If you like, I can take a sample and send it to the lab." She returned to the autopsy table. "It might take a couple of days, but—"

"I don't think that will be necessary," Adam said. "Just have a quick look to satisfy my partner, will you?"

M.K. didn't like the way he had phrased that. He made it sound as if her request was somehow out of line, or at the very least, unnecessary. The doctor, however, seemed nonplussed.

"Let's see," Dr. Wood murmured, lifting the brown hair in her gloved hands. "Looks like a lock about an inch wide, oh, six inches long, was cut."

M.K. looked over her shoulder. "Edges look jagged to you?"

"A little, maybe, but that would be consistent with a home haircut." She threw a glance over her shoulder. "I used to cut my hair all the time when I was a teenager. Always used Mom's dullest scissors."

M.K. didn't smile. "Can you tell if it's a fresh cut?"

The medical examiner leaned over the autopsy table again. M.K. waited.

"We really would need to send a sample to a lab for confirmation," Dr. Wood said after a moment. "And I'm not a licensed beautician, but I'd say no. It's not a fresh cut. The ends look a little dull—maybe some hair product buildup." She straightened up. "I really don't think this has anything to do with the death, but I don't mind putting a hold on the release of the body if—"

"That won't be necessary, Dr. Wood." Adam tucked the photo into the envelope he'd brought with him. "We won't keep you any longer. Thank you again for getting to this so quickly."

M.K. backed away from the autopsy table, from Jessica's cold body that would soon be interred underground. "Yes, thank you."

On the stairs, she stayed right behind Adam. "I wish you wouldn't do that," she said.

He looked over his shoulder down at her as he climbed the steps. "What now?"

"Make me sound like I'm being a pest or something. You have to admit, that slice of hair that's been cut off is odd."

"It is odd," he agreed, reaching the landing and opening the door for M.K. "But it has nothing to do with the girl's death, which is what Crackhow sent us to investigate. We have our cause of death. It is in no way associated with the Palmer boy's death." They walked side by side through the public lobby of the county building. "Senator Palmer's office cannot possibly suggest there was any connection between the death of his son and this girl. We did our job. We move on."

"You're right." M.K. sighed. "I suppose I just feel bad for Mr. and Mrs. Lawson. They didn't even know their daughter used drugs."

"It's a scary world out there when you're a parent of a young adult," Adam agreed, surprising M.K. by the emotion in his voice. "You hope to God you've raised them right, hope you can protect them, but that isn't always the case."

She looked up across the wide hood of the car to say something, but as quick as that, the moment had passed. She could see it on his face.

"So where do you want to stop for lunch on the way

back?" Adam asked, climbing in behind the wheel. "Roast beef or Italian sub sandwich? Name your poison."

"Mom? You here?" Liza Jane walked in through the unlocked front door, through the dark hallway. Lights were on in the kitchen.

"In here."

Liza Jane dropped the keys to her lime green VW bug on the cluttered counter and walked up behind her mother standing at the stove, kissed her on the cheek. "Savannah already gone to bed?"

"Yup," her mother said, stirring a big pot of boiling water with metal lids in it.

"Shoot, I was hoping I would catch her, but I got hung up at the newspaper." She looked over her mother's shoulder. "I know you're not the best cook in the world, Mom, but are you making lids for dinner?"

Her mother laughed and wiped her perspiring forehead with the back of her hand, then pressed her hand to her back the way pregnant women do. "Very funny." She pointed to the mason jars full of tomatoes lined up on the counter. "Just canning the last of my tomatoes. Mark loves fresh tomatoes in his marinara."

Liza Jane wandered to the refrigerator and pulled the door open. "Then I would think Mark ought to be canning his own tomatoes instead of getting the preggers woman with the swollen ankles to do it."

Her mother looked down at her bare feet. "They're not so bad today."

Liza Jane grabbed a little Tupperware container off the top shelf, popped up the lid, sniffed it, and put the lid back on, wrinkling her nose. Health food was fine but she didn't do tofu. She opened another container. "The point isn't the ankles, Mom. The point is, you shouldn't be doing that kind of stuff for him." Green beans with red peppers. Bingo. She went to the utensil drawer, taking the container with her, letting the fridge door close.

"I like home-canned tomatoes, too, and so does Savannah." Her mother took a pair of long metal tongs and started chasing the metal rings and their caps around inside the pot. "And if I recall correctly, so do you, missy."

Liza Jane grabbed a fork and pushed the drawer shut with her hip. She climbed up on a bar stool. "He home?"

Her mother shook her head.

"He coming home?"

"Probably."

Liza Jane hesitated. "Look, Mom, I know it's none of my business, but—"

"You're right. It's none of your business." Her mother dropped two jar rings onto a dish towel she'd laid out on the counter beside the stove. "I appreciate your concern, but—"

"Mom, you're forty-two and you're getting ready to have another baby. You've got a five-year-old upstairs who needs you. You don't have time for his bullshit."

Her mother didn't turn around. Didn't say anything. She just started fishing for jar lids again.

Liza Jane poked a green bean in her mouth. "I'm sorry. I know you love him. He's a good guy."

"He's been very good to you," her mother said stiffly.

Liza Jane looked at her mother. She was standing at the stove, barefoot, in a calf-length skirt and a loose peasant kind of blouse, her back to Liza Jane. She had her long blond hair pulled back in a messy ponytail and long, dangling earrings with multicolored wooden fish on them hanging from her ears. And her bare ankles did look puffy.

"I've got another front-page article coming out in the paper Monday. It's about the dead girl." She munched on another cold green bean. "I got a photo, too."

Her mother whipped around, tongs in hand. "You took a

picture of a dead girl? You ought to be ashamed of yourself. That's disrespectful to publish such a thing, to the girl and her grieving parents."

"Mom, I didn't take a picture of the dead girl." Liza Jane rolled her eyes, swinging one foot. "This is a cool picture of the yellow tape the police put up and behind it you can see this big green Dumpster where they found her body."

"Your father going to be as upset about this article as the last?" Her mother turned off the stove and grabbed two flowered hot mitts from a drawer.

Liza Jane shrugged. "Who knows? He shouldn't be, but that doesn't mean anything."

Her mother began placing the lids on the canning jars, fumbling in the big mitts. "I'm glad to hear you're doing so well. You making new friends?"

"Yes, Mother. Packing my lunch and taking it every day, too."

Her mother gave her one of those looks that said, *knock it off, smart-ass, before I knock it off for you.*

Liza Jane offered a quick smile, cramming the last of the green beans into her mouth, leaving the red peppers. "Actually, I've met a lot of people, mostly at the paper, but at the station, too."

"The station?"

"The cable station the college has. They're taping that reality TV frat show every week."

"*Fraternity Row*—I've seen it." Her mother waved a hot mitt. "Everyone who comes into my store is talking about it. They think it's great."

"It's okay." Liza Jane carried the dirty dish to the sink. "But there's this guy, Cameron, who directs the show. Cam."

"It's directed? I thought that the point of reality TV is it's real life; there isn't any direction." Her mother picked up a jar of tomatoes and tightened the cap down. "I thought it was unrehearsed, taped as it happens."

"Well, it is." Liza Jane parked her butt against the counter.

"But they still kind of know what they want to happen. They manipulate the scenes—you know, egg people on, sometimes."

Her mother made a clicking sound between her teeth. "Nothing is ever what it seems, is it?"

"Nope." Liza Jane watched her mother struggle with the lid of the canning jar in her hands. "Let me do that." She scooted her over with a swing of her hips, taking the jar from her.

"Careful—it's hot, honey."

"Mom." Liza Jane stared her down while gingerly fastening the hot ring and flat lid down on the warm jar of tomatoes. "I'm not a child anymore."

Her mother backed up and plopped on the stool. "You're *my* child." She smiled and rubbed her lower back.

Liza Jane moved on to the next jar. "Why don't you go up and take a shower? You look beat. I can finish these."

Her mother looked around the kitchen that was strewn with dirty pots and pans, piles of tomato skins, empty jars yet to be filled, and assorted toys belonging to Savannah. "The kitchen's a mess. I really should—"

The sound of the garage door going up made her halt midsentence.

Liza Jane was really hoping to avoid Mark tonight, but at least he'd come home.

Her mother slipped off the stool, pushing a stray lock of blond hair away from her face. "Be nice," she whispered.

"Always," Liza Jane answered sarcastically under her breath.

The door from the garage into the laundry room off the kitchen opened, hitting something just inside the door.

"Just a second, Mark," her mother called, almost running across the kitchen. "It's Savannah's bike."

Mark shoved the door open, flinging the pink plastic Big Wheel against the washing machine. "Why the hell can't she put this stuff away?"

"I'm sorry," Sophie said quietly, trying to push the little

bike beneath the utility sink. "Look, hon, our Liza Jane's here."

Not for long, Liza thought. Not tonight. She could see that look in Mark's eyes. Hear it in his voice. What her mother said was true: Mark had been good to her. Liza Jane even loved him, but that didn't mean that she had to put up with his behavior. She didn't think her mother had to, either, but so far, her opinion didn't seem to matter much to her mother. All Liza Jane knew was that whatever the hell his problem was these days, she wasn't going to enable him.

"You make dinner?" Mark demanded, walking into the kitchen.

"It . . . it's after nine. Savannah and I ate hours ago, but I can heat something up if—"

"I don't want any fucking leftovers!" Mark slammed his hand against the back of the chair and it pitched forward, striking the table and knocking some of Savannah's wooden blocks down. They skittered across the floor and he kicked one, sending it flying across the room to bounce off the refrigerator.

"Mom," Liza said quietly, stepping behind her mother. "I'm out of here. You going to be all right?"

Her mother nodded. She smiled, but Liza Jane knew it was a fake smile. "I'll be fine. Go." She kissed her daughter on the cheek and gave her a little push toward the door.

Liza Jane grabbed her keys off the counter and walked out of the kitchen and out the front door.

"What the fuck's wrong with her?" Mark bellowed as she closed the door behind her.

Chapter Six

"Can I get you anything else, hon?" the waitress asks.

I glance up, smiling. The grilled chicken sandwich was excellent, as was the Caesar salad. There was once a time in my life when I was uncomfortable going to a restaurant or a little bar like this one alone, to eat alone, but I no longer feel that way. In fact, I enjoy these solitary meals. It gives me time to think . . . to watch.

"That'll be all. Just the check, please."

"No problem."

I watch the college girl slide my plate off the table, grab the fork and knife and straw wrapper, and head for the kitchen. She is cute. Friendly, but not overly so. I glance around the little pub not too far from O'Shea's. The College Park Bar & Grill played directly into the hands—or pockets, as the case might be—of the college students who attended Chesapeake. The whole place was decorated with the college's memorabilia with a sports theme: footballs, softballs, soccer balls, cheerleader's pom-poms, and old sports uniforms on the walls above the tables. Old banners and photographs. Photographs everywhere.

And the photographs are what I hate most about this

place. They repulse me . . . and yet I cannot stop myself from coming here. Staring at the pictures. Just as I cannot stop myself from looking at the young men and women who come and go in the sports bar. I imagine what it would be like to make love to one of them and then kill her . . . or him.

I close my eyes for a moment as a shudder of recrimination passes through me. This is dangerous, these thoughts. I need to write them down for Dr. Fisher. It is my assignment for the week, to keep a diary of the unwanted feelings, the urges. And because I am a good patient, because I truly do want to get better, feel better, I will dutifully mark these thoughts down in my journal. Not the part about wanting to kill them, of course.

I watch a young woman rise from the table across from me, brush her fingertips against a young man's face, and then sashay away. She has pretty hair—long, brown, straight, the way college girls like to wear it. Her hair reminds me of Jessica's, of the exquisite lock I now possess. The part of her I now possess. I breathe deeply, letting my eyes drift shut again. The bad feelings, the worries, wash away in an instant and I am filled with joy. With happiness and a sense of confidence. No, it is more than confidence, it is *power*. Jessica had been a selfish, unkind, mean girl, but her hair . . . her hair is perfect.

I smile.

"Here you go." The waitress walks by, dropping the check on the table. "You can leave it there or pay up at the bar."

"Thank you." I smile.

"Sure." She smiles back.

She has a pretty smile and seems nice, but she is probably just like Jessica. Not what she seems.

I watch her go and then rise. I consider moving to the bar. There is a young man with tousled hair sitting there alone, waiting for someone. Smoking a Marlboro. Another kid who can't read the surgeon general's warning on the side of the package. Stupid idiot. Did he think he was immortal? Did he not know how fragile life is? How easily he could be involved in a fatal accident and burn to death . . . or meet the wrong person on a bar stool?

He realizes I am looking at him and he lifts his chin. An invitation, perhaps? I am tempted, sorely tempted, but I know I have to control my urges. We talked about that, Dr. Fisher and I, during my second visit. While never making a judgment, he says that if my urges disturb me, if I don't want to follow through on them, I need to resist from the beginning. Before they take over and become . . . overwhelming.

The young man at the bar has a nice nose—and it isn't surgically enhanced, either. As a student of the human form, I can recognize a rhinoplasty or a breast augmentation from across a crowded room. I'm not interested in the surgically enhanced, or the artificial. I want the genuine thing. I want what I will never be, I suppose.

I leave cash on the table and a twenty-five-percent tip. I waited tables in my college days and I know what it is like. I know how customers treat you, like you're some kind of servant. Fellow students always seem to be the worst, too, as if they look down on you because you are making your own way in the world, paying your own tuition and room and board instead of Mommy and Daddy doing it.

I dare one more glance at the young man with the lovely nose. Someone has joined him, a carrottop with a scruffy red beard. I like red beards.

I make myself turn away from the bar and the young man I hunger for. At the door, the bulletin board catches my eye. Here, students are permitted to post their own snapshots, and they are replaced regularly so there are new photos up each time I come. It is my favorite thing about College Park, besides perhaps their excellent grilled chicken sandwich. I pause at the bulletin board and gaze up at the laughing faces. There are news clippings, too, mostly about games won, titles in the division won, but there are also announcements: a student who has been granted a fellowship in physics at

Oxford, a second-place win in a robotics competition in Ohio.

A woman in her late forties is standing there, too, smiling. "My son," she says proudly, pointing to a photo of a young man on the bottom of a human pyramid in front of the media and broadcasting wing of Elton Hall. "Cameron. He's producing that new show, have you seen it? *Fraternity Row*."

I feel the muscles in my jaw tighten, and I make a conscious effort to relax. "No, I don't believe I have."

"You really should tune in. Tuesday nights. Tomorrow night, nine o'clock. It's on the college's cable channel—twenty-seven, I think."

I stare at the young man's beady eyes in the photo. He is laughing. At who? Me?

"Everyone is talking about it," the mother gushes. "Everyone is watching it."

My gaze shifts from one bright smiling face to the next in the human pyramid. Eight students. Four on the bottom, all male. Then three, two girls and a guy. On the very top, a smiling young woman with a pink bandana. I know the pink bandana.

The entrance door opens and a man in his late forties walks in carrying a newspaper under his arm, glasses perched on the end of his hawk nose. He is in need of a rhinoplasty.

"John," the woman beside me calls.

"Cameron here yet?" he asks without smiling.

"No, but I'm sure he'll be here any moment." The proud mother looks to me. "It was nice talking to you." She hurries after her grumbling husband. "You really should turn on *Fraternity Row*," she calls over her shoulder in one last pitch to secure another viewer for her future Spielberg.

I nod, smile. My face feels like plaster and I fear it will shatter at any moment, revealing my true self to everyone in the restaurant. To the world.

Is this some kind of conspiracy? Anger begins to bubble

up inside me, acidic and foul-tasting. Everywhere I go, that TV show is thrown in my face.

I look up at the photographs and the faces blur for a moment. I swallow the bile that rises in my throat. My fingers ache to rip the photo from the board, tear it into tiny pieces. But the mother of Cameron will surely notice if it is gone, become suspicious.

I glance at another photo. This one is of a young man in a football uniform—Chesapeake's colors of course, green and white. Beside him is a cheerleader in a skirt and sleeveless tank top, pom-poms extended. She has red-gold hair and the top is formfitting. She has perfect breasts, no augmentation there. They are pert, rounded, and I imagine the feel of one of them in the palm of my hand. The weight of the breast. The smoothness of the skin.

I study the football player's face, taking deep, cleansing breaths in my nose, out my mouth. His features are too craggy. He reminds me of the character Gaston in Disney's Beauty and the Beast. I have seen the show on Broadway.

My gaze shifts to the football in his hand. He raises it high as if he is about to make the winning pass. The pass that will win the game and the cheerleader and her perfect breasts. That is when I notice his hand and the perfect form of it. A masculine hand; long, tanned fingers unmarred by scars or moles. I am amazed that God can create such perfection in such an obviously imperfect human being.

I glance around. No one is paying me any mind. I pluck the photo from the wall, tack and all, and I walk out the door with it concealed in my hand. I don't yet know what I will do with the photo. I only know that I must have it.

"Good evening, love. I'm sorry I'm so late." Jerome approached the bed where his wife lay propped up on pillows.

On her bald head, she wore one of her African print scarves, the one with the elephants dancing across it.

"It's all right," she said, her pale face lighting up at the sight of him. She reached out her arms to him.

After all these years, Sela still made his heart patter when he saw her. "Bertrice gone?" He sat on the bed and leaned over to take her in his arms and kiss her forehead. Bertrice was the hired nurse who spent several hours a day with Sela, helping her with her personal needs, driving her to doctor appointments, whatever was needed.

"Mm-hm." She lifted her chin until their lips met. Lingered.

Jerome closed his eyes for a moment, enjoying the feeling of her warm, full mouth pressed against his. "You must be feeling good this evening. You're feisty."

She tipped back her head, laughing. "Well, not quite as feisty as I would like to be feeling."

He leaned back, placing her hand in his and stroking it. "Don't worry, that will come back. You'll start feeling better."

"Jerome . . ." she said softly.

He knew she was looking at him with her cinnamon eyes, but he couldn't bear to meet her gaze.

"We need to talk about this."

He shook his head. "We should give it some more time. The body is a miraculous thing. You never know—"

"Jerome," Sela said firmly. "You're not listening to me."

He smoothed her hand, marred by all the IVs she had endured in the last year. "I'm listening."

"You're not hearing, then."

He closed his eyes for a moment and then opened them, forcing himself to look at her. "I'm just not ready to talk about it, okay?" he said quietly. "I'm not as strong as you are. I never was."

She held his gaze for a moment, her eyes filled with love and a little sadness. "All right, we'll table it for tonight. But we do need to talk about it and soon. We need to make plans while I'm still able."

He nodded.

She lay back against the pillows, fatigued from just sitting up that long. "So tell me how your day was."

Jerome rose from the side of the bed, loosening his tie. He walked to his closet and began to disrobe. "Good. Uneventful. The hospital ball meeting was quick and relatively painless. I took notes for you." Sela had been the assistant chairperson for the fund-raising event before she'd become ill.

"You see many patients?"

"Five." He hung his blue tie with the tiny red circles on the wooden tie rack in the closet. "I saw my new patient again."

"And how did that go?"

Jerome unbuttoned his shirt slowly, going over in his mind the conversation he'd had with Blue. "I'm not sure."

"Now, dear, you know there's rarely immediate progress. Sometimes there's even a regression when treatment first begins. Why has the patient come to you?"

"Concerned with newly discovered bisexual urges."

Sela nodded. "You've dealt with many bisexuals. It can be a difficult time in one's life. Especially if it's just emerging."

"I know." He slipped out of his oxford shirt and tossed it in the laundry basket bound for the dry cleaners. "But somehow this is different." He shook his head, slipping out of one Italian loafer and then the other. "I'm concerned."

"Why?"

"I'm not exactly certain. Well educated, an established career. The actual sessions have gone well. The patient has complied with my request for a journal, the patient is forthright in expressing the feelings which lead to the undesired behavior, but . . ."

"But?" Sela urged.

Jerome backed up to sit on the edge of the bed and remove his argyle dress socks. "It's just a feeling, I suppose. And you know me, I don't usually have an iota of intuition when it comes to these things." He glanced at her and she was smiling. "What?" he asked.

She shrugged her thin shoulders inside her emerald green silk pajama top. "It's just that you sound like me, Dr. Jerome Fisher, talking about *feelings*, your *intuition*."

He tossed his socks into the dirty-clothes basket one at a time from where he sat on the bed. "Which is exactly why our practice is struggling, my dear. Because everyone knows it's Dr. Sela Fisher who's truly the brilliant psychiatrist. I've just been riding on your coattails all these years."

"Come on. Put on your pajamas and join me." She patted his side of the bed and then reached for the TV remote control. "The show's about to start, and I don't want you jabbering through it. I can't wait to see who Katie's going to choose. She was Casey's high school sweetheart, you know, but Ty's got it all over him in the brains department and he is an older guy."

Jerome stood, unbuckling his leather belt. "I cannot believe you've gotten hooked on a soap opera."

She clicked the remote and the large TV in the armoire on the far side of the room came on. She began to flick through the stations, filling the bedroom with bits of the evening news, weather predictions, and the last seconds of a sale on topaz bracelets on a home shopping channel. "*Fraternity Row* is not a soap opera. It's reality TV. You've been known to watch a *Survivor* episode or two."

"You're right—it's not a soap opera because it's worse." He stepped out of his navy dress pants and hung them on a wooden hanger. "And the only reason I ever watched that show was for the location shots."

Sela laughed. "Right. That and the half-naked women."

"Hey there, welcome to another episode of *Fraternity Row*," the handsome blonde on the TV screen said. "I'm Axel, and we're glad you tuned in—and you'll be glad, too, when you see what's going down between Ty and Casey. Plus, Samantha, the rush chair from Delta Zeta, has got a bone to pick with the Pi Beta Phi gals." The young man winked.

"I'm thinking we might be in for a catfight tonight," Axel says, looking right into my eyes. That boyish grin. "Kind of sexy, don't you think?"

I stare at the TV screen, only half hearing what the young man is saying. I despise him. I despise his fraternity and all it stands for and I despise the college that allows the Greek organizations to continue to operate on campus. Some colleges are actually beginning to wise up and ban them.

I flip through the pages of the magazine in my lap. I know I should turn the TV off. I know without even asking Dr. Fisher that watching the show, even listening to it, could be potentially dangerous to my psyche right now, but it is one of my urges I cannot control.

On the glossy magazine page on my lap I see a white Jeep and I pick the scissors up from the pile of files I should be attending to. I have notes to copy. I's to be dotted, t's to be crossed.

Instead, I am cutting pictures from magazines. I already have a pair of green pom-poms and a nice scientific calculator. The white Jeep is quite a find.

The photographs on the wall of the pub I saw the day before have enlightened me. My little chat with Cameron's mother has made it clear to me that it is not only the inane, self-centered, harmful fraternity brothers and sisters on the TV screen that are imperfect, but they all are. All imperfect creatures. The young men and women who placed in the robotics competitions, even the boy headed for Oxford.

I place the neatly trimmed white Jeep next to the pom-poms on the floor in front of me so I can see them, and I think of the photograph I have stolen from the pub. I slide it out from under the pile of files and I again study the face of the football player, then his hand poised on the football.

I know him. His name is Charles, and when I close my eyes I can still see him, I can hear his laughter. Gym was a required class in those days. I took the easiest course available. It was badminton, for heaven's sake. How hard could it be to play badminton? How athletic did one need to be?

"Weak shot," I hear Charles say from the other side of the court.

Through the holes in the net, I see his leering face. "Game point, pansy-ass. Again."

Tears fill my eyes. I see the birdie fly over the net. I hold my racquet as I have been instructed; I swing with the appropriate arc and still the little toy floats by me. There is laughter from those lined up along the sides of the gym. Spectators. Girls I would like to date.

"Hey!" my opponent calls, sauntering off the court. "Good game. You ever think about going out for tiddledywinks?"

I open my eyes and Charles is gone, but I still feel the tightness in my chest, the pain of my embarrassment. I sniff. Then I very carefully cut the photograph in half, separating the football player from the cheerleader.

I feel better.

The phone rang and M.K. checked the caller ID. Against her will, she smiled. "Hello," she said into the phone, lowering the volume of the TV with the remote.

"Hey, it's Adam. I wasn't sure if you'd be home."

"Yeah, well, Thursday is usually my night to hit all the transsexual bars in Baltimore, but I just wasn't up to it tonight," she quipped. Then she pressed her lips together; she couldn't believe such a thing had come out of her mouth. She thought things like that all the time, but she never said them.

She was letting her guard down too often with Adam. She found herself enjoying his company, enjoying the person she could be with him. Unlike the other male agents she'd worked with, he actually seemed to be receptive to her alternative methods of investigation. Well, relatively receptive. Crackhow had assigned her to work the dockworkers case with him and she'd actually convinced him this morning that breaking heads might not be the most prudent way to get the information he needed.

"I was playing catch-up myself. You know, it didn't used to be this way, when I first joined the Bureau," he grumbled cheerfully. "There wasn't all this paperwork. Anyway, I was just checking to see if you were going to meet me at B & P Shipping in the morning, rather than at the office."

"Yeah." She removed her reading glasses. "We said that this afternoon, right?" She knew he knew she intended to meet him there, so why the call? Was Special Agent Thomas fumbling for an excuse to speak to her after hours? She felt a flutter in the pit of her stomach that she hadn't felt in a very long time.

"Right." He paused. "That's right." He chuckled. "Liza Jane says I'm getting old, forgetful—guess she's right."

M.K. nodded. Waited, having no intention of making this too easy for him. It was too much fun to hear him squirm. "So . . . was that all you needed?" she asked, after a moment of deafening silence on the other end of the line.

"Yeah. That's all. Well, no. While I have you on the phone . . ."

He had her smiling. "Yes?"

"I was wondering . . . There's a home football game tomorrow night at Chesapeake Bay College. Liza Jane asked me if I wanted to join her. She's not into sports, but she said she was hoping to pick up a local-interest story. The whole community turns out for the games: grandparents, neighbors of students, neighbors of neighbors of students. Ashview loves its football."

"I'm not much of a sports fan either," M.K. said. Then she almost groaned out loud when she realized how that must have sounded. Here the guy had called to ask her out . . . sort of, and she was cutting him off at the knees.

"How about a beer-and-hot-dog fan? You one of those?"

It was a good recovery on his part. He had her smiling again.

"I don't know," M.K. said, drawing out the time she had to respond.

"Come on, Melanie Kathleen, it's not like a date or anything."

Of course he wasn't asking her on a date, she chastised herself. Why would he do that? "I didn't mean to suggest I thought you were—I just—"

"M.K. You and I are partners—at least it looks like it for the time being. This is the way it's done. Partners do stuff together. Social stuff sometimes. It makes the partnership, the job, go more smoothly."

"Right. Of course."

"So meet me at the stadium at six thirty tomorrow night. At the ticket booth, and I'll buy you a hot dog, okay?"

She pressed her lips together, upset, and she didn't even know why. "Sure. Okay."

"See you tomorrow."

M.K. hit the "off" button on her phone and set it on the end table beside her chair. Then she stared at the silent TV screen and wished she had more of a life than she did.

Chapter Seven

"Mom." Liza Jane stood up on the bleacher bench and waved both hands, trying to catch her attention. "Sophie! Up here! Come sit with us." She looked down at her father, who was seated on the bench next to the woman cop. She was nice enough, and her father seemed to like her. They squabbled a lot, but Liza Jane knew her father liked to argue. He saw it as a sign of intelligence if a person could argue a point well, even if the point was whether or not foot-long hot dogs tasted better than the regular ones.

"You don't care if Mom and Savannah sit with us, do you?" Liza Jane asked. She craned her neck. "Hell, Mark's with them, too."

"One big, happy family of divorce," Adam quipped.

"I've got one of those and my parents have been married to each other for thirty-two years," M.K. remarked dryly.

Liza Jane watched her mother slowly make her way up the bleacher steps, her big baby belly protruding, while holding Savannah's hand and carrying a backpack with the other arm. Savannah was dragging her constant companion, Boo Boo Bunny. Boo was nice, as stuffed animals went; the problem was it was almost as tall as the five-year-old . . . at least it was before its ears began to droop and the stuffing inside began to settle. Her little sister took the monstrosity everywhere she went.

"Savannah Banana, what's up?" Liza Jane put her arms out to her half-sister and the little girl released her mother's hand and bounded up the last two steps, Boo Boo Bunny in tow.

"Liza Piza!"

Liza Jane got a hug from her sister and the stuffed rabbit. "Hey, Mom," she said, leaning out to kiss her mother on the cheek as she steered Savannah past her to sit on the wooden bench between her and her dad, just to give her mom a break.

"Hey, Mark." Liza Jane lifted her chin in her stepfather's direction.

He had his hands stuffed down in his jean pockets. "Hey, sweetie." He almost sounded like his old self. "Adam."

"You remember M.K.," Adam introduced.

Mark nodded and he and the woman cop exchanged some kind of polite conversation.

"Aren't you going to sit down?" her mother asked Mark, scooting over closer to Liza Jane. "There's plenty of room, hon."

"Nah, I think I'll go grab a couple of dogs." He pointed to his daughter. "Hot dog or nachos?"

"Nachos," Savannah squealed.

Sophie gave Mark one of those health-food-nut looks. "Mark, really! It's not even real dairy."

"I'll eat most of them, Mom," Liza Jane said, trying to defuse the disagreement before it turned into a shouting match in front of a couple of thousand people she went to school with every day, worked with, or saw in line at the cell phone store downtown.

Mark disappeared into the crowd of students and parents carrying meals on cardboard trays and jockeying for seats before the game started.

"Can you believe it's October and still this warm?" Sophie pulled a Chinese paper fan from the backpack at her feet and waved it in front of her face.

"How are you, Sophie?" M.K. leaned forward, parting Boo Boo Bunny's ears so she could see.

Sophie went on about the heat and a mixup with the tofu and bean sprout deliveries at her store that morning.

Liza Jane looked at her dad in his jean shorts and yellow hibiscus shirt and then at his friend. They weren't dating or anything. At least he hadn't said they were, and he was usually pretty up-front about that kind of stuff. They did seem pretty into each other, though. When Liza Jane first met M.K. at her mom's house, she thought maybe the cop was a lesbian. Lesbians didn't bother her—it was just an observation. But hearing her dad mention his new partner a couple of times on the phone and now seeing her again, Liza Jane wasn't sure anymore. Maybe she just had a bad haircut, didn't know what kind of clothes to wear. At least tonight she wasn't wearing one of those shapeless suits. She was wearing blue jeans, an FBI t-shirt, and sneakers. Nothing like advertising you're the feds, but she looked pretty normal.

The kickoff signaled the start of the football game and everyone around Liza Jane stood up and shouted, clapping. Savannah clapped, too. Liza Jane stood up just so she could see over the crowd.

"Dad, you catch my news piece after *Fraternity Row* this week? About the dead girl?"

He nodded. "Not bad."

"I didn't say anything that pissed you off?"

He sipped his beer from a plastic cup. "I'm sure you did, but all in all, it wasn't bad. I liked the statistics on drug overdoses you gave with the shot of the local cemetery."

"A lot of people were pretty shook up about her death. This girl down the hall from me knew her. She said she didn't even know she did drugs. Apparently no one did. It's pretty hard to believe."

"They found the illegal substance in her possession," M.K. said. "And unfortunately it only takes once, especially with synthetic drugs."

Liza Jane nodded. Everyone else was beginning to sit down. She sat down, too.

Her father leaned forward, past the bunny, past Savannah, who was chowing down on the last of his fries. "How's Mark doing, Sophie?" The tone of his voice was as serious as it ever got.

So he did know something was going on.

"He's good." Liza Jane's mom bobbed her head, her blond ponytail whipping in the air. Her hair was much longer than Liza Jane's now and it was pretty, even with the little bit of gray at her temples. Liza Jane was glad her mom hadn't cut it the way most moms did by her age.

"Yeah?" Liza Jane's dad kept looking at her mom. "Because he didn't seem great last week at the barbeque. Not last week when I saw him at headquarters, either."

She shrugged one shoulder. She was wearing a tie-dyed tank top that was really tight across her big belly. She kept fanning herself. Liza Jane didn't know why her mother was so hot; she thought it was nice tonight. She'd even put on jeans instead of the usual shorts.

"No, really. I think he's better." Sophie glanced out over the sea of bobbing heads in front of her. "Thanks for asking, though, Adam."

He looked at the field, too, and just nodded. He knew his ex was telling him to mind his own business.

Just then, Chesapeake scored a touchdown and the crowd went crazy. Savannah climbed up on the bench seat and jumped up and down, clapping her hands.

"Whoa there." Adam caught her just before she pitched forward onto the back of an elderly gentleman listening to the game on headphones as he watched it.

Adam set Savannah on her feet and tickled her belly. Savannah laughed. "I'm hungry," she said.

"Hungry?" Adam teased. "Hungry? But you just ate all my fries. How can you be hungry?"

Savannah burst into giggles again. "Boo Boo Bunny is hungry, too."

"Sit down." Liza Jane pushed on her sister's shoulder. "People can't see over your big head. Your daddy will be back in a minute with your nachos."

"Big head, big head," Savannah sang.

M.K. caught Liza Jane's eye. She was obviously amused by Savannah's antics. "You have kids?" Liza Jane asked.

She shook her head. "Not married. But I have seven sisters—I'm the oldest."

"Seven. Wow." Liza Jane adjusted her pink bandana. So far, neither of her parents seemed to have noticed that under it she had dreadlocks. Just baby ones right now, but she knew they were going to flip when they saw them—at least her dad would. So the easy solution was to put off the flip-show as long as possible.

"I can't imagine having that many sisters." Liza Jane tugged on one of Savannah's braids. "Just one is too many."

"Shut up." Savannah used her bunny's floppy paw to give her sister a playful push.

Liza Jane pulled her onto her lap to keep her occupied and asked her mom about the new organic drinks she was getting in her store. Liza Jane knew a lot of kids on campus who were really into organic and were always interested in new products available in the small town.

The quarter ended and the teams switched sides on the football field. There was a little excitement when one of the fans tried to run across the field, but he was escorted off by a young Ashview cop Liza Jane knew from high school.

Then a girl Liza Jane had met at the newspaper stopped by and they discussed the new news show. There was gossip that Professor McKinley, head of the media department, was looking to expand the new show if it was successful. As they talked, Liza Jane kept her eye out for Cam, half hoping he'd stop by. They weren't going out or anything, but she really liked him, and they had a lot in common. He wanted to go into media broadcasting; she wanted to be a reporter. He was nice, not like a lot of guys she met on campus.

"I'm hungry," Savannah whined. "Boo Boo's hungry."

Liza Jane waved to her friend, who was taking off, and glanced at the clock on the scoreboard. Only three minutes and twenty seconds remained in the half. "Mom, where'd Mark get to?" she asked quietly.

"To get us something to eat." Her mother dug into her backpack and pulled out a homemade granola bar that resembled a lump of dried animal dung and passed it over to Savannah. "Eat this, honey bunny. He'll be back soon. Line must be long."

Liza Jane looked at her mom, lowering her voice. "Maybe he won't be. I can go for Savannah's dinner."

"He'll be back."

"I don't like this," Savannah said, scraping raw rolled oats off her tongue with dirty fingernails. "I want nachos. Daddy said I could have nachos."

"I'll get 'em, sweetie." Liza Jane's dad stood up and passed in front of them, making his way to the aisle. "Anyone want anything else?"

"Adam. You don't have to." Sophie dropped the Chinese fan into her bag. It was dark now and there was a cool breeze coming off the bay. "I'm sure Mark'll be back any minute."

"I need to hit the john, anyway. Mariette Karen." He pointed to M.K. "Anything else? A beer? Another foot-long?"

She shook her head.

Liza Jane turned to her as her dad made his way down the bleachers. "What's with the names?"

"Long story," M.K. said. "Suffice to say, your father has too much free time on his hands."

"You're telling me." Liza Jane laughed and scooted over closer to M.K. so she could hear her over the screaming fans and the obnoxious guy with the air horn two rows up.

* * *

When Adam reached the bathrooms, he found a line of men snaking out the door. From behind the bleachers, he couldn't even see the football field. As the line moved forward slowly, he kept his eyes peeled for Mark. Where the hell had he gotten to? Even if he did run into someone he knew, which no doubt he did because everyone in Ashview was here, he knew Savannah was waiting for her nachos.

When Adam was almost at the restroom door, he noticed a familiar balding head in line in front of him. "Dad?"

The man kept talking to his companion, his back to Adam. He was getting hard of hearing but refused to even consider hearing aids.

"Yo, Dr. Thomas!"

The man turned and sure enough, it was his dad.

"What are you doing here?" his father asked, he and his companion allowing several men to move ahead of them in line.

"Same thing you're doing. Where's Mom?"

"Her bridge night. You know how much she despises football." He indicated the distinguished African-American gentleman in a forties-style cabbie hat next to him. "Jerome is keeping me company. A colleague of mine. Dr. Jerome Fisher, my son, Special Agent Adam Thomas. FBI," he said proudly.

Adam shook the doctor's hand. "Dad, you don't have to broadcast it. You'll create a mob scene with students trying to get the hell away from me." He smiled at his dad's friend. "You a surgeon, too?"

"No." The man raised both palms with a grin. "I can't imagine the dedication, the hours. The blood." He pretended to shudder. "Psychiatry."

"Well, it's nice to meet you." Just then, Adam spotted Mark. He was leaning against a cement abutment, drinking a beer. No nachos for his daughter to be seen. "Mark," he called.

His ex-partner turned. Sophie said he was fine. He didn't appear fine. There were dark smudges beneath his eyes and he looked like he was losing weight.

Adam waved him over. "You remember my dad, Art, and this is Dr. Fisher."

The men shook hands.

Just then Liza Jane and M.K. showed up. Liza Jane was leading Savannah by the hand. M.K. had the bunny.

"I was afraid you'd been taken by aliens, too," Liza Jane told her dad. "And the banana had to pee." She indicated her little sister.

Adam made introductions again, kind of glad he had run into his father and could introduce M.K.

"I want nachos. Where's my nachos, Daddy?" Savannah whined.

"Coming right up." Mark smiled as if nothing had happened, as if he hadn't been gone an hour and a half.

"I'll take her to the bathroom. You get the food," Liza Jane ordered. Then, under her breath, "And if you're not going to do it this time, just say so."

Adam noted the strain in his daughter's voice and made a mental note to talk to her about Mark sometime this week. She had always gotten along so well with him that he was concerned about what was going on and how it was affecting Liza Jane.

"I said, I'm going." Mark finished off his beer in the plastic cup and tossed it into the closest garbage can. "Nice to see you again, Art, Dr. Fisher." He waved as he walked off.

"See you back at the seats," Liza Jane said, leading her sister toward the ladies' room, where there was also a line.

As M.K. walked by, Adam tugged on the sleeve of her t-shirt. "This is boring, huh?"

"Boring? Football, hot dogs, and a four-foot stuffed bunny?" She gave him a little smile, hugging the stuffed animal to her chest. "How could I not be having fun? See you up top."

Adam was pleased she was beginning to loosen up a little, not take herself so seriously. As she disappeared around the corner, he watched the way her hips swayed as she walked.

I stand in the aisle looking over the rail. Behind me, I feel the crowd pressing against me. I smell their popcorn and hot dogs and French fries with vinegar. I watch the football players line up for the next play, noting the quarterback. He is on tonight. Chesapeake is ahead by fourteen.

I have had enough football and want to go home. I have had enough contact with others, smiled enough, exchanged pleasantries. Introduced and been introduced. But I am nervous. I am afraid that if I move, I will see him again. Dr. Fisher. I knew when I started sessions with him so close to home that there was the possibility I might run into him outside his office. It was why I had chosen the name for myself. To keep myself and my position separate.

I don't know why I am so upset. Dr. Fisher is very professional. He pretended we weren't acquainted.

My gaze drifts to the quarterback again. His name is Bart Johnson and he is a senior at Chesapeake. There is gossip that he might be drafted by a professional football team, but it is just that, small-town gossip. He is not that good, because if he was, he would be playing for USC or Notre Dame and not a small arts and sciences college in Nowhere, Maryland.

Bart clasps the football in his perfect hand, and I watch the ball sail. It is a thirty-five-yard pass, I hear the announcer say over the loudspeaker. Everyone is on their feet clapping, patting each other on the back as if it is they who have made the successful play against their arch rivals, the Blue Hens.

Another play and the Chesapeake Mariners score again. I watch as the star quarterback walks off the field, his chest thrust out like a brightly colored peacock in his green-and-white uniform. Other players are congratulating him. The cheerleaders circle around him. He is laughing with them. They press their half-naked bodies against him and I am disgusted. He is flaunting his perfect hands without any regard for those who were not created so perfectly.

Bart turns his head, gazing up into the crowd in the bleachers. I think he sees me. We make eye contact and I am sure he is mocking me. I turn away, angry. Perhaps a little hurt. I make up my mind then that I will pay Bart Johnson a visit. I will see then how he mocks me.

Bart adjusted the plastic safety goggles on his face and grabbed the starter cable on the chipper-shredder. One good pull and it started right up, filling the backyard of the rental house with the deafening sound and stench of a small engine. He knew it was silly, but he liked the stink, the rumble of the engine; it reminded him of home and when he was a kid.

His dad, across the bay, over in Federalsburg, had a small engine shop. When Bart was growing up, he had always loved that smell of burning oil because it meant he was right there with his dad—mostly getting in the way, probably—but that had never been a problem for Clyde Johnson. Bart had been what his mother called a late baby, born an only child when Helen was forty-five.

Bart leaned over and adjusted the choke on the engine, taking care to keep his hand away from the large red aluminum chute. It was really a bigger chipper-shredder than he needed to clean up the little bit of brush in the backyard, big enough for four-to-six-inch-in-diameter trees. But this was the only chipper-shredder his father had had in the shop right now where he repaired lawn mowers and other small engines and sold a few used ones on the side. Bart's landlord was going to give him a cut on the rent this month for doing the work, and he knew his father always appreciated that.

With the piece of equipment running smoothly, Bart slipped on his leather work gloves and began to feed a pile of branches into it. It made a horrendous, satisfying sound as it grabbed the branches, sucked them into the chute, and sliced and ground them with a spinning drum with razor-sharp blades. Fine sawdust and wood chips no bigger than Bart's thumbnail came out the other side.

He fed another branch—a big, fat one—into the chute and grinned, reaching for a beer he'd left in the grass with the long-bladed shears he was using to trim back the bushes along the privacy fence. He emptied the can and crushed it in his hand, tossing it into a pile of empty cans. He needed to get to the recycling place, or at least get his roommates to come out and pick up the cans; most of them were theirs, anyway.

Grabbing another can out of the old cooler in the grass, he popped the top and stuffed another branch into the chipper-shredder. He didn't mind doing the work alone; in fact, he liked this kind of work. Two of his roommates were gone, one at work, one at some chick's house. The third, Buddy, who dropped out of college last semester and hadn't told his parents yet, was asleep upstairs. He had his alarm set to get up in time to get to work by four at the pizza place where he was a delivery man, but Bart knew very well he'd sleep right through the alarm if somebody didn't wake him. A parade of big-wheel trucks driving through his bedroom wouldn't wake up Buddy.

Bart took another drink of the beer and wiped his sweaty forehead. It was hot for the first week of October. Football practices in this heat were killing him. They were so bad that he was actually looking forward to Thanksgiving when the season would be over. He didn't really even like football any-more; he'd just done well in high school and when Chesapeake had offered him a partial scholarship to play for them, he hadn't been able to turn them down. Not with his dad working so hard in his shop, the economy not being so good, and his mother getting worse.

Bart set down the beer. He'd talked to his dad last night after the game. His dad usually drove over to see his games but Bart's mother was worse. She had Alzheimer's—early onset, they called it. She'd only been fifty-five when the symptoms started. Now, when Bart went home, his mother didn't even recognize him. She kept telling him about her son who played football for the local high school and how proud she was of him.

Bart pulled off one leather glove and wiped at his stinging eyes that had teared up. The engine on the chipper-shredder was smoking a little; it must have gotten in his eyes. Maybe he'd have a look at the engine tomorrow after church. Cut his old man a break and repair it for him. He'd probably be able to get a decent price for one this size if it was running right.

"Excuse me!"

A voice behind Bart startled him. He turned around, beer can in one hand, one leather glove tucked in his armpit. "Yeah?" he hollered. He'd never even heard the stranger approach, the engine was so loud.

"I was wondering if you could tell me where the Lockes live. It's 111 Porter Street."

Bart set the beer can down on the cooler and fed another branch into the chipper-shredder. He needed to get a move on. He'd told his girlfriend, Sara, that he'd go to some foreign film with her tonight. Neither of them was into partying, so it was a good way to get out of whatever his roommates had planned for the evening without looking like a bigger wuss than he already did. "This is 111," Bart told the stranger, "but it's a rental. Hmm . . . Locke. I don't know the name." He tried to think of who else was on the street. This was the third year he had rented here. He liked it because it was close to campus but not on the party street where most of the guys liked to live. Bart didn't even drink that much except for a couple of cold ones on a hot afternoon like this. "Kind of old people? A lady that walks all hunched over? That might be the people down two houses and across the street. Little blue house. I don't know their last name, though—I just call them Miss Emma and Mr. Ralph." He fed another branch into the chute.

Mr. Ralph was in a wheelchair with bad emphysema, so Bart would carry their groceries in from the car once in a while and roll their trash Dumpster out on Wednesdays after classes and roll it back the next day. Miss Emma was always really nice to him, always asked him how his father was because she had met him once when Bart was moving in.

The stranger took a step closer to be heard above the grind of the wood. "Yes, an elderly couple, Emma and Ralph Locke."

"That must be them but you could use the phone if you want." Bart pointed toward the house with a thick branch and eased it into the chute, watching the sharpened barrel suck the branch up inside. "I can run in and get it or I could just walk over and—"

Bart felt something strike him hard in his side, and, suddenly off balance, his right knee buckled.

It all happened so fast that he didn't even have time to scream. His knee hit the ground, his right arm instinctively shooting out. He felt the blade catch his gloved fingers and an excruciating, white-hot pain flashed through his entire body. He screamed, turning his head, his eyes wide with fear.

The stranger had pushed him.

I knew that it was divinity the moment I walked around the side of the house. There he was, the star quarterback, the young man so full of himself and his accomplishments, his fame in the community, his perfect hands.

He was alone in the backyard, his back to me, feeding branches into a large, gas-powered machine meant to grind up logs. It was much bigger than the average homeowner would ever need. It was overkill, like everything else about Bart Johnson. He was just like Charles in gym class, all those years ago. I knew that even before I came, and now it was confirmed.

As I approach, a plan forms in my head. Such a perfect plan. Again, surely divine. I have brought no weapon with me. I have left the moment up to chance, just as with the young men in the Jeep, Jessica on the bar stool. And I am rewarded.

I walk up to Bart and he turns to me, a great hulk of a young man, and utterly without suspicion. He is drinking beer, has had quite a few from the look of the pile in the grass. He is just like every other football jock. Just like Charles. Getting drunk, taking advantage of young men and women under the influence of alcohol he has provided them. Underage students. Vulnerable, wanting so hard to be included in the fun, to be part of a group of his or her peers, any group.

I ask Bart about the whereabouts of a fictitious family. I give his address. I step closer and he bumbles his way through a reply, still feeding branches into the chipper-shredder.

I watch with fascination as the branch as thick as my wrist is violently jerked into the mechanism. In a split second, the limb is sheared off again and again, ground and spit out on the grass, little more than dust.

I do not even know if I make a conscious decision. One moment I am standing there, smiling; the next, Bart turns away and I am throwing my weight against him. He is caught off balance and he falls. His right hand is sucked into the spinning, grinding blades. He screams, but it barely comes out as a grunt above the noise of the monster pulverizing flesh and bone.

Some blood spatters onto my clothing, but not much. Because of the way he has fallen, much of the blood spray is redirected by the open chute meant to feed the limbs into the machine.

Bart stares at me in horrified shock. I cannot take my gaze from his eyes as he digs one knee into the grass, trying to escape. The chipper-shredder has eaten his arm up to the elbow and yet it still hungers.

I take a step back. I know that I should go. He will bleed to death in minutes. That is when the gleam of the cutting shears in the grass catches my eyes. Again, it is utterly unplanned and yet somehow feels right.

The chipper-shredder has pulled Bart to his knees against it. The blades seem to be slowing as they grind his upper arm.

As I pick up the shears, I stare at his perfect left hand slapping helplessly at his side. He had tucked the glove under his arm, but it has fallen to the grass now. He is no longer screaming. His eyes are open, but he does not seem to see me. He is convulsing, but the churning blade is relentless.

I open the shears, placing a hand on each handle as it is meant to be used. I lean over and make a perfect cut.

Bart screams one more time.

Chapter Eight

By the time I reach my car, I am shaking all over. I manage to unlock the door with one hand and, looking up and down the shady, all-American-hometown street, I slip into the driver's seat. It is Saturday afternoon and the neighbors must be inside taking an afternoon nap or perhaps out shopping. There is no one on the street, no occupied cars. No one sees me. I am sure of it.

I take a shuddering breath, knowing I must calm down. My hand, clenched around the object, is trembling. I should not have taken it. It is dangerous. And yet when I think of Jessica's hair at home in my drawer, I know that the hair is not enough. I thought it would be, but it's not, just as leaving the young men alongside the road screaming as the fire reached them, had not been enough.

I force my brain to send a signal to my fingers and they unclench. The object falls to the seat beside me. It is not as bloody as one would think it would be.

That is when I catch a glimpse of my face in the rearview mirror. A blood spatter, just one tiny droplet, rests on my cheek. I raise my hand to wipe it away but I stop myself. I look down and see tiny spatters on my dark t-shirt. No one would even realize what it was if they saw me. I gaze out through the windshield, my hands on the steering wheel.

Through the closed window I still hear the engine of the chipper-shredder. It sounds as if it is trying to cut through thick bone again. The other arm still, perhaps. I had to cover myself for what I had taken. Bart, the quarterback, is probably already dead. Charlie is dead.

I must go. I must go home and destroy my clothes. I must shower and then I must clean out my car. I must wipe down the seats and anything I have touched, ridding myself of any DNA evidence.

I take another deep breath, amazed by the calm that is settling over me. I still feel that adrenaline rush, but I am not afraid. I start the car engine, thinking of the cool shower I will take when I get home. I feel the water hitting me in the face, streaming down my arms, my legs, washing away the evidence of Bart Johnson's sins against mankind.

"Liza! Phone!" Muriel's voice echoed in the tiled bathroom. "Liza!"

Liza Jane came out of the shower and grabbed the beach towel hanging on the hook in the little dressing area outside the stall. She gave her dreads a shake and wrapped the towel around her, stepping out of the puddle of water into the main bathroom all the girls on the dorm floor shared. "Tell them to call me back."

"It's Cam," Muriel sang, on her way out the swinging door. "But sure. I'll tell him to call back."

"It's Cam?" Liza Jane hurried across the floor, her green plastic flip-flops slapping on the tile, leaving wet footprints behind. "Wait. No! Muriel, I'll take it."

Liza Jane raced out the door, down the carpeted hall, and darted into the dorm room she shared with Muriel. The college had paired them up as roommates, but so far, so good. Liza Jane liked the biology major and they were fast becoming best friends.

"Hey, Cam," Muriel said into the phone. "Liza says she can't come to the phone right now. Actually, she says she never wants to speak to you again, so—"

"Give me that!" Holding on to her towel with one hand, Liza Jane snatched the cordless phone out of her roommate's hand with the other.

Muriel giggled, backing off so Liza Jane couldn't swat her.

"Cam. Hey. Sorry about that. That was some crazy, homeless woman that lives behind my dorm in the alley." This was the first time he'd ever called Liza Jane. She didn't even know how he'd gotten the number. She always gave out her cell. "What's up?"

"You're not going to believe this, man," Cam said, out of breath. "Can you get over to 111 Porter Street, like this minute?"

"Sure." As she talked, she raced to her closet and dug through the pile of clothes in the basket on the floor. "What's going on?"

"I've already sent the camera crew. I doubt you'll be able to actually get any shots of the scene, but even one of you standing in the front yard would be kick-ass."

Shaking out a pair of wrinkled blue jeans, Liza Jane cradled the phone between her shoulder and cheek and stepped into them. She was still wet, so it was a fight to get them up and buttoned. "Cam, what's going on? What's the story?"

"Bart Johnson is dead."

"The quarterback beef? You're kidding me." She dropped the towel and pulled a t-shirt over her head, skipping the bra. She didn't have any boobs, anyway. "Too much partying after the winning game last night? Death by kegger?"

"No, man, way weirder than that. Just meet me there."

"Okay." Liza Jane slid her feet into a pair of Muriel's

clogs sticking out from under her bed. "I'll be there in a few minutes—111 Porter."

"Hot date?" Muriel asked.

Liza Jane tossed the cordless phone on the closest unmade bed, grabbed her messenger bag off the doorknob, and ran out the door. "Not hardly. Looks like there's been another *accident*."

"I'm sorry, it being Saturday and all. I hope I did the right thing calling you." Police Chief Seipp wiped his sweaty forehead with a white handkerchief neatly folded into a palm-sized square. "I mean, I know you feds don't usually do this kind of work, but the governor is breathing down our mayor's neck something fierce. I'm just tryin' to cover my a—, bases."

Adam stood in the center of the backyard of the house Chesapeake Bay College quarterback Bart Johnson had rented, birds chirping in the old oak and maple trees that dotted the property. The body had already been removed after the assistant coroner had declared the young man dead, but the scene of the accident was still fresh. He could smell the blood in the warm, late-afternoon air, and he had to concentrate not to let it get to him. Not let it remind him of another time when he had smelled this much blood. It struck him as odd that birds could still chirp in the trees overhead after something like this had just happened. "You were right to call us, Buck," he told the police chief.

"Looks like an accident, plain and simple, to me." Chief Seipp carefully unfolded, then refolded his handkerchief and mopped his brow again. "Kid was cutting up brush with that big-ass chipper-shredder, trips, and goes down." He used one pudgy arm to demonstrate, giving it a violent jerk at the last second. "Next thing you know, you're getting sucked into the thing and your arm is gone. I had this cousin, she used to like her afternoon gin and tonic before the kids got home from school. Every one of 'em brats. Anyway, she tripped one day vacuuming and somehow got her hair sucked up in one of those roller heads. Ripped it right out of her scalp, big hank of hair. She was bald on the one side. Eventually, she cut the other side and let it grow back." He shrugged his thick shoulders, armpits stained with perspiration. "But these things happen."

Adam was only half listening to the police chief as he watched M.K. circle the chipper-shredder, taking care not to walk in the blood. There was almost no blood at the point of entry where the quarterback's body was found. At the opposite end, however, where the piece of machinery spit out the wood chips and sawdust, the ground looked like a massacre had taken place.

"The funnel redirected the blood spatter," Adam said, pointing it out to M.K.

"I can see that, *Special Agent Thomas*."

Okay, so she had loosened up when she was off duty the night before; that didn't mean she didn't still take her job seriously.

"You see where the grass is torn up?" she observed.

No, but he had noticed that she'd left her jacket in his Jeep. He'd picked her up at her place on his way over. "No. Where?"

She pointed, and he walked away from Seipp, leaving him to deal with his perspiring forehead.

"Here." M.K. stood close to where branches would be fed into the machine, and squatted down. "Look like there was a struggle to you?"

He took a step closer. The grass had been dug up as well as some dirt. "I'd sure as hell hope so." He glanced down at her. "Wouldn't you struggle if the thing was eating your arm?"

She gave him the *you're cursing in my presence again* eye and rose. "What I mean," she said quietly, "is, does it look to you like a sign of struggle, as if someone pushed him and he tried to get away?"

Adam frowned, studying the pattern of the upturned grass. "Not really, but it's such a small area." He glanced over his shoulder, back at the house. It was an old, farmhouse-style white clapboard built at the turn of the century but relatively well maintained. "Hard to believe his roommate slept through it. No neighbors heard him scream, either."

"I wouldn't let the Ashview police start the thing up because Dr. Wood will want the tissue from inside, but apparently it's pretty loud," M.K. said. "One of the cops said he had a smaller version of this brand and he wears the same ear protection using it as when he's on the shooting range." She covered both her ears with her hands and then let them fall.

"Think we should talk to the roommates? Make sure everyone was getting along, hunky-dory?"

M.K. nodded. "As long as we're here."

"Damned if this isn't bizarre." Adam shook his head, glancing around the backyard again. The EMT and ambulance crews were gone but there were police still milling around, as well as several firemen. He had no idea why the firemen had been called. Or the EMTs, for that matter. Apparently the poor kid had died from blood loss within minutes of the accident, but had lain there, propped against the chipper-shredder, for a good two hours.

The roommate who had been home had gotten up at five in the afternoon and come out looking for Bart, hoping for a ride to work. According to one of the firemen, the machine had only shut off when it ran out of gas. The roommate said he'd heard it cut off when he was in the shower, about five minutes before he went outside looking for Bart.

"You don't happen to have a camera in your car, do you?" M.K. asked.

"Actually, I do. My new digital. What do you want to shoot?"

She rested a hand on her hip. "Obviously this is an accident, but while we're here, I just thought I'd take a couple shots." She wrinkled her nose, lowering her voice. "Seems the camera Buck uses for crime scenes is out of film again."

"Used them up taking naked girlie pictures of his woman, maybe?" Adam grinned, turning away before she had a chance to chastise him. "Be right back." He slid his hands into his shorts pockets and walked around the side of the house.

Out front, a crowd of students had gathered on the sidewalk and neighbors were huddled in small groups in the middle of the blocked-off street. Staring at the house, they talked in hushed tones. There was a local news truck parked in the driveway next door, and a camera crew was rushing to get set for a shot, their reporter pulling on a sports jacket.

As Adam turned onto the sidewalk to go to the Jeep half a block away, he spotted a familiar pink bandana. To his surprise, his daughter was standing on the open front porch of the old rental house, a student shooting her with a video camera as she spoke. He glanced at the orange wooden barriers the Ashview police had put up that were holding everyone, including the professional news crew, back from the scene. What the hell was his daughter doing crossing police barriers and what the hell had she done to her hair?

"Liza Jane!" Adam called.

If she heard him, she gave no indication.

Adam cut across the lawn that had recently been mowed.

"Initial reports from Ashview Police Chief Buck Seipp state that the star quarterback from Chesapeake Bay College, Bart Johnson, was found dead, right here in his own backyard." She gazed directly into the camera held on the shoulder of a young man wearing jean cutoffs, a Radio Head t-shirt, and flip-flops. "Ashview police released a statement stating the young man died in an accident involving a large piece of lawn-maintenance equipment." She paused for dramatic effect. "The question students are asking is, what's happening here? Six students don't just die *accidentally* in seven weeks' time on a campus of only three thousand students."

"Liza Jane, that's enough," Adam barked, heading up the sidewalk.

She took a quick look at her father and then gazed into the camera lens again. "This is Liza Jane Thomas on Porter Street in Ashview. We'll keep you up-to-date."

"Cut," a young man with a blond ponytail ordered. He walked up to Liza Jane, putting his arm around her shoulder. "Great. Listen, I already talked with Prof McKinley. He'll meet us at the studio tomorrow to edit for Tuesday night." He grinned, stray strands of hair in his eyes.

Adam had just reached the steps when Liza Jane came off the porch. "What are you doing here?" she demanded.

"What am *I* doing here? What are *you* doing here?" He gave the ponytailed guy the once-over.

"A problem, Liza?" the ponytail asked.

"No, it's cool, Cam," she called over her shoulder. "My dad." She returned her attention to Adam, planting both hands on her hips, reminding him of Sophie years ago when she had been a size six and worn a bandana around her head.

"What's it look like I'm doing? I'm reporting the campus news. Rather disturbing news, at that."

"What do you think those police barricades are for?" He pointed. "I'll tell you what they're for." He went on without giving her a chance to respond. "They're to keep civilians away from—"

"From what?" she demanded, not backing down one inch. "A crime scene?" She crossed her arms over her chest. "Besides, Jesse let us by. He said it was okay if we shot my piece on the front step."

"Who the hell is Jesse?"

"Ashview cop." She pointed to a pimply-faced young man in an Ashview police uniform. He was talking nervously to a woman in a housedress hunched over a walker at the house next door where the news van had parked.

Adam turned back. "Well, he shouldn't have let you by. Any of you." He waved at the three young men hastily packing up their equipment. "Liza Jane, no crime has taken place here!" Realizing that people across the street were staring at them, he grabbed her arm none too gently and led her off the sidewalk to a clump of rhododendrons. "This poor kid died in a horrible accident and you're trying to take advantage of his death to boost your ratings on your little news show."

"If there was no crime,"—she met her father's gaze— "then why'd someone call the feds? On a *Saturday*. I know procedures, Special Agent Thomas."

"Hey, hey, hey, what's going on here?" M.K. approached them, hiking across the lawn, glancing over her shoulder at the news reporter and camera crew next door looking in their direction with great interest. "Think we could take this family squabble elsewhere?"

"My daughter was just leaving." Adam grabbed her by her arm to escort her behind the barricades. "And you, with the camera." He pointed, then gestured. "Get the hell off that porch and behind the barricades before we haul your asses in."

"Adam," M.K. said calmly as she pushed in between him and Liza Jane. "Go easy there. Cameras could be on." She shot a glance in the direction of the news van with the satellite dish now turning on top. "You don't want to end up in Crackhow's office first thing Monday morning, do you? Not if he hasn't had his bran muffin."

M.K. looked to Liza Jane. "Why don't you take off?"

"Take off?" Adam grunted, pissed at M.K. now, too. "She's not taking off anywhere. I want to talk to you, young lady." He shook his finger at Liza Jane.

M.K. grabbed Adam's sleeve and led him across the lawn. His daughter cut across in the opposite direction. "Adam, knock it off. People are looking," M.K. told him.

He was surprised by how strong she was. "I don't care if they're looking. It's irresponsible of her to be saying the things she's saying on the air. I don't want her—"

"Adam," M.K. said sharply. "You get the neighbors and

the students riled, make them suspicious, and we're going to have a problem."

He halted on the sidewalk, now out of earshot of everyone. "For Christ's sake, it was just an accident."

She glanced away, but he made no apology for his language. "I know that," she said, turning back, speaking to him as if he were a small child. "*You* know that. But all this community, these kids, know, is that six college-age students have died here in the last seven weeks. That's scary. When people are scared, they like to point fingers."

Adam exhaled, pushing his hair off his forehead, thinking absently that he needed a haircut. "You're right."

She released his arm.

"You're right," he repeated. "I'm sorry. Just seeing Liza Jane on that porch. Hearing her say that crap . . ."

"Kind of makes you temporarily lose perspective."

He glanced down at M.K., then away, annoyed with her now because she was probably right. "Something like that."

"Come on. Let's get that camera. I'll get a couple of shots and we'll get out of here." They started down the sidewalk toward his Jeep. "You know, Special Agent Thomas," she said, a hint of amusement in her voice, "you and I aren't as different as you'd like to believe."

He looked at her, calm again. Focused. "What's that supposed to mean?"

"Just that you're not quite the laid-back, easygoing guy I think you want everyone to believe you are."

He frowned.

"You flew off the handle pretty quickly there. And," she said, stopping at his Jeep parked along the side of the street, "I've seen the file folders on your desk. That's color coding on them, isn't it?" She watched him as he used his key to unlock the glove box, where he kept the camera.

Adam couldn't believe she'd noticed his color coding. He'd been doing it since he was fresh out of Quantico. It helped him keep his desk organized, the cases straight in his head. He pulled the camera out of the glove box. "You want to get something to eat after we're done here?"

"I'd like that."

If he hadn't still been so damned annoyed with her, he might have thought she was cute the way she said it. Almost shyly. "I know this great place on Main Street. It's called The College Park Bar and Grill." He lifted one shoulder. "Burgers, beer." He offered her the camera. "You know how to work one of these things?"

She snatched the camera out of his hand. "You want a dinner partner, you wait here. I'll be back in five."

Adam fought his first impulse to follow her, as if he had something to prove. They were partners and she was just looking out for his best interest the way partners should, the way he and Mark once had. He leaned against the hood of the Jeep and watched M.K. go up the sidewalk. He wondered if she had a boyfriend, then almost laughed aloud. She didn't strike him as the kind of woman who had a lot of time for dating. But who knew? She was certainly more complicated than he had first thought.

Adam kind of liked complicated.

Chapter Nine

All day, I have been consciously aware of the fact that it is Tuesday and *Fraternity Row* will be on TV tonight. I hear two employees in the stairwell discussing it. I catch a snatch of conversation on the radio before I change the station.

As I go about my workday, taking particular care to be efficient in my duties, compliant with my supervisor, pleasant with my co-workers, I tell myself that I will not watch the show tonight. I know that it upsets me. I know that it fuels my urges.

And yet here I am, watching the fraternity brothers of Phi Kappa Alpha and Theta Chi play tag football in a field behind the gymnasium that has been hosed down until it is a quagmire of mud. Students from the campus line both sides of the field and they are laughing and clapping, egging them on. I study the crowd of onlookers carefully, the remote control squeezed tightly in my hand.

I know how some of those watching must feel. I know what it is like to be outside, wanting so desperately to be inside. The camera catches the image of a young woman in a long-sleeved Phi Kappa Alpha t-shirt and shorts. Someone has thrown mud on her and it runs down the front of her pink

shirt. There is a plump girl in unattractive glasses standing
beside her, laughing as if she thinks it is funny, but I know
that inside she is not laughing. She behaves the way that others expect her to behave. She is what they want her to be,
and yet she will never be that. Never be one of them, and I
know it eats at her. I know that over the years it will eat at her
until she cannot sleep, cannot eat, and then she will look
back at the young men playing football right now, the girl in
the too-tight pink t-shirt cheering, and she will know that
this is all their fault. That they are responsible for who she
has become . . . a person foreign to her. A person she does
not like.

Our host, Axel, appears in the corner of the screen, raising a plastic cup of beer in a toast. Mud streaks one side of
his handsome cheek. He is signing off until next week when
we will learn if Bruce really is failing biology, if Doug's girlfriend back home is pregnant, and if the brothers at Phi Kappa
Alpha will oust the pledge, Ricki, for telling a friend in his
English class what he did with the brothers during a secret
meeting Saturday afternoon.

I am glad when the television screen flickers and Axel is
gone because I am sick of him. I am sick of his handsome
face and his falsehoods.

I lift the remote to change channels. I like to listen to the
light rock station while I put the finishing touches on my paperwork for the day, but the screen flickers again and a young
woman appears, standing on the front porch of Bart Johnson's
house. I am immediately mesmerized. The clip was obviously
recorded Saturday. I can see the crowd on the street, the news
van in the driveway next door. The picture is a little grainy,
the sound not as sharp as network TV's. I hold my breath,
listening.

"Ashview police released a statement stating the young
man died in an accident involving a large piece of lawn-
maintenance equipment," Liza Jane is saying. She pauses,
looking right at me. "The question students are asking is,

what's happening here?" she continues. "Six students don't just die *accidentally* in seven weeks' time on a campus of only three thousand students."

I stare at her lovely face, not certain what I am to think. Not certain how I feel about her.

"This is Liza Jane Thomas on Porter Street in Ashview. We'll keep you up-to-date."

The last camera shot is jerky, and my first thought is that if she is going to be a news reporter, if this station is truly going to make something of itself, it must get better equipment.

Liza Jane appears again, this time in the studio in the Media Broadcasting building on campus. My mouth is dry. I move forward in my chair to draw closer to her.

"We had hoped to bring you an update on the death of Bart Johnson," Liza Jane says, looking directly at me.

She is not wearing what most news reporters would wear, but instead, a tight pink t-shirt advertising a company that makes surfboards. She is not wearing her trademark bandana, so I can see her blond hair that has been twisted into little knots. I do not like it. The hairstyle seems beneath her.

"But we have been unable to uncover any more information than what has been in the local papers," she continues. "The autopsy is still pending, but apparently Bart Johnson died when his arms were amputated in a chipper-shredder, a large machine used to cut up small trees and branches. The quarterback died at the scene of blood loss."

She continues to look directly at me, not even needing the notes in front of her. "Local Police Chief Buck Seipp has been unavailable for comment, so the cause of death at this time is still believed to be accidental. However . . ."

Again she pauses. For dramatic effect, no doubt. It is an excellent technique. She has my attention.

"Students on campus are anxious. Parents are calling dorms, concerned. At least two students have applied for transfers to other colleges this week as a result of these accidents. Six accidental deaths of Chesapeake students in seven weeks? Prior to the automobile accident in August, there have only been seven deaths of students in the fifty years this college has been in existence. Need there be further investigation into these deaths? This reporter believes so."

The camera angles shift and she is no longer looking right at me.

"This is Liza Thomas for CCAS News. Good night."

The screen flickers and then goes black. The college station has gone off the air. I change the channel to a light rock music station and slide back in my chair. I loosen my grip on the remote, realizing that my fingers hurt from holding it so tightly.

I am concerned by what Liza Jane has said, the suspicions she might generate with the authorities. At the same time, I cannot help but be impressed. All six deaths were obviously accidents, but she looks beyond what is obvious. She looks beyond the deceit, the untruth of society, of humanity, without fear of reproach.

I wish that I could be Liza Jane.

"Here we are again," Adam said, plopping himself down in front of Dr. Wood's desk.

It was only ten-thirty in the morning, and M.K. was already annoyed with Adam. He didn't seem terribly interested in the Bart Johnson investigation, hadn't really even agreed that they needed to follow through. Crackhow, however, had heard about Liza Jane's broadcast the previous night after *Fraternity Row*. Apparently his wife or mother or someone had watched it. M.K. had seen it, too. She agreed with Adam that while her technique was perhaps not the best, she had to give the teen one thing—she was sincere.

"Here we are again," Dr. Wood said, chuckling. She had the same playful tone in her voice as Adam.

Nothing like a little workplace flirtation to get through hump day.

M.K. ignored them both. It wasn't her business if Adam was interested in the coroner, or she in him. They were both single, consenting adults. She shifted in her chair, reaching for the preliminary autopsy report in its now-familiar manila folder. The envelope beneath it, she knew, contained autopsy photos. She had a matching envelope in her briefcase on the floor beside her containing eight-by-tens from the scene of the accident that had worried her all night.

"The report is self-explanatory," Dr. Wood said, leaning back in her leather executive chair. "Excuse the typos. Don't worry, I'll spell check the final one."

She smiled; she had perfect white teeth. M.K.'s parents hadn't been able to afford braces for any of the Shaughnessy girls, or bleaching. Surely teeth that white had to be bleached.

"I'm not a great typist." She cut her dark eyes at Adam. "The county keeps talking about getting me some help with all this paperwork required by them and the state. I'd even take someone part-time, but they just repeat their mantra. The budget is tight."

M.K. skimmed the report.

"So what, Doc?" Adam asked lazily, as if inquiring about the weather. "He bled to death, right?"

"Exactly. The amputations were so severe that he bled out in a minute or two. Not enough blood to circulate, heart stops."

M.K. set the report down and reached for the envelope. "Is there any possibility, Dr. Wood, that foul play could have been involved?"

She and Adam both laughed at the same time. M.K. didn't appreciate it from either of them.

"Death by homicidal wood chipper?" Dr. Wood said, tucking a lock of her blond hair behind one ear to reveal a sparkling diamond stud. "Not hardly. Death by six-pack-induced stupidity is more like it."

M.K. offered a quick, perfunctory smile. "The body still here?"

"Sure is. You want to see it?" Dr. Wood started to get out of her chair.

"That won't be necessary," Adam said. "I think we have all we need. This is just another wild-goose chase the boss is sending us on."

"Actually, I would like to see the body." M.K. stood up, glancing at Adam, then the M.E., ignoring the jars of body parts lining the shelves on the walls. She reached for her briefcase. "If it's not too much trouble."

"No trouble at all." Dr. Wood walked around her desk. "If you'll follow me this way."

M.K. turned in the doorway. Adam was still in his chair. "You can go bring the car around, if you want. I just want to have a quick look."

"So now I'm your chauffeur?"

She shrugged, handing him her briefcase with the photos and reports stuck in the outside pocket. "Suit yourself." She followed Dr. Wood through the tiled exam room into a smaller room with a wall of what appeared to be large file cabinets, only the drawers were flush to the wall. They were stacked four on four.

"My only customer today," Dr. Wood said, grasping the handle of a drawer and giving it a jerk. "Which is a good thing because I'm up to my eyeballs in death certificates that need to be issued. I just can't seem to get caught up these days."

M.K. winced as the drawer glided open to reveal the pale, nude body of the young man who had been Bart Johnson. Beside the usual Y autopsy incision that had been stitched with black thread, there were lines of black stitches on what was left of his left arm.

M.K.'s stomach did a flip-flop. She breathed through her nose, exhaling from her mouth. His arms were barely recognizable, misshapen and waxen, with rows of black stitching in every direction. "Really did a number on him, didn't it?"

"Power tools are dangerous in the wrong hands." Dr. Wood tilted her head, considering her work. "We were actually fortunate that we got as many large pieces as we did. Nothing left of the right arm but I was able to put quite a bit of the left arm back together. Bone from the right arm caught in the blades, so it shredded the left less efficiently."

M.K. glanced at the place where the young man's right arm should have been attached, then at the body again. Dr. Wood had done a good job of cleaning him up; there were no bloodstains and the stitches were neat and orderly considering the grisly task. She looked at the left arm, which was missing chunks of flesh, but at least still looked like an arm. As her gaze reached his hand, she noticed at once that his entire index finger was missing.

"Missing digit," M.K. mused aloud.

"Yeah." Dr. Wood grimaced. "I didn't realize it until I had most of the pieces put back together."

M.K. looked across the gruesome drawer at the coroner. "Just ground up, you think?"

"Very possible. Or the dimwits with the Ashview police didn't find it in the chipper-shredder when they dismantled it." She rolled her eyes. "I don't mean to disparage your profession, Agent Shaughnessy, but those guys on the Ashview police force are not the brightest bulbs in the pack, if you know what I mean."

"No offense taken." M.K. took one last look at Bart Johnson and then looked away. "Thank you for your time. Once again, you've been very helpful."

The doctor pushed the drawer closed and M.K. turned away, getting a flash of what it would be like to be inside that drawer, sliding into the cool darkness. It made the hair stand up on the back of her neck. As a kid growing up, she'd never been afraid of heights, or dogs, or even bugs or snakes, but close quarters . . . She even avoided elevators, taking the stairs whenever it was feasible.

"Let me know if you need anything else," Dr. Wood called

as M.K. saw herself out of the morgue. "Tell Agent Thomas to feel free to call me. I gave him my personal cell number . . . just in case."

M.K. didn't miss the implication. The doctor wanted to go out with him, probably wanted to sleep with him. She pushed through the swinging door, into the hallway, glad to be out of the morgue, away from the medical examiner and her perfect white teeth.

Adam was waiting for her in the car that had been permanently assigned to them. It was a light blue Crown Victoria and, as he had warned, screamed *feds*. She climbed into the passenger side and lowered her briefcase behind the seat before fastening her seat belt.

"Dr. Wood said you should feel free to call her." She reached for her sunglasses on the dashboard. "Apparently she gave you her personal cell phone number."

"I think we've got all we need to satisfy Crackhow, even if my daughter isn't satisfied." He pulled out of the parking lot and onto the street. "Don't you?"

M.K. couldn't help but laugh.

He glanced at her. "What?"

She couldn't help thinking how good-looking he was in the wraparound sunglasses, his blond hair slightly shaggy. "Didn't you hear me? She was hitting on you, Adam. She wants you to ask her out."

He made a face. "Nah."

"Yes." M.K. looked at him, then away, shaking her head. Men could be so clueless sometimes, especially when it came to women. "She gave you her personal phone number, Adam."

"In case we had any questions on the autopsies." Taking his hand off the wheel, he gestured. "She knows we're still getting heat from the senator's office, and apparently the chief coroner in Baltimore called her after his office got a call from the governor and the president of the college."

"That may be true, but she was still hitting on you."

"Nah," he scoffed. "She's not my type."

"Not your type? You were flirting with her!"

"I was not." He hit his brake and the horn as a huge SUV cut in front of him on the ramp to get on Route 301/50, headed west.

"You most certainly were. Right there in her office. Laughing, making eye contact."

This time he looked at her. "I always do that. I'm just a friendly guy."

M.K. laughed, telling herself she shouldn't care who he flirted with. "Hey," she said, changing the subject entirely. "Did you notice in the autopsy report that the guy's finger was missing? Left index."

"I didn't really read it. Hell, I could have written that report. It was pretty obvious from the scene what happened and how he died. Liza Jane's gone right off the deep end with this whole investigative reporter thing."

M.K. tried to consciously ignore his swearing. She knew her reaction annoyed him and that her feeling on the matter prevented her from being *one of the boys*. It was just that in James Shaughnessy's house, growing up, the use of swear words had been strictly forbidden and resulted in a squirt of liquid dish detergent in the mouth. She'd gone through a time in her life when she was fourteen that her mother should have owned stock in Dawn dish detergent. To this day, every time she heard a word that was not acceptable in the Shaughnessy home, she tasted the soap on her tongue.

"What do you think happened to Bart's finger?" M.K. pushed.

"I don't know. Ground up in the machine, I guess. What did Dr. Wood say?"

"Same thing. She wondered if maybe the finger got lodged inside, and the guys who took apart the chipper-shredder missed it."

"Possible, I guess."

She took a quick look at him through the dark lenses of

her sunglasses. "You mind if I give them a ring—before we turn the report into Crackhow?"

"Mind? No? Do as much extra work as you like, Manuela Karen." Again, he looked her way, this time grinning. "Am I getting close?"

M.K. crossed her arms over her chest and looked out at the highway and cars in front of them. "Nope."

Jerome studied the patient in the chair across from his. Blue was restless today. Not as communicative as in the past two sessions. He made note of that in the margin.

"Can you tell me about the week since we last met?"

The patient's legs crossed, uncrossed, and crossed again. "Work has been busy. Stressful. I feel great demands on my time and energy."

Jerome nodded. No one had to tell him about stress and how it could affect one's work. "Do you find that stressful situations lead you to thoughts, behaviors you find unacceptable?"

The patient glanced down. "Sometimes."

Jerome let a moment or two pass. "Did you experience any of these thoughts or actions you've expressed that you wish to avoid this week?"

This time the patient's gaze shifted to the bookcases that lined the wall behind his desk. "You have a lot of books."

Jerome smiled patiently. "My wife and I are avid readers."

"Have you been married a long time?"

"Since we were in medical school together," Jerome said proudly.

"And that's her. The photo on the desk? She's very pretty."

"She is," Jerome said, not unkindly, "but you're not here to discuss me or my wife. You came to me of your own free will with some concerns that obviously are worrying you a great deal." He kept his gaze focused on the face in front of him. "You didn't say if you felt any of these urges this week."

"No, I didn't."

Jerome smiled. He liked intelligent patients. He liked the idea that he might possibly be able to help someone so bright and able to contribute to the world. "I can't help you if you're unwilling to provide what I need, to offer my help."

"I went to a bar the other night. One very close to home."

The patient's gaze lost focus, and Jerome sensed they were moving back in time.

"I had the chicken sandwich. It was very good. The College Park Bar and Grill. Have you been there, Doctor?"

"I believe my wife and I have."

"After my meal, I considered going to the bar. Having a seat . . . trolling."

"An interesting term." Jerome checked the small brass clock on the coffee table in front of him, left in plain view of him and his patients. It always seemed as if just when he was beginning to reach a certain level with a patient, time was up. But he had learned from trial and error that appointments of more than an hour could actually be counterproductive. He had to be patient. "What do you think you meant when you said *trolling*?"

"I don't fish, if that's what you're asking." Blue chuckled. Sighed. "I suppose I see them, on some level, as prey."

"And you find that disturbing?"

Blue's gaze met Jerome's. "Don't you, Doctor?"

There was something about the tone of the patient's voice, the reflection in the eyes, that Jerome found unsettling. He shifted in his chair, hoping it wasn't obvious. "Blue," he said, deciding to take a different tack. "Did something happen this week? Something you'd like to talk about?"

Again, the patient looked away. Eyes glazed over. "There was this guy who made fun of me."

"This week?"

"No. A long time ago. I just met someone who reminded me of him."

"If those feelings are not resolved, they come back to us, sometimes at the most inopportune times." Jerome set his notebook on his lap and tented his fingers, sensing he needed to tread carefully here. "Did you have these feelings, these urges, at the time that you knew this person?"

"I think I've always had them." Blue's voice was eerie, almost chilling. "In the past, I could control them, though. Usually."

Jerome glanced at the clock again. Time was up, but he was tempted to let the patient go on.

No, there were reasons for these rules, as Sela liked to remind him.

"Blue, our time today is up, but I'd like to pick up our conversation next week here where we're leaving off."

"My past."

Jerome rose. "Yes. Please feel free this week to note any recollections of the past that seem to upset you, or possibly trigger these urges you're fighting."

Blue rose. "I'll do that. Thank you, Dr. Fisher."

Jerome watched the patient go out the door, still sensing the oddest feeling of unrest. Almost doom. Logically, he knew this feeling had no place in a psychiatrist's office, and yet he was having a difficult time dismissing it. He, too, like the patient, had had a stressful week. Sela had been feeling poorly since the weekend, and he knew the blood tests taken today would not return optimistic results. Maybe it was just the stress of the last few days, his wife's worsening condition. He knew it was time he began dealing with the idea that she would not live another year. With that thought, how could he look forward without the feeling of impending doom?

Chapter Ten

"It's Liza Jane. Leave a message, and I might call you back."

"Damned irreverent teenagers," Adam murmured. He never knew whether he should be pissed at her or proud of her. Probably both. "Hey, it's your dad again. Thursday, noon," he said, when the phone beeped in his ear. "You still avoiding me? If it's about Saturday or your newscast Tuesday night, I'm over it." He hesitated. "Call me back, hon. I worry when I don't talk to you for a few days."

He was just sliding his cell phone across his desk when M.K. sat down right in front of him. She had a nice derriere for a chick carrying a gun and an attitude.

"The finger's missing."

"What?" Adam tried to slide a file out from under said derriere. She refused to shift her weight.

"The kid's finger. Dr. Wood said it wasn't in the body bag. Ashview police say it wasn't in the chipper-shredder. Apparently they had the whole thing taken apart and spread out on tarps on someone's garage floor."

Adam gave the file one last tug and surrendered, sitting

back in his chair and tucking his hands behind his head. "Maybe it just got ground up."

"Maybe." M.K. studied him, her eyes narrowing. "But isn't that odd? Just one finger missing on the left hand. If one finger got chewed, wouldn't other fingers have gotten chewed up, too?"

He closed his eyes for a moment and rubbed them. For some reason Crackhow had been piling old case files on his desk all week to be reviewed and then officially closed. There were so many that he'd started sending some over to M.K.'s desk. She was getting through her pile faster than he was, even when he stacked her desk up higher than his own. He figured she had to be staying awake all night reading them.

"A missing finger."

She crossed her arms over her chest. Today she'd come to work in a pair of gray slacks and a form-fitting white t-shirt; it was plain but revealed that she actually had a nice figure. Small, round breasts, a narrow waist, and nice hips, not too wide, but not so small as to be boyish. Her hair looked different, too, longer, lighter, something. Whatever it was, Adam approved. She just seemed to be growing on him. She annoyed the shit out of him some days, but he looked forward to each weekday morning, knowing he'd have the opportunity to work with her, possibly spar. She was an excellent sparring partner.

"Okay," Adam said with a sigh that obviously meant he was only humoring her. "Let's say the finger is missing. So what?"

"So what?" She dropped her hands to her hips, nice butt still on his desk. "What if his head was missing? Would you say 'so what' then?"

"Of course not." He rubbed his temples, feeling a killer of a headache coming on as a result of either too many beers last night or not enough. "Where are we going with this, Mother Teresa?"

"I know this is going to sound crazy."

"What makes me think you're right?"

"Just shut up for a minute and listen to me." She raised her foot and gave his chair a push. "What if Bart's accident wasn't an accident?" She went on before he could stop her. "What if the hair is missing from Jessica's head and Bart's finger is missing because someone killed them both? Someone killed them and is taking trophies."

"You saw my daughter's newscast Tuesday night?"

She looked away, then back at him. "So I caught the end of *Fraternity Row* and then her little news brief. She's actually pretty good, Adam."

"Great. Maybe she can get a job with the *National Enquirer*. Do they do a news program, too?"

"I know. It's crazy." She lifted one hand and let it fall. Then she looked back at him. "I just keep getting this weird feeling about this."

"Listen, M.K., let me give you a little advice on the whole cop intuition thing. Basically, it's a bunch of made-for-TV crap. As officers of the law, we have to follow leads based on evidence. We can't trust our *feelings*. You only have to look at the divorce rate to see that. What we can trust is evidence."

"But what if, on the outside chance, Liza Jane is right? Weren't you just telling me the other day that part of being a good agent is being able to think outside the box?"

"Oh, you're outside the box, all right."

She scowled.

"Look, his finger was not removed from his hand," Adam insisted impatiently. "It got eaten up in that big meat grinder."

"You're probably right."

"I know I am."

"But just to be sure, just to humor me, would you mind calling Dr. Wood and asking her to have a look at the hand? Just a quick look to verify that his finger was chewed off in the chipper-shredder and not cut off."

"Or eaten off by a rabid badger?"

"Very funny. Come on, Adam. I'm serious. It just strikes

me as weird that one digit would be completely missing. Don't you think it's weird?"

He met her gaze. "Any weirder than the couple who kidnapped their boss's four-year-old for ransom and buried her underground, forgetting she needed to breathe? Any weirder than a man strapping bombs to a life vest and walking into a federal office building and detonating himself? Any weirder than—"

"Okay, okay." M.K. held up her hand. "I get what you're saying. I know I'm new at this. Untrained, and you've been doing it for years."

"Seems like a lifetime," he mused.

"But couldn't you just humor me? Just this one time, Adam?"

The look she gave him made him want to do anything on earth she asked.

What was with him and the women in his life? Why was he such a weak-kneed sorry excuse for the male species?

"Just call her and ask her to have a quick look. That's all I'm asking."

He frowned, already knowing he'd do it for her. "Why don't you call her?"

"Because she's really busy and I've already been a pain in the butt and she likes you."

"She does not." He rolled his chair forward and poked her with his pen. "You going to move or not?"

She jumped off the desk. "Thanks, Adam. And ask for a copy of the autopsy report."

"I thought we got a copy of the autopsy report."

"Nope. Just the death certificate."

"Right. Okay. Whatever. Now get back to your cubicle." He pointed. "We get the transcript on that warehouse phone tap yet?"

"Working on it." She walked away. "Let me know what she says."

* * *

Adam left a message on Dr. Wood's voice mail and she called him back less than half an hour later.

"Thanks for getting back to me so quickly," he said. "I know you're swamped."

"Not a problem, Adam. And please, call me Valerie."

He spun his pen on his desk. "Okay, Valerie. Listen, I've got a big favor to ask. It's really more for my partner than me."

"But you volunteered to call me."

He smiled, thinking maybe M.K. was right; the doctor did have a little thing for him. "Yeah, something like that. Anyway, she—we were wondering if you could take another quick look at our gardener's hand. Ashview police can't seem to find the damned finger."

"I'm not surprised. I don't think Seipp could find his ass if it wasn't tied on."

He laughed. "Yeah, exactly. Anyway, my boss is being pretty pissy about this whole thing with the accidents at the college and we just want to be sure the finger was, you know, chewed up in the chipper-shredder and not . . . cut off or something."

"Cut off?"

"I told you it was a favor." He straightened out the picture frame on his desk, meeting his daughter's smiling gaze. "My partner is new—she wants to make a good impression, be sure she's covered all her bases."

"I'd be happy to help you out."

Adam leaned back in the chair. Dr. Wood was nice, a hell of a looker. She was certainly the kind of woman he had dated in California, when he had the time and opportunity to date, at least. But something was holding him back from asking her out, even when she was making it obvious from her tone of voice that she was interested. "Great."

"One problem, though," she said.

"What's that?"

"The body's already been released to a funeral home in, let's see . . ." She paused. "Federalsburg, Maryland. You want me to try and catch them? It says here that the body is to be cremated."

"No, no, that's all right." Adam glanced in M.K.'s direction. She wasn't going to be happy. "I'm sure you did a thorough exam. You would have noticed if the finger had been cut off cleanly . . . wouldn't you?"

"I like to think of myself as being quite thorough, Adam."

The temperature on the phone call seemed to have dropped several degrees rapidly.

"Of course," he said quickly.

"Anything else I can do for you, Adam?"

She was warming up again. "No. That's it. At least for today. You have a good day."

"You, too."

Adam hung up and he wasn't out of his chair before M.K. appeared around the corner. "She going to take another look?" she asked.

"Can't. Body's already been released. On its way to be cremated."

M.K. snapped her fingers. "Darn it."

He laughed. "You know, you're a grown-up now, one that carries a Glock. You can say *damn*."

"I'm still my father's child." She looked up at him, then away. "I guess Dr. Wood would have noticed anything suspicious about the hand, anyway, don't you think?"

He leaned against the frosted glass of his cubicle. "I'm sure she would have."

"But the report? She'll send it?"

He thumped his forehead with the heel of his hand.

"You forgot to ask." She turned away.

"I'll call her back."

"I'll do it myself."

He followed her, cutting in front of her and walking backwards. "I'm sorry. I'll call her right back."

She looked at him the way all the women in his life looked at him when he screwed up.

"Let me make it up to you," he said, putting out his hand to try and stop her. "Dinner tonight."

"I'm not having dinner with you. I have a lot of work to do. Work you put on my desk, I might remind you."

She kept walking, forcing him to continue walking backwards which was tricky in the main aisle with other people coming and going.

"Come on. A quick dinner. We can discuss the Muribito case, make sure we're on the same page."

"I'm not having dinner with you tonight."

"Tomorrow night, then," he said quickly. "Surely you're not working on a Friday night."

She stopped, eyeing him up and down. "You going to wear that shirt?"

He looked down at his Hawaiian flowered shirt and ran his hand over his chest. "I like this shirt."

"I guess that means yes." She walked past him.

He turned. "Yes, you'll come?"

"Seven-thirty. But I'll meet you somewhere."

"O'Shea's?"

"Absolutely not. I won't be able to eat for thinking of that dead girl in the parking lot."

"Then College Park."

"Fine, I'll be there." She pushed the door into the ladies' room. "But don't wear that shirt."

As Liza Jane walked up the dark driveway, the garage door went up. She heard Mark start the engine of his extended cab pickup truck and saw the red taillights come on. She walked through the cloud of exhaust, to the sidewalk, her backpack slung over her shoulder. Her mother was waiting for her at the front door.

"Hey, honey, thanks for coming on such short notice."

"Mom, you know I'll watch her anytime. I keep telling you that."

Her mother look tired and swollen, but she'd dressed in a cool, filmy skirt and top and she'd even put some lipstick on. "Savannah's all ready for her bath. Just waiting for you."

"Liza Jane!" Savannah called from the top of the staircase.

Liza Jane looked up to see her sister bare naked, stuffed bunny in her arms. "Eek!" she cried. "Banana's naked!"

The little girl shrieked with glee and raced down the hallway.

"Don't get in the tub until I get up there," Liza Jane warned. She looked back to her mother, who was retrieving her Peruvian wool purse. "You guys have a nice dinner. Go for a walk. Just sit in the car and talk. Whatever you need. I can crash in my old room tonight."

"Mark and I just need some time alone, to sort things out. He's got a lot of things going on right now. The stress at work is exhausting."

"You know, he needs to get some help, Mom."

"We're working on that."

"He can't keep doing this to you. You not knowing where he is, when he'll come home. You know very well he's in bars. Picking up women, probably."

"Honey, please." Her mother walked by, pressing her palm to Liza Jane's cheek. "Cute dreads, by the way."

Liza Jane grinned. "Thanks," she called as her mom went out the door.

"Hey, you talk to your father?"

Liza Jane caught the storm door, shaking her head. He'd left four messages on her cell in the last two days; she just hadn't been ready to call him and listen to the ration of crap she knew he was going to give her. He'd been pretty angry

Saturday at Bart Johnson's house. "No, why?" Liza Jane said sweetly. "What's up?"

"I don't know. You know your father. Call him."

Mark had backed into the driveway and was waiting, motor running. He laid on his horn.

"Asshole," Liza Jane muttered as her mother ran down the sidewalk.

I sit at the kitchen table. I am supposed to be writing an entry in my journal this time of evening, but I have found something else to occupy myself. Something I am beginning to think might be more therapeutic than Dr. Fisher's journal. I have known for some time that I should find a hobby, something fun to do to help me relax in the evenings and on weekends. I think that I may have found that hobby.

I have gathered magazines. I have been tearing out pages I like, saving them for when I have time to cut the pictures out. As I reach for my scissors I catch a glimpse of the TV in the living room. *Fraternity Row* is on the screen and even though the sound has been set on "mute," I can hear Axel's voice in my head.

I touch the top of my head and I feel the green Chesapeake Bay College ballcap. I finger the strand of perfect hair I have carefully, cleverly attached to the hat. On the table, beside my clippings, is the perfect finger placed in a small white cardboard jewelry box. I know that it is unwise to keep these things. I know that I cannot continue to do so. But for tonight, at least, I have them. They comfort me.

I reach for a glossy page I have pulled from a women's magazine and I carefully cut out the face of a young man who reminds me of Drew Palmer. Same color hair. When I have trimmed it to my satisfaction, I pick up the glue stick I was told in the craft store was perfect for scrapbooking. I remove the cap and find that I like the scent of it.

I apply just the right amount of glue to the head and then

I carefully place it on the white Jeep I have cut out and glued on my posterboard. I use tweezers I also purchased in the craft store to adjust the face just so. When I am satisfied, I sit back in my chair and smile.

In the white Jeep I have placed the faces of four young men. I am particularly pleased with the two I have placed in the rear seat area. Their mouths are open as if they were laughing. Or are they screaming?

For several moments I sit and admire my handiwork. But I have more to do so I set the posterboard aside and pick up the photo I removed from the bulletin board at the pub. I have debated whether or not I should cut the photo and risk making a mistake and ruining it; it is such a treasure. But I have a steady hand.

I painstakingly cut Bart from the photo and holding him in my hand, I try to decide just where he belongs in my collage.

"I'm glad you came," Adam said, lifting his beer mug in a toast.

M.K. raised her mug to meet his before drawing it to her mouth. He made her uncomfortable saying things like that. She didn't know how to respond, maybe because she didn't know how she felt. "And I'm glad you didn't wear that hideous shirt."

"You can be pretty funny when you loosen up a bit." He eyed her across the table. "You know, you're not at all what you seem to be in the office, either."

"And what's that?"

He shrugged, leaning back. He was still wearing his sunglasses though it had been dark for hours. He wore them pushed back on his head, pinning back his hair that was getting shaggy. "You know, uptight, hard to get along with, break-your-balls kind of—"

"Lesbian type?"

He pointed his finger. "I didn't say that."

"You didn't have to. I see the way most of the guys look at me. It's like you have to be one kind of woman or the other, as if there's nothing in between." She fiddled with the damp cocktail napkin. "Like you have to either be Dr. Wood, all curves and breathy voice, or a dyke." She looked up at him, not sure she should have said that, especially since he was obviously attracted to Dr. Wood and women like her.

"In all fairness, you did come on a little strong during your first days of school."

She couldn't help but smile at the way he worded things sometimes. She liked his sense of humor that seemed different from most men's, certainly her father's. She usually associated men and humor with farting and The Three Stooges.

"I didn't know what to expect," she admitted. "And you know very well that the Bureau isn't an equal-opportunity employer—not yet. Sure, women are getting equal pay, but we're not getting equal treatment, especially from our male fellow agents." She studied him across the table, daring him to challenge her statement. To her surprise, he didn't.

"Some of us have just been burned, is all." He shrugged.

"And some of you are just male chauvinist pigs."

He laughed and she found herself laughing with him.

The waitress brought them their chicken sandwiches, and Adam ordered another beer. "So tell me why you decided to become an agent." He removed the lettuce and tomato from the sandwich. "You said you had a good job at Quantico."

M.K. didn't like lettuce and tomato, either. "I don't know." She slid the lettuce and tomato out from under the sesame-seed bun. "I saw all those cool movies and wanted to be like the FBI chicks you see on TV? I wanted to set my father off again? I was bored with my neat little office and all my neat little facts and figures?"

"Maybe a little of each?" He took a bite. "Divorced?"

She shook her head, looking down at her sandwich. "Never been married. Don't think I ever will be."

"Maria Katrina, that's just crazy." He took a gulp of beer. "Everyone needs to be married. I loved being a married man, being a husband and a partner."

She took a nibble of the bread and reached for the ketchup. "So why are you divorced?"

He looked her right in the eye. "Because I screwed up. Classic male mistakes. A whole dump truck full. I didn't know what was most important until it was too late. I put my job before my wife and child every time I had the chance. Sophie got lonely. Liza Jane needed a father."

She squirted ketchup on the side of her plate and handed the bottle to Adam. "And that's when your best friend stepped in?"

"It's not how it sounds." He was quiet for a moment as he squirted ketchup all over his fries. "It is, but it wasn't. Sophie and I were long done, even if I was still in the house, before Mark showed up."

"I didn't really get to talk to him much at your ex's that evening, but he seems like a nice guy."

"Mark? He's great." He pushed fries into his mouth. "So back to this you not getting married. You're too young to be making choices like that. Don't you want children?"

She reached for a fry on her plate. "Just don't know if it's in the cards for me," she said quietly.

"Well, I loved being a father, still do. I wish we'd had another. I wish we'd had a dozen, but . . ."

"But things just fell apart before that could happen?" she asked.

"I went undercover. I was gone a lot. We considered applying to adopt again, but no one is terribly receptive to sending babies home to live in one-parent homes while the other one lives among drug dealers and crime bosses."

M.K. pointed with a fry. "You said adopt *again*. Is Liza Jane *adopted*?"

He nodded. "I can't have children." He busied himself

mopping up ketchup on his plate with a fry. "Faulty plumbing."

"But she looks like you," M.K. said in amazement. "Like you and Sophie."

He looked up, smiling. "I know. Guess she was meant to be ours, huh?"

She smiled back. "Guess so."

After that, the conversation turned less serious. They talked briefly about the Muribito case they had been assigned to. M.K., again, mentioned the quarterback's missing finger but Adam just didn't think it was significant. He was ready to move on to new cases.

Adam had the second beer and then they both switched to water with lemon. M.K. felt unsteady enough as it was with Adam; she didn't need to add alcohol to the mix.

All evening as they talked, M.K. tried to tell herself that there wasn't really anything going on between them. They were just partners, getting to know each other, like Adam said. But she knew she was attracted to him and by his second beer, she was beginning to suspect that the attraction was mutual.

Though she protested, Adam paid the whole bill and then walked her out. The days were finally beginning to grow cooler, so the evenings were cooler, too. Almost overnight, it seemed as if fall was in the air.

"Well, here I am." She leaned against the door of her Honda. "Thanks for dinner."

He moved closer, watching her. The only light was from a security lamp a row over in the pub parking lot. "You're welcome."

M.K. knew that was the signal for her to get in her car, but he kept looking at her. She kept looking back. It wasn't until she realized he was leaning over to kiss her that she knew it was what she had been waiting for.

His mouth barely brushed hers, and she didn't know what came over her. The last year and a half of celibacy maybe?

Adam's arms closed around her waist and she found herself pressing her hips to his, wrapping her arms around his neck, lifting her chin to meet his mouth. She kissed him hungrily, her tongue intertwining with his. He tasted of beer and maleness and the forbidden.

When M.K. finally pulled away, she was dizzy and breathless. Instinctively, she ran her hand over her mouth, looking down at the dark pavement as she stepped back to lean on her car again.

"I . . ." He chuckled, glancing away. "I have no idea where that came from."

"We can't do this," she said, afraid to meet his gaze. Afraid she'd kiss him again.

"I know. I shouldn't have. It was wrong of me."

"Office policies. Safety issues." M.K. had no idea what she was muttering.

"Right, right." He ran his fingers through his hair, at last removing his sunglasses. "Look—"

"Adam, it's okay. Really." She slid to one side to unlock her car door. "I'm a big girl. A consenting adult."

"I know. I just—"

"I'll see you Monday morning." She opened the door and jumped inside. "All right?"

"Yeah. All right." He turned away, then back to her as if he wanted to say something else.

M.K. still couldn't catch her breath. She could still taste his mouth on hers. She slammed the door shut and started the engine.

Adam just stood there in the middle of the parking lot, hands pushed down in his cargo pants pockets, and watched her go.

Chapter Eleven

The phone rang as M.K. came down the hall, pulling her pajama top over her head. She'd stayed home all day doing wash, cleaning out her already clean refrigerator, slogging through paperwork, hoping Adam might call. They hadn't spoken since dinner the previous night, since their kiss.

All day M.K. had obsessed about the kiss. She knew she shouldn't have done it. Knew he shouldn't have. It was a bad idea in so many ways. He was a twenty-year veteran, she was a newbie; they had to work together without concern for personal issues, not to mention the fact he was more than ten years older than she was. M.K. knew all that. Knew it then. Knew it now. Yet the feel of his mouth against hers had made her feel more alive than she had in months . . . maybe years.

As M.K. picked up the phone, she looked at the display screen. She knew the number, and it was not the one she'd been hoping for. "Mama. I thought you weren't calling tonight. Didn't you have something going on at the church?"

"Certainly not anything that would keep me out past ten," she said indignantly. "What woman belongs out after ten at night? It's what your father says is the cause of so many of these crimes. Women are out on the streets at all times of the night and then they wonder why when terrible things happen to them."

M.K. sighed, wishing she hadn't picked up when she saw that it was her mother. Of course, every Saturday night after she picked up the phone she wished she hadn't and the next Saturday night she would pick up again, anyway.

M.K. wandered into the dark kitchen and opened the refrigerator. She wasn't really hungry, just bored. Anxious. The interior light from the refrigerator cast a V of light over her bare foot and across the clean tile floor. "That's right, Mama. Those young women who are raped and murdered, they deserve what they get. That's certainly fair punishment for having a late dinner, or, God forbid, an evening class at the college."

"Don't use that tone of voice with me, young lady," her mother said. "And take care how you use the Lord's name."

M.K. knew her mother was crossing herself right now, whispering a little prayer for the salvation of her eldest daughter's soul. M.K. didn't care. It was one of those weeks when she and God weren't getting along so well.

She released the handle on the refrigerator door and it swung shut, leaving her in darkness. She needed to get out of the house, go for a walk, tempt a rapist or murderer, something . . . anything to find her way out of this funk.

"Mama, how are the girls?"

"They're fine. Everyone is fine. If you came home more often, maybe you would see for yourself."

M.K. stood in the middle of the small, dark kitchen, the phone to her ear, her other arm hanging at her side. "And Da?"

"Fine," her mother said crisply. "His spastic colon has been acting up but he's fine other than that. Blood pressure is good."

"And how about you, Mama? How are you?"

"Fine. I'm always fine. Except that my oldest daughter never comes to see me. I cleaned the oven today. I made apple pie earlier in the week to take to Father Houlihan and it bubbled over, the way it does sometimes. The smell of the smoke in the house was awful. We had to open all the windows."

"So Father Houlihan is getting ready to retire." M.K. grasped at some subject to discuss with her mother other than her short-comings or the oven or her father's colon. "Any word of who will replace him?"

"Certainly not," her mother exclaimed indignantly. "It's not up to the parish who the diocese sends us."

"I know that, Mama. I just wondered—"

"Your father's calling," she interrupted. "I had better go."

"Okay." M.K. brushed her bangs out of her eyes. She needed a haircut but she was toying with the idea of letting it grow out a little. Maybe add some highlights. "Thanks for calling, Mama."

"I don't suppose you'll be coming for supper tomorrow?"

M.K. took a second before she answered, knowing that anger or bitterness was a waste of time in this conversation and just about any other she had with her parents. All it did was make her feel guilty after she hung up. "No, Mama. Not tomorrow. Soon, though."

M.K. hung the phone up on the counter and stood there for a moment, alone in the dark, before heading back down the hall to change out of her PJs. Adam wasn't going to call, and if she didn't get out of the house for a few minutes, she was going to go stark, raving mad.

I had no intention of going to the campus. I went out for cream for my Sunday morning coffee is all. But instead of pulling into the minimart near home, I found myself parking on Main Street. I locked my car and walked down the brick sidewalk. I passed students going to and from their dorms and houses to the pubs downtown, to parties elsewhere on the campus and in town. They walked right past, taking no notice of me. Talking. Laughing. Paying no attention to the pain they have caused me.

I follow the quaint brick path to the rectangular mall that is lined with the distinguished red brick buildings of the college: Elton Hall, Carver Hall, Wooten Hall, Locke Hall. I am familiar with them.

There are lovely trees planted around the mall, with benches beneath many of them. There is a crisp edge to the night air and I know that autumn is upon us again. The leaves on the trees are already beginning to change colors, curl, and soon they will fall to the ground . . . drift.

As I walk along the sidewalk, taking care not to study any one passerby too long and draw attention to myself, I struggle with the mounting urgency inside me. At first it was only a pulse in the very center of my abdomen, but now I feel it in every fiber of muscle and tissue in my body. I almost tremble with the intensity of it.

It has only been a week since the quarterback, and I know that I must control my compulsion. I must be careful, make no mistakes, protect the life I have built, no matter how false the walls are. After all, what would I have left if those walls tumbled?

I take a seat on a bench under an old elm tree at one end of the mall, looking across at the oldest building at the college, which is now a student services building, but I know that once it was not. There is a street lamp nearby but it does not cast light directly on the bench.

I sit, trying to gather my thoughts. My knee jiggles uncontrollably. I wish that I had brought the journal I keep for Dr. Fisher. Perhaps I would find comfort in it. I use the journal as Dr. Fisher has instructed, to explore my thoughts, my feelings. He does not ask to see it; he only inquires as to what I have written, and I am free to share as I please. I have been as honest with Dr. Fisher as possible so far, but during our last session I sensed he knows that I am hiding something. Something too terrible to speak of. I am ashamed that I have not been as truthful as I could be with him; after all, the good doctor is only trying to help me. And he *is* a good doctor, or at least it seems so to me. He appears so compared to the others I have known.

I rest my hand on my knee to cease its movement. I wonder why I am so restless tonight. Why I could not stay home. Why I was drawn here.

I know why, of course. It is that damned TV show. I know I should not have taped it. I did not even recall doing so, but there it is in my VCR/DVD player, where I can play it over and over again, giving me the opportunity to obsess.

And obsess I do. Even when I am not watching it, I know that it is there. There inside my TV. In my gut. Churning. Rotting.

How deranged is that?

I chuckle out loud at the absurdity. How is it that I am intelligent enough to recognize my disorders but unable to alleviate them or at least control them? A curse, I suppose. Yet another of God's sick jokes.

Against my will, my mind strays back to thoughts of the ridiculous *Fraternity Row* television show. Everyone in the community is talking about it. Last Sunday, the *Baltimore Sun* ran a feature on it. It angers me the way people are drawn into the lives of the students, into the lies. It is called a reality TV show but it is not reality. It is not the way the real world is, or even the college world. Yes, the fraternity brothers and sisters say they are concerned with each other's problems, but I know that they don't really feel that way. I know that Katie does not really care for Casey or Ty, and Samantha is not sincerely concerned with the fairness of how pledges were chosen for Pi Beta Phi.

My knee begins to shake again and this time even pressing down on it with my hand does not stop it. I watch a couple walk by, hand in hand, and in my mind's eye I see myself following them. I see myself raking out the young woman's eyes with the car keys in my pocket. I see myself dragging the young man behind Locke Hall and—

The images frighten me.

My hand trembling, I reach into my pocket and I take out my cell phone. Dr. Fisher has given me a number to call if I need him, any time of the day or night. It is a number for the hospital where he has privileges. I give my name to the woman with the pleasant voice on the other end of the line. My voice is amazingly calm, even as I tell her that this is indeed an emergency. She takes my information and says that she will relay my message to Dr. Fisher.

It is only five minutes before the phone rings, even though it's almost midnight now. I knew that Dr. Fisher was a good man.

"Blue?" he says on the other end of the line.

"Doctor, thank you for calling me back." I am so relieved that I cannot control the emotion in my voice.

"Blue," the doctor says calmly, "tell me what's happening."

"I . . . I went for a ride. Just to get cream for my morning coffee," I say, already feeling calmer. Just the sound of Dr. Fisher's voice has made me see that I can direct my actions.

"But you didn't get the cream?"

"No, no," I say. "I'm sitting on a bench in a public place." I know better than to give too many details. I would not want the doctor to feel he is in any way responsible if I am unable to remain in command of myself. "I am watching . . . people and I want to . . . I need to . . ." I don't know what to say.

"You are feeling the urge to behave in a way you don't want to behave?" he asks gently after a moment of silence.

"Yes," I say excitedly. "I feel the urge and it's wrong. I know it's wrong. I know that I can't live this way." I tighten my grip on my cell phone. "I will not live this way. I will not ruin my career, my life," I say passionately.

"Blue, I understand how you're feeling. I hear your frustration and we'll talk about that, but first I need to ask you . . . In your state of unrest, are you contemplating suicide?"

"No," I say, and I am being honest. "Not tonight. Not now.

I'm beyond that. But other nights, other times, I am ashamed to tell you that I have considered that option."

"Would you like to tell me about those times?"

"I don't know." I gaze up into the tree branches overhead. I study a twig with leaves, thinking how perfect they are in this imperfect world. "There were so many times . . ."

"Perhaps just one time. Do you think you could tell me about one incident?"

Dr. Fisher's voice is so kind, and I remind myself that he is here to help me. I sought out his help. "High school was hard for me," I hear myself say.

"As it was for many of us."

Memories flash in front of my eyes like frames from an eight-millimeter film. Silent, ugly scenes. "But college was worse," I say.

"Worse how?"

"In . . . in high school I just kept my head low. Stayed under the radar. I made no attempt to do anything but get through each day. Survive."

"Sometimes it's all we can do, Blue." Dr. Fisher's tone is soothing.

"But college . . . that was when I began to go against my parents' wishes, my father in particular." I swallow the bile in my throat, the echo of their angry voices banging around in my head. "I didn't want to disobey them or even disappoint them, but I couldn't go on that way. I began to emerge once I was in college."

"It's a time when we, as young adults, begin to climb out of our cocoon, if you will, Blue. Become our own person away from our parents. It's a very scary period in our lives."

"Scary, yes," I agree. And then out of nowhere comes a shard of memory and with it the pain that I feel as sharply as I did that day. "I . . . I had to take physics and it was hard for me," I confess, still not knowing where the memory has come from or why it has surfaced. "I was always better with biology."

Dr. Fisher chuckled. "Me, too."

"There was this big test . . . midterm exam, I think. I studied, I did," I tell him. "But it was hard. I went to check my grade. You know, they post them in the hall. Or at least they used to." I close my eyes for a moment. Open them. "We weren't supposed to know who was who but we knew, of course. We learned each other's social security numbers pretty quickly. I went to look at . . . at a time when I should have been alone. Should have been the only one there, but—" I have to stop. Have to catch my breath.

"It's okay, Blue," Dr. Fisher says. "Take your time. Breathe deeply."

I breathe in through my nose. Out through my mouth. A technique I learned years ago. "I failed the exam. Failed it miserably. I was just turning away when he came up behind me." I cannot hide the emotion in my voice now.

"Who, Blue?"

I close my eyes again, fighting tears. "Carl . . . Carl Curry, Carl Cary, something like that." I shake my head. "He looked right over my shoulder. He knew the failing grade was mine and he laughed."

"It was very rude and unkind, Blue. He shouldn't have laughed."

I sniff.

"What did he say?"

Again, I shake my head, trying now to obliterate the sound of his laughter from my mind. My life. "I . . . I don't remember. Stupid idiot. I'm not sure if he said it, I just—" I stop. Start again. "He thought I was stupid. That I couldn't pass the class. That he was smarter than I was."

"He called you a stupid idiot, Blue?"

"I don't know," I retort. "I don't remember. It was a long time ago!"

Dr. Fisher is quiet on the other end of the phone for a moment, quiet long enough that I want him to say something. Anything.

"Blue?" he speaks finally. "Would you like to meet me at the office? Would you like to come in to talk?"

"No. Thank you, Doctor. I feel much better now." I take another deep breath, feeling guilty that I have snapped at him. He is only trying to help me. I really am feeling better, though. "I've already kept you long enough. Long enough from your wife." I think of the pretty, intelligent face in the photograph on his desk.

"It's all right, Blue. This is what I do. I'm glad you called and I really think we need to talk further."

"I said that won't be necessary, Doctor." I stand up. "I'll see you Wednesday. Thank you again." I hit the "off" button on the cell phone and walk back up the sidewalk, headed for my car.

"There you are." Adam appeared in the doorway of the small room filled with copiers, printers, and fax machines. "I've been trying to catch up with you all day." He leaned against the door frame, effectively blocking M.K.'s getaway. "You trying to avoid me or something?"

She glanced at him, and then back at the copy machine that was flashing lights at her. *Paper jam*.

"No, of course not." She was, of course.

"Because I'm really not the kind of guy who needs to be avoided. Not usually, at least." He stroked his clean-shaven chin thoughtfully. "Of course, Liza Jane was avoiding me last week and now you—"

"I'm not avoiding you." M.K. crouched in front of the copier to open the service door. He was wearing one of his ugly flowered shirts, as he had been more frequently in the last two weeks. She wondered if Crackhow had just given up saying anything about them.

"Because if it's about Friday night . . ."

"Adam—" she said more sharply than she intended. She stole a quick glance at the door to be sure no one was in earshot and then returned her attention to the copier. She thought she could see the corner of a piece of paper in one of the likely paper jam spots.

He didn't say anything, which was almost as bad as saying too much.

"Look," she said quietly. "The other night was an error on my part. I flirted with you, I—"

He took a step toward her. "M.K.—"

"Adam, please, let me finish." She snagged the piece of paper and tugged. It tore, leaving her with a quarter of the piece in her hand, three quarters still jammed in the copier. "Adam, I just don't think this is a good idea." She looked up into his blue eyes that were entirely too blue. Entirely too penetrating. "Not with us working together."

"You're probably right."

She nodded, fighting a sinking feeling in the pit of her stomach. What did she expect him to say? She *was* right. "Good." She nodded again, then, after a moment of awkward hesitation, turned back to the copier. "I'm glad we're straight, then."

"Me, too."

She couldn't read his tone, tell if he meant it or if he was disappointed, too.

"Anyway, um . . ." He backed toward the doorway again. "I just wanted to see when you wanted to get together and listen to those wiretaps. There's not a lot there, from what Jimmy in surveillance has to say, but it would be good experience for you. Hear what kind of things we're listening for."

"I'll meet you down there in ten minutes, okay?" She grasped the piece of paper and jerked it as hard as she could. When she turned to look at Adam, torn paper in her hand, he was gone.

Chapter Twelve

When I leave home, I have a vague idea of where I'm going. I tell myself that there is no premeditation because I do not carry a weapon, not even a card of roofies. It's dark, but not yet late. I cannot stay out late because I have a full schedule tomorrow. There are others depending on me and I must be at my best.

I park my car on the quaint, tree-lined Main Street and follow the brick path onto the campus. I approach the mall and its majestic buildings, thinking that few students probably realize the importance of this institution, or what their education will mean to their futures.

I follow the brick path, walking beyond the rings of light cast by the street lamps. Now that I am here, I do not know exactly where I am going or what I will do. I only know that there is a tension building inside me, a fury that must be discharged.

Peter cut across the marble floor of the central lobby in Wooten Hall, stuffing his lab sheets into his messenger bag, his footsteps echoing overhead. He was a little creeped out to be the last one in the building. He hadn't intended to stay so late, but it had taken him longer to get the work done than he'd thought. It had been nice of Dr. Connelly to let him make up the lab he'd missed for Biology without penalizing him a grade point, but the professor had had a dinner engagement at eight so he told Peter to just close and lock the lab door behind him when he left. He said he trusted Peter not to rip him off.

The sound of a door closing startled Peter and he halted, glancing over his shoulder. All the lights were still on in the lobby, but most of them had been shut off down the intersecting hallways as well as on the second floor, where he could see the open balcony. He'd thought he'd been alone in the building, but obviously he wasn't. Had to be a janitor around somewhere; that must have been where the sound came from.

Peter shifted his bag on his shoulder, still feeling a little uneasy. He was such a chicken; he didn't even like sleeping in the dark. He'd been that way his whole life, always afraid of the boogeyman or the chainsaw massacre guy jumping out of the darkness. That was why he'd gotten a single room in the dorm this year. Now he could leave the monitor of his computer screen on at night and no one had to know. It gave off the perfect amount of light to sleep by.

Suddenly eager to get out of the building, Peter took a shortcut out of Wooten Hall, down the back staircase marked EMERGENCY EXIT ONLY. As he pushed out through the fire doors, he half expected some kind of alarm to go off, but it didn't. Outside, he stopped on the concrete landing, illuminated by a single bulb on the building beside the door, and reached into his bag to nab a pear and the handy-dandy Swiss army knife his grandfather had given him when he was ten.

Peter had been starving all evening, but he'd resisted the urge to go to the vending machines down the hall from the lab and get the Coke and cheese curls and Snickers bar he wanted. This summer, after finishing his freshman year at Chesapeake

Bay and enduring the usual wisecracks about his weight, he'd decided to do something about it. He was tired of being a geeky fat guy. He figured he couldn't do anything about the geek part; he liked science and he loved chemistry, that's all there was to it. But he didn't have to stay fat, even if he did come from a family with *big bones*. At home, in Easton, he'd gone to the public library and gotten some books on nutrition and read them. He'd made out a meal plan for himself and stuck to it, even when it hurt his mother's feelings that he didn't want to pack scrapple sandwiches on squishy white bread for work or eat her fried potatoes anymore. He'd gotten a job at a country club as a lifeguard and bicycled back and forth every day the seven miles to work. He'd also gotten permission from his old gym teacher at the high school he'd once attended to use the weight room that was open a couple of nights a week for student athletes. In eleven weeks, he'd lost twenty-five pounds, and now that he was back at school and girls were beginning to notice him, he wasn't returning to his old eating habits. Hence the pear.

Peter cut off a slice of pear and pushed it into his mouth, savoring the sweet juice that ran from the corner of his mouth. God, he was hungry; it seemed like it had been a long time since he had the garden salad, chicken breast, and broccoli. He should have brought two pears from the dining hall.

Again, he heard a sound behind him—footsteps maybe. He looked back, but he didn't see anything. Maybe a shadow, but he wasn't sure. He had a pretty vivid imagination when it came to the dark and what he envisioned was lurking out there.

Slicing off another piece of pear, he went down the cement staircase and followed a dirt path made from so many students taking the same shortcut. He'd have to walk all the way around the building to pick up the sidewalk on the mall. He walked a little faster. He'd taken this shortcut before but always during the day; he hadn't realized how dark it was out here at night. He took a quick look at the dark line of trees

behind the building and the twinkling lights beyond them
that he knew were the Groveworth dorms. They were brand-
new and co-ed by floor. Nice. Usually there were students
cutting through the woods there, but he didn't see anyone
tonight, didn't hear anyone. He walked a little faster, munch-
ing his pear and going over some of the element symbols in
his head that he needed to know for his quiz tomorrow. That
kind of tedious thinking usually worked when he was nervous, whether it was because he wanted to ask a girl in class
if she wanted to join his study group, or because he had to
go down into his grandparents' dark cellar in the old farmhouse and check the fuse box.

Peter heard a sound behind him again, and this time he
was sure it was footsteps. Maybe there'd been another student
in the building making up a lab somewhere else; maybe he
or she had had that stomach virus last week, too. Or maybe
someone had cut through the woods from the dorms and he
just hadn't seen them in the dark. He munched on his pear,
debating whether he should turn around and look, but he felt
funny doing it. He didn't want anyone thinking he was some
kind of stalker or something.

I do not know what led me up the steps of Wooten Hall. I
cannot fathom why I would want to tread these hallways, but
I find myself there, standing in the marble lobby looking up
at the balcony on the second floor overhead, listening to the
deafening silence of the empty building.

Then I hear footsteps, and before I know what I am doing,
I am stepping behind the curving staircase so as to remain
unseen. The young man appears before me, bag of books on
his shoulder, flipping through a stack of lab papers.

I know who he is at once. I recognize the haircut, probably still done in a barbershop. I see the mechanical pencils
poking out from the pocket of his plaid shirt. I watch him
halt in the center of the lobby as he tucks the papers into the

bag and glances in the direction of the front doors I have come through only a moment ago.

When the young man turns away, I know that I should stay put. That I should wait until he has exited the building and hurry back out the doors before I am spotted by a janitor or a night watchman. But when he disappears down the staircase marked as an emergency exit, I cannot stop myself. My heart pounding in my ears, I follow him.

I watch him go out the back door and I wait there in the darkness. Wait for what, I am unsure.

Then he pulls the knife from his bag and I feel my breath catch in my throat. A knife. Carl has brought me a knife. That is why I have come to Wooten Science Hall, why I have been led inside.

Even in the dim light, I can see the gleam of the blade; I can almost feel its sharp edge as he slices through the piece of fruit.

The young man glances my way and I freeze in fear, then realize how foolish I am. I am standing in the dark, he is in the light. He cannot see me.

He walks down the steps, taking his knife with him, and I have no choice but to follow. In my head, I hear his laughter, I feel the shame of the failed exam and the pain of his cruel gesture. I fall into step a distance behind him, in the shadows of the three-story brick building, barely noticeable. As I walk softly, taking my time, remaining patient until the right moment, scenes flash in front of my eyes as if someone is changing television channels in my head with a remote control. I see the classroom where I took physics all those years ago, then the path I followed to class each day. Bart Johnson's face flashes by. The young men in the Jeep. I hear Axel on that stupid TV show, laughing. But Bart and the boys are not laughing. Jessica is not laughing. They are buried in the ground, dead, rotting with worms crawling out of their skulls.

I lean over and pick up a rock from along the dirt path students have cut across the well-maintained grass. It is the size of a small melon and jagged on one side; it fits perfectly in my hand. There are no other rocks that I can see in the darkness, so I do not know where it came from. I only know that it is mine and what I must do with it.

Peter tossed the pear core into the woods to his right and nervously wiped the blade of his penknife on his pantleg. There was definitely someone behind him. Maybe a couple of people. He thought he heard a girl's voice—in the woods, maybe.

He was almost around the building now. It was pretty dark here, pretty creepy, but just up the bank, around the side of the building, were street lamps. Lights from Wooten Hall, too, that stayed on all the time to keep kids from doing goofy stuff like trying to break into lab rooms and steal the baby pig lab specimens.

Peter heard the person behind him walk faster, and suddenly he felt him or her behind him. Students did that all the time—walked right behind you, and then went past you because you weren't going fast enough to suit them. It was easy to let his imagination get away from him in these kinds of situations, picturing a man with a bowie knife or a ghoul with an axe.

Peter's stomach gave a little nervous flip; then suddenly, out of nowhere, he felt this incredible pain on the back of his head. He grunted, pitching forward, falling to his knees. He felt the penknife his grandfather had given him fly out of his hand.

Peter's knees hit the dirt first, then his hands. He felt his messenger bag with the lab sheets he had just completed swing forward under the weight of his biology books. He didn't want to lose the knife. Grandpa Jack had just died two weeks ago. Coronary while mowing his lawn on his new tractor. A good way for an old farmer to go, people said.

Peter didn't know if that was true or not; all he knew was that he had loved his grandfather and he really missed him.

Peter caught himself before his forehead hit the ground, and he reached out blindly in the dark for the knife. He was dizzy, confused, and his head really hurt. Something wet was running down his neck. Down his back.

He lifted his head and the excruciating pain came again. That was when he realized someone was hitting him from behind.

The second time his assailant hit him so hard that his forehead slammed into the ground. His mouth filled with dirt and he felt his body jerk uncontrollably; one hand flew out from under him. The unbearable pain came once more, and this time when Peter's head hit the ground, he could not lift it. He felt like all the muscles in his body were jumping. His whole body was jerking. The pain in his head was gone, but there was a fuzziness filling it now.

He felt a hand on his back. Someone grabbed the collar of his shirt and twisted, flipping him over. He couldn't feel his legs, but he could see them jerking in spasms and suddenly he was afraid.

There was someone there in the dark, but Peter's vision was blotchy now. Bright lights sparked in the darkness. "Please," he managed weakly, trying to reach out but unable to control his limbs.

He watched, paralyzed, as the person stepped away, leaned over, and picked something up from the grass. The knife! His grandfather's red Swiss army knife. Thank God it wasn't lost.

Then, out of nowhere, Peter saw the rock come crashing down on his face. He didn't even have time to scream before the pain and the blackness descended.

I stand for a moment above him, trembling all over. I slowly turn my head to look at the rock in my hand, not even sure how it has gotten there. I loosen my fingers and it falls to land beside the convulsing body.

My heart is pounding, but I realize I am not afraid. I am exhilarated.

I feel the handle of the penknife in my other hand, and I look at it as if I have never before seen a cheap little penknife. Again, even in the dark, I can see the shiny blade, feel the sharp edge, the bite of it.

I look down at the body that is now still, and I know that he will never laugh again at a student who is not as smart as he is.

I hear a voice and my heart rate increases. I know that I must go, but I still stand there with the knife in my hand, unsure yet as to what its purpose is.

Then, in a flash of brilliance, I realize why the young man brought the knife for me. I lean over and make quick use of it.

"You're quiet tonight. What's up?"

Cam rested his arm casually around Liza Jane's shoulder as they walked along the path that would lead through the woods and up behind the science building where she was currently flunking her Bio 101 class. Cam's touch felt kind of good.

"I don't know." She shrugged, glad she'd grabbed her jean jacket on her way out the door. The air was chilly.

Cam had just showed up at her dorm room and asked if she wanted to go for a walk. He said something about talking about the show for next week, but she knew it was just an excuse to see her. Pretty cute excuse, but an excuse nonetheless. Of course, she should have stayed and studied for her bio quiz tomorrow, but how often did a cute guy show up uninvited at your dorm? Besides, maybe a little fresh air would clear her head and then she could get back to studying all those plant cell parts when she returned to her dorm.

"Just have a lot on my mind. Family stuff. School stuff," Liza Jane answered. She didn't know him well enough yet to say too much about biology or her mother's marriage. She wasn't the kind of person to spill her guts to just anyone. Something she'd gotten from her father, she thought. It was funny, because her dad appeared to be such a fun, open kind of guy, few people ever seemed to notice how careful he was about talking about himself or his feelings. He wasn't anything like her mother, who wore her heart on her sleeve and got it smacked around on a regular basis.

"Good show last night," Cam said, after they walked for a minute in silence.

"Thanks." She looked up at him and smiled. "So was yours. *Fraternity Row*, I mean. We all sat around and watched it before we ran the news shot. Everybody is talking about it. Not just kids on campus. My mom says all these people who come into her shop to buy stuff are saying how they're hooked on it. People her age."

"It's kind of stupid, I think. Guys arguing about whose turn it is to dump the beer cans, girls arguing over who took whose makeup."

"But I heard it was your idea." She poked him playfully in the waist with her finger.

"It was." He gave her a silly grin. "That doesn't mean it wasn't a dumb idea. I just wanted to come up with something people would watch. You know, with all these other reality shows on TV, I thought it just might work. It was just my way to get into directing, filming."

"Well, I'm not really into the whole fraternity and sorority thing, although they do throw great parties." She laughed. "But it was a good idea." She smiled up at him as they came out of the woods behind Wooten Hall.

"Thanks." He stopped. "I don't usually come this way. Which way?"

"Either way around takes you to the mall." She grabbed his hand and tugged, going left. "Let's go this way. We can go up to Main Street and get some ice cream, but then I need to get back and study."

"Hey, that's cool." They took another couple of steps and he looked at her. "I'm just glad I got up the nerve to come by and see what you were up to."

Liza Jane laughed. "Me, too." She dared a quick glance at him, and then walked a little faster. It was dark at the back of the building, and being raised the daughter of an FBI agent made her cautious in places like this.

They walked up the short incline to the brick sidewalk that ran in front of Wooten Hall, where there was plenty of light from the street lamps and the lights around the building.

There were quite a few students walking the mall—some alone, others in groups. A pizza delivery guy carrying a red insulated bag in each hand came down the steps from Wooten and cut in front of them, walking so fast he was almost trotting. Liza Jane recognized him as the creepy guy who delivered pizza at the dorm, always asking girls if they wanted to party, offering them Jamaican weed.

"Must be running behind," Cam whispered in her ear.

She giggled, glad he hadn't noticed her. Somehow she was always the lucky one who had to meet him at the door, so he was always hitting on her. "Afraid he might owe a free pizza."

Cam laughed at her stupid joke. "Okay, here's the real deal with the major network asking about the show. Problem is, you have to swear you won't say anything, even if people tie you to a red-ant hill or something."

"I'm not afraid of ants." She looped her arm through his. "So tell me."

"I'm not kidding, Liza. My dad just hired some kind of fancy entertainment attorney. The guy said a deal like this could take months, maybe a year, and we don't even know yet if there's going to be a deal offered."

Liza Jane hopped up and down as if she were her little sister. "Okay, you've got my curiosity. Now you *have* to tell me."

Chapter Thirteen

"I can buy my own, you know," Liza Jane said, licking the cold, sweet butter pecan ice cream.

"I know." Cam handed her his cone so he could pull his wallet out of his cargo pants. "You can buy mine next time." He offered the girl at the register a five-dollar bill.

She rang up the two cones and the register drawer popped open. "Shoot. I've got to get quarters from the back." She rolled her eyes. "Sorry."

Cam took his cone from Liza Jane. "No problem."

While they waited for the change, Liza Jane turned around to check out who else was there. The deli was open late making sandwiches and salads. It served good coffee and hand-dipped ice cream, so it was a popular place with students. It was only a block down from her mom's health food store, so she'd been coming here since she was twelve, when her mom bought the place.

A young Ashview cop sitting at one of the booths caught her eye and he nodded.

Liza Jane nodded back. "Hey, Jesse."

He grabbed his cop hat off the table and got up. "H . . .

How are you, Liza Jane?" His face turned bright red the way it always did when she spoke to him.

"I'm good." She'd known him in high school. He'd graduated the year before her and had always acted like he had a thing for her. She wasn't interested; he wasn't her type, too redneck-y. But she was always nice to him because she didn't see any reason not to be. Besides, now that he was with the Ashview police and she was working for the paper and the TV station, it didn't hurt to have acquaintances like Jesse.

"Working a late shift?" she asked and glanced at Cam. He was still waiting for his change, thumbing through a *Rolling Stone* magazine at the counter.

"Just until midnight. I come on at three this week."

He grasped the large buckle on his belt with both hands and adjusted his pants and holster; she wondered if that was something they taught them in cop school. They all did it, even on TV.

She nodded, licking her cone. "Hey, listen, it was nice of you to let me past the picket lines or whatever you call them there at Bart Johnson's place. I got some great shots."

"Barricades, we call them." He somehow managed to swagger while still standing in place, his hat clutched tightly in his hand. "I saw you on TV, right after *Fraternity Row*. I . . . I love that show, tape it when I'm working." He blinked. "I mean, I love your show, too. You're good. Really good. I knew back in high school you'd be famous."

She couldn't help but smile. He was so goofy, but harmless goofy. "Well, I'm not exactly famous yet. We probably have a viewing audience of all of about ten, but thanks." She reached out and tapped his arm.

Jesse's radio on his belt went off in a burst of static and he jumped. Liza Jane didn't know what had startled him more, her or the radio.

"All available units," a monotone voice came over the radio. More static. "Possible 187 at 1001 College Drive. All available units are asked to respond."

Jesse reached for the transmitter on a strap on his shoulder, tried to punch a button, missed and tried again. Again came the static. "This is unit 21, responding, 10-4 on the 187. ETA three minutes."

Liza Jane's eyes widened with interest. "A 187 on College Drive?" What was a 187? "What's that code, Jesse? That's on campus. I have class there. 1001 College Drive is Wooten Hall, isn't it?"

"Sorry, police business." He started to walk backwards toward the door, dropping his Smokey the Bear hat on his head. "It . . . it was nice talking to you, though, Liza Jane." His red face had gone white.

Liza Jane watched him back out the door, then turn and hurry toward the police car parked a short distance up the street.

"Cam." She reached out and tugged on the hem of his sleeve, watching through the window as Jesse threw his big boat of a police car into gear and pulled out, cutting off a kid in an old Miata. "Come on. We have to go. Quick." She grabbed his arm, hustling for the door. "You think we can get into the building and get a camera?"

"Yeah. I've got a key."

They stepped out onto the brick sidewalk. "You hear those sirens? What's going on?"

"I don't know yet." She dropped her ice cream into the nearest trash can. "But I think we're going to be there to find out."

"Holy shit." Buck Seipp stood over the dead kid, holding his flashlight beam on him. He'd ordered Maglites for the entire force. They came in different colors, different sizes. His was the mother of all Maglites, eighteen inches long and fire-engine red. The other officers all got the twelve inchers, blue.

He studied the figure at his feet, getting a bad feeling.

Terrible bad. He was so close to retirement. All he wanted to do was retire from the city, play with his grandkids, and take the camper to follow the NASCAR season. It was his life's dream, but he needed his pension to see it through, and to get his pension he had to keep his job another fourteen months. Just fourteen months . . .

Buck felt the bile rise in the back of his throat and he swallowed against it, not sure if it was the sight of the dead kid making him nauseous or the thought of losing his pension. There was a dark puddle that went around the kid's head like some kind of gruesome halo. Blood. The eyes were open, but they were never going to see anything again. Not on this earth.

"Who found him?" Buck demanded, covering his emotion with gruffness.

"Campus Security, Patrick Purnell," Sedowski said. "I got him up there on the steps. Told him he wasn't to move and he wasn't to talk to anyone else, not even his supervisor, until you got here." The cop, late-thirties, ex-military, wiped his mouth with the back of his hand and hooked his thumb in the direction of the back stairs that led up into the building. There was a silhouette of a figure there, someone sitting.

Buck turned his head to listen with his good ear. In the distance, he could hear the wail of sirens: ambulance, EMT service, hopefully more of his own guys if they'd gotten up off their asses in the deli on Main Street and answered the call for all available units.

He turned back to his officer. "He see anything?"

"Nope."

"So what the hell was he doin' back here in the dark?" Buck barked.

"Apparently he was making rounds. Says he's supposed to walk all the way around each building." Sedowski pointed his smaller Maglite toward the woods. "A path there that kids use to cut across to the mall from the new dorms they just built."

"And you're sure he's dead?"

"The security guy checked for a pulse. Me, too. But look at him, Chief." He flashed the beam of light across the face and it reflected off the kid's pupils. "He's dead, all right."

"We know who he is?"

"I didn't touch anything else," Sedowski said quickly. "I knew you wouldn't want me to."

"Here, hold this." Buck handed him his flashlight. "Put the beam right on him. Not yours, damn it," he snapped. "Mine. I need as much light as I can get."

"Yes, Chief. Right." Sedowski directed both beams on the body.

Buck grasped his belt and holster and hiked up his pants, slowly sinking down to a squat. It was a long way down to the ground, and Buck didn't get as much exercise as he once had. He heaved a breath, pressing on his gut as he struggled to lower himself. Maybe Kitty was right—maybe he did need to cut back on the Budweiser.

"Let's see," he grunted, trying to rock the boy over to reach into his pocket. He came up with a smooth leather wallet. Not one of those cloth or canvas ones like most kids carried these days. It looked just like Buck's, same make and everything. He flipped it open and Sedowski was smart enough to direct the beam on the wallet.

Buck pulled a student ID from the clear plastic window and squinted to look at the photo, read the name. He didn't know where the hell his reading glasses were. Most likely on his desk at the station, or on the dash of his car.

"Says his name is Peter Wright. Sophomore here at Chesapeake." Buck glanced down at the kid again and suddenly realized something wasn't right. His face was smashed in something awful. Forehead dented. Blood covered his features, washing them out in shadows. "More light." He waved the wallet at the boy's face.

Sedowski took a step closer and the two overlapping circles of light grew larger. "Where the hell's his ear?" Buck demanded, using the edge of the ID card to move the wet hair back. There was definitely no ear there. "Where the hell's the ear?" he repeated.

"I don't know." Sedowski began moving the flashlights up and down the path and in circles around the body.

"You see it?" Buck groaned as he heaved himself to his feet, his heart pounding in his chest so hard that he felt like it was going to bust out. Standing upright again, he grabbed his handkerchief from his back pocket and began to mop his sweaty forehead. It was cool out, but he was a sweater, especially when things got tense.

"It's not here." Sedowski was now whipping the flashlights back and forth wildly. "It just ain't here."

The sirens were louder now. Closer.

"You," Buck shouted, pointing to the shadow on the steps. The figure stumbled down, hurrying toward them. "Me?"

"You seen his ear?"

The security guy stopped several feet from the dead kid. "What?" He sounded dazed. "His ear? No. What do you mean?"

"I mean he's missing one of his goddamned ears! He missing one when you found him?" Buck panted. He had to catch his breath or he knew he was headed for a coronary. He had a cousin who did that just last year, two months from retirement, and he fell over dead while filling a baby pool with water for his dogs in the backyard. Buck had been planning his NASCAR dream too long to fall over dead so close to reaching it. He pressed his hand to his pounding chest and tried to take deep, even breaths.

"What I'm saying, boy," he said, carefully leaning over and laying the kid's wallet and ID on his chest, "is that this dead kid is missing an ear. You checked for a pulse before you called 911, right?"

Patrick Purnell stood hunched over in his cheap security police uniform, which was a full size too big for him. "Yeah, right, but I didn't see no ear."

"Of course you didn't see it," Buck snapped, just about

out of patience. "That's what I'm saying. The damned thing's gone!"

Sedowski was now walking in a wide circle around the body, leaving Buck and the security guy in darkness. "It's not here, Chief, but we got a suspicious-looking rock here. Might be what was used to bash his head in."

Buck took one more look at the dead kid and stepped back out of earshot, reaching in his pocket for his own wallet where he knew he'd put that business card. He didn't know why he'd put it in there instead of leaving it in his desk like all the others he'd kept over the years, but tonight he was glad he had. All he could think about was Kitty. The NASCAR trip was her dream, too. She'd had a hard time of it these last couple of years; their youngest son had put her through hell. Buck had to do the right thing to get this mess cleaned up as fast as he could.

He punched the numbers on his cell phone and mopped his brow with his handkerchief as he waited for the call to go through.

When the call came in, M.K. hadn't been home long. The phone had startled her. It wasn't Saturday night. No one called her that late.

She'd listened to the Ashview police chief and spoken calmly to him, promising to come at once. She had no idea what the protocol on something like this was; she just knew she needed to get there quickly before those local yokels screwed up any evidence.

She'd changed quickly and then grabbed her car keys and ID and headed for the college. She started calling Adam the minute she was in the car, and she kept trying him all the way there, his cell phone and home number. Nothing. As she was parking her car on the street that ran the length of the mall, she called in to the office and just gave the guy she was patched through to the basic details. She knew Crackhow wouldn't be in until morning, but she was confident he would want her and Adam on this at once.

It wasn't hard to find Chief Seipp and the dead student. M.K. just headed for all the flashing lights. She showed her FBI ID, making it quickly past the wooden barricades that several Ashview officers were putting up as she arrived. She found the chief leaning against the brick building. Someone had set up floodlights to illuminate the scene, but the generator that was running them was so loud, M.K. couldn't imagine how anyone was hearing anyone else.

Seipp's face was bright red and he was sweating profusely, even worse than in the parking lot where Jessica Lawson was found. "You all right, Chief Seipp?" she shouted.

He nodded, wiping his forehead with a perspiration-soaked handkerchief like the kind her father used. "Where's Special Agent Thomas? You track him down? Like I told you on the phone, I tried him first."

She took no offense at the fact that it was Adam he had attempted to call first. She chose to think it was because Adam was the senior partner, the more experienced of the two of them, and not that she was female. "I'm still trying to locate him." She hesitated, then took a step closer, not because she wanted to smell his sweat but because she didn't like having to holler. "Able to locate any witnesses?"

He shook his head. "Dead kid's name's Peter Wright. Janitor inside the building said he was doing something in one of the labs. Had permission from the professor."

M.K. glanced back at the body sprawled on the dirt path; even from this distance, she could see that he'd been bludgeoned to death. It was obviously a murder; premeditated or not didn't necessarily make it FBI business. What made it FBI business was the chilling detail Seipp had related to her over the phone.

She looked back at the police chief. "I see you've got some light here, now. You find the ear?" She was amazed by how nonchalantly she said it. She was really beginning to wish Adam would hurry up and call her back. She didn't know where he was at this time of night, or with whom. Didn't care. She just wanted him here.

He shook his head. "No, but we did find a penknife. Wiped clean, folded up nice, and laid in the grass beside him."

M.K. pressed her lips together, thankful it had been hours since she'd eaten. She wasn't positive, but she could guess that upchucking in front of the locals was not good for the Bureau's image.

"*Trophy* is what they call it. I saw it on TV, one of those cold-case files cops dig up from years ago. It was about this guy who raped and killed women along some Mississippi highway. He always took their underpants right off 'em." Seipp wiped his mouth with the damp handkerchief. "But they said on the show that some killers did worse. Took body parts. You saw that *Silence of the Lambs,* didn't you? The movie with that guy making that dress or whatever the hell it was from their skin? Sick bastards—'scuse my French."

M.K. didn't know if she wanted to laugh or cry. The police chief was obviously uneducated, obviously over his head with this case, but he certainly summed it up pretty well.

"I think I'm going to go ahead and call our crime scene guys in, if you don't mind," she said.

"Not a bit, ma'am." He raised his hands. "That's why I called you."

"I want to hurry up and get some photographs taken so we can get the victim out of here." She turned to stand beside him, her back to the brick wall so she could get a better look at the scene. "I see the news vans are already moving in." She nodded in the direction of the side of the building where there was a small parking lot. "I don't want some poor mother to see her son's face on the morning news before we've had a chance to contact the family."

"Already had a little trouble with that, but I sent them packing." Chief Seipp unfolded the handkerchief that was now soaking wet and began to refold it. "Those kids running that news show. You know, the one after *Fraternity Row*. Me and the wife, we don't miss it."

M.K. had only been half listening to him but suddenly he had her attention. "You had some trouble? What do you mean? With whom?"

"Cute girl. Little blond twisty pigtails everywhere." He pretended to lift locks off his own balding head. "You've seen her on that news show, haven't you? Feisty thing."

"She was here?" M.K. knew, of course, who *she* was. How many blond, dreadlocked girls could there be on the local cable access news?

He began to mop his brow again. Because the handkerchief was so wet, he seemed to just be moving the sweat around. "Her and another kid. Guy with a ponytail. Sneakin' around the building, trying to get the dead kid on film, I guess. We run them off, and then she tried getting into the building to take pictures from the windows, I guess. Once I dangled my handcuffs in front of them"—he jangled them on his belt—"the boy got smart and hauled her and her camera out of here."

"They get any shots?"

"Nah, I don't think so. Just the same as what the others out front are getting. The building, ambulance, police lights flashing. And I haven't said a thing to any of them. For all they know, we got a cat up a tree."

M.K. couldn't manage anything more than a grimace. "Look, I'm going to go ahead and call those evidence guys in and we'll see what we can do to get this cleaned up."

"'Preciate that." He hesitated. "You know, I'm not far from retirement. Something like this, especially after those accidents, it don't look good on my record."

"You can't be held responsible for something like this, Chief. The others were just accidents. They can't possibly be connected."

"That's what I told myself when I was standing here waiting for you," he said. "I mean, those were accidents, mostly about kids bein' stupid, and this . . ." He gestured toward the body. "Probably a bunch of drunk kids got into a tussle, somebody got pissed off, things got out of hand." He looked back at her. "Don't you think, Special Agent Shaughnessy?"

He sounded so hopeful that M.K. couldn't disagree with him. "I'm sure you're right, Chief." She reached for her phone. "Let me give these guys a call." She walked away, praying to her mother's God that he was right.

It was just after eight in the morning and had been daylight for almost an hour when M.K. spotted Adam trudging up the dirt path that had been trampled all night by police, EMTs, and the FBI crime scene investigators. Almost everyone was gone now, except for a couple of Ashview officers guarding the barricades that remained up. M.K. was just sitting on the cement steps of the building, studying the crime scene, when Adam appeared.

"I tried you several times," she told him as he walked around the area that had been staked off where the body had been found. "I left messages on your home phone and your cell phone." She was tired. No, *weary* was a better word.

"Sorry. Sometimes I turn the phones off. You know, just to get a break."

She tried to hide her annoyance. "So I guess you've heard what's going on here." She got up off the step to stand in front of him.

"After I got your message, I called in to the office. Spoke to Crackhow on my way over here."

She rubbed her hand over her face. "Did you realize he gets into the office at, like, six? He called me at five after."

"What do I care what time of day he starts pushing his papers?" Adam turned to face the crime scene. "I got the bulletin, but I want to hear the whole story from you. Start to finish."

He had on a pair of khaki slacks and a striped oxford

shirt. His hair was still damp from his shower, but he looked nice. He was wearing his usual wraparound sunglasses, but they didn't hide the fact that he looked tired. M.K. tried not to think about what he'd been doing all night, or who he had been doing it with.

"We're pretty much done here. I called our guys in to make sure the evidence was collected and logged properly. I got plenty of still photos and some video."

"Crackhow said the kid's ear was missing. Presumed taken."

M.K. nodded, walking back toward the front of the building, giving Adam no choice but to follow. "Sliced off with a penknife that was wiped down and left behind."

"What the hell—" Adam shook his head.

"Trophy, I'm guessing."

"I know what that is," he snapped.

M.K. looked him directly in the eye, too tired this morning to take any crap from him or anyone else. "Okay, you know whoever killed this kid with the rock also cut off his ear as a souvenir. So tell me, Mr. Know-It-All. Do you know if the same guy who killed Peter Wright also killed Bart Johnson?"

"Bart Johnson fed himself into that damned chipper-shredder!" Adam clenched his fist at his side. "You saw the blood alcohol level on him."

"I did." She nodded, looking up to meet his gaze. "But what I never saw was any part of his missing finger."

Chapter Fourteen

When Adam heard his cell phone ring and saw who it was on the caller ID, he was tempted not to answer. It had been a long day and he wasn't in the mood for what he knew was coming.

He reached for the phone, pressing the "talk" button, and lifted it to his ear.

"Okay, Dad, I've given you all day to call and you haven't, so I'm calling you," Liza Jane said in his ear. "So what the hell is going on here?"

"How am I? Fine, dear, thanks for asking," he said, in his best faux-pleasant voice, leaning back in his chair. "How about you? Have a nice day? Pass that bio quiz you were worried about?"

Liza Jane groaned. "That's not going to work with me today, so you might as well hang it up. No, I probably did not pass my bio quiz. I didn't pass it because I didn't study enough. I didn't study enough because I was up all night worrying about a serial killer stalking my college campus, murdering my fellow students. So I'm going to ask you again, *Dad*. What the hell is going on here? More importantly, what are you guys doing about it?"

"You know, you've got a mouth on you." He closed his eyes, hoping to fend off the headache that was building. "Where did you get that mouth? I know your mother never let you talk to her that way."

"I got it from you, Dad, and you still haven't answered my question. What happened to Peter Wright?" This time she didn't bother to give him a chance to answer, she just went on. "I'll tell you what happened to him. Someone hit him over the head with a rock and bashed his brains out, then cut his ear off, probably with the kid's own penknife."

Adam groaned and reached into his desk for a bottle of super-strength, over-the-counter pain reliever. They hadn't even yet released the fact that the penknife found at the scene, wiped clean of fingerprints, had belonged to the victim. There were only two ways his daughter could have known that: either someone was running their mouth who shouldn't have been, or she was there last night, listening in on conversations civilians had no business listening in on. "Please tell me you weren't there last night," he said, popping three tablets and swallowing them dry.

"What, your girlfriend tattle on me?"

Now Adam was really pissed. It *had been* a crappy day and seemed to be getting crappier by the moment. So she *had* been there; worse, M.K. had known it and not told him. "She's not my girlfriend, she's my partner and you can go ahead and be disrespectful to me because I know I've probably earned it somewhere along the way, but she hasn't, so lighten up, kiddo."

This time he was the one not giving her a chance to speak. "You know, you might have had a bad day today, but I'm guessing mine's been worse, and you know what? Neither of us is having as bad a day as Peter Wright's parents."

Liza Jane was silent on the other end of the phone for a moment, and then Adam felt bad. He was always hurting the people he cared about the most.

"Dad," she said after a minute, not nearly as fired up as

she had been. In fact, now she sounded a little bit scared. "This guy took his ear, for God's sake. I know you guys are still sticking to your stories about those other students all dying by accident, but you can't tell me Peter died by accident. Somebody murdered him."

"I'm not saying nothing happened. I'm saying we don't know what happened or who was involved yet. I've been officially put on this case—M.K. and I."

"At least someone realizes there *is* a case."

So much for his daughter's momentary vulnerability. She was all mouth again.

Adam sat back in his chair again, tucking one hand behind his head, and stared at the generic ceiling tiles that seemed to be in every FBI office in the country. All day, he'd been fighting a niggling guilt concerning the Bart Johnson case. He'd actually teased M.K. about seeing murderers in the shadows. He still didn't think there was anything to the chipper-shredder accident, but he was, at least, now willing to entertain the idea. Not because of the *weird feeling* she'd been getting. That was bullshit. But because the facts warranted it.

Earlier in the day, he'd agreed with M.K. that the Bart Johnson case was at least worth looking into again to compare to the new case. He'd even gone into Crackhow's office to get him on board with them and called Dr. Wood . . . twice. He still thought the whole idea was far-fetched, but he was willing to give his new partner the benefit of the doubt because she was smart and she was going to be a good agent, and maybe just a little because he wanted her to like him. What he was not willing to do was discuss any of this with his daughter. "Liza Jane," Adam said firmly into the phone, "I'm warning you, stay out of this."

"Stay out of it? What do you mean?" she flared. "I can't stay out of it. It's my job as a journalist to report the truth."

"No. You're wrong." He slapped his hand on the desk. "Your job, young lady, is to have fun in college, get to know people, get to know yourself, get a degree, and be able to support yourself and your own family someday. That's your job."

"I don't even know why I called you, Dad. I guess just professional courtesy. I want you to know that I'll be continuing to investigate Peter's death."

"You keep it up, young lady, and you'll be transferring to Our Lady of Perpetual Sorrow in Galveston. I understand it's a nice private women's college where they let you out on Friday nights to go see a movie—with a nun as a chaperone, of course."

"You can't make me transfer colleges," she scoffed.

"Sure I can. I'm the one paying your tuition, your room and board. I'm the one giving you an allowance so you don't have to work, so you can have your newspaper and news hobbies."

"I'm hanging up now, Dad."

"Liza Jane—"

"'Bye, Dad."

Adam heard the click of the phone as she disconnected, and for a moment he just sat there with it still pressed to his ear. She'd hung up on him. His daughter had actually hung up on him. He cursed under his breath and tossed the phone on the desk.

"That mean Dr. Wood's not going to get back to us today?"

Adam wondered how long M.K. had been standing there. He sat up in his chair and rolled forward, not making eye contact with her. "No, she's not getting back to us today— probably not tomorrow, either. She's swamped and has some kind of court thing and she doesn't know how long it will take. But that wasn't Valerie." He sighed. "It was Liza Jane."

M.K. just stood there.

"You didn't tell me she was there last night." He jerked open the file on the top of his desk, not even sure which one it was. "At the scene."

She came around the corner of his cubicle and parked her

butt on his desk, right on the file. "She was gone by the time I got there. The chief ran her off."

"You should have told me."

"Probably." She kept looking at him, not giving an inch. "But I figured you'd find out soon enough."

He laughed, but it was without humor. "What? On the evening news?"

"I don't think she really saw anything."

"Maybe not, but somehow she already knew about the penknife."

"You ask how she knew?"

"Nah." He pushed back in his chair again and looked up at her. Her hair was definitely longer than it had been. It was starting to curl around her ears and seemed to be lighter in color—like she'd been out in the sun. It was nice. A little less severe, softer-looking than before. "I was too pissed."

"It probably wouldn't hurt for us to know how she found out."

"Yeah, I know. I'll ask when she's speaking to me again."

M.K. smiled and glanced at her watch. She'd ditched the suit jacket hours ago. Maybe hadn't even worn it into the office, he couldn't recall. "It's six. You want to go out and grab a bite to eat? We can start drawing up any parallels we can find between Bart and Peter. I've got a list of people to interview—Peter's teachers, friends, family. It wouldn't hurt to know ahead of time if any of them knew Bart."

"I don't know. I don't think I feel like going out tonight. This kind of stuff doesn't leave me anxious to be among my fellow men." he said.

"Okay, so come to my place. I'll make pasta."

M.K. had no idea what had made her say that; it just came out of her mouth before she could stop it. She glanced away, almost hoping he didn't take her up on her offer. They'd worked well together today, and she didn't want him thinking she was hitting on him, trying to pick up where they'd left off in the parking lot that night. Besides, he'd probably been with someone else last night. Maybe he had a date with her tonight. Maybe it was Dr. Wood. M.K. had no intention of fighting her for him; she knew the coroner was way out of her mousy-brown league.

"Sure. Why not?" He looked up at her with those blue eyes of his that she was seeing at night when she closed hers.

"Yeah?" She tried not to sound too surprised, or too pleased.

"Why not?" He opened his arms. "What can I bring?"

She got off his desk, thinking she'd have to stop at a grocery store on the way home. She didn't have anything to make anyone a pasta dinner. She had mustard, skim milk, and some old Chinese food in her refrigerator and coffee beans and low-fat cherry vanilla ice cream in her freezer.

"How about some wine?" he asked.

"I don't know, Adam. I never went to bed last night. A sip of wine and I might fall out of my chair, out like a light."

"Don't worry," he teased, back to his old self again. "I'll catch you before you fall."

M.K. rushed out of the office, carrying everything she could scoop off her desk in her briefcase. She stopped at the grocery store and bought linguine from the refrigerated section, fresh vegetables for the sauce, and a pound of shrimp. She didn't even know if Adam liked shrimp in his pasta, but she did. She also bought bagged salad, salad dressing, and, on impulse, flowers for her table. Daisies. She didn't know what had made her buy the flowers. It was so unlike her. But by the time she got home, changed into jeans and a t-shirt, picked up the living room, and started the sauce, she was glad she had. Other than her houseplants, her place was so bare that it bordered on pathetic.

What kind of person lives in a house with no pictures on the walls, no throw rugs on the floor, no food in the house? she heard her mother whispering in her ear. A person with no life but their work. A person no one loved. Could ever love . . .

The doorbell rang and M.K. turned the flame down on the sauce and went to let Adam in. He was carrying a bottle of wine and a freezer bag with ice cream in it. "Dessert," he told her, handing her the bag. "I thought about bringing flowers, but I was afraid that might be crossing the partner line." He followed her into the dining and kitchen area, his gaze falling to the table she'd set. "Looks like maybe someone else beat me to it." He fingered one of the daisies. "Your boyfriend?"

"Not hardly." She laughed, opening the freezer and pulling the ice cream from the bag. "Cherry vanilla. Perfect. I've only got a scoop left in the freezer, and I was afraid you were going to make me share it with you."

"I brought a merlot." He held up a wine bottle. He'd changed, too, into blue jeans and a light sweater. He wore clothes well. Of course, he probably knew that.

"Opener is there on the counter. Wineglasses, too." She didn't tell him they were the only two wineglasses she owned or that she'd had to dig them out of a packing box in the spare bedroom. She just hadn't gotten to unpacking a lot of things since her move from Virginia.

While M.K. drained the pasta, Adam opened the wine. He came around the corner of the galley kitchen, carrying a glass in each hand. "Here you go. It's been one of those days when you definitely earned this, Special Agent Shaughnessy."

They raised their glasses, but there was no toast. M.K. knew that the image of the dead student was still too fresh in both their minds. "Mmmm. Not bad." She took another sip. "You know wine?"

"A little. Just mostly what I like and what I don't like. I don't like whites." He leaned against the counter and in the small kitchen she had to step around him. "Friends don't let friends drink white zin."

She laughed. "It's almost ready. Another five minutes."

"You want me to do something?"

She was pleasantly surprised by his question. He didn't strike her as the kind of man who peeled carrots or washed dishes. "Nope. Have a seat in the living room if you want."

He wandered out of the kitchen. "Nice place."

"It's okay." She opened the salad bag and began to divvy it up between two bowls.

"Not much into home decorating, are you?"

She glanced over the counter, through the dining area, to see him standing in the middle of the living room. "I haven't picked up my Renoirs and Monets from the vault at the bank yet."

"Renoir is nice. I'm not a fuzzy flower kind of guy." He sipped his wine. "Nice TV, though."

The large flat-screen was her one guilty pleasure. "I know, it looks silly in the room. I could barely get my chair back far enough to see it." She ducked to see him moving toward a bookcase beside the TV that was filled with VCR tapes.

"Wow. You tape a lot of stuff," he said, tilting his head to try and read some of the carefully labeled tapes.

"Yup. Always things on I'm going to watch when I get the time, so I record them." She grabbed the salad bowls and came out of the kitchen. "You ready to eat?"

"Sure." He glanced back, seeming reluctant to join her.

"Why don't you grab the salad dressing and butter in the refrigerator. I'll get the pasta and bread."

They lingered over the meal, drinking most of the bottle of wine. They talked some about the new case, but only briefly. They were both worn out and it felt good to relax, talking about nothing important. They both read the newspaper regularly so they found plenty to talk about and before M.K.

knew it, almost two hours had passed and she was beginning to yawn.

"Well, looks like I've outstayed my welcome," Adam said, getting up and taking both their dirty plates with him.

"I'm sorry." She covered her mouth. "I didn't mean to be rude."

"You aren't rude." He leaned over, looking at her across the counter that separated the tiny kitchen from the eating area. "You're just beat."

She picked up the wineglasses and carried them into the kitchen, feeling a little light-headed. She wasn't even thinking when she reached around Adam to place them in the sink. "Don't worry about the dishes. I'll just run some water in the sink and wash them in the morning."

He turned around to face her and the next thing she knew, she was in his arms. M.K. was so tired. Or maybe it was the wine. But when he wrapped his arms around her waist and drew her against him, she found herself pressing her body to his, molding her hips against his. She parted her lips in a sigh, closing her eyes, taking in the heady scent of him, the taste of his mouth on hers, the feel of his body as his mouth covered hers.

Adam teased the hair at the nape of her neck with his fingertips, sending little sparks of pleasure through her whole body. It had been so long since a man had made her feel this way. Who was she kidding? No one had *ever* made her feel this way.

Somehow they got turned around in the kitchen and she felt the edge of the counter against her back. He drew his mouth over hers, across her cheek and down her neck to the small V of skin revealed by her t-shirt. The heat of his mouth made her shiver. "Adam," she whispered.

Even through his jeans, she could feel he was hard for her. M.K. had never been one for jumping into bed with a man. She could count on one hand the number of men she'd slept with and still have two fingers to spare, but suddenly all she wanted was Adam. She knew it didn't make any sense. They couldn't have a relationship; they'd already agreed on that. Not and work together.

But seeing that dead teenager, coming home alone to her bare apartment, made M.K. realize she wanted more out of life than she was getting. Maybe even if it was just for one night.

She tore her mouth from his, panting hard. "This counter's hurting my butt," she whispered in his ear. "Want to go in the bedroom?" When he didn't answer right away, she knew she was in trouble and she wished she could have taken back her foolish words.

He kissed her mouth, then her cheek, and pulled her against him. "M.K., I'm sorry. I swore I wouldn't do this again. I didn't mean to—"

She caught his chin and turned his face, forcing him to look at her. "Is that a nice no-thank-you?" she whispered, praying she didn't burst into tears.

"It's not like that." He smoothed her cheek with his hand, kissed her again lightly on her mouth. "It's not you, M.K., I swear it's not."

She looked down at the floor, fighting the lump in her throat and the tightness in her chest.

"I'm not someone you want to get involved with," he said, taking a step back. He gently brushed her hair off her forehead.

"It's okay, really." She turned around, flipping on the faucet to run water in the sink to give herself a minute. She was still breathing hard and felt dizzy again. She didn't know how many glasses of wine she'd had, but obviously the answer was too many. She could still taste Adam's mouth and the merlot. Still wanted to taste his mouth again. She was becoming the person her mother warned her single women in their thirties became. Desperate. Needy. The next step was apparently closer than she realized. Slutty.

"M.K., you're not listening to me." He halted, then started again. "I . . . I've got a lot of things going on. I'm attracted to you. I really am, but I'm not in a place right now where I can give you what you deserve."

"How about I see you tomorrow?" She remained facing the sink, taking care with the tone of her voice. "It's been a long, hard . . . emotional day."

He stood there for a minute and then turned away, brushing his hand against the small of her back as he walked out of the kitchen. "See you in the morning."

"You okay to drive?" she called, leaning around the corner of the kitchen cabinets.

"Sure. You drank most of the wine." He turned to her, giving her one of those boyish grins, and then he walked out, closing the door behind him.

M.K. cleaned up the kitchen, shut out the lights, and went to bed, trying not to feel like she was alone in the world.

Sophie turned over in bed, startled by a sound. She opened her eyes and stared at the digital clock on the nightstand. It was two-forty. She rested her head on the pillow for a moment, listening, her heart rate a little faster than it needed to be. Sometimes she heard sounds at night when she and Savannah were home alone. It had been the same way years ago with her and Liza Jane.

Again she heard a sound, but this time she knew what it was. She slid her swollen feet over the side of the bed and heaved herself up into a seated position. Bare feet on the carpet, she pushed down her thin nightgown and padded out of the bedroom, down the hall past Savannah's closed door, and down the staircase.

There were no lights on in the house except for the eerie glow of the TV in the family room. It was a huge TV, flat-screened and a complete waste of money, she thought. But Mark liked it. He liked having it to watch football, basketball, whatever sport season it was. And it seemed a tiny concession to let him have his little pleasures.

She approached the easy chair he sat in, his back to her. He didn't look at her, not even when she walked by him and sat on the edge of the couch. She glanced at the TV, rubbing her belly. The sound was off. He watched that way a lot, something else she didn't understand. "What are you watching?" she murmured, glancing at the screen again. It was some old Spencer Tracy movie.

Mark sat stock-still; the only thing moving was his finger on the remote control. "I don't know. Nothing." He clicked the remote and the channel changed. Home shopping.

Sophie pushed her long, blond hair off her shoulder and clasped her hands, looking at him. "Mark, you've been gone two days."

His only response was to change the channel again.

"I was worried. I didn't know if you were all right. If you'd gone to work or not."

"You didn't call there?" His voice was without emotion.

Again, the TV flashed as he changed the channel.

"No. No, of course not. You asked me not to, and I've respected that request."

"I don't miss work. I never miss work."

"I know." She closed her eyes, pressing her palms to her cheeks, fighting the urge to cry. Crying didn't work for women in a marriage. It hadn't worked with Adam, and it didn't work with Mark either. "I . . . I'm just so worried about you."

"Don't be."

She took a breath, her gaze straying to the TV. CNN. Shots of a bombed-out building somewhere in the Middle East. A reporter wearing one of those photojournalist vests she'd thought about getting Liza Jane for Christmas. "Mark, that's easy for you to say. You're not here alone trying to care for a five-year-old, run a business, and worry about whether your unborn child will have a father."

The TV flickered in the dark room again, sending eerie, bouncing shadows off the bookcases that lined the back wall.

"Mark—"

"Sophie."

For the first time tonight she heard some emotion in her husband's voice. At this point, she would even welcome anger.

"I told you, I'm getting things under control."

Against her will, tears slid down her cheeks. She loved Mark so much that it broke her heart to see him this way. She felt a physical ache for him, for herself. What was wrong with her? She hadn't been able to help Adam. Her marriage had failed because she hadn't been able to help him, hadn't been able to keep their family together, and now it seemed as if it was happening all over again. She sniffed, wiping her running nose with the back of her hand.

"I wish you wouldn't do that," Mark said, his hand still on the remote for a moment.

"I know," Sophie whispered, sniffing again. "I just . . . I just don't know what to do. How to help you."

"You can't help me, Sophie," Mark said, his voice barely above a whisper. "Only I can help myself." He was quiet for a second. "And I'm trying."

Again, just a sliver of emotion.

"I know you are," she said, looking up at him by the dim light of the TV.

"Now go to bed. Get some sleep." Mark continued to stare straight ahead.

"Okay." She got up from the couch, trying to dry her eyes with her hands. "You coming?"

"Soon."

Sophie hesitated for a moment. She wanted to scream at Mark. She wanted to demand to know where he'd been. What he'd been doing. But she knew how fragile he was when he got like this. She knew how close to a breakdown he could be.

"Come to bed," she whispered, rubbing her hand over her swollen abdomen. And then she left him alone in the dark with his silent TV.

"Dr. Wood."

"I thought you were going to call me Valerie. Are we going to have to start all over again, Special Agent Thomas?"

Adam cradled the phone on his shoulder, glancing at M.K. parked on his desk. He'd agreed to call the coroner because M.K. had left three messages in the last two days and Dr. Wood still hadn't returned her call. That, and because he still felt guilty about the other night at her place. He really hadn't intended to make out with her again—it just kind of happened, the way things did sometimes when situations got tense. What he really felt bad about was her wanting to sleep with him and him turning her away. He really did have a thing for her, which was the main reason he'd beat feet out of there that night. He was afraid he'd screw up everything if he slept with her.

"I stand corrected. Valerie," he said into the phone, then chuckled.

M.K. narrowed her gaze disapprovingly, her arms crossed over her chest in not-so-difficult-to-read body language. He knew she was still upset about the other night. Pissed at him, though she hadn't mentioned it and neither had he. Still, things had been a little cool between them in the office the last few days.

"It's just that since this was a professional call . . ." he explained.

"That would lead me to believe you might be calling me for reasons other than professional." Her chuckle was husky. Sexy. "Promises, promises. Okay, Special Agent Thomas, I know why you're calling. Please tell your partner how sorry I am that I didn't get back to her. I wanted something definitive before I talked to you, and things are crazy down here."

Adam covered the receiver. "She's got the autopsy results."

M.K. waited.

"Nothing exciting here," Dr. Wood said.

He heard the crackle of paper.

"The victim died of blunt-force trauma to the head. You had to have gray matter on the ground. Poor kid."

Adam covered the receiver again. "Nothing exciting."

M.K.'s dark eyes widened. "Except that the kid's ear is gone!"

"Anything you can tell me about the missing ear?" Adam said into the phone.

"Not really. I received the penknife from your evidence guys. It was a match. It was definitely the one used to remove the ear. I took some swabs, hoping for some DNA evidence, but I'm not hopeful."

"And that's it?" Adam asked. "That doesn't give me anything to go on that we didn't already know . . . which is damned little."

"Sorry, Adam. Wish I could be of more help, but I just sit in my little basement room with my dead bodies and report what I see."

"Yeah, I know."

"So you haven't got any leads at all?" she asked. "Crazy fraternity pledge night? Fight over a girl? A Van Gogh fetish, maybe?"

He laughed. She was clever. "Checked out the first two. Nothing." He picked up his pen, tapping it on his desk. "But the Van Gogh thing, that's a thought. You ever consider becoming an FBI agent?"

"No, thank you. I prefer my dead people to the living. Far more cooperative. I'll send a copy of the final autopsy to you as soon as I can get to it."

"Tell her we want copies." M.K. poked him in the foot with the toe of her shoe.

Adam nodded.

"Anything else I can do, any questions you might have, let me know."

"And tell her we want copies of the audio tapes, too." M.K. whispered loudly.

Adam glanced at his partner, then looked away. "Hey, Val. There is one thing. I know you make audio tapes during your autopsies. My partner was wondering if we could get copies."

"All of them," M.K. said. She poked him again with her shoe, this time harder. "Jessica, Bart, and Peter."

"All three of the college students, if that's not too big a pain in your derriere," he said.

"What on earth does she want those for?"

He shrugged. "I don't know. She's new. Wants to impress the teacher, I guess."

This time when M.K. kicked him, she kicked him so hard in the shin that he flinched. "Ouch!"

"You okay?" Dr. Wood asked in his ear.

"Yeah, fine. Just klutzy. Listen, thanks."

"You bet."

Adam hung up the phone. "There. You happy?"

M.K. got up and walked out of his cubicle. "Nope. And I won't be until I figure this out."

Chapter Fifteen

Liza Jane looked up from her latte when the bell over the deli door signaled another customer's arrival. When she saw Jesse Connor, she raised her hand to get his attention.

He glanced around the shop, spotted her, and approached the booth. He was dressed in jeans, a flannel shirt, and a down vest. Definitely not the look she liked in a man, but she had no intention of dating him.

"Thanks for meeting me," she said.

"Yeah. Sure." Standing at the end of the table, he slipped his hands into his jeans pockets. "I . . . I was surprised when my mom gave me the message that you'd called." He scuffed his boots, looking down. "At first, I thought she had the name wrong." He gave a laugh. "She does that sometimes. You know, says the cable company called about the bill being late when really it was the phone company."

Liza Jane laid her hand on the middle of the table. "You want to sit down?"

"Um. Yeah. Sure." He sat on the edge of the fake leather bench, then slid over so he was sitting directly in front of her. He'd somehow managed to get his hands in his pockets again.

"I'm having a latte." Liza Jane closed her hands around the paper cup, enjoying the warmth on the chilly morning. "You want one?"

"Um. Nah." He shook his head.

"I know. You just want to know why I called." She released the cup and reached into her backpack beside her, pulling out a notebook. "I called because I'm doing a little work for the campus newspaper and maybe the TV station, and I was hoping you could help me out."

He eyed the notebook and the pen. "What . . . what kind of help?"

"You realize, it's been almost two weeks since Peter Wright was killed, and do you know how much the students on our campus know about that death? Zilch. Nothing more than what was released that week. Peter was attacked from behind by an unknown suspect, hit in the back of the head, then in the face with a rock found nearby. Then the killer cut off his ear with Peter's own penknife and took his ear, leaving him to die. That's all we know."

He pulled his hands from his pockets to rest them on the table, where he fiddled with his fingers. "The FBI was brought in by the college's president or the governor or something."

"I know that, Jesse." She nodded, looking into his pale brown eyes. "My dad's an FBI agent, remember? He was assigned to this case. I know you probably talked to him after the murder."

Jesse bobbed his head. Half-smiled. "He was nice to me. I . . . I really didn't know anything."

"Jesse, my point here is that students are scared, and the FBI is refusing to cooperate. No one's said exactly why they were even called. Obviously it must have something to do with Bart Johnson's death . . . maybe even Jessica Lawson's."

"I wouldn't know anything about that."

Liza Jane tapped her hand on the table. "Students want more information. They want to know if this was something personal, like if someone who was mad at Peter killed him, or if it was random. If it was random, students need to know there could be a killer out there right now. They need to know they should be careful."

"Actually, they should be careful at all times. Not walk alone at night. Especially girls. Know who they're getting into a car with. Know—"

"Jesse," Liza Jane interrupted, reaching across the table to still his hand. "You know what I mean. Now listen, I've been talking to everyone who knew Peter, who saw him in the last couple of days before he was killed, and I've got a list of people I think we need to take a second look at." She slid the notebook across the table. "I was wondering . . . do you know anyone on the list? I mean, have you seen them in the Ashview police station?"

He glanced quickly at the list, running his finger down the page. "Um, Buddy Caruso—I've seen him at the station."

"You have?" She pulled the notebook back. "You're kidding! Has he been brought in for questioning by the Ashview police or the FBI? Because you know, I saw him leaving Wooten Hall the night Peter was killed and he seemed like he was in a big hurry."

"You tell the police that?"

"I tried. They said he'd already been questioned. He was just delivering pizza to the janitor working in Wooten Hall." She looked him in the eye. "But you know, according to a girl who works at Tony's with Buddy, he also delivered pizza to Bart Johnson's house the night before he was killed."

"What I meant was that I used to see him all the time. Not so much now, though."

Liza Jane frowned. "What do you mean?"

"Well, he's the chief's stepson."

She laid down her pen. "You're kidding."

"His wife's son from a previous marriage. He was in such trouble a while back but they say he's doing fine now. Working and all."

Liza Jane picked up her pen again and made a note beside the pizza guy's name. She didn't know if the fact that he was Seipp's stepson mattered, but she wrote it down anyway. "Okay. My next question is, is there any way you could take this list of names and tell me if any of these people have ever been arrested for anything? I mean, I don't need to see their records or anything. I just wondered—"

"I can't do that."

Liza Jane looked up. "You can't? Don't you have computers to run people's records?"

He sat there for a minute, then slid out of the booth and stood up. "I . . . I guess I mean I won't. I could lose my job doing something like that." He crammed his hands into his pockets and looked down at the floor. "Besides. It wouldn't be right. Me being a man of the law and all. I mean, I'm supposed to be protecting them, too. Right?" He dared a quick look at her. "So, if that's all you wanted, I think I'll go." He turned around and started for the door, looking like a puppy someone had been kicking around.

All of a sudden Liza Jane felt like a real jerk. "Jesse, wait!" She grabbed her backpack, sliding the notebook and pen into one of the pockets as she hurried to catch up with him. "You're right."

He stopped at the door and looked back at her. "I am?"

"Yeah." She looked at her own feet. "It was wrong of me to ask you to do that. That's not the kind of reporter I want to be. Here I am, worrying about injustice, trying to get you to do something that wouldn't be just at all." She let her hand fall to her side. "It's just that I really am worried, and,"—she glanced up at him—"and I really do want to be a good reporter."

Jesse was quiet for a second. Someone opened the door behind him to come into the deli, and he and Liza Jane both stepped aside. He waited until the two young women walked up to the counter.

"So if you want to be a good investigative reporter," Jesse

said quietly, "you should use all the resources available to you."

"What do you mean? I swear, I've talked to half the students and professors on the campus in the last two weeks."

"Try the Internet?" He looked up with this goofy grin.

"What do you mean?"

He shrugged, hands in his pockets again. "I mean, did you Google them?"

Her eyes widened. The thought had never occurred to her. "I could find out if they'd ever been arrested by Googling them?"

"Maybe." He shrugged. "If not, there's other databases the public is welcome to access. You just have to know where to look."

She glanced up, grinning. "And I bet you know where to look, don't you, Jesse?"

Another shrug. "Maybe. Look, you see what you can find. You find anything interesting, you need more, you call me and I'll see if I can point you in the right direction."

"Thanks, Jesse." Liza Jane glanced at her watch. "Listen, I have to get to class, but I really appreciate your help and . . . well, you not letting me screw up and sacrifice my integrity."

He pushed open the glass door and held it open for her, the big grin still on his face. "You have a good day."

She flashed him a smile as she passed him, throwing her backpack over her shoulder. "You, too, Officer."

I have given up fighting the urge, and like so many other citizens of Ashview and the surrounding county, I turn on the TV Tuesday night in time to see Axel Cunningham's handsome face. I have used the remote control to set the timer on my VCR and I hear it click on and begin its steady hum. I sit in my chair, my eyes glued to the television as people I have come to know, fraternity brothers and sorority sisters, parade across the screen.

I know the truth and yet I am powerless to turn away. The show is broadcast, I know, to perpetuate the lie. I hear what others say about the show, about the students who attend Chesapeake, and I know that they have been successful. The viewers have all been fooled. They do not know the true nature of these young men and women. It is almost as if they are being brainwashed.

I am not so foolish—so deranged, of course—as to think that it is only fraternity brothers and sorority sisters who have a propensity for cruelty. After all, I am educated and well traveled. I know that one must take care with generalities. I know that the same behavior, the same attitudes, can be found in any dorm and in any hall of learning on that campus.

My gaze falls to the magazine cutouts I have spread on the floor in front of my chair. It takes time for me to decide what I will add to my collage next, so I spend a great deal of time thinking, studying. I linger over the half of the photograph I took from the pub that has not yet been added to the posterboard. I read somewhere—the local paper, perhaps—that her name is Tiffany Faulk. She attended Bart Johnson's funeral and apparently gave a rather moving epitaph, but I know that is not really her name. Her name is Cheryl, Cheryl Cleaves, and she once invited me to a movie.

I return my attention to the TV, listen, watch, as Axel and his friends go about their day, their night. There is laughter and roughhousing, opportunities lost and gained. As the hour progresses, I find that watching it is physically painful to me, but I cannot stop myself. There is talk of planning a Halloween party at Phi Kappa Alpha and I find myself actually becoming nauseous at the thought of it. I know what goes on at those parties.

I am saved by the end of the show and the college's newscast that directly follows.

Liza Jane Thomas appears on the screen with those piercing blue eyes of hers that tonight, I fear, look straight into my eyes. Into my heart. Her newscast has been expanded to fifteen minutes. She appears in several previously taped clips, talking about a blood drive students sponsored, an upcoming film festival, and a cute piece on a stray dog that has been adopted by one of the sororities. Then she appears live in the newsroom, and I slide to the edge of my chair to listen to each word she utters.

More than two weeks have gone by since Peter Wright's passing, she tells me. She uses a different word than *passing*, but I ignore her unkind implication. Accusation. She is, after all, still a child. Well, perhaps not a child, but she is certainly not an adult, either. She tells me that she is still investigating the death of the fellow student and that while local and federal police agencies claim to be working on the case, she and other students are working on it as well. She cuts to a previously taped interview with the janitor on duty in Wooten Hall that night and one with an angry parent who had taken his son out of Chesapeake College and had him transferred to a place where he will be "safe" to walk the campus at night. Then, back live in the newsroom, she again meets my gaze, vowing to students that she will not give up her investigation until Peter's killer is found. She finishes off by mentioning that she is following a lead that might possibly link Peter Wright's death to Bart Johnson's.

The news show ends and the cable station signs off, leaving my TV with nothing but a dark screen and the white noise of static. I am concerned by what I have heard tonight, what Liza Jane has said. She is very bright, very inquisitive, with an air of fresh honesty. She could potentially cause me great harm and I know that I must be more cautious. To fall at the hands of a nineteen-year-old girl would be tragic. The idea angers me, and yet at the same time I cannot fight a certain feeling of something akin to envy. She has the kind of mind I admire.

I wish that I had known Liza Jane all those years ago. I wonder if a friend like her, just one, might have made my life turn out differently.

* * *

Jerome was reading some notes into a dictating machine when Mrs. Elright buzzed him. He glanced at the large clock on the wall. He still had another half-hour before his afternoon appointments began.

He pressed the "pause" button on the dictation machine. "Yes?"

"I'm sorry to disturb you, Dr. Fisher, but a Patricia Williams is calling from your home. A nurse, I believe. I thought you would want to take it."

"Yes, of course." Jerome felt a tightness in his chest. His pulse fluttered. "Thank you."

"Line one."

Jerome punched the red button on his phone. "This is Dr. Fisher. How can I help you?"

"Dr. Fisher . . ." The nurse hesitated. "Your wife specifically requested that I not call you. She didn't want to bother you. She thought it could wait until you returned this evening."

He removed his glasses, relief washing over him. At least Sela wasn't dead. Every time someone called him about her these days, he feared the worst. Her condition was deteriorating quickly, faster than either had anticipated. But if Sela was able to tell Patricia not to call, she couldn't be too bad off, could she? "What's the trouble?"

"She's having difficulty breathing again. Severe difficulty."

"I see." He rubbed his eyes. After her last MRI, they had learned that the cancer had metastasized in her lungs as well as her bones, but she'd begun to have trouble breathing only last week. "And the oxygen isn't helping, even if you turn it up to a higher percentage?"

"I think she needs to go to the hospital, Dr. Fisher. There could be an infection that's preventing her from utilizing the oxygen we're giving her." She hesitated again. "I really am sorry to call you and I feel terrible going against the other Dr. Fisher's wishes. She's such a nice lady."

"No, no. You did the right thing. You know how stubborn

she can be." He paused for a moment, thinking. "How about if I come home for a surprise visit? A late lunch. I do that sometimes. If I find her doing poorly, I can be the one to suggest we go to the hospital. That way she doesn't even have to know you called me."

The nurse laughed, but it was a sad laugh. Jerome knew Patricia was having a difficult time dealing with his wife's deteriorating health, too. They had grown quite friendly in the last few months, though they were of different races, different religions, different social classes. Sela was like that; everyone loved her.

"I'll be there in twenty minutes. You just look surprised to see me."

"Thank you, Dr. Fisher."

As he hung up the phone, he got out of his chair, leaving his file open on his desk. He walked to the far corner of his room where a Victorian wrought iron coatrack stood and grabbed his overcoat and hat. It was the last week of October and it was chilly out. There was even talk of snow flurries this weekend. Jerome felt silly in the old-fashioned woolen bowler hat that looked like one his grandfather had worn forty years ago, but Sela had insisted this morning that he wear it and there was no denying her when she got something in her head.

He walked out into the intimate, tastefully decorated waiting room, and Mrs. Elright rose from her desk. She was a tiny white woman from New England with close-cropped gray hair and a no-nonsense attitude. She'd been keeping him and Sela straight for seventeen years.

"I have to go home."

"Is Dr. Mrs. Fisher doing poorly?"

It was the name she had created years ago to differentiate between the two of them when they had shared the practice. For years, Sela had tried to get her to simply call them by their first names, but Mrs. Elright was a force to be reckoned with, even with Sela.

"I may have to take her to the hospital." He strode across the room. "Difficulty breathing." He pressed his hand to his chest, trying not to think about what it must feel like to inhale and not get oxygen. To be slowly suffocating. "A little bug or something, perhaps. Some antibiotics, a breathing treatment or two, and I'm sure she'll be fine."

"I'm sure she will be, Dr. Fisher."

He rested his hand on the doorknob. "I'll need you to cancel the rest of my afternoon."

"All of your appointments?"

He hesitated. He was supposed to see Blue at five. He hated to have to cancel that particular appointment. Blue was the one patient worrying him these days. There always seemed to be one he couldn't shake, couldn't leave behind at the end of the day, and Blue was that patient right now. Nothing seemed to be following the pattern of typical bisexual behavior, and it concerned Jerome that his intuition was right and that there were underlying problems, perhaps even greater than the issue of bisexuality.

But his Sela needed him. "Yes, cancel all of them. Reschedule as you or the patient feel necessary. I'll stay late tomorrow if I need to."

Mrs. Elright settled in her chair behind her immaculate desk again. "Yes, Dr. Fisher. Of course. And please give Dr. Mrs. Fisher my regards."

He forced a smile, lowering his wool bowler hat to his head. "I will, Mrs. Elright. Thank you. I'll see you in the morning."

The phone call came out of nowhere, blindsiding me. Dr. Fisher has never cancelled on me. Never. He wouldn't do that. He is a good doctor. Conscientious. He knows how important our weekly appointments are. In fact, only last week we had discussed increasing my visits to twice a week. He said he sensed we were about to hit *a bump in the road* and he would feel more comfortable seeing me more often.

As I hang up my cell phone after speaking with the Puritan-like Mrs. Elright, I am surprised by a feeling of fear that passes through me. I am afraid to go the week without my visit with Dr. Fisher. It is my weekly visits that keep me in check . . . or at least keep me from crossing a line that will truly put me, my life, in jeopardy.

How dare he! How dare he, I think, substituting my fear with anger. It is a far more palatable dish, one I am confident I can handle. One I can control.

And I have been doing so well, recording in my journal, examining my thoughts, my feelings. A bump in the road, Dr. Fisher said.

I feel it coming, too.

Chapter Sixteen

Coming down the steps of the Phi Kappa Alpha house, Liza Jane tripped on a rubber rat parked on the last stair tread. Fortunately, a clown grabbed hold of her before she totally wiped out on the landing.

"Whoa, there—easy, babe." He caught her in his arms and helped her stand up.

He had nice arms for a guy with a bulbous red nose, but he was staring right at her chest. She doubted he realized it was mostly fake under the tight sweater, thanks to a Victoria's Secret sale rack. "Sorry about that." She extricated herself from his embrace and checked to be sure her very short pleated skirt was covering her fanny.

"You sure you're okay?" Bozo tipped back a beer can to chug.

Two guys from the station were rolling cameras, hoping to get some good shots for the show, she was sure. She lifted her hand to block their view of her face. How great would that look, her on *Fraternity Row* stumbling drunk, then ten minutes later appearing as a newscaster? That would be great for her credibility. The fact that she wasn't drunk wouldn't matter a bit.

"I'm great. Fine. Perfect," she told the clown. She backed away, bumping into a lacrosse player with a goalie mask and a guy in flesh-colored tights and a woman's wig similar to the one she was wearing, only his mouth was painted into a big O like he was one of those blow-up, sex-toy dolls. "Sorry."

"Not a problem," the blow-up doll said. "Give me a T, give me an I, give me another T, give me a—"

"Funny." She steered clear of him and wound around behind the camera guys. "Not funny at all," she whispered under her breath. "Cretin."

At last she reached the front door of the old Victorian house. It was hot and super-crowded inside, because everyone wanted to party with Axel and the celebrities of Phi Kappa Alpha. Everyone was hoping for a split second of fame with a spot on *Fraternity Row*. That was not the kind of notoriety Liza Jane was looking for.

She needed some air. What she really needed was a walk outside, a cup of her mother's herbal tea, and her Mickey Mouse PJs.

She had only come to the PKA party because one of the girls on her floor didn't want to go alone, and there was some guy she'd seen in an episode of *Fraternity Row* who she wanted to check out. Apparently she and the guy had hooked up, because Liza Jane hadn't seen her for more than an hour. At first it had been okay being alone. She knew a lot of people here, not just frat guys, but people she'd met on the newspaper staff and at the TV station.

She liked Halloween, dressing up, being silly and stuff, but somehow this year it just didn't seem right. It didn't seem right to her that everyone was laughing and drinking and having a big time when students who could have been at the party were dead. The idea just freaked her out a little bit. The president of the college had actually tried to ban Halloween parties as a way to appease some of the students' parents, suggesting that until Peter Wright's murder was solved night activities would be severely curtailed. In the end, the students won out and all the parents got were additional security officers and lame promises from their sons and daughters that they wouldn't walk alone in the dark.

She stepped out onto the wraparound porch, ducking a mass of fake spiderwebs. A couple of the sticky strings caught her in the back of the head and she tried to wipe them away.

"Hey, Liza," somebody called from a group standing around a tub of water with half-eaten apples floating in it.

She looked up to see Cam approaching her. He had a cool costume: breeches and a white shirt with a long, wooden saber stuck in a black leather belt.

"Oh, good. It *is* you. I wasn't positive with all the long yellow hair."

"Wig," she said, giving her do a flip. "So what are you? A pirate?"

"Captain of an eighteenth-century sailing ship, thank you," he said haughtily, tugging on his real ponytail pulled back with a velvet ribbon. "I was hoping I'd run into you. Your roommate said she thought you'd at least stop by here." He lifted his chin, indicating her costume. "Don't tell me you were a cheerleader in high school."

She laughed, running her hand over the sweater with the big C across her enhanced chest. "Not hardly. I found it in a storage room off the studio. Apparently a bunch of stuff got sent there instead of the theater last year and no one ever came for it. Prof McKinley said we could borrow anything we wanted as long as we put it back."

"Well, you do make a cute cheerleader." He waggled his eyebrows.

She laughed. "Hey, listen, I think I'm going to head back to my dorm." She leaned against the step railing where someone had glued a bunch of rubber spiders. "I've had enough fun for the evening." She stepped back to let another blow-up doll pass. Apparently that costume was popular this year. Of course she'd also seen at least half a dozen cheerleaders in Chesapeake cheerleader uniforms, guys and girls.

"What's up? Some guy diss you?" he teased, moving in a little closer.

She rested her hand on his chest, feeling all warm and dizzy all of a sudden. She'd taken a couple of hits on a bong upstairs. Maybe that was what was making her feel all weird. Or maybe it was Cam; she liked him more than she cared to admit. "Nah," she said, flattered he would care. They had talked about keeping their relationship open and easygoing. Neither of them was looking for anything serious right now, so spending time with each other when they had a chance seemed to be working out. "I'm just beat." She took a step down the stairs.

"You want me to walk you back to your dorm? You heard what the prez said. No one should walk alone under any circumstances."

"I'm too smart and too mean for anyone to get me." Her dorm was close to a mile from the frat house. She didn't want him to walk all the way to her dorm and then back again. Besides, she really had had enough company tonight. Sometimes she just needed time alone. "I'm fine, really. The street's well lit and there will be plenty of people out wandering around."

He grabbed her hand. "And you haven't had too much to drink?"

"Nope. Like half a beer, a Jell-O shooter, and a couple of hits on Bill's Willy bong."

He laughed. "Then I'll see you tomorrow at the studio if you're sure I can't walk you home."

"Yup."

He took her hand, bent over, and made an event of kissing it like she was some kind of royalty or something.

She laughed and pulled away, backing down the last two steps. "See you tomorrow."

He leaned on the porch rail, really looking like a captain on a ship. "Good-bye, fair cheerleader wench."

Liza Jane was still laughing when she skipped across the street and cut through the backyard of one of the sorority houses that was also having a big party. Through the windows, she could see two guys dressed as hula dancers, complete with coconut bras, dancing on a table, throwing leis at a bunch of girls. Liza Jane knew some the sisters of Pi Beta Phi because of the show. Most of them were actually pretty nice, she'd been surprised to discover. Not like what she thought they were, and certainly not how they were portrayed on *Fraternity Row*.

Reality TV wasn't really reality, Cam had explained to her the other night, while sharing tacos on the front steps of Elton Hall. His case in point had been Axel, president of Phi Kappa Alpha. Yeah, he was a fun-loving, spontaneous guy, but he was also a political science major who intended to go to law school next year. Eventually, he'd join his father in a law firm in D.C. that focused on fighting for indigent people's rights all over the country. Hearing that, after seeing Axel on the show, was forcing her to look at the sorority sisters differently. Maybe everyone she met. She was always so big into not having people judge her by her hippie clothes or her dreads, but she was beginning to realize that maybe she was just as guilty of those kinds of judgments, just in a different way.

Despite the goofy blond wig, someone on the front lawn of the Pi Beta Phi house recognized her and waved. "Liza! Want to come in?" the girl dressed like some kind of furry, four-legged animal called.

"Thanks, but I'm on my way home."

"Party pooper!" the animal brayed.

Liza Jane turned to wave and almost ran into a guy carrying an armful of pizza boxes.

"Oh, gosh, sorry." She reached out to help him steady them and he peered around the side of the boxes.

It was Buddy Caruso, and she instinctively took a step back.

"Hey," he said.

"Sorry," Liza Jane repeated and hurried down the sidewalk.

"Pizza's here!" someone shouted from the front lawn of the sorority house.

Liza Jane kept going, wanting to put as much distance as possible between her and Buddy before he got back into his old pickup with the giant pizza sign lit up on top of the roof. It was chilly outside, but the air felt good. Only her bare legs were cold, and her head felt better now that she was out of that stuffy house, expending too much energy dodging guys trying to check out if she was wearing anything under her skirt.

At the end of Sugar Maple Drive, Liza Jane halted, trying to decide which was the best way to go home. She could continue up this street, pick up Main that was well lit, and be home in fifteen minutes or . . .

She considered the path that cut through the woods behind Wooten Hall. The shortcut would take a good five minutes off the walk. Then she thought of Peter Wright's body lying in the dirt in the puddle of blood. She hadn't caught more than a glimpse of him that night before the EMTs covered him with a sheet, but it had been a good enough look to scare the bejesus out of her.

She glanced behind her, thinking she heard a sound. "What the heck?" she muttered. Then she heard it again. It was like a pop and then a little rattle. It wasn't until she spotted the third acorn rolling past her sneaker that she realized what it was. Acorns falling from the tree overhead. What a dunce.

She laughed at herself with relief and headed for Main Street, figuring the decision as to which way to go had been made for her. If falling acorns scared her, she certainly didn't have any business cutting through the dark woods on Halloween night.

Liza Jane hadn't gotten a block from the sorority house when she heard something behind her again, this time something like a whirling sound. She knew it wasn't acorns and she whipped around. There was nobody there, but she had the strangest feeling that someone was watching her. She glanced around and started walking again, a little faster than before.

There were street lamps along the sidewalk, but they were farther apart than they needed to be so she would walk in the light for a few steps, then the dark. She passed a couple of guys standing on the sidewalk on the other side of the street: a Raggedy Ann, a Freddy Krueger and Jason, the killer from one of those eighties slasher movies. Freddy waved his claw hand. Raggedy stopped to take a leak against someone's trash Dumpster.

She waved back, though she couldn't tell who it was, and kept walking. She was almost on Main Street and there would probably be more people there. She'd expected more people to be out. None of the students seemed to be taking their parents' or the college's advice about not walking alone at night. Her mother said it was because kids her age thought they were invincible, right before she made Liza Jane swear *she* wouldn't walk alone. Maybe the late movie was just getting out. There would be foot traffic and cars moving.

Alone again on the street, she walked faster, cold again. She hugged herself for warmth. A dog barked and she thought she heard someone calling "kitty, kitty" on the residential street a block over.

She heard the weird whirling sound again and whipped

around, wishing she'd taken Cam up on his offer to walk her home or just driven her car and taken the chance of getting a parking ticket.

A piece of paper blew across the street. There was nothing there.

She started to walk again; then, out of the corner of her eye, she spotted something white and heard the whirling sound right behind her. She spun around, totally spooked.

It was one of the golf carts security used to patrol the campus. There was a guy in it dressed like one of the orcs from the Tolkien movies, and Liza Jane jumped, startled. She knew logically that it wasn't a real orc, but it still scared her for a second. She didn't smoke weed often; now she knew why.

"Hey, it's okay," the orc called, waving one grotesque hand. He stopped his cart and pulled off the rubber mask. "It's Patrick Purnell. You remember me. I helped you get your keys when you locked them in your VW bug a couple of weeks ago."

She nodded, taking a step back closer to the street lamp. She did recognize him now that she could see him better. He was skinny and had a bad complexion. He was also on her list in her notebook of people to check out on the Internet. He'd been the one who found Peter Wright.

"Yeah, of course. Hi." She gave a nervous laugh.

"You okay?" He took a step toward her, tucking the rubber mask under his arm.

"Yeah, fine. Thanks. I was just headed home."

"You shouldn't be out here alone, pretty cheerleader like you." He chuckled at his joke. "You want a ride to your dorm?" He pointed to the two-seater golf cart. "We're supposed to be available to give any student a ride home who feels the need of an escort. Students are not to be walking alone at night." He sounded like he was quoting from some instruction manual. She had a feeling Patrick wasn't the kind of guy who said things like *who feels the need of an escort*.

She shook her head. There was something about the guy she didn't like. Maybe it was the bad teeth. Maybe the costume. Maybe the combination. He'd creeped her out the night he'd helped her get into her car, too, the way he kept looking at her. In the five minutes it had taken him to get her car open, he'd asked her out like three times, then tried to find out what building she lived in, what floor and stuff. At least then she'd been with some of her girlfriends.

"Really, I'm fine," Liza Jane said. "But, hey. There's some guys taking a leak on the sidewalk up there. You better nab them before the town police do."

"That way?" He tossed the mask on the seat of the cart and jumped in. "Thanks."

"Sure," Liza Jane mumbled, walking in the opposite direction as fast as she could. Next Halloween, she decided, she was staying home at her mother's house and passing out candy.

I do not know what possessed me to buy this ridiculous costume or put it on, but now that I am out, walking around the campus, a part of the nighttime festivities, I am beginning to enjoy myself. I find that wearing this mask, there is something exhilarating about my anonymity. I am free to walk these streets without fear of anyone recognizing me or thinking me out of place in any way. I move among the students, greeted by some, invited to parties by others who mistake me for a fellow student or are too intoxicated to care. I find it interesting that after what happened to Peter Wright, there is not more fear in the eyes of the students.

On the sidewalk on the mall, I pass two students dressed almost exactly like me; it seems the Freddy Krueger costume from the *Nightmare on Elm Street* slasher movie has become another retro fad. Or perhaps the costume never went out of style. What an interesting conversation that might be to have with Dr. Fisher. Did more people than we realize fantasize about killing?

As my identical twins pass, they both raise their clawed hands in greeting. "Dude," one calls.

I want to call back, but I do not.

I forwent the claw hand in the costume store. It was an additional thirty-five dollars and made poorly of plastic and polyester. Instead, I carry a Bowie hunting knife with a splendidly sharpened blade.

I find that tonight I do not question my impulses. Dr. Fisher was concerned with a bump in the road in my therapy, but I am not. I know what I am doing tonight. I know why. Perhaps I will be able to treat myself in a way no physicians, no psychiatrists, no family counselors have been able to.

I follow the sidewalk along the mall and then cut across a familiar street. I have driven my car here many times. I have also seen shots of this street on TV. I am on Fraternity Row.

I take my time walking along the sidewalk in the dark, taking in the full ambience of the night without allowing myself to remember another night similar to this. I pass one fraternity house after another: Sigma Pi, Delta Chi, Theta Chi. The last house on the street, the largest, an old Victorian, is home to Phi Kappa Alpha and our own local celebrity, Axel Cunningham. I stop on the walk out front. The porch is filled with students in costumes: ghosts, movie stars, politicians, characters from movies. Through the window I watch students dance and laugh. Alcoholic beverages are being served, of course, and I am quite certain that there are underage drinkers inside. I am tempted to call the police and instigate a raid, but then I realize how foolish such a call would be, on so many levels.

A young blond woman in the window catches my eye. She is dressed in a Chesapeake Bay College cheerleader's costume. I think I recognize her. I remember the other cheerleader, Cheryl. I remember the scent of her clean hair and how she made my heart pound in my chest every time I laid eyes on her. I had truly thought myself in love with her and I think she knew it.

Standing here on the sidewalk, I can still recall how hurt I had been that night when I waited in the lobby of the movie theater for her the length of the entire movie. After ten minutes I knew she wasn't coming. Knew she had stood me up, probably never had any intention of meeting me, but I was young and still believed there was some good in the world, some tiny glimmer of happiness, even for me. It took time for me to realize that young women like Cheryl were too self-centered, too overly confident of their good looks to ever be interested in a person like me. A person far from perfect.

I feel tears sting the backs of my eyelids and I blink to clear them because I cannot remove my mask of the hideous burned villain to wipe them.

I watch the cheerleader speak to several drunken partiers and then walk out the front door. I step behind a large bush and watch her. She speaks to someone else, a pirate, and then backs down the stairs with a wave.

As I watch her cross the street, I feel a tightening in my chest. All those years ago she hurt me. How many more people will she shatter with her beauty and cruel intolerance for those who are less beautiful, less perfect?

I follow her.

On Sugar Maple Drive where the sororities are located, I fear that she will stop and go inside, but she only greets friends and keeps walking. I notice that she is not entirely steady on her feet, and I guess that she is either drunk or high on something, or both.

I continue to follow her, staying well back on the opposite side of the street. Once, she stops and looks over her shoulder, as if sensing me after all these years. Just looking at her lovely young face makes me angry. Jealous, too, I suppose. How does a young woman of such poor character deserve such a perfect body? My gaze is drawn to her tight sweater as she stands beneath a street lamp, seeming to contemplate where she is going.

Cheryl had the most beautiful breasts, breasts I had longed to touch . . . to taste.

I tremble under the intensity of my desires.

Cheryl begins to walk again and unwisely chooses a deserted street rather than one more traveled. Once again, a sign of what is preordained?

I begin to shorten the distance between us by crossing the street. My heart rate is beginning to increase, my brow perspiring slightly. Her gait stiffens and I know that she senses that I am following her. I wonder if she will remember me.

She stops beneath a skeletal tree, devoid of leaves. "What do you think you're doing, buster?" she demands, resting one hand on her hip. Her words are slightly slurred; she has had too much alcohol. "Why are you following me?"

"I wondered if you remember me," I hear myself say.

She looks at me for a moment and then twists her mouth in an ugly frown. "How would I know if I remember you? You've got that stupid mask on."

I take a step closer, moving my hand to the inside of my jacket where I placed the knife.

"I was wondering why you stood me up," I say.

"What are you talking about? Are you nuts?" she snarls.

"The movie." I try not to sound too pathetic. "I just wanted to be your friend, was all. I understood if you weren't interested in me in . . . in any other way, but—"

"Look, I don't know who you are," she tells me, pushing down the hem of her sweater that had ridden up to show a part of her bare belly, "but you better take a hike before I start screaming."

"You don't remember me?" I whisper, fighting my tears again. All these years, and I still remember her . . .

I pull off the hot rubber mask and she stares at me for a moment in shock. She does recognize me, doesn't she?

I lunge forward. She opens her mouth to scream, but I am

fast. Strong. I am glad that I am finding time to go to the gym and get in better shape. I wrap my arm around her throat and I tighten it until no sound is able to escape her lips. She gasps, kicks, as I drag her into a hedgerow. All I have to do is tighten my grip and she ceases to struggle.

The football field is just on the other side, and I know just the place where we can go.

Chapter Seventeen

"Ah, Jesus," Adam murmured into the phone.

"You okay?" M.K. pulled the phone away from her ear long enough to drop a thin tank top over her bra. She'd obviously woken him up, which meant he wouldn't have made it to work on time if she hadn't. He'd been late one day last week, too, but he hadn't offered any explanation and she hadn't felt as if she could ask. "Adam?"

"Yeah, sure."

She hesitated, not sure how far into personal territory partners went. "Because you don't sound all right."

"I . . . I've been having trouble sleeping."

"Who doesn't?" M.K. glanced at herself in the mirror, tucking a lock of hair behind her ear. "Listen, why don't I come by and get you? There's no sense in us both driving over—the streets will be blocked off and parking will be a pain, anyway."

"I . . . I need to get a shower. Maybe you should go ahead. Let me catch up."

M.K. hesitated, reaching for the mini-holster on top of her dresser that she had just bought to wear under her shirt. It kept her minuscule Kel-Tec .32-caliber pistol secured in the small of her back so it was almost impossible to see, unless she was wearing a skintight t-shirt, and there was no danger of that happening anytime soon. The personal weapon had been her gift to herself when she graduated from the academy; it had just taken some time to find the right holster on the Internet. She didn't know why she had decided that today was the day to start wearing it, but she didn't have time to think, just to go with her gut instincts.

"Adam," she said into the phone, holding it with her shoulder as she slipped on the gun holster and buckled it in place. "This sounds bad, from what Seipp said. Really bad. He was so shook up he couldn't talk." She took a breath, forcing herself to stay calm; it was the only way she knew she could do her job effectively. "There can be no doubt in our minds now of what we've got here."

"Damned serial killer," he murmured, still sounding as if he was only half awake.

She wanted to say something about her instincts being right, but somehow, an *I told you so* didn't seem appropriate. Not when it meant another dead twenty-year-old.

She heard him knock something over, then the sound of running water.

"Okay, M.K. Give me time to grab a shower. You know where my place is?"

"Of course. I checked your personnel file, even if you didn't check mine." It was a lame attempt at a joke under the grim circumstances. "I'll be there in twenty minutes. You're not more than ten from the campus."

He hung up without answering. M.K. finished getting dressed, got her car, and stopped at a donut place for coffee. She was guessing neither would have the stomach for food. She arrived at Adam's town house just after eight-thirty. Leaving the car running, she ran up to the door and rang the doorbell, his coffee in her hand.

The door opened and Adam stepped out, closing it behind

him. He was wearing his usual khakis, and a sweater with a sport coat over it. His hair was still wet from the shower, and he was wearing the sunglasses, so she couldn't see his eyes. If he'd been out late the previous night, she couldn't tell; he cleaned up pretty well.

"Didn't figure you had time to make coffee." She offered up the large paper cup.

"God bless you." He reached out and, at the same time, leaned over and kissed her on the mouth. It was just a quick peck, more of a greeting than anything sexual, but he took her by complete surprise.

M.K. looked up at him, frozen for a second. She didn't know what to say. What to do. After the way he had left her apartment last week, she thought that had been the end of anything brewing between them. Now she didn't know what to think.

"I wonder where the hell that came from." He smirked, bringing the coffee cup to his lips.

"I was wondering the same thing."

He took a sip of the hot coffee. "I don't think we want to talk about this now."

She shook her head. "No," she murmured.

"So let's go."

In the car, it was back to business, and in less than ten minutes she was parked in the Chesapeake Bay College stadium parking lot.

The Ashview police were already there in full force, of course. Campus security was there, too, in cars that looked similar to the town's. An ambulance and an EMT van were pulled in on the grass next to the fence. There were also two golf carts, with the college's emblem painted on the side, parked at the entrance gate that M.K. and Adam had walked through weeks ago to see the football game.

There was a chill in the air as she got out of the car. She knew it was her imagination, but she thought she could smell blood.

"I already called for our crime scene guys," she told Adam. "I expect they'll be here any minute."

"You talk to Crackhow?"

"Out sick. I checked in with Duffy. He's in charge today. He's going to let the guys upstairs know. Apparently, Peter Wright's missing ear wasn't enough evidence for them to classify this as a killer taking trophies. It was still up for review. I think this puts us beyond the *review* stage."

Adam looked at her over the roof of her Honda. For a second she thought he was going to say something. Maybe offer an apology for not listening to her sooner, but he just tilted his head in the direction of the gate where Chief Seipp waited.

"We've put this off long enough," he said. "We better get going."

M.K. met Seipp just inside the gate. They didn't shake hands. He looked pretty upset; his eyes were red, as if he'd been crying. He kept wiping his mouth with his ever-present handkerchief, and she could have sworn she smelled a hint of vomit when he spoke.

"It's bad. Worse than it sounds." He shook his head. "I didn't let anybody even close to her. We got the call from campus security. I came over right straight from my breakfast table. Left my scrapple and eggs on the field over there." He wiped his mouth again.

M.K. glanced away, thinking she was a pretty good detective. Of course, if she really was, she'd have figured out by now who killed Peter Wright. Maybe then this girl wouldn't be dead.

"Who found her?" she asked. She and Adam hadn't really discussed in the car who would be in charge here, but when they'd met Seipp at the gate, he'd fallen back. She was in charge, at least until she started screwing up. They walked down the corridor beneath the bleachers where M.K. had met Adam's father that night.

"Groundskeeper. Saw the blood first. Followed the trail.

Then there she was. Poor old guy. You'll have to wait on talking to him. We ended up having an ambulance take him to the hospital. Heart palpitations." Seipp pressed a pudgy hand to his chest. "'Course, I'm feelin' a little short of breath myself. We all are. EMT who checked for a pulse did what he had to, then had to sit down. Right there in the grass in front of her. Said he served over in Iraq as a medic, picked up bodies off I-95 with a shovel, never saw anything like this."

M.K. swallowed hard. "Our forensic evidence team ought to be here any minute. We'll get them to do what has to be done and get her out of here just as fast as we can. We have a name?" They had exited the stadium and were walking across the brown grass toward an open area off the side of the field. A line of police officers, EMTs and ambulance crew members were standing in a row, facing away from her. M.K. didn't allow her gaze to move beyond them, to what they were looking at, not yet.

"Name's Tiffany Faulk. Senior. Twenty-one years old, from Hagerstown. Parents haven't been notified yet, but someone's gone to the *register's* office to get the phone numbers."

"We'll be needing that information from the *registrar's* office as well."

"Here, you're going to need these," Adam said quietly, pushing into her hands a pair of gloves like the ones Dr. Wood had offered her in the morgue that day.

They had almost reached the line of medical personnel and police officers.

A man in a gray, three-piece suit walked up to them, addressing Adam. They'd met him after the Peter Wright murder. He was William Gumble, director of campus security. "What the hell's going on here?" he demanded. "Do you have any idea what this will do to us? I won't be surprised if more parents are arriving by this afternoon to remove their students from our program. We've already lost half a dozen since the Wright boy."

"Can't say just yet," Adam said coolly. "Let us do our jobs

and we'll get back to you." He and M.K. walked through the line of bystanders who parted like the Red Sea.

"Like you were going to get right back to me on the last one?" Gumble shouted after them.

M.K. fiddled with her gloves. She couldn't get one to go on over her thumb. "I've called him four times in the last week to update him, even though we don't have any leads," she told Adam under her breath. "And it's not like he's been terribly cooperative. If I'd had my way, we would have questioned every student on this campus after Peter's death, but he was completely against it. He said it would cause *unnecessary panic* among the students."

"Parents footing the tuition bills is who he's concerned about. Ignore him. He's just trying to cover his ass. Make this our problem and not his."

He rested his hand on her shoulder for a minute, and it was just enough to help M.K. get her head straight again.

"You ready?"

She nodded.

The body was not actually right out in the open, but behind a small shed used to store equipment. M.K. walked around the shed, steeling herself. She halted as the body loomed ahead, a blur for a brief moment when she thought she recognized the dead young woman. She let her eyes adjust. Focus. It wasn't who she thought it was.

Thank God.

"Jesus," Adam breathed. "Ah, Jesus."

"Don't take the Lord's name in vain," M.K. heard herself whisper. Her hand went for the tiny crucifix and the Miraculous Medal she had worn around her neck since her first communion at the age of seven.

Adam, standing beside her, lowered his head, pressing his hand to his forehead. "Jesus," he whispered again. "What's she doing in a cheerleader's costume? There were no games last night."

"Halloween." M.K. gave herself a moment before she

moved closer, taking care not to step in the blood. "Remember?"

"For a moment, I thought it was . . . I thought it looked like—"

"I know." M.K. still couldn't manage anything above a whisper. "Actually, it's not even a costume. She is . . . *was* a cheerleader for the college. We probably saw her the night we came to the game. She was captain of the cheerleading squad."

Adjusting the rubber gloves one last time—though why, M.K. didn't know—she walked up to the body.

The beautiful, blond young woman was hanging by a canvas strap attached to the apparatus used by football players to practice tackling. Her old-fashioned black-and-white saddle shoes dangled above the grass. Her throat was cut and there was blood everywhere. Obviously a struggle had taken place. She had not died at once like Peter Wright.

But the worst part, the most horrendous, was that her sweater had been cut open and . . .

M.K. pressed her lips together and glanced away, her stomach turning over again and again. It was cool outside, but she was suddenly sweating.

She returned her gaze to the body. The young woman's breast had been cut off. M.K. didn't have to look around in the bloody grass to guess that it was gone.

"Sweet Jesus," she whispered. Only she wasn't swearing, she was calling Him for help.

"Sick bastard," Adam grunted, obviously still not quite in control of his emotions. "We have to get her down from there." He stepped forward, but M.K. grabbed his arm, stopping him. "Stay out of the blood." She pointed. "We've got footprints here. Probably the EMT's, but we don't know."

"We can't just let her hang there."

M.K. closed her hand around his arm, looking into his face, getting him to look at her. She could only imagine how difficult this had to be for him, having a daughter almost the same age. Having Liza Jane look so much like the dead girl. "Just a few more minutes and then we'll get her down. Okay?"

He nodded, glancing down at the bloody grass.

"Listen, if you want to go talk to Seipp, see if he can give you anything else, I don't mind staying here and—"

"M.K., I'm all right now. I apologize. I shouldn't have—" He gestured lamely toward the body. "It's just that—"

"I know. For a minute I thought it was her, too." She pushed her hair out of her face. "Listen, I know Dr. Wood usually sends that assistant coroner out to declare the bodies, but do you think we could get her out here? I'm thinking it would be a good idea for her to see the girl as she was left. It might help with her examination of the body."

"I'll call her now." He pulled his cell phone out of his jacket pocket and scrolled through the directory.

M.K. wondered why he had her number keyed into his phone, but she didn't ask. He walked away so she couldn't hear the conversation, and she glanced up at the young woman hanging in front of her, covered in blood, her eyes half closed. "I'm sorry," M.K. whispered. "I'm sorry this had to happen to you."

"Special Agent Shaughnessy?" someone called from behind her.

M.K. turned around, wiping the moisture from her eyes. It was the FBI forensic team. "Let me tell you what we've got," she said, approaching the man and woman in dark blue jumpsuits. "Then I'll let you get to work."

Adam spoke with Valerie and she agreed to come to the crime scene herself, but she said he would have to give her an hour as she was right in the middle of something. Just as he was hanging up the phone, he caught a glimpse of a pink bandana in the bleachers.

Stuffing the phone into his pocket, he walked around the

railing and took the steps two at a time, the aluminum clanging under his feet.

"Agent Thomas?" someone called from down on the field.

Adam glanced over his shoulder. The cop was pointing into the bleachers. He'd spotted her, too. "I'll take care of it."

When he reached Liza Jane, she was seated on a bench, scribbling in a notebook. Obviously she knew she was busted, but she made no attempt to get up or explain herself. In fact, she didn't even look at him.

Adam sat down beside her. He didn't know if he wanted to hug her or smack some sense into her. "Liza Jane," he said, in a tone he thought was amazingly calm. "What are you doing here?"

"It's a crime scene." Her voice was shaky. "I'm here to report."

"You're not allowed to be here."

"I didn't see any barricades or yellow tape," she defended, taking on an adversarial tone.

"That's because we didn't have time to get the damned tape up yet!"

He felt her tremble beside him and he slumped forward, resting his hands on his knee. Seeing that girl hanging there had scared him. It hadn't been his only child . . . but it *could* have been. It wasn't that either, and he knew it.

He'd been upset before M.K. called him this morning. Upset for days . . . weeks. He just couldn't stop thinking about the Lombardo case. It wasn't similar to this one, it really wasn't, but it had gone bad. Somehow he couldn't shake the feeling, even though he knew his feelings couldn't be trusted—knew they were worthless—that this one was going in the same direction.

Adam lifted his head. Below, on the football field, the Ashview cops and the medical people were milling around, talking in hushed tones. A couple of state troopers were on the scene now, too. He glanced at Liza Jane, who had stopped writing and was just staring at the notebook on her lap.

"How'd you get here so fast?" he asked her. "How'd you know?"

"You'll flip."

"I won't flip."

"Police scanner. I borrowed it from some guy."

"Liza Jane, you have no damned business—"

"See, I told you you'd flip."

They were both quiet for a minute, then she glanced up at him. "This is really awful, isn't it, Dad?"

He realized suddenly that she was very pale. "You saw?"

She nodded.

He glanced away for a moment, thinking that of all the things he wanted to spare her from in the world, seeing that young woman's body hanging, her breast brutally cut off, had to be at the top of the list. But he was learning pretty quickly that sometimes parents couldn't protect their kids, no matter how badly they wanted to.

"Why would someone do that?" she whispered. "It's so . . . so cold-blooded. So . . . so callous."

Adam slid his arm around his daughter's shoulders and hugged her against him. "I can't tell you how many times I've asked myself the same thing over the years."

"So why do you do it?" She looked up at him with the innocent blue eyes he remembered from her childhood. "Why do you have to be a cop?"

"Because it's my job. Not just the way I get a paycheck. It's what I was meant to do, no matter how horrific it is sometimes." He hesitated. "Someone has to do it."

She folded her hands on her notebook, seeming to shrink up inside a bulky, hand-knit blue sweater he knew Sophie had made for her a couple of winters ago. "That's the way I feel about reporting, Dad. It's, like, what I need to be doing." She looked up at him again. "And I'm good at it. Just like you're good at this." She lifted her chin in the direction of the equipment shed and the body.

Down below, M.K. appeared and waved, signaling she needed him to come down.

"Look," he told Liza Jane as he rose, "I have to get to work and you have to get out of here. You didn't take any pictures, did you?"

She shook her head. "Cam didn't answer his cell." She frowned. "I think he's sleeping over at some girl's. So I couldn't get him to bring the camera. I brought a digital but when I saw her, I couldn't—" Her voice caught in her throat.

"Good. And what have you got there?" He nodded to her notebook.

"Not much. I don't even know her name yet. I was thinking I would go to the library and look for her in a yearbook. I know she's an upper classman."

"Pretty clever. Look, I have to go and you definitely have to go. I'm closing the whole stadium and the parking lot, which means neither you nor the news vans that I'm sure are on their way are going to be able to get near this crime scene." He glanced overhead at the clear blue sky dotted with fluffy clouds; it seemed too pretty a day for such an unspeakable crime. "I'm closing the air space, too. I don't want any of those clever guys from the Baltimore stations sending their helicopters in."

Liza Jane stood up, throwing her backpack on her shoulder. "You can do that?"

"Sure. I'm one of the feds." He gave her the best smirk he could muster.

"I'll go out the back way." She turned away to go up, rather than down.

"Good idea. And Liza Jane?"

She turned back. "Yeah, Dad?"

"Would you mind calling me before you run anything in the school newspaper or on your news show? Professional courtesy."

She hung her head, her little white-blond dreads falling from the pink bandana to cover her face. "I'll call you, Dad."

He started down the steps. "Love you, Liza Jane," he called without turning to look at her.

"Love you, Daddy."

Chapter Eighteen

"I'll just be another moment." Jerome covered the receiver with his hand. "I apologize profusely for asking you to wait. Under normal circumstances, I would never do this, but my wife is very ill." He paused. "She's terminal, and I've been on hold for twenty-five minutes. I'm bringing her home this evening from the hospital. I just needed to talk to her doctor about pain management."

Jerome didn't usually speak about anything personal with his patients, but he was rattled today. Tired. Worried, and feeling sorry for himself, at least just a little. He didn't know how he was going to live without his Sela.

"I understand. It's quite all right." Blue smiled with kindness, and Jerome realized he liked the patient, a judgment he usually tried not to make.

The phone connection clicked in Jerome's ear. "Yes?" he said.

"Dr. Fisher?" a female voice inquired.

"Yes, this is Dr. Fisher, still holding for Dr. Attiya." He tried not to sound impatient.

"I'm sorry, Dr. Fisher, but Dr. Attiya will have to return your call. He's unavailable right now."

"I just need to speak with him for a moment," Jerome intoned, glancing up at his patient, who was seated, legs crossed.

"He asked me to give you a message. He asked if he could call you at home this evening. Say, eight-thirty?"

Jerome checked the clock on the wall. An hour with his patient, an hour to get to the hospital and pick up Sela. He'd have to hustle to make it. "Yes, yes, that will be fine. But I'll be picking up my wife to take her home, so let me give you my cell phone number. If I don't answer at home, please tell Dr. Attiya that I want him to call my cell."

"I certainly will. And that number?"

Jerome gave her the number and hung up. "Again, I apologize," he told Blue as he came around his desk.

The patient raised a hand. "Apologies aren't necessary. I'm very sorry to hear about your wife's illness. Is . . . is there no hope?"

Jerome picked up Blue's file from the edge of his desk. "I'm afraid we've passed that point." His voice was devoid of any emotion. He was slipping into psychiatrist mode and there was no place for sentiment. "We've stopped treatment. Now." He took a seat in his comfy leather chair. "Tell me how your week has been." He flipped open the file. "Two weeks, really." He glanced up. "I'm sorry about having to reschedule; my wife had to be hospitalized suddenly."

The patient smiled. "I knew how to contact you if I needed you. Really, Dr. Fisher, it was all right."

"And your week? Did you go out often?"

"To bars, you mean?"

Jerome nodded.

"No." The patient smiled with pride. "Actually, I didn't. I . . . I haven't had sex in weeks. Months now."

Jerome nodded. "So you feel you're making progress?"

"Of sorts."

"Meaning?"

"I . . . I've been able to stay away from bars." There was a hesitation. "But . . . but I seem to have picked up another . . . habit that I fear could be destructive, as well."

"I see." Jerome looked up and the patient's demeanor changed almost before his eyes. The attractive, intelligent person sitting across from him seemed to draw up in the chair, almost shrivel. The face seemed to soften until it was almost childlike.

"Would you like to tell me what you've been doing?" Jerome asked gently, setting his pen down.

The office was quiet for a moment except for the tick of the clock on the wall and the muffled sound of the copy machine on the other side of the door.

"I don't think so."

"Blue—"

"I lied."

Jerome waited.

"I lied," the patient repeated. "When . . . when I said I hadn't been treated before by a psychiatrist."

"I see."

"No. No, I don't think you do. When you asked me about my psychiatric history, I lied. I've been treated on and off my whole life."

Jerome was not entirely surprised; he had been certain more was going on here than met the eye. He had told Sela that, hadn't he? "Would you like to tell me about it?" Jerome gave Blue another opportunity to speak, then went on. "I take it you were treated for the particular concern you came to me to address?"

The patient's head shook rapidly. "Not for this. For . . . for other things." There was a shuddering exhalation. "It's very complicated."

Jerome smiled, not unkindly. "Life is, isn't it?"

The patient's gaze lifted. Jerome still saw the child, but Blue's demeanor was shifting again. The mature, reasonable person who had entered the office only minutes ago was reappearing.

"I want to tell you. I want you to help me, but I . . . I don't know that I can say it."

Jerome was quiet for a moment. "We have some options, then. Perhaps you'd just like some time. We could talk about it next week."

"I . . . don't know that I would know where to start next week, either, and . . . and I'm concerned that my behavior could . . . *worsen.*"

Jerome contemplated their options, choosing to offer the best first. "Then what would you think about my requesting your previous psychiatric records? You would have to give permission, of course, but then I could acquire copies. I could read them and then I would know where you and I should start." He hesitated. "Because, Blue, I've suspected for a number of weeks that we were not starting in the right place."

Tears filled the patient's eyes. "It's not that I didn't want to tell you."

"I understand. Sometimes it's hardest for us to say what is foremost in our minds." Jerome hesitated, glancing down at his notebook and file on his lap. "Do you know that when I told you a few minutes ago that my wife was terminally ill, that's the first time I've told anyone?"

Blue's eyes were filled with compassion.

"It's all I have thought about day and night since she has been in the hospital, but I haven't been able to actually say it." Jerome chuckled. "Now Sela, she has no difficulty discussing the subject."

"Sela—that's a lovely name."

Jerome lowered his head. "For a lovely woman. Now tell me, would you be willing to give me your previous psychiatrist's name? Mrs. Elright could bring in a consent form. We have them already printed up for just this type of situation."

"I think that would be best."

"Excellent." Jerome rose from his chair. "I don't think you'll regret this. It's a wise step in gaining the control you seek over your life." He opened the door. "Mrs. Elright, could you please bring a patient's records release form?"

"Certainly, Dr. Fisher."

Jerome closed the door and headed for his chair again. "That will be just a minute—now, why don't we talk about something else? Something you're more comfortable with." He sat down. "Tell me how you made out this week with your journal entries."

"So what do we have?" Adam walked into the conference room M.K. had commandeered as her own the day after Tiffany Faulk's murder. He took a chair across from her. She had the conference table covered with files and stacks of legal-size notepads set in orderly rows. Around her chair were white cardboard file boxes she was beginning to fill with information she'd gathered on the Chesapeake Bay College case. All week he'd been letting her get as far as she could alone, doing the legwork on the case, while he worked the wiretap at the docks and plowed through the old files Crackhow kept leaving on his desk.

M.K. sat back in her chair, pushing her hair aside on her forehead and reaching for a diet soda. "What have we got? Nothing," she said, gazing over the paperwork, files, folders, and legal pads in front of her. She tipped the can, taking a drink. "That's why I thought we needed to talk. This isn't working. I don't know what to do. What direction to go. I've got a big, fat bunch of nothing."

"That isn't true. You've worked hard for days, and we've got a list of possible suspects now, right?"

She sighed, nodding as she set down her can. "Right."

She looked tired to him, not quite so tough, maybe just a little vulnerable. He liked that side of her. "So let's go over them," he said.

She grabbed a yellow legal pad and began to scan her notes.

"We've got Patrick Purnell, the security guy. He found Peter Wright's body. He was also conveniently within a block of the football field when the groundskeeper called Tiffany Faulk's body in. He was first on the scene, even before the Ashview police."

Adam tented his hands, nodding. Processing the information. "Okay, the guy's definitely got possibilities. Let's think about what we know from Serial Killers 101. We know they often like to be directly involved with the discovery of the bodies. They like to stand in a crowd of bystanders and watch, call in tips, offer to help with the investigation. I can't tell you how many cases have been solved by starting with a photograph of the bystanders. If our killer's really got co-jones, he'll even be the one to report the deaths."

"I know. I've interviewed Purnell twice now, first in person, then on the phone, but he just doesn't seem right." She pressed the forefinger and thumb of one hand to her temples. "He doesn't appear to be bright enough to be a serial killer, if you want to know the truth. They usually have IQs well above average."

"Okay. Who else?" Adam prodded. He was proud of how well M.K. was doing on this investigation. She really had a head for the order of things, the patience it took to see each and every detail through. That was what it took to work these cases. Not intuition or feelings. Just hard work. It was the best way. The only way.

"Buddy Caruso. Pizza delivery guy." She glanced up. "Come to find out, he's Chief Seipp's stepson."

"You're kidding."

She shook her head. "Don't know that it has anything to do with anything, but . . ." She shrugged. "Seipp sure never mentioned it. Guess how I found out."

He lifted his brows.

"Our own campus sleuth, Miss Liza Jane Thomas. I spoke with her yesterday. She has an excellent memory for details. She was the one who told me she had seen Caruso leaving Wooten Hall the night of Peter's murder. "

"Please tell me she isn't reporting he's a suspect."

"You don't read her articles in the campus newspaper? Watch her news show?"

He reached for her soda. "A swallow left in that can?"

She handed it to him. "It's hot and flat. And no, she didn't give any names, but I feel like she's got a better handle on this investigation than I do. You know, you should watch her show. Read her articles. She's good."

Adam ignored her advice on being a good father. "You're doing fine. You know I wouldn't hesitate to tell you if you weren't." He took a sip of her soda. She was right, it was flat. He drank the rest of it anyway. "So, what have we actually got on this Caruso?"

"Nothing, really, except that he's creepy as all get out. Delivered pizza to the janitor working in Wooten that night." M.K. ran her finger down the page of notes. "And he's got a record. Assault and battery. Minor marijuana possession. He's on probation. And I'm almost positive his record was expunged more than once prior to his eighteenth birthday, so I have someone looking into that."

"Excellent." Adam shot the soda can into the trash bin in the corner of the stuffy room. "Records that are no longer supposed to exist are always fun to read."

"Get this, also thanks to Miss Liza Jane. Caruso delivered pizza to Bart Johnson's house that Friday night after the football game. The night prior to his death."

He frowned. "How the hell did she know that?"

"Talked to some girl she knows from her psych class whose sister works at the pizza place. I didn't get a thing out of them, but Liza Jane is less intimidating, I'm sure. Caruso also delivered pizza to Tiffany Faulk's dorm the week prior to her death."

"No shit."

M.K. frowned.

He groaned inwardly, but it didn't bother him as much as it had a couple of weeks ago. So she had her quirks. Didn't they all? "Sorry."

"Trouble is," she continued, "he's probably delivered pizza to every dorm, and every frat and sorority house on campus. Shoot, he's probably delivered to your place. Liza Jane said he even delivered to your ex-wife's once in a while."

"Doesn't matter." Adam leaned back in his chair, parking his ankle on his knee. He enjoyed this part of the work. He liked trying to outthink these bastards. And he was finding out that he liked doing it with M.K. "It's a place to start."

"I know." She set down the legal pad. "I just feel like we have so little. Something as big as this, I would just think there'd be more."

"Maybe something will come up with the forensic testing," he offered.

"Maybe, but you heard what Belker said. There wasn't that much evidence. A hair on her sweater that could have come from anywhere. No follicle, though. Footprints we couldn't match to anyone at the scene, but we have to have suspects to compare to and I don't have enough on anyone for a judge to let me confiscate shoes. There's no DNA anywhere." She opened her arms wide. "I'm telling you, we've got nothing."

"Who else is on your list?"

"Let's see." She looked down. "Arthur Connelly, professor of biology. Jessica, Peter, and Tiffany were all either presently taking a class from him or had taken one of his classes in the last three years." What she didn't tell him was that Bart had had Connelly, too. She wasn't ready to push that button yet.

"Liza Jane has him, too," Adam said thoughtfully. He looked up. "How'd you get that information?"

"Requested all their schedules, cross-referenced them."

"It must have taken hours." He met her gaze across the table.

She looked down. "It did."

"I notice you just included Jessica in your list of those who had contact with this professor. Why are you connecting her death with these last two? The official cause of death was an OD. For God's sake, M.K., we found the roofies in her purse."

"I know, but everyone said she didn't do drugs, including her roommate. What if someone put them in her drink? It's how it's used as a date rape drug. And we never found any explanation for the missing lock of hair. Her roommate knew nothing about it. I know there's no direct evidence, but I just have the feeling her death is connected."

More of her damned *feelings*. M.K.'s stubbornness annoyed him. It could get in the way of the investigation. An agent couldn't afford to stubbornly stick to certain thoughts or assumptions, not leaving the door open to other possibilities. "I'm still not buying it," he told her firmly. "I'm not buying the idea that someone fed Bart through the chipper-shredder, either."

"Who said anything about Bart? Anyway," she said, "I was thinking about interviewing this professor, but I don't know what my approach should be. I don't know what reason to give him for the interview or how to proceed once I've got him. If it is, by chance, him, which I don't think it is, obviously I don't want him to think he's a suspect."

"We'll do it together. I'll run the interview, you sit back. We all develop our own techniques with time, but I can show you the general direction to follow when you talk to a possible suspect that's way outside the perimeter."

She tapped her pen on the table. "I feel like I'm really grasping at straws here with no physical evidence to go on. No witnesses, no forensics that will help us . . ."

"It's how we do it in these situations, M.K. You heard Crackhow yesterday morning. He warned you these serial killer cases can take years."

"We haven't got years! The president of Chesapeake

College has called Crackhow twice. Parents of students are holding news conferences. Kids are dropping out left and right." She slapped down the pen and leaned forward, pressing her hands to the table to move closer to him. "Adam, this guy's on a hot streak. He's going to kill again, and you know it. We've got to find him."

Her gesture came pretty close to getting in his face, but he didn't get pissed off because he knew her anger wasn't directed toward him. It came out of her frustration with the case. He'd been there too many times not to cut her a break. "But the only way we're going to find him," he said, "short of him leaving us a calling card, is by following through on every possible lead, every hunch, no matter how insignificant or far-fetched it might seem."

She glanced away, folding her arms over her chest, staring at the wall painted government-green behind him.

"So let's talk about our killer," Adam pushed. "Tell me what we know about him."

She threw up her hands, still angry. "Are you not listening to me? We don't know anything!"

"Sure we do. We know more than you think. I know you've been reading up on everything the Bureau has printed on this subject. I've seen the piles of stuff you're printing to read. You're killing entire pine forests with your printouts. Mother pine trees are weeping everywhere. Now tell me what we know, statistically."

She hesitated for a second, then reached for a different legal pad in front of her in one of her neat rows. "Male, Caucasian. Either employed during the day, or the night, but not a shift-worker."

"Why?"

She glanced up. "What do you mean?"

"I mean first, how do we know he's male and Caucasian?"

"We know it's a male because more than ninety-seven percent of serial killers are male and only males take trophies," she said, as if he was an idiot.

"Excellent."

"He's Caucasian for the same reason. They almost always are, and the fact that the victims are Caucasian ups the percentage to almost guarantee it."

M.K. leaned back in her chair, her jacket falling open to reveal her Glock service weapon in her shoulder holster and the thought crossed Adam's mind that he liked a woman packing a weapon. It was kind of sexy, somehow. "Tell me about his job."

"He probably works days since all the deaths occurred at night." She lifted a finger. "Unless, of course, he's killing them while on the job."

"Like if he was a night security cop or a pizza delivery guy."

She tapped her nose with her forefinger, then scanned her list again. "Let's see . . . what else? He's smart, because they are, but also because he's leaving no physical evidence behind except the body. Being outside helps—the elements make it more difficult to collect evidence, but these are very well planned murders. If not well planned as in forethought, at least well executed. Both the penknife and rock at the Wright scene were wiped clean. He didn't leave the weapon at the Faulk scene."

"Who are the victims?"

"If we only look at Peter and Tiffany, all we can really say is that they're college students at Chesapeake." She chewed on the end of her pen. "I mean, they never even knew each other."

"You're sure?"

She nodded. "Peter was a sophomore, undeclared major, but going into some kind of sciences. Tiffany, a senior, was a communications major. No extracurricular activities for Peter, and he roomed alone. He had a small group of geeky friends from the science department, but he was kind of a loner. Tiffany, on the other hand, was a cheerleader, a member of all sorts of clubs and committees, and shared a dorm apartment in the towers with three other girls. She was Miss Popularity. She told friends when she graduated, she was going to go west to try out for a position as a Laker girl."

Adam shook his head at the notion of such unrealistic goals. And to think, the poor girl's family had been putting her through college so she could be a half-naked cheerleader. He was thankful his own daughter had more lofty objectives. He shifted his focus back to the investigation. "The actual murders are very different, though, aren't they?" he thought aloud.

She nodded. "With Peter, the killer used an object he found lying around."

"Which suggests it was unplanned."

"But with Tiffany, we found no weapon. We know it's a large knife, but it wasn't left behind, which makes us think he brought it with him."

"And the knife used to kill Tiffany was not the same type of knife used to cut off Peter's ear?"

"Nope. According to the M.E., the killer definitely used Peter's own penknife to cut off his ear." She looked up. "Speaking of which, did we get a written report from your buddy, Dr. Wood?"

"Nah." He shook his head, wondering how the coroner had become his *buddy*. "But she's been backed up. She told you she couldn't get right to it."

M.K. glanced down at her notes again. "We haven't gotten those audiotapes from her autopsies that she promised, either."

Adam frowned. "So I'll give her another day and if we don't hear from her, I'll give her a ring. Don't get so pissy. Why do you get so pissy with me every time her name comes up?"

M.K. flipped the page on her legal pad so hard that the paper made a loud pop. "I don't."

"You do."

She shot him another one of those killer looks. "I am not being *pissy*. What do I care if you're dating her?"

It was bad enough to be in trouble for things he did. "I'm not dating her."

"I don't want to talk about this. You have a right to date who you want. We already agreed that you and I,"—she kept her gaze on the notepad—"that it wouldn't work out."

What a mess. Adam knew better than to allow himself to become attracted to a co-worker. He knew agents made lousy partners. The fact that he was attracted to her was just getting in the way here. "M.K., I said I'm not dating her."

She flipped another page. "If you are, it's fine. She's nice. Pretty. I'd kill for that body of hers."

"I thought you didn't want to talk about it."

"I don't." She slapped the notepad down and grabbed another one. "What do you think about the trophies? From Peter, he took an ear, from Tiffany, a breast."

"Dam—*darned* gruesome, isn't it?" He put emphasis on his better choice of words. "And with Tiffany, it seems as if it escalated. An ear—I mean, that's not so hard to do. Just slice it off. But a breast . . ."

"It's definitely a pattern, especially if we include Jessica's hair." She raised her hand. "I know you don't think they're connected, but how can we know for sure? It's a pretty well documented fact that serial killers have often killed sometime prior to becoming serial killers. I'm just afraid of what we're going to find next if we don't catch this creep." M.K. scribbled something down and looked up. "And why? Why would a person do such a thing?"

Adam looked down at his hands on the table, suddenly feeling like a dark cloud had drifted over him. *Why would a person do such a thing to another person?* Against his will, memories of the past were coming back, pushing at the walls of his mind where he had so carefully constructed barriers. He wiped his mouth with the back of his hand, suddenly feeling like he couldn't breathe. Ten years. How in ten years could he still feel this way?

"I think you're doing a great job here, M.K." He got out of his chair. "I think we're definitely moving in the right direction." He kept nodding as he went to the door. "See what you can do about making arrangements to speak with the professor."

She followed him with her gaze, his sudden retreat not going unnoticed. "Okay . . ."

"I've got something else to take care of." He hooked his thumb in the direction of the hall . . . the world beyond the building. "Let me know." In the hall, he walked straight to the elevator. It was only three-thirty, too early to leave, but he was beginning to break out in a sweat. The memories weren't just pushing on the walls anymore. They were banging on them. Breaking through. He saw the flash of the gun. The look on Mark's face.

He punched the call button, and when it didn't light up at once, he punched it again. The doors sprang open and he hit the button to take him down with his fist. The doors closed and he leaned back against the wall, closing his eyes, thankful no one had seen him.

FBI agents losing their marbles ended up losing their jobs.

Chapter Nineteen

Sela stirred beside Jerome in the bed, startling him, and he glanced over his reading glasses at her.

She turned to him and slowly lifted her hand to lay it on his arm, the effort so great that it seemed to him as if it took forever. "It's very late," she murmured, her words slightly slurred by sleep and the strong painkiller she was taking.

He nodded, glancing at the digital clock beside the bed, then back at her. "Almost three."

She sighed, closing her eyes, and pushing down on the mattress with both hands, trying to sit up.

His first impulse was to help her, but the rule was that she would ask for help if she needed it. "I'm sorry I've disturbed you," he said.

"Don't be ridiculous, Jerome." Leaning back on a pile of pillows, she kept her eyes closed for a moment and breathed deeply.

He knew she did it as a way to cope with the waves of pain that now washed over her with every movement.

"You're not disturbing me. It's this damned cancer in my bones that's disturbing me!" When she opened her dark eyes, they danced with defiance.

He couldn't help but smile.

"So what are you doing up so late?" She shifted, trying to find a comfortable position. "It's not like you to bring work home like this."

Jerome stared at the records in his lap. "A very disturbing case. My patient I call Blue."

She reached up to straighten her head scarf that had slipped askew while she slept.

He disobeyed the rules and put out a hand to help her, covering her hand with his.

"I hate you seeing me bald as a baby," she said, sliding the scarf down over the smooth, dark skin that was just beginning to get fuzzy. Once chemo was discontinued, even dying patients apparently began to grow hair again.

"I don't know why. I told you you're lovely bald. You have such a perfectly shaped head." He ran his hand over it.

She pushed him away with as much playfulness as she could muster. "Tell me about your case."

"You know I shouldn't."

She settled against her pillows and closed her eyes, folding her thin hands on her hollowed belly. "Tell me anyway. What are they going to do? Take away my license to practice?"

"They could take away mine."

She smiled, eyes still closed. "I'll never speak of the matter to anyone. I'll take it to my grave. Now tell me. It'll give me something to think about."

"You're hurting?" he asked, reaching out to rub her thin arm.

"Tell me," she repeated.

He returned his gaze to the file on his lap, hating this feeling of helplessness. And now that feeling was extending to his work. What he had read in the records transferred from a psychiatrist's office in Texas had been so disconcerting that he had been unable to sleep. After lying awake for more than an hour after Sela had drifted off, thinking about the patient, he'd gotten up and retrieved the file from his briefcase.

"Tell me what you know about hermaphrodites," he said quietly.

Sela opened her eyes, startled. "Your patient is a hermaphrodite? You're kidding. You didn't tell me that before."

"I didn't know. The patient appears quite normal—good-looking, even."

"Fascinating," she breathed.

"Now, I know the basics, but you're better at remembering these obscure conditions, Sela. You always were. What do I need to know?"

"Let's see. There are three kinds of hermaphrodites," she began to recite, as if from a text. Then she looked at him, excitement in her eyes. "You know, this is remarkable. There are probably only three hundred and fifty known cases in the United States right now."

"So you think I'm in over my head."

"Certainly not, Jerome." She patted his hand beside hers on the bed. "Let's see, there are three kinds of hermaphrodites." She went back to her recitation. "A true, a male pseudo, and a female pseudo. A female pseudo is born with XX chromosomes and normal female organs, but with masculinized genitalia. They can appear more male or more female or a combination. Then there is the male pseudo with XY chromosomes and testes that are usually in the abdomen rather than descended. The external genitalia is usually female, although it can be ambiguous."

"How do you remember all this?" he asked.

"I went to class more than you did, remember?" She smiled slyly and then went on. "The last and the rarest of the hermaphrodites is the true hermaphrodite. This person is born with both ovary and testicular tissue. The genitalia can appear to be all male, all female, a combination of both or ambiguous in appearance. What are interesting are the chromosome combinations, if I recall correctly." Sela pressed her finger to her lips in thought. "You know, not more than a year ago there was an article on this in one of the psychiatric journals. The karyotype can be XX, which is female, of course, XY, which is male or XX/YY which is called . . ." She snapped her fingers, trying to remember. "This damned morphine, Jerome—this is why I hate taking it. It clouds my memory." Her face lit up. "Mosaic!"

"Ah, mosaic, that's right," he agreed, scribbling a note on a legal pad beside him on the bed. "My patient is a true hermaphrodite. I haven't found it yet, if it's noted, what the chromosome makeup is." He paused. "What's the history of treatment of these individuals?"

"We've not done well by these troubled souls, I can tell you that. For years, of course, we didn't know a person could appear to be one sex and be another genetically—we just made the assumption that they were what they appeared to be. And as for those with a combination of both types of genitalia, we simply cut off anything that didn't look right and called that child a female." Sela shook her head. "We're learning now that these are the most tragic cases of all. The gender identity confusion can take a tragic toll on the psyches of these individuals." She turned to him. "I'm almost afraid to ask, but how was your patient treated?"

He shook his head, pulling off his glasses to rub his tired eyes. "I don't have any medical records, just psychiatric, but this patient has been disturbed for a very long time, I suppose as a result of the gender confusion. Apparently the patient's parents did not agree with the medical practice of altering the genitalia to make their child male or female, so the patient was forced to live with the idea of being neither . . . both, I suppose."

"Actually, true hermaphrodites can be. You need to go on the Internet tomorrow and see what you can find out about the most recent treatment of true hermaphrodites. I believe that some doctors are now beginning to take the position of doing no surgery and allowing the individual to develop as God . . . or nature"—she chuckled—"depending on where you stand, has created him or her. These individuals are a third sex, a combination of both male and female inside, and now, sometimes, outside as well." She closed her eyes, her facial muscles tightening in a spasm of pain.

"I'm sorry, sweetheart." Jerome dropped the file on the floor beside the bed and rolled toward her, trying carefully not to jostle her. "I shouldn't be troubling you with this."

"Don't be ridiculous," she said in a small voice. "You give me a reason to continue to live a while longer, Jerome."

He picked up her left hand in his. She had had him tie a string to her wedding band so she could wear it without having it fall off in the bed. "I think it's time for more pain medication. It's been more than four hours."

"I know, but I hate it," she said in an almost child-like voice. "It knocks me out. It steals from me much of the time I still have left with you."

Her words brought a lump to his throat. "I know." He rubbed her hand between his. Her skin seemed so thin now, and blotchy. She'd always had the most beautiful, rich ebony skin. "But at least you're not in pain. And at night, I'm asleep anyway."

She sighed. "I suppose it is time."

He placed her hand on the bed and climbed out, going around to her side. They had brought a small end table in from the living room and it was stacked with her many medications. He turned on the bedside lamp and grabbed a syringe and a bottle of diamorphine. Glancing down at her, he filled the syringe. "I think you need to consider an IV pump for this. You'd be more comfortable with a steady flow of medication."

She shook her head slowly. "Not yet. You know how that works—once you take that step, quality of life is severely reduced. Patients on diamorphine drips just mostly sleep."

"Maybe with a lesser dose—"

"Jerome, just give me the damned shot and get in bed. If you don't get some sleep you'll be cranky tomorrow and Mrs. Elright will blame me."

He wanted to tell her that Mrs. Elright would never blame her for anything. She worshiped Sela. Instead, he opened an alcohol prep package and removed the little square of gauze. "Left or right?"

She slowly rolled over to present her bottom to him.

Jerome slid her silky lavender nightgown up over her hip, wiped a spot of skin with the alcohol prep, and gave her the injection. As he rubbed the injection spot with his fingers, he tried not to think about how painfully thin Sela had become. She was nothing but skin and bones. Even her buttocks, which had always been so full and muscular and feminine, had lost its tone. He felt tears sting the backs of his eyelids and he fought it. "There you go, my love."

"Thank you," she whispered, not moving.

He slid her nightgown down and the sheet up. He then disposed of the prep pad and popped the syringe into the red plastic hazardous waste container he'd had to pick up at the medical supply store. "You sleep now," he whispered, shutting the light off and leaning over to kiss her cheek. "I love you, Sela."

"Love you, Jerome," she breathed.

He walked back to his side of the bed and stepped over Blue's files on the carpet. Climbing into bed, he shut off his light and lay back, consciously pushing all thoughts of his patient from his mind. Tomorrow he'd do as Sela suggested and go on the Internet. Perhaps he'd even look up some colleagues. He was very concerned about whether or not he could treat Blue, and even more concerned about what the patient might do if he couldn't.

"Hey, I thought you'd gone home." M.K. walked around the wall of Adam's cubicle, a white cardboard box filled with files and her notepads in her arms.

"Just going back over Professor Connelly's statement." He pushed back in his chair, tucking his hands behind his head. "He's a weirdo, I'll give him that."

She propped the corner of the box on his desk to relieve her arms of the weight for a minute. "But he's not our killer."

Adam shook his head, staring at the notes on his desk. "I don't think so."

M.K. nodded. "Dr. Wood call? I'd really like to see Tiffany's autopsy report. The real thing, not the preliminary. Something might stand out to us that she didn't realize was significant."

"I was just getting ready to give her a call. She's been working nights, even later than we have. Some kind of big inspection coming up. Apparently she has to provide procedure manuals that haven't been written yet, plus the morgue has to be perfectly up to code, hacksaws and liver scoops in the right drawers, and so on."

"You want me to wait for you? We could grab something to eat. I'm just going home to go through some of these statements again. The interviews with the students' friends."

Adam wanted to say yes, but he knew he shouldn't. Couldn't. Not tonight. "Thanks, but I think I'll stick around here. Crackhow's on me to get those notes to him on the dock wiretaps. I should listen to a couple of them again."

She gave the box a heave, lifting it into her arms again. "Guess I'll see you Monday, then."

He thought she seemed disappointed and he felt bad. He didn't want to hurt her, but he was sure the best way to prevent that was not getting too close. He'd already hurt enough people.

When Adam heard M.K. step into the elevator, he picked up the phone and dialed Valerie Wood's office. She answered the phone on the second ring.

"Friday night, seven o'clock, and you're answering your phone yourself," he said, pushing back in his chair again and propping his feet on his desk.

"Adam."

He grinned. "How'd you know it was me?"

"Because you're the only smart-ass I know who is also working at seven o'clock on a Friday night. Besides, we've got caller ID."

He laughed with her. "Listen, I was calling—"

"I know, I know," she interrupted. "The autopsy reports. I'm sorry, Adam. I feel like I'm drowning in paperwork down here, and I've got this inspection coming and the county swears they're going to find a clerk for me, but right now it's just me and my deputy coroner and his wife's getting ready to have a baby and—"

"All right, all right. I get the picture." Adam chuckled. "A public servant's work is never done. I still can't believe you're not out on a Friday night. Don't you have a guy who wants to take you out, wine and dine you?"

She chuckled, her voice husky. "I wish. I can't remember the last time I went on a real date."

He chuckled, too. "I hear you."

"But actually, I'm starved," she went on. "I could definitely use a little dine, if not the wine. You want to get a bite to eat? I hate eating alone in restaurants, and I don't think any of my friends here in the cold-storage drawers are going to go with me."

Adam smiled at her sick sense of humor. He supposed you had to be that way to do what she did. "Sure," he heard himself say before he even thought about it. "I can meet you. I have to run by my ex's house in Ashview for a second, but then I'm free. Want me to come to Annapolis?"

"I could meet you in Ashview. There's this great little pub that has the best—"

"Grilled chicken sandwiches," he interrupted. "I know the place. College Park. I go there all the time."

"Great. Eight-thirty?" she said. "That will give me enough time to wrap something up here."

"Eight-thirty. See you then, Val."

* * *

Adam left the Baltimore office and, despite Friday evening traffic, was at Sophie and Mark's by seven-forty-five. On the ride over, he decided he wouldn't let himself feel guilty about not going out to eat with M.K. and then agreeing to meet Valerie Wood. Two entirely different situations, he told himself. Right now with M.K., he felt as if he were walking a tightrope. There was no denying the chemistry between them, and the fewer opportunities he gave himself, the better chance he had of not ending up in bed with her. Valerie was safe. While he liked her and certainly found her attractive, the tall, beautiful blonde just didn't hold a candle to M.K.'s more petite, subtle femininity. The coroner just didn't light his fire the way his partner did.

Walking up the sidewalk, Adam took note that the lawn needed mowing one last time before winter. It wasn't like Mark to let something like that go. He was always so fastidious about this lawn. The first thing he'd done after he moved in with Sophie was reseed the whole thing. Apparently he hadn't cared for the Kentucky fescue Adam had planted. He was fond enough of Adam's wife and child, though. *Whatever*.

At the door, Adam didn't knock, he just walked in. He found Sophie in the kitchen in fuzzy slippers, her ponytail to him, stirring a pot of spaghetti sauce that smelled great. "Hey, fatty," he called, walking up behind her to put one arm around her and give her a peck on the cheek.

"Hey." She turned to him, smiling.

He frowned and reached out to brush her temple. The area around her eye was a deep purple, beginning to turn green around the edges. "What happened to you?"

"Oh, that?" She laughed and turned away. "I'm getting so clumsy with this belly of mine. I swear there have to be two or three babies in here, but Dr. Ritter says it's just one."

He watched her as she went to the refrigerator and began to pull out vegetables for salad. "So you fell?"

"Ran into the corner cabinet." Without looking at him, she pointed to the end cabinet near the laundry room.

"Ouch."

"Yeah." She carried the vegetables to the counter.

"Well, I just came by to drop off the check. Sorry it's late."

She waved a cucumber in his direction. "You always pay, Adam. Who cares what day you give me the check so long as you give it to me and Liza Jane's tuition, room, and board get paid."

He laid the check on the small counter near the refrigerator that served as a desk. "You okay?" he asked, not entirely sure he believed she'd run into a cabinet. It looked to him like someone had punched her.

"Sure." She was peeling the cucumber. "Why wouldn't I be?"

"I don't know. You look tired."

"I'm forty-three and eight months pregnant, Adam." She began slicing the cucumber into a large wooden salad bowl. "I *am* tired."

He stood there for a minute. "Okay. Well, you ought to take it easy. Mark here?"

She turned to him, a smile lighting up her face. "He's been sticking close to home for days. Just work and home. He's out in the backyard with Savannah. She wanted to show him how well she could swing all by herself now."

He crossed the kitchen toward the French doors that led out onto the deck. "Little dark and chilly for swinging in November at eight at night, isn't it?"

She rolled her eyes. "We have coats and lights here. She wanted to show her daddy."

Adam walked out onto the deck and closed the glass door behind him. In the shadows beyond the lamplight coming from two sconces he'd wired on either side of the doors himself, he spotted a hunched figure in a dark jacket sitting on the steps. Across the yard, illuminated by a large security lamp, Savannah sailed on a swing.

"Adam!" she shouted excitedly. "Liza Jane come?"

"'Fraid not," he called. "Sorry. Just me." He walked over to the step and sat down beside Mark, who didn't look at him. "Hey, buddy, how's it goin'?"

"Goin'," he answered flatly.

Adam nodded, watching Savannah swing higher and higher for a moment.

"Look at me, Daddy," she squealed with delight. "Look, I fly!"

Mark raised one hand. "I see you."

"How was your week?" Adam asked.

"Fine."

Adam reached down and buttoned up his jean jacket. It was chilly tonight. Winter was definitely on its way. It smelled like rain. "I saw Sophie inside. Brought the support check. She looks beat."

"She works too hard." Mark's tone remained without emotion. "She's doing inventory at the store."

Adam turned the ball of his foot back and forth on the step. "Saw her eye. Pretty nasty."

"She's gotten clumsy with this pregnancy. I tell her she needs to slow down."

Adam hesitated. He hated to voice what he was thinking, but he'd hate himself even more if he didn't ask, and there was something to his concern. "So that's what happened? She ran into the cabinet?"

Mark turned to look at him. "What are you asking me, Adam? Did I hit my wife?" he growled.

Adam glanced out over the dark yard. He'd always loved this yard. Once upon a time, he'd sat here on these steps and watched Liza Jane swing. "Did you?"

"I can't believe you would ask me such a thing."

Mark's bitterness was plain in his voice, and the bitterness wasn't about Sophie or her eye. It was about what had happened. About Laura. About how Adam had failed her. Failed Mark. Mark. He'd never been able to forgive Adam. Not any more than Adam could forgive himself.

"Of course I didn't *hit* her."

"Sorry, buddy." Adam rested his hand on Mark's shoulder for an instant. "I know you're having a rough time." He sighed, wishing now he hadn't asked. Of course Mark hadn't hit Sophie. He would never do such a thing.

Mark was watching Savannah again, or maybe he was just staring out into the dark.

"So how have you been doing? I mean it, man." Adam rubbed his hands together to warm them up. "I've been worried about you. You get some help like we talked about? A lot of people do. It's nothing to be ashamed of. Hey, if a guy like me—"

"I'm getting some help." He stood up abruptly. "Savannah, dinner." He walked up the steps, across the deck, and into the house.

Savannah leaped off the swing in midair and raced toward Adam, all bundled up in a pink coat and hand-knit gloves. In the dark like this, she looked so much like Liza Jane had at this age that it was eerie. What was really eerie was that they weren't even related by blood.

"You stayin' for dinner?" Savannah demanded. "We're havin' *pasghetti*."

He put out his hand, catching her smaller one. "Can't." They crossed the deck and he opened the door for her.

"Mama, Adam says he can't stay for dinner. I told him we was having *pasghetti*."

"We *were* having *spaghetti*," Sophie corrected. "Hang up your coat and wash your hands." She looked to Adam. "You sure you don't want to stay? There's plenty."

"Can't."

She set the salad bowl on the table. "Date?"

"Sort of." Adam halted in the doorway to the front hall. "Where'd Mark go? I should take off."

"Bathroom, I guess." She gave him a quick smile, opening the refrigerator to get something. "I'll tell him you said good-bye."

Adam took one more look at her black eye, but he didn't say anything. "Okay. Catch you later." He followed the sidewalk out to his Jeep, ignoring the too-tall grass that he sometimes wished still belonged to him.

Chapter Twenty

M.K. sat in her chair in the dark in front of the TV, volume turned down. Around her, she'd spread the files and notes she and Adam had so far amassed in the Chesapeake Bay College murders. On the end table beside her lay a frozen lasagna dinner she'd barely touched. A commercial had advertised that it tasted just like Mama Zito's; to M.K., it tasted mostly like cardboard and ketchup.

She sipped a glass of wine, but even that didn't taste particularly flavorful. She set down the glass and stared at the silent TV, watching the images come and go across the screen. An old John Wayne movie. While she normally enjoyed his movies, this one didn't seem to suit her any better than the lasagna or the wine.

She groaned out loud, frustrated. She had hours of work to do on the case, but tonight she just couldn't bring herself to reread another interview. She couldn't even bring herself to turn on the light beside the chair. The clues that would lead her to this killer just weren't here. She'd missed something, she was certain of it. She just couldn't figure out what.

She rubbed her tired eyes, refusing to allow herself to

think about Adam. It was stupid of her to have asked him out to eat tonight. He'd made it clear that he wasn't interested, for whatever reason, when he'd come for dinner, hadn't he? But then there'd been that kiss the morning she'd picked him up to go to the Tiffany Faulk crime scene. If he wasn't interested, why had he kissed her?

She closed her eyes. She had told herself she wasn't going to obsess over this like a thirteen-year-old, and she wasn't. She had a killer somewhere out there—close, she sensed— and she needed to find him before he found his next victim.

What she needed was a break. She needed to set the investigation aside for a day or two and not think about it.

It was a great idea—the question was, what was she going to do? She had no friends to speak of; a couple of women she'd worked with back in Quantico, but that was it. She had no hobbies. She belonged to no clubs or organizations, just the gym—and that was just another solitary activity. At least, she made it one.

On impulse, she picked up the phone and dialed her parents' house. Her mother picked up, of course; as far as M.K. knew, her father had never answered the phone in his life.

"Mama?"

"That you, dear?"

"Yeah, it's me. It's M.K."

"I really wish you'd use your given name."

M.K. drew her sock-covered feet up beneath her in the chair, feeling as if she was twelve again. That was as great a reprimand as her mother ever gave but, as a child, it had been enough to send her crying to her room. "I know, Mama."

"Is there something wrong?"

M.K. wiped at her eyes, fighting the lump in her throat. "What do you mean? Why do you ask?"

"Well, it's Friday," she said, as if it was obvious.

M.K. didn't understand what her mother meant for a moment; then she got it. She leaned forward, her free hand to her forehead. "Mama, I've told you before. We can talk any night of the week you like You can call me anytime. It doesn't have to be Saturday night."

"You're very busy." Her tone was cool. "You work long hours."

M.K. could hear water running. Her mother was probably cleaning up the kitchen. "I do work long hours, but I'm usually here at night."

"You should join a singles group at your church. Our singles group does nice things. They go out for coffee. Go to movies. Volunteer at the soup kitchen. It's not healthy for you to spend so much time alone. Not an unmarried woman your age."

M.K. closed her eyes for a moment, surprised her mother hadn't called her an old maid to her face. The fact that her eldest daughter was unmarried at thirty, and might well remain so, was a cross Mrs. James Shaughnessy found hard to bear. "How's Anna, Mama?"

"She's fine."

M.K. fiddled with the toe of her sock. "I . . . I was thinking about driving up tomorrow. Maybe taking Anna to a museum or something. Maybe spend the night tomorrow night," she said hesitantly. "If that would be all right."

"You could go to Mass with us Sunday morning," her mother answered excitedly. "And you'd stay for supper, wouldn't you? I got a nice ham at the Super Mart. And cabbage and potatoes."

"I'm not sure if I can stay that late Sunday."

"But you'll come tomorrow?"

M.K. heard a sound as if her mother was placing her hand on the receiver. "James, our daughter the FBI agent is coming to visit tomorrow," she heard her mother say, her voice muffled.

"Mama," M.K. said into the phone.

"She's staying the night and going to Mass with us Sunday

morning. She doesn't know if she can stay for ham and cabbage."

"Mama," M.K. repeated, trying to remain patient. She wasn't even in her parents' home yet, and she was already upset with them. "Maybe I can stay. We'll just have to see."

"Maybe she can stay for ham and cabbage," her mother called to her father in the den. "I'm so glad you're coming," she then said, this time directly into the phone. "You'll get a chance to say good-bye to Father Houlihan."

"That will be nice, Mama. I should be there by ten or eleven tomorrow. Can you have Anna ready? Maybe we'll go to the Franklin Institute of Science. She likes the activities there."

"She'll be thrilled," her mother said.

M.K. smiled. "So I'll see you tomorrow, Mama."

"I'll pray to St. Christopher and St. Valentine for traveling mercies for you."

"Thanks, Mama. Think you could pray to the patron saint of FBI agents in search of serial killers, too?"

"What, dear?"

"Never mind, Mama. I'll see you tomorrow."

M.K. hung up the phone as she got out of her chair, then poured her wine down the drain and dropped the frozen entrée into the trash can in the kitchen. As she went back through the living room, she snatched up the remote control off the end table. She punched the "power" button and the TV faded, leaving the room and the files scattered on the floor in darkness.

"So you know this place, too?" Adam sat back on the booth bench as the waitress walked away, taking their menus with her.

Valerie smiled across the table at him. "It's a good place to come. I don't quite feel like I'm committing a crime, the way I do in some places if I come in alone."

He grinned, nodding his head to an old tune by The Band. It was funny how kids Liza Jane's age were listening to the same kind of stuff he once listened to. "I know what you mean."

"So you're divorced, I take it?"

"Almost ten years." He glanced at the TV over the bar to see several familiar faces gathered to watch the basketball game. He hated basketball. "You?"

"Never been married."

"Two Labatts on tap," the waitress said, walking over to the table, a mug of beer in each hand. "Those sandwiches will be coming right up."

Adam grabbed one of the beers. "No hurry. Thanks." He lifted his mug. "How about, to solving this murder together before the bastard hits again?"

"To solving the case together." She tapped her mug to his and they both drank. "You know, not that I would wish anything so horrible on anyone, but I have to admit, it's been interesting to do these autopsies, work with the FBI. It can get pretty dull alone in that basement with mostly geriatrics who just die of old age." She took another sip of her beer and set the mug on the cardboard coaster that advertised a lager. "I mean, I do get the occasional coronary in a fifty-year-old."

"And auto accidents. You had those kids in August."

She fiddled with the coaster. "Yeah, that's true. And there's at least one drowning every summer."

"Damn, you make my job look cheery."

Her laugh was almost a giggle.

"I know, it does sound rather morbid, doesn't it?" She glanced around the pub as if she feared someone might hear her. "What would even be more morbid," she whispered, leaning over the table, "would be to say that I actually enjoy my work. Most of the time, at least. When I'm not pushing papers."

"We've certainly got our share of that with the Bureau."

He took another drink from his mug. "But you have that assistant, right?"

"He's only part-time. He helps out going to the scenes, declaring people dead, but he doesn't do the autopsies." She looked around and chuckled, cutting her eyes in the direction of a table of college students nearby trying to listen in on their conversation. "Maybe we should change the subject."

"Maybe," he agreed with a grin.

For the next hour, they talked. Not about anything in particular. A little about the Chesapeake Bay College murders in vague terms so no one who overheard them might be able to follow along, but mostly they talked about nothing in particular: what was in the newspapers, the price of gas, the cold winter the Farmer's Almanac was predicting. Adam found it easy to talk to Valerie. She wasn't just beautiful and sexy, she was obviously very intelligent and had a great sense of humor. Their chicken sandwiches and fries came and they ate. The waitress took away their plates and brought them their check.

Adam looked at his watch. In the past two hours, the pub had gotten busier, more crowded and louder, so they had both found themselves leaning over the table to be heard. "I guess I should get going. I've got this old sailboat I've been restoring. I'm supposed to be meeting a guy at the shipyard early tomorrow. He's going to give me a price on some teak."

"I used to love sailing." Valerie began applying her lipstick.

Adam had always been fascinated that women could do that without a mirror. He couldn't keep from watching as she outlined her sensual mouth. "Oh, yeah? Used to, meaning you don't sail anymore?"

She shrugged, pursing her lips as she twisted down the thin silver tube and dropped it into her purse. "It never seems like I have any free time anymore. At least not lately. This upcoming inspection at the morgue is running me ragged."

"Well, I don't get out much, either. Not like I'd like to."

He chuckled, finishing the last of his beer. "And my boat probably won't be done until I'm headed for a nursing home, but maybe we could go out sailing some time. I have some friends who'll let me borrow a sailboat for the day."

She met his gaze. "I'd like that, Adam," she said, laying her hand over his on the table.

For a second he wasn't sure what to do. He guessed he knew Valerie was interested in him. M.K. certainly brought the subject up often enough, but it hadn't occurred to him that she might make a move on him. Now he felt stupid. Was this why she'd asked him out to eat in the first place?

Adam looked down and then up again. "Look, Val . . ."

It must have been his tone, because she slid her hand off his and across the table. "Oops," she said.

He smiled. "I'm sorry. I didn't mean to—"

"No, no." She held up her hand, obviously a little embarrassed, too. "It's my fault. I asked you out and made it sound like it was a work thing."

She made eye contact again, which he respected. This was no shrinking violet, Dr. Valerie Wood. She went after what she wanted, but she wasn't a spoilsport. While he knew now he really wasn't interested sexually, his admiration for her grew.

"It's not you, Val." He leaned back in the booth. "It's just that I'm sort of involved . . ." He stopped and started again. "Thinking about getting involved, although it would be a really bad idea. Career-wise, at least."

"Aha," she said. "Your partner, Special Agent Shaughnessy. I thought I spotted a little glimmer in her eye the last time I saw the two of you together."

"Oh, yeah?" He grinned, looking down at the table. "It's just weird, you know. Working together. She's very different from my ex-wife, from the women I've dated in the past."

"Tough nut to crack, is she?"

"I suppose. I mean, it's not like she doesn't have a lot on

her mind. We are in the middle of a case involving a serial killer."

Valerie nodded, grimacing. "True. But I can see her appeal, why you find her attractive. She seems very smart and . . . vulnerable in a way men like."

"I don't know about that." He lifted his brows. "You should see her firing range scores."

She chuckled. "Anyway, I apologize if I've embarrassed you." She reached for the check lying on the table between them.

"You haven't embarrassed me. I'm flattered. What man wouldn't be? You're a very attractive woman, Valerie. Now, let me pay that." He reached for the check in her hand. "It's the least I can do."

She snatched it away before he could get hold of it. "Most certainly not. I invited you out. I practically leaped into your lap. I'm paying." She grabbed her leather jacket and purse. "Do me a favor, though?"

He reached for his jean jacket. "Sure."

"You swing and miss with Special Agent Shaughnessy, will you give me a call?"

He grinned. "You bet."

Valerie paid the bill at the bar, and Adam walked her to her car, which was parked on the street. After they said good night, he continued to his Jeep half a block away. Inside, he started the engine and turned up the heat full blast. He felt antsy. Restless. His mind was flying in a hundred different directions. He wished he'd accepted M.K.'s dinner invitation. He hadn't heard from Liza Jane all week. He was worried about Mark. About Sophie. The case was eating at him. The case ten years ago was eating at him, too. He wished he had gone out to eat with M.K.

Adam stared out the windshield. He wasn't ready to go home to his place. It was dark there, lonely. All he'd do was sit in the dark and stare at the TV. He thought about going back into the pub for another beer, or maybe down the street to O'Shea's. He felt like talking to someone, even if it was the guy or girl on the bar stool beside him.

Instead, he pulled his cell phone out of his jacket pocket and dialed M.K.'s number. After three rings, he pulled the phone away from his ear to hang up. Obviously she'd found someone willing to have dinner with her. Served him right.

"Hello?"

It was M.K.'s voice. Sleepy.

"Hello?" she repeated.

"It's Adam," he said, not even sure now why he'd called. Just needed to hear her voice, maybe.

"Hey," she said.

"You asleep? It's only"—he checked his watch—"five after ten."

"Yeah, I know. Just beat, I guess. Long week."

She sounded more clearheaded now. He imagined her lying alone in her bed in the dark. He imagined himself lying beside her. He missed not having anyone to hold at night. To hold him.

"I'm sorry. I didn't mean to wake you."

"Adam, it's okay. What's up? You still at work?"

"On my way home." It wasn't a lie. He was. "I was thinking about the case."

"You come up with anything brilliant?"

"Not hardly. I was just wondering if we needed to have a chat with Patrick Purnell." It actually had been on his mind.

"Why do you say that?"

She was fully awake now. He had her attention.

"I don't know. He comes and goes all over that campus on that damned golf cart of his. People see him all the time—they see him so often that he's sort of invisible. You know what I mean?" He flipped the car heater to defrost. He was fogging up the windows.

"Yeah, I guess so. You wonder if someone saw him or saw

something and doesn't even remember it. But . . ." She was quiet for a second. Thinking. "The same goes for Buddy Caruso, doesn't it? Creepy pizza guy. Running all over town after dark. Coming and going in dorms, even the school buildings."

"Maybe you're right," he conceded. "We'll just be rehashing what we already have."

"I really think we're missing something, Adam. Something right under our noses. Did you catch Dr. Wood before she left her office? I'd really like to see the autopsy reports, not just the death certificates. I'd like to go over the details." She was quiet for a second and then she sighed. When she spoke again her tone of voice was different. More intimate. She was speaking to Adam the man rather than Adam the FBI agent. "This is really worrying me, Adam. I know we're not supposed to let it get personal, let it get to us, but . . ."

"I hear you." He found himself gripping the steering wheel with his free hand. It was the eeriest thing, but he felt as if he was experiencing a flash of déjà vu. He and Mark had had almost the same exchange of words what seemed like a million years ago. "But . . . but you shouldn't," he managed. "You can't be as effective as you need to be if you let yourself get too close to the case."

"I know. You're right."

She sounded so solid. So grounded. Adam envied her youth. Her strength. "Hey, you want to get together tomorrow? I know it's Saturday, but we could go back over Purnell and Caruso's statements? Get a jump-start on Monday?"

She hesitated long enough before answering for him to think what a jerk he was. She'd asked him out tonight and he'd declined because he was afraid of having a relationship with her. Now he was trying to hook up with her because he was afraid if he didn't, nothing would ever come out of whatever it was they were feeling.

"Um. Can't. I promised my mom I'd come to Philly tomorrow. Take my little sister to the Franklin Institute. She has Down's syndrome. It's hard on my mom. I feel like I need to help out more."

"I understand. I didn't even know you had a sister."

"Seven."

"Seven?" he choked.

"Good Catholic family."

"Of course, Mildred Karen. Why am I surprised?"

"You really need to give up on that."

He grinned, enjoying the fact that he could still get her goat with his juvenile game. He eased his grip on the steering wheel. "Yeah, I know."

"So I'll see you first thing Monday A.M.?"

He could almost hear her smiling. He liked it when he made her smile. It made him smile. "See you Monday A.M., bright and early."

"'Night, Adam," she said softly. Kind of sexy.

"'Night." He hung up and headed for home, no longer feeling the need to warm a bar stool or talk to strangers.

Sophie stood in front of the bathroom sink, looking into the mirror as she squirted goat-milk lotion into her hand. Rubbing it in, she grimaced at the face in the mirror. She thought the prenatal vitamins were supposed to be so good for your hair and complexion. She had more zits these days than she had when she was Liza Jane's age. So maybe they were only good for you up to a certain age . . .

With a sigh of resignation, she flipped the bathroom light off and, still rubbing the cream into her dry hands, walked into the dark bedroom. She was so relieved that Mark hadn't gone out tonight. She'd get a good night's sleep, not having to worry about where he was or what he was doing.

She sat down on the edge of the bed and listened to his steady breathing. "You still awake?" she asked quietly. She missed him. Missed the closeness they'd shared before.

"I'm still awake," he answered.

She slid under the flannel sheet and bull's eye quilt she'd made. "Adam was acting strange tonight, don't you think? I thought he was acting strange." She didn't want to push Mark. She certainly didn't want to anger him. But she felt like she had to try to act normal. Otherwise, how would they ever feel normal again?

"No. I didn't think so. He seemed fine," Mark's voice came out of the darkness emotionless, as if he had no feeling left inside.

Pleased that he answered at all, she rolled over on her side to face him, her arm around her belly that seemed more like a beach ball under her shirt every day. "No, he was definitely acting strangely. I'm worried about him."

"Adam can take care of himself."

"I know." She stared through the dark at Mark and hesitantly reached out to lay her hand on his bare stomach. He'd lost weight, but he was still muscular. He had a good body for a man in his mid-forties who worked a desk job pushing papers. "Liza Jane said something about him dating his partner. You know, M.K."

"He's not the kind of guy who dates other agents. He usually likes his women a little slow, preferably with big tits."

"Well, thanks a lot," she joked, not really offended. She knew what he meant. Since the divorce, he preferred to be unencumbered.

Mark didn't laugh.

Sophie rested her head on her pillow again, her hand still on Mark's stomach. His bare skin was warm. It felt so good beneath her fingertips. She missed him so much . . . missed making love with him. It had been months since they'd made love.

"Do you think he told her?"

"Sophie, I'm beat."

"I know," she whispered. "But do you think he did?"

"Told her what?"

There was an edge to his voice now, and for a moment she considered just letting it go. Just rolling over and going to sleep, her back to her husband the way they had been doing for months. But something inside couldn't let it go. She wasn't in love with Adam anymore. But she still loved him. She still cared about him and he was still their daughter's father. "You know, Mark," she whispered, "it's coming up on ten years."

"You think I don't know that?" he spat.

She rolled onto her back, fighting the tears that welled suddenly in her eyes. Pregnancy made her emotional. She'd been the same way with Savannah.

"Sophie." Mark's voice startled her.

"Yes?"

"He didn't tell her. It's not his way. Don't worry about him. He's dealing with it just fine."

She wanted to say, *Just like you are?* but she didn't because she knew that would anger him, and then . . .

Sophie closed her eyes. "I'm glad you're here, Mark. Here with me."

"Are you?"

"Yes," she whispered. And she meant it. "We'll get through this. We'll be happy again. You'll see. You'll be happy again."

"I hope you're right."

She closed her eyes, praying fervently. "I hope so, too," she whispered.

Chapter Twenty-one

I try to sleep, but I cannot. I open my eyes and stare at the dark ceiling.

I try to pretend that everything is all right. That it will be all right, but I know that it is not true. I know that Dr. Fisher's treatment is not helping. I know that I am getting worse.

I feel as if I am two people, torn apart during the day when I must go to work and do what must be done, be who the people around me expect me to be. I find myself actually pursuing my tasks, because they are expected of me, in a way that could be harmful to my very existence. I suppose I am a perfectionist in everything I do.

After work, I come home and I must meld these two people into one. Find myself again. Only I am finding it harder and harder to bring them together at the end of each day.

I rise quietly. Slip out of bed.

I am lonely and the TV calls me. The screen is dark now. Silent. But I have only to turn it on, hit "play" on the VCR, and they will all be there. The companions I feel I know now, just as I knew those companions years ago. It's funny how people can pretend to be your friends and then turn on you when you are the most vulnerable.

I do not remember putting on my robe or entering the dark living room. I do not remember turning on the TV, but suddenly Axel is there. He is speaking directly to me, inviting me to stay tuned next week for a big announcement concerning the show.

The announcement worries me.

I hit "pause" on the remote and stare for a moment at the screen, at his handsome face. I want to hate him for what he has done to me, the memories he has stirred, but I cannot. I cannot hate him because he seems to be all that is wonderful in the world. All that is right. I long to be Axel. But there are others I long to be.

Anyone but myself.

"Mmm, dinner smells good," M.K. said, walking up behind her mother to kiss her cheek in an unusual demonstration of affection. She loved her mother, but they had never gotten along. Not when M.K. was the oldest child in a household with too many children and not enough money. Not now.

As M.K. grew to adulthood, the fissure between them only widened. Neither seemed to ever be able to understand the life choices the other had made. M.K. could not fathom why her mother would devote her entire life to being James Shaughnessy's wife and a mother to his children, and her mother could not understand M.K. wanting to be something, *someone,* more than that.

Her mother turned and smiled, her drab navy Sunday dress covered with a flowered apron that made her look far older than her fifty-two years. "So you'll stay?"

M.K.'s gaze drifted to the 1970s wallpaper with the red roosters behind the stove that was so out of place in the South Philly row house. She always thought that the pattern, which had once been a bright red, belonged in a farmhouse in a big country kitchen. She remembered when her mother had bought it on sale at Woolworth's and put it up herself. Now it was faded by time, stained with grease and water damage from the leaky roof. It seemed as worn out and without hope as Margaret Shaughnessy. "I'll stay, Mama."

"Good, because I've invited Mrs. Crosier and her son over. You know them—they live on the next block over. You went to St. Francis with Joey."

M.K. leaned on the back of the old wooden chair pulled up to the same Formica table that had been here when she was a child. She'd offered to buy her mother a kitchen table last Christmas, and the Christmas before that, but Margaret Shaughnessy would take no *charity*, not even from her daughter. "Mama, why would you invite Mrs. Crosier and her son? I thought this was just going to be a family dinner. Just us."

"Mrs. Crosier's daughter-in-law passed away last year, God rest her soul." She crossed herself. "Left poor Joey with the twins and a seven-year-old. He's had to move in with his mother so she can help with the children."

"Mama, that's all very sad, but why would you invite them?"

Her mother wiped her chapped, red-raw hands on her apron, not making eye contact. "Joey's looking for a nice girl. Martha knows what a nice girl you are. She remembers you from St. Francis."

M.K. closed her eyes for a moment, mortified. "Mama, you didn't tell Mrs. Crosier I was looking for a husband."

"He's such a nice boy. He didn't deserve this." She shook her head as she opened the glass-front cupboard and pulled out a stack of chipped dinner plates. "A welder. Did I tell you he's a union welder? Makes good money. Benefits. A good provider."

M.K.'s first impulse was to jump all over her mother for suggesting she needed a man to provide for her, but she knew exactly where the conversation would go from there. They'd get into an argument over Mrs. Crosier's son that really wasn't about him at all, but about the fact that M.K.

would never be who her parents wanted her to be. She would stomp off, get in her car without saying good-bye. Her mother would stand at the stove with her stinking ham and cabbage, hurt, too proud to consider she might be wrong.

M.K. lifted her head. "Where's Da?"

She pointed to the back door.

"Still sneaking smokes?"

"I don't know what he does out there," her mother snipped. "It's not my concern. Not when I still have the biscuits to make."

M.K. stepped out onto the crumbling brick patio and closed the door behind her. It was cold out and the wind whipped through the gaping holes in the stockade fence that separated the backyard from the alley behind the row houses. She hugged herself for warmth, glad she had brought the navy suit to wear to Mass this morning instead of the drab flowered dress she knew her mother would have preferred.

She spotted her father from the back, his bad leg propped on a broken picnic table bench, hunched inside his stained canvas jacket, a wool cabby's hat on his balding head. "Not smokin' those fags again, are you, Da?" she called.

He didn't even look over his shoulder at her; he just took another puff of the unfiltered cigarette. Smoke curled over his head, dissipating in the wind that stank of ham and cabbage and burning leaves. "No need to tell your Mama. It will only worry her." Forty years in Philadelphia and he still held dearly to his Dublin accent.

"I'm not going to tell," M.K. scoffed. "You've been hiding out here, smoking, for as long as I can remember."

"She says it's not good for my health," he grumbled.

"Hasn't killed you yet." She walked over to stand beside him. "I guess we all need our little indulgences." She stared over the weatherworn, gray fence to the empty lot across the alley that seemed to hold her father's attention. It was filled with brown weeds, clogged with fast food wrappers, old newspapers, beer and soda cans. "We all need a little something to get us through the day, don't we, Da?"

Her father hooked his forefinger around the cigarette in his mouth and turned to her, his plaid cabby's hat pulled low over his forehead. His craggy face was as worn and gray as the fence. "Been reading in the paper 'bout your wee problem."

M.K. arched one brow. This was the longest conversation she could recall ever having with her father. Certainly the first he'd ever initiated. "That right? And what little problem would that be?" She didn't know why what he said put her on the defensive. Maybe because she'd been defending herself, her ideas, her choices since she was old enough to cross the street without him.

"The one killing the college kids."

"I see." M.K. buttoned up her jacket and slipped her hands into the pockets. "So what do you think?"

He gazed out over the fence again. A pink bubblegum wrapper flitted through the trampled weeds where kids had cut a path through the empty lot. "What would I know you feds don't already know? C'mere, I'm naught but a retired beat cop. Naught but an Irish Mick."

M.K. found herself fingering the Miraculous Medal given to her by her long-dead Aunt Katherine. It gave her something to do with her hands rather than strangling her father. "Da, you have something to say or not?"

"You don't know who it is?"

"We have suspects." She chipped at the frozen dirt under her feet with the toe of her sensible loafer. "But no, we don't know who it is—otherwise, we'd have arrested the son of a gun."

"Show some respect, lass. Shot in the line of duty, I was."

"I know, Da. Twice. But you refused to retire on a disability, didn't you? You put in your twenty-five years, never taking a sick day once, except the days you were in the hospital. Didn't matter how much pain you were in, did it?"

He drew on the cigarette and the end glowed. Smoke eased from his nostrils. "It be one of your own."

"What?"

He took one last pull on the cigarette glowing dangerously close to his gray lips, and then skillfully flicked it to the bench with his finger. "You heard me." He ground it out with the toe of his work boot.

"Da, how—"

"Look at the evidence, lass."

"There isn't any."

"My point." He cut his gray eyes at her.

"Da, I don't understand."

He leaned closer to her. "Look around you, daughter. This killer knows the work of a cop. Knows how an investigation is done."

"Da, that's crazy."

He shrugged, smaller than he had once been inside the old coat.

M.K. gazed out over the fence again. The idea was crazy. A cop? Like who? One of the Ashview police? Chief Seipp? The rookie who was at every scene? An FBI agent?

It was ludicrous. Absurd.

But it would explain why there was never any evidence at the scene. Why each murder had been without a single witness. The perpetrator was smart; he was smart, and he knew what the cops would be looking for when they showed up.

M.K. was already cold, but the thought chilled her to the very bone, a kind of chill you couldn't shake.

He was wrong. He had to be. What did James Shaughnessy know about serial murder cases? He was a street cop. He walked the beat, kept an eye on South Philly businesses, broken up the occasional domestic disturbance, directed traffic on holidays and parade days. He wasn't a detective; he hadn't been trained to investigate as she had been.

"I better go inside," her father grunted. "Your mother will worry."

M.K. watched him cut across the tiny yard, surrounded by the high fence and the poverty of his generation of Irish immigrants who had worked hard, giving up their own dreams, to put their children through college.

She fought a pang of regret, knowing what a disappointment she was to him, and hurried to catch up and open the door for him.

M.K. was barely out of the old neighborhood, on 95-South, when she punched Adam's number into her cell phone.

"'Lo."

"It's M.K."

"Hey. What's up?" He sounded glad to hear from her.

"I had a thought today." She switched lanes, around a slow-moving paneled van, and started again. She didn't want to tell him it was her father's idea because she didn't want to talk about him. Not with Adam, not with anyone. "I know this is going to sound crazy, but—"

"What's that?" Adam said louder than he needed to. "I'm only getting every other word. A lot of static."

She pulled the phone from her ear, keeping one eye on the road as she checked out the phone's display panel. Two bars; he should have been able to hear her, but she could hear the static, too. "Adam? Any better?"

"A little. Maybe. What's up?"

She wasn't even positive she wanted to offer the new theory, even if it actually did make sense. Maybe she needed to think it through. She was so desperate that maybe she was grasping at straws, taking her father's notions for lack of her own.

But that was what partners were for, weren't they? To bounce ideas off?

"M.K.?"

There was a little static, but she could hear him just fine. "Yeah, I'm here."

"Here, where?"

She glanced in her rearview mirror, switching lanes again. Traffic was pretty light and she was anxious to get home, to start going over notes again. Applying the new theory. "I'm in my car."

"I know that!"

"Adam, listen to me. We have almost no evidence, right? First, the murders look like accidents. The evidence we do have, the autopsies, the tox reports, they all come back appearing to be accidents. Then, when our killer loses his control and just goes out and murders, even then, there's almost no evidence left behind. The murders take place outside, where physical evidence is difficult to collect. There are no witnesses."

"So our guy's smart. Right. We already know that. Serial killers are smart—often they're geniuses. What's your point?"

"Adam, what if the killer knows police procedure? What if he knows how we collect evidence, what we look for? He knows this information, it makes it harder to get caught, right?"

He didn't say anything. There was more static.

"You still there?" she asked.

"M.K., that's crazy."

"It's not crazy," she insisted. "We're supposed to look at every angle, right? I'm just trying to look at what we have from a fresh angle. That's all."

"It's not a cop, M.K.," he said dryly. "No one on the Ashview police department is bright enough to chew his tobacco and drive his cruiser at the same time. They're certainly not bright enough to be serial killers."

She groaned, switching her steering wheel and phone hands. "So maybe it's not one of them. What if it's—"

"One of us?" he laughed. Only it wasn't a funny-haha laugh. He was making fun of her.

"Or someone from the sheriff's department or the campus police," she pressed on. "A state trooper. A security cop who used to be a policeman? I don't know, Adam."

"M.K. . . . " He started to say something, then stopped. "Why don't we talk about this tomorrow?" he asked after another stretch of silence. "It might have to be later in the week. I've got to take a personal day or two to take care of something, and I may have to fly to New York to meet with someone in connection with this damned dockworkers' case that won't go anywhere but won't go away."

M.K. didn't like being put off by him, but maybe it was better to do a little investigating herself first. After all, it was just a theory. Her father hadn't seen any of the evidence. All he had was what he'd read in the *Philadelphia Inquirer.*

"You still there?" Adam asked.

M.K. turned up the heater in the car a notch. "Still here."

"We'll talk about it as soon as I get in the office. Now listen, while I have you, I was wondering . . ."

She waited.

"There's this benefit ball my dad's in charge of coming up. Big hoopla at the hospital where he works. It's next Saturday night. Everyone in my family goes. We always have. Even Sophie, even though we aren't married anymore."

"This coming Saturday night?"

"Yeah."

"And you're asking me out? To go?"

"No. Well, yeah, sort of, I suppose."

She was short on patience tonight. Her parents had wrung just about the last drop of it out of her over the ham and cabbage supper with guests Mrs. Crosier and her wonder son, Joey. "It's a simple question, Adam. A yes or a no."

"You have a bad weekend?"

"Adam!"

"Okay, okay. Yeah, I guess I am asking you out. It's black tie. You could pull one of your fancy, low-cut gowns from your closet and—"

"I don't have any fancy gowns, low-cut or otherwise."

"So buy one. Borrow one. Come on, M.K.," he begged, using that tone of his that she just knew other women fell for. A tone she could easily fall for if she didn't watch herself. "All work and no play make FBI agents dull boys and girls."

"You want me to go to a *ball*?" she asked dryly.

"Yeah. It could be fun."

"I somehow doubt that."

"So that's a yes?"

"Sorry, losing the reception again," M.K. lied. "Talk to you later." She hung up the cell phone and tossed it on the seat beside her.

Where in heaven's name was she going to get a ball gown?

Chapter Twenty-two

Jerome sat at his desk, tapping his pen on his blotter, waiting for the door to open and Mrs. Elright to announce his patient's arrival. He was nervous about this appointment with Blue, unsure quite how he would undertake the subject of the patient being a hermaphrodite. Ordinarily, he didn't lack confidence in his abilities, but the issue, mixed with his concern that the patient could be far more mentally ill than had first appeared, and the fact that he had been up all night with Sela, led to a discomfort he couldn't shake.

Sela had been in a great deal of pain last night and the usual dose of the diamorphine had seemed to barely touch it. It was the first time he'd seen her cry in all these months of her torturous treatment, and he'd ended up calling her physician at three in the morning. When the on-call doctor didn't return his call, Jerome had increased his wife's medication anyway, guessing at how much would put her to sleep without making her comatose. He'd felt guilty because even though he was licensed to prescribe medication, he didn't know enough about pain management to prescribe such a powerful and potentially lethal drug. One could have made a case for incompetence if something, God forbid, had happened. But Sela had fallen asleep at last, and Jerome had realized at that moment that he would have been willing to surrender his practice, even rotted in jail, to give her just those few hours of pain-free sleep.

The sound of the doorknob turning startled him and he glanced up.

"Dr. Fisher—"

"Yes, show the patient in," he said, rising from his desk, not allowing Mrs. Elright to complete her sentence.

Blue entered the office and took the appropriate seat.

Jerome retrieved the file folder from his desk as well as his notepad and sat in the other chair. "So how were you this week?" he asked, adjusting his glasses on his nose as he poised his pen over the notepad.

Blue's gaze shifted to the thick file on Jerome's lap, labeled with the patient's name in bold-print letters on the tab. "I see the records arrived." It was a soft voice. Hesitant.

"Yes, yes, they did, and I must say, I wish you had told me from the beginning that you were a hermaphrodite," Jerome chastised gently.

"Because it changes everything."

"No, not everything." He glanced up over the black frames of his glasses. Sela had picked out the half frames for him on the last trip she had made to the mall. The last she would probably ever make.

She had once loved shopping, but had become too weak to walk and refused a wheelchair in public. She had said the new glasses made him look scholarly. He hoped that right now they at least led to an air of credibility.

"It answers some questions, though," Jerome explained. "Especially since you are a *true* hermaphrodite." He hesitated, shifting in his chair. "Blue, because you possess both male and female chromosome make-up, it only makes sense that you would experience an attraction to both males and females."

Blue gazed at the expensive Oriental carpet at their feet.

"I assume you take hormone treatments."

Blue nodded.

"And there is mention of surgery, but not performed when you were a child as is generally done in these cases."

A head shake. "My . . . my parents refused to take the doctors' advice and choose a sex for me at birth because I had both male and female genitals. They . . . they thought it would be better to allow me to mature, become the person I would become, and then make a choice on my own."

"How old were you when you made the choice?"

Blue did not respond immediately, and Jerome had to fight the sense of empathy he felt for his patient. It was not the proper way for a psychiatrist to treat an individual. Usually, he had no problem controlling his sentiments, but today— no, with Blue in general—he had to constantly check himself. He supposed it was due to the raw emotions being stirred each day with Sela's illness.

"I . . . I suppose I was a senior in high school when I knew for sure, or thought I did. It wasn't until after my sophomore year in college that the surgery was performed."

When Blue's gaze met Jerome's, he felt the full force of his patient's anguish. He also saw a flash of anger beyond the pain. Anger so intense, so frightening, that Jerome gazed down at his notes to sever eye contact. He cleared his throat. "Well, with this development, I may need to shift our strategy slightly, but I don't want you to be concerned. I've spoken with my wife, also a psychiatrist, and she assures me there is protocol for patients such as yourself. I have already—"

"You discussed my case with your wife?" Blue demanded.

The patient's alarmed tone made Jerome glance up again. "Yes . . . but she's also a psychiatrist. She must follow the same rule of physician/patient confidentiality."

"Dr. Fisher," the patient said tensely, gripping the arms of the leather chair, "I made it very clear to you from the beginning that it was my utmost priority not to allow what you see here, what is in those records, to go beyond these walls. My career could not tolerate disclosure."

There was something about the manner in which Blue spoke that was eerie . . . almost frightening. Jerome struggled to maintain his composure. He shouldn't have come to work today, not after being up most of the night. He just wasn't himself. "I assure you, Dr. Sela Fisher is required by law to follow the very same regulations concerning patient confidentiality that I am. Sometimes it is necessary for a physician to consult with another physician. I would never, however, ever disclose your name. Not even to my wife," he promised.

"It's just that I have taken a great risk in coming to you," Blue said quietly, looking down again. "My risk increased by allowing you full disclosure of my previous treatment. My . . . condition."

"I understand that, and I appreciate your desire to help me help you." Jerome tried to smile reassuringly. "Now let's start the way we like to start every week. Tell me about your journal entries and we'll go on from there."

For the next forty minutes, Jerome tried to engage his patient in conversation, but Blue seemed either unwilling, or unable, to participate. While talkative and relatively adept at expressing feelings in previous sessions, the patient barely said more than a dozen words throughout the remainder of the time they had together.

When their time was up, Jerome escorted Blue to the door. "I'd like to see you again before the weekend. Would that be possible?"

The patient did not meet his gaze. "I'll have to check my schedule. I'm finding my job . . . my personal life stressful presently."

Jerome nodded. "That's perfectly understandable. Perhaps you could check your schedule and call Mrs. Elright. I don't normally have hours on Friday, not since my wife became ill, but I'd be happy to meet you here Friday if it would be more convenient."

"I'll call if it's possible."

Trying to fight an oppressive sinking feeling in the pit of his stomach, Jerome watched the patient leave the office. He had not brought up the subject of suicide, and he was concerned that perhaps he should have.

The phone rang as Jerome stood in the doorway, and Mrs. Elright answered it with her usual cool efficiency.

"The nurse on line three, Dr. Fisher," she said.

Jerome stepped back into his office, closing the door to take the call.

I sit in my chair watching the TV, unable to concentrate even though *Fraternity Row* is on and there has been a serious development at Phi Kappa Alpha. A fraternity brother, Jason, was caught cheating on an English exam and it is suspected by college officials that one of the brothers in the house provided the answers. Axel has insisted that if anyone provided Jason, who has already been expelled, with the copy of the test, then they should give themselves up. School officials are threatening to break up the fraternity and close the house.

I am sincerely interested in what will become of Phi Kappa Alpha because I know that they deserve to be shut down. They all deserve to be expelled, if not for this incident, then others they have not been caught for. I know firsthand that this is the case among all fraternities and sororities. Among students this age.

Axel is talking to his father by telephone, but Mr. Cunningham, who is an attorney, will not allow the students to tape the conversation, so the audience is only able to hear one side of the exchange.

I glance down at the pictures I have cut out from a magazine and spread across the floor. I am recording the show, as I have recorded all of them, so I will watch it later when I am not so distracted.

On the floor are several pictures that caught my eye in magazines, but the one that I cannot stop thinking about is that of a distinguished-looking African-American man. It is not as good a picture as I would like; I had to cut away an attractive female who was seated on the couch beside him.

My session with Dr. Fisher today did not go well. I feel I have made an error in judgment in agreeing to allow him to see my previous records. I should have given him more time, been more patient with myself. I could tell by the way he looked at me that he is more concerned for the state of my mental health than he was previously.

I lean over in my comfy chair and pick the picture up off the carpet. He is a handsome man, Dr. Fisher. Intelligent. Caring. Compassionate. That is obvious in the way that he is caring for his dying wife. I pity him. Losing a loved one to such a terrible disease as cancer. I know that it cannot be easy to watch a loved one die in such pain.

I shift my gaze to the collage propped against the table beside the chair. I have been smart enough to realize I could not keep the objects, at least not here, any longer: the ballcap, the lock of hair, the ear, the finger, and the breast. They have been safely tucked away. The collage is all I have now readily available to remind me of my accomplishments.

I study the boys in the Jeep, the blonde on the bar stool, the football jock, the spectacled young man with the calculator, and the cheerleader, now reunited with the football player in my work of art. I have even added some appropriate props to fill in some of the white spaces: pom-poms, a calculator, a chilled margarita glass.

I look down at the picture in my hand, then back at my collage. The doctor does not fit.

Not tonight, at least.

* * *

Liza Jane sat on the edge of her bed in her dorm room and looked at the cell phone in her hand.

"So, are you going to call him or not?" her roommate, Muriel, said, drying her wet hair with a striped towel. "You've been sitting there for ten minutes with the phone."

"I know." Liza Jane twisted her mouth in indecision. "I was just thinking I shouldn't go."

"No way! Cam stands you up at the last minute and you're just not going to go?"

"He's not standing me up. I told you, he had something really, really, really important come up. Besides, it's not like he's my boyfriend or anything." She hadn't told Muriel about her suspicion that he was sleeping with someone. Maybe because she didn't care that much. She liked him, but she didn't like him that much.

"I know. And he has to fly to New York tomorrow and he won't be back until Sunday." Muriel frowned. "He's standing you up."

Liza Jane looked at the cell phone again, the number already called up on the screen. "Maybe I just shouldn't go. It's really not my thing, getting all dressed up, rubbing elbows with doctors, bigwigs from the college and stuff."

"You said you've been going since you were fifteen." Muriel dropped her wet towel on the floor. "Your grandfather will be disappointed if you don't go."

"I know," Liza Jane moaned. "I've just . . ." She jiggled her foot. "I've never come out and asked a guy out before, not like this."

"Then here, give me the phone and I'll do it for you, you chicken." Muriel tried to snag the phone, but Liza Jane jumped up off the bed, turning her back to her roomie.

"Okay, okay. I'll do it." She wrinkled her nose. "You really think I should? He's older than I am."

"So's Cam."

"Okay, so he's geekier."

Muriel laughed as she began to spray gel into her wet hair and run her fingers through it. "I've got news for you, Liza. You're a geek, too. Just one with cool dreads. Now either you call him and ask him to take you to the hospital benefit ball right now or I'm calling him. You have to give the guy time to rent a tux."

Liza Jane took a deep breath. Muriel was right. She knew she was. Her grandfather would be so disappointed if she didn't go to the ball. Besides, she wanted to talk to the dean of students and see what she could find out about what had happened at Phi Kappa Alpha. Even though nothing official had been announced yet, there were too many rumors going around for people not to know it wasn't just a rumor. If the college shut down the fraternity, that might be the end of Axel and Cam's deal and the positive publicity Chesapeake Bay College would get out of it. Needless to say, the college could use some positive publicity right now. A girl who worked as a clerk in the dean of students' office told Liza Jane there'd been a big meeting the day before and a lot of shouting had been involved.

The ball would also be a good opportunity to talk with her father's new not-girlfriend about the murders at the college. As far as she could tell, the FBI had made no progress in the investigation, but she knew they were working long hours on it. There was stuff on the news and in the papers every day. Surely they knew *something*, and while her father might not give it up, talking girl to girl with M.K., she just might. Especially after she'd had a few glasses of the champagne that always flowed so freely at these things. Maybe she'd try to get in good with Liza Jane the way her father's girlfriends always did, but maybe Liza Jane would actually get something out of it for once.

She hit "send" on the phone. It rang twice.

"Hello?"

"Jesse, hey, it's Liza Jane."

"You go, girl," Muriel whispered loudly.

Liza Jane waved her hand for her friend to be quiet and turned her back on her.

"Hey, Liza Jane. You makin' out okay with that Internet research?" he asked. "I was thinking about calling you to ask, but I didn't want to be a pest or a jerk or anything about it."

"I haven't found a lot, but yeah, I'm doing okay. I haven't had as much time as I'd like to spend on it right now," she went on, stalling as she tried to figure how to ask him out without making him feel like he had to go with her if he didn't want to. "You know, the semester will be over before I know it, and things have been crazy at the newspaper and the station—"

"Ask him!" Muriel insisted.

Liza Jane glared at her roommate and turned away again. "Listen, Jesse, the reason I called—and you can say no, no problem, but . . . I was wondering. I have this benefit ball to go to. It's for the hospital and it's kind of a big deal in my family. I've got free tickets and my grandfather is in charge and, well—"

"Liza Jane, are you trying to ask me out?"

She was amazed at how different he seemed to her now than he had when they'd first started talking a few weeks ago. He said he'd just been nervous with her at first. To her, he almost seemed like two different people. "You really don't have to go with me. I mean, I know, a tux is expensive to rent and—"

"Yes."

"Who likes wearing a tux?" she went on. "I have this long gown I wore last year. I don't see why I couldn't wear it again, but—"

"Liza Jane." He was laughing, but not really *at* her. "Did you hear me? I said yes, I'd like to go."

"You would?"

"Sure."

"And, actually, I have a tux so it won't cost me a cent."

"You do?" She put her hand on the phone so he couldn't hear. "He has a tux."

Muriel made a face like she was impressed.

"So when is it?" Jesse asked.

Liza Jane dropped her hand. "Saturday night. This Saturday night. If that's too short a notice—"

"What time do you want me to pick you up?" Jesse asked. "Or would you feel better me just meeting you there?"

"No. Sure. You can pick me up. My dorm. Groveworth, building two, first floor, room twelve. I can drive myself if you'd rather, though."

"Where are we going and what time do we need to be there?"

"The Ashview Country Club. Um. Eight o'clock."

"I'll be there Saturday, seven forty-five."

"O . . . okay. Great."

"Thanks for asking me, Liza Jane."

She wondered if she ought to explain to him that the date didn't really mean anything. That she and Cam were sort of . . . But then she realized she and Cam really weren't sort of anything. He was too busy wrapped up in his show these days to even meet her for coffee. And as much as she hated admitting it, she did kind of like Jesse. He wasn't really what she thought he was.

Liza Jane smiled. "Thanks, Jesse. See you Saturday night."

"He said yes?" Muriel asked the minute Liza Jane hung up.

She nodded, surprised she was excited. "And now what am I going to wear?" Liza Jane tossed the phone on her messy bed.

"I thought you were going to wear that gown you wore last year."

"I can't wear that," Liza Jane exclaimed. "Come on. You

have to get dressed." She reached for her backpack hanging on the end of her bed. "I know this cool secondhand clothes store."

"I have class in an hour."

"Muriel, skip class." Liza Jane grabbed her roommate's arm. "Can't you see this is a fashion emergency?"

Chapter Twenty-three

Liza Jane had been nervous about going to the ball with Jesse. She had been afraid they wouldn't have anything to talk about during the car ride over; she thought she might feel uncomfortable, or even bored, because he wasn't her type, but she realized before they even got to the country club that it was going to be a great night.

Jesse showed up with a cool wrist corsage of white lilies that had been organically grown in a hothouse in Annapolis. He looked great in his tux, and he complimented her right away on the funky teal gown she'd bought at the thrift shop. He said it made her look like an exotic blond Gypsy. She was still smiling when she walked into the ballroom on his arm.

She heard her father's voice the minute she walked through the archway of fake bubbles. The ball's theme this year—there was always a theme—was *Under the Sea*.

"Liza Jane."

"My dad," she murmured to Jesse. "FBI, so watch out."

Jesse chuckled. "I know. We've talked, remember? I'll try to keep my nose clean, though."

"You look gorgeous, daughter," her father said, taking her

by her hand and twirling her around the way he used to when she was a baby.

"Thanks, Dad." She twirled out of his reach to stand beside her date. "This is Jesse Connor."

"We've met, right?" Adam pumped his hand. "Ashview police officer." His eyebrows knitted. "Hey, aren't you too old for my daughter?"

"We went to high school together, sir. I was two years ahead of her, but actually, I'm only a year older." He let go of her father's hand, adding sheepishly, "I skipped a grade in elementary school. I am an Ashview cop, but only while I go to school. I'm hoping to work for the state police." He looked her father right in the eye. "Or maybe the FBI."

Her father made a face, exaggerating how impressed he was. "Decent guy. Much better than the one with the ponytail longer than yours. Why would he want to go out with a hippie like you?"

"Dad." She rolled her eyes. "There's no such thing as hippies anymore. Haven't been for, like . . . forty years."

"She's a hippie, isn't she, Jesse?" He swept his hand toward her. "She dresses like a hippie. Drives a VW bug like a hippie."

"I think I should stay out of this conversation, if you don't mind, sir. So far, the date is going pretty well. I don't want to screw things up."

Her father busted out laughing, reaching for an appetizer on a tray a waiter offered. "Smart move, Jesse."

"Diet Sprite," M.K. said, walking over to them, handing the drink to Liza Jane's father. "And white wine for me. It's been a heck of a bad week." She lifted her glass in a toast and turned to Liza Jane. "Nice to see you again."

Right behind her came Liza Jane's grandfather. "And there's my favorite granddaughter. I'm so glad you came." He wrapped her in a big bear hug, not in the least bit worried that he might ruin her thirteen-dollar gown. "Your father said your date backed out and he was afraid you wouldn't show up."

Liza Jane felt her cheeks get warm. Thank God she'd told Jesse about Cam. "Thanks, Gramps." She hugged him back. "Can you promise me this will be the only time you totally embarrass me tonight?"

He kissed her cheek and backed up. "Afraid not."

"Jesse Connor, this is my grandfather, Dr. Paul Thomas. He's responsible for this extravagant affair and the forty thousand dollars that will be raised tonight for the hospital."

"Nice to meet you, sir."

Her grandfather shook Jesse's hand. Liza Jane guessed he'd already had several drinks by the way he held Jesse's hand too long, pumped it a little too enthusiastically.

"Well, I hope you young people enjoy yourselves. There are sushi appetizers here somewhere." He opened his arms wide. Slightly overweight and entirely gray, he always reminded Liza Jane of a big teddy bear. He had always been so nice to her. Not just generous on birthdays and Christmas, but fun. And kind. Her dad had never said why he had never gotten along with his dad, why he had actually acted for years like he hated him, but Liza Jane had always suspected it was her dad who was the problem, not her grandfather.

"There will be dancing, too," Liza Jane's grandfather went on as he stepped back. "If you'll excuse me now, I have a big, fat donation check to track down."

Liza Jane looked up at Jesse. "Sorry about that. He can be a little overwhelming."

"No problem." He stepped forward, offering his hand to M.K. Shaughnessy. "Good evening, Special Agent Shaughnessy. We've met before, although you probably don't remember me. Officer Jesse Connor. I'm with the Ashview police. Unfortunately, I responded to the calls when Peter Wright and Tiffany Faulk were killed."

Her father's date passed her wineglass to her left hand and shook Jesse's. "I do remember you. Nice to see you under better circumstances."

"Your gown is pretty," Liza Jane said, surprised how nice

her father's partner looked. She'd never been wearing makeup any of the times she'd seen her before. The well-fitted navy gown with a high neck and cutaway sleeves was actually pretty sexy on her. She had seriously nice shoulders, very muscular. "You get your hair done differently or something?"

M.K. laughed and tucked a curl behind her ear. "I've been trying to let it grow out a little. You think it looks okay?" She lowered her voice, leaning forward so that they were talking woman to woman. "I lightened it and I used this stuff to make it curlier. Fluffier. Too much?"

Liza Jane shook her head. "Nope. It really does look great. I don't know if I even would have recognized you; you look so different than you do in your FBI clothes."

M.K. eyed Liza Jane's father.

"You know what I mean," Liza Jane said, not meaning to insult her or anything. "You just look different."

"You do, too, without that pink bandana around your head."

Liza laughed, then touched the teal headband that had been a fabric-with-beads belt that she'd tied around her head, letting the ends fall down her back. "Thanks. I feel funny. Like I'm wearing my mom's clothes or something."

"Not like you could wear any of my clothes these days." Liza Jane's mother walked up to them, offering her hand to Jesse. "Hi, I'm Sophie. That's my daughter, your date."

"Now *this* is the hippie," Liza Jane told Jesse.

"Jesse Connor. Nice to meet you." He shook her hand.

"Mom's not married to Dad anymore," Liza Jane explained. "She's married to Mark. You'll meet him later." She cut her eyes at her mother. "Mark *did* come, didn't he?"

Her mother smiled. "He most certainly did."

Liza Jane nodded, glad to hear it. She didn't care what Mark's emotional issues were, she just wanted him to be the husband her mother deserved. "As you can see, she's about to pop," Liza Jane told Jesse, indicating her mother's huge belly, barely covered by the tight, crazy-colored blouse over her ankle-length, sleek black skirt and cute flat ballerina slippers. "I have a stepsister, too. Savannah. She's home. Babysitter."

"She was pretty put out when she found out her big sister wasn't coming over," Sophie said. "Well, it was nice to meet you, Jesse." She nodded cordially. "Have a nice evening, and just remember when you walk my daughter to her dorm that her father does have a license to carry a concealed weapon."

"Mom," Liza Jane groaned.

Jesse laughed. "Actually, I'm licensed to carry one as well, ma'am, but I have no intentions of dueling with anyone. Not even for Liza Jane."

"I'm going to the bar to make sure my husband is *not* there. Can I get anyone anything?" her mother asked. "Liza Jane, how about you guys?"

"What can I have?" Liza Jane asked.

"Anything you like."

"A glass of champagne, then."

"Anything that is *not* alcoholic, that is," her mother corrected.

"Damn." Liza Jane snapped her fingers.

"We're fine. I'll get her a soda later," Jesse said. "Nice to meet you."

"Well, I think that's about everyone here who can possibly embarrass me," Liza Jane said as her mother walked away. "Dad, M.K., if you'll excuse us, I think we're going to track down the sushi guy before it's all gone."

"I like her," M.K. told Adam, taking a drink of her wine as she watched Liza Jane in her crazy, funky blue gown walk away with her date.

"Yeah, I kind of like her, too." Adam sipped his soda.

"I'm not saying that because she's your daughter," M.K. said. The room was beginning to fill with people, and she backed against a wall decorated with big blue paper waves to get out of the stream of traffic. "She's smart and she's funny. She's got your wry sense of humor."

"My *wry* sense of humor, is it?" Adam stepped closer, leaning over to look into her eyes. It was definitely an intimate gesture; she just wasn't sure what to make of it.

A waiter with a tray of dirty dishes walked behind Adam and M.K. She finished off the last swallow of wine and put her glass and his on the tray as it went by. "Yeah," she said, tucking her hands behind her and leaning against the wall. "Your wry sense of humor and your good looks."

She was feeling a little light-headed. She'd barely eaten in two days for fear the gown she'd bought on sale at a department store at the Annapolis Mall would be too tight across her stomach or rump. She guessed she should have had a little something to eat before she had the wine, though.

Adam leaned forward, lowering his head to brush his lips across her cheek. "God, you smell good." He looked down into her eyes. "I mean, golly, gee willikers, you smell good."

She lifted her lashes enhanced by Maybelline. "You know, you can't keep doing this to me," she whispered, surprised she actually had the guts to tell him what she was feeling. Shaughnessys weren't big on expressing feelings; in her house, not feeling at all was preferred.

"What's that?"

"You know." She looked up, trying not to lose herself in those blue eyes of his. "Making me feel one minute like there's something between us, the next minute as if there isn't. As if you hate my guts."

"I don't hate your guts." He paused. "Yeah, I know," he said quietly, resting his hand on her waist, gazing out at the crowd of well-dressed men and women.

Music drifted from the far side of the enormous room. It was a waltz. Classy. It made M.K. feel like she was waltzing through life tonight.

"I keep telling myself I should back off. I'm not the kind of guy you need to get involved with."

"Don't you think I should be the one to decide that?"

He didn't look at her. "Probably. It's just that there's this thing eating at me."

"We'll get this killer, Adam."

"It's not that. I mean it is." He looked at her, then away. "But it's something else. I almost think that if you know . . . you won't feel the same way about me." He waited and when she didn't say anything, he looked at her. "That's when you're supposed to say that you don't care what I've done. What I am. You're hot for me, anyway."

She smiled, touched. It was possible this was the most intimate conversation she'd ever had with someone. It made her feel good. Alive. Adam made her feel alive. "I guess it depends on what you've done. What you are. You aren't a homicidal maniac, are you?"

Again, he glanced away, that boyish grin she loved on his face. "You're funny."

"Am I? No one ever told me that before."

"Well, I'm telling you now." He leaned over and kissed her mouth. "Now listen, I need to walk around. Schmooze. I see my dad's friend Dr. Fisher over there and I should say hello. You remember him? I introduced you at the football game."

"I remember. He seemed nice."

"His wife's ill," Adam explained. "Cancer. It's bad. My dad says she's in unbearable pain now and Dr. Fisher's beside himself. Doesn't know what to do." He ran his hand down her rib cage, over her hips before stepping away. "You going to be okay for a few minutes?"

"I'm a big girl, Adam. Go. I think I'll get another glass of wine, maybe even champagne. You are going to be able to drive me home, right?"

"Strictly diet soda tonight." He gestured. "Sort of for a friend. Long story."

"Go." She waved him away. "I think I'll get that drink and

find Liza Jane. Maybe she's got something new for me on the investigation."

"No plying her with champagne," Adam warned, walking away. "Remember, she's only nineteen and I do have that license my wife mentioned."

"Got myself my own concealed weapon." She winked. Again, totally out of character for her. "See you later."

M.K. watched Adam walk away, feeling warm from her freshly manicured toenails to the top of her curly head. She knew tomorrow that she'd come up with a hundred good reasons why she shouldn't get involved with him, but tonight she was just going to enjoy his company and enjoy the flirtation between them. Shoot, she might even sleep with him.

M.K. moved away from the wall and wound her way through the crowd of men in tuxes and women in lovely ball gowns. She was surprised how many people she knew there, people she'd run into during their investigation at the college, even people she worked with. Captain Crackhow nodded to her as she walked by. She noticed he had a double of what appeared to be scotch on the rocks in his hand. She also saw another agent from the Baltimore field office, the endodontist she'd just had a root canal with, and Dr. Valerie Wood, dressed in a sexy black calf-length gown. She avoided all three of them, making a beeline for one of the bars decorated to look like a ship.

"Hello there, little lady," someone said from behind as M.K. got into line at the bar.

She turned around to see Chief Seipp dressed in a cheap, too-tight tux. She smiled but only enough to be polite. There was something about him that she didn't like. "Chief. Nice to see you."

"Please." He held up a chubby hand. "It's Buck. Social event here, no need for titles and what not."

She nodded. "Then no need to call me Special Agent Shaughnessy."

"Right." He chuckled, pointing his finger, pulling his thumb back and then pushing it down, as if shooting her.

M.K. despised that gesture and found it inappropriate coming from a law-enforcement officer.

"Everyone in Ashview's here tonight," Chief Seipp said as they moved closer to the bar. "Big fund-raiser. They always have the best food. Got my ticket free. Being an employee of the city, and all. They say it goes for two hundred a head."

She didn't even bother to smile this time. "Do they?"

"May I help you?" the bartender, dressed as a sailor, asked.

M.K. turned around, thankful for the reprieve. "Chardonnay, please."

"The good stuff, Tommy," a voice said from behind her. "Not the cheap house wine."

M.K. turned to see Sophie beside her, big belly to the bar. It was so crowded, she hadn't even noticed her. M.K. laughed. "Thanks."

"You bet."

Sophie accepted her glass of tonic water with a twist of lime and M.K. picked up her wine. The two women walked away together.

"Phew. It's warm in here." Sophie fanned her face with a blue cocktail napkin.

"You feeling okay?"

Sophie was a striking woman, even almost nine months pregnant and pushing forty-five.

"I just get a little overheated in places like this." She sipped her drink.

"You need to get out of here?" M.K. asked, genuinely concerned.

"Actually, there's a balcony that overlooks the golf course." Sophie pointed to large French doors beneath a canopy of twinkling lights.

M.K. nodded. "We can step out there for a minute, then."

"You won't be too cold?"

M.K. looked at one bare shoulder as they weaved their way through the crowd and around the dance floor, where couples were beginning to dance. "Nah. It might feel good. It's pretty warm in here. Besides, I'm trying to duck Chief Seipp."

Sophie chuckled, leading the way. "Actually, I kind of wanted to talk to you alone, anyway." At the far wall, she opened the glass-paned French doors.

The two women stepped out into the chilly, dark night and M.K. closed the door behind them. Two dim lamps left the balcony mostly in shadow.

"You wanted to talk to me?" M.K. wasn't sure she liked the sound of that.

"Mark says I should keep my mouth shut." Sophie set her glass on the rail and, leaning against it, gazed out into the darkness. "But I can see there's something between you and Adam and I'm concerned. For you and him."

M.K. didn't know what to say so she didn't say anything.

Sophie glanced at her. "Which is good. Don't take me wrong. Adam's been going out with bimbos, running away from a real relationship for too long." She shrugged. "Guess that's my fault. You know, hurting him the way I did when I divorced him and ended up with Mark."

M.K. still didn't know what to say so she just listened.

"That whole thing is complicated. Way too complicated to explain now, but anyway." Sophie turned around, leaning against the rail, cradling her big belly the way pregnant women always did. "Has Adam said anything to you about what next month is?"

M.K. shook her head. "Next month?"

"Maybe about an anniversary or something?" She laughed but obviously it wasn't a subject that was actually funny.

"He hasn't said anything."

"No, I didn't think he would. He and Mark, they're so much alike in so many ways." She shook her head. "I swear, sometimes I think I exchanged one man for a photocopy.

Wouldn't you love to investigate the psychology of that one?"

"Sophie, look," M.K. said, "I'm not sure I'm comfortable with you telling me things from Adam's past. It's not terribly fair to him."

"No, no, this is something you need to know." Sophie lifted her hand from her belly. "Or at least be aware of. I'll give the gist of it, and then if you feel like you want to know more, you can ask Adam."

"Sophie, I—"

"Has he been acting strangely? Not sleeping? Saying he'll take care of something and then not getting to it?"

"No." Then M.K. thought about how tired he seemed some days, about the autopsy reports and tapes she was still waiting for. "Well, maybe a little."

"Talking nonsense about not deserving you? Being afraid you won't love him anymore if you knew who he really was?"

M.K. looked away. She knew she shouldn't listen to this. It was wrong of Sophie to tell her any of Adam's secrets. Wrong for her to stand here and listen. But Sophie had used the word *love,* and all of a sudden it was buzzing around in her head. She'd never been in love with anyone before. Not really. But when she thought about Adam, the word came to mind. Scared her silly. Did Sophie think Adam was in love with her?

M.K. turned to lean against the balcony and stare out at the dark golf course. "I'm listening."

"Fancy meeting *you* here, handsome," Adam heard a female with a sexy voice say. He glanced over his shoulder to see Valerie Wood in a very revealing black gown, her lovely blond hair piled up on her head with little wisps of hair curling beguilingly around her face.

He grinned. "I'd say the same about you, but that would be silly, wouldn't it? The place is packed with doctors."

She leaned past him, brushing her breast against his elbow. "*Glenfiddich*, neat." She looked at Adam, and then his glass.

"Diet Sprite," he told the young male bartender in the silly sailor hat.

"Comin' up."

Valerie leaned against the bar with her elbows. In the high heels, she was taller than he was. "Hard drinker, are you, Special Agent Thomas?"

He shrugged, tucking two dollar bills into the jar hand-labeled by one of the for-hire bartenders: *Tips appreciated. College fund.* "Been drinking more than I should. Drinking alone too much. Time to cut back."

"You don't have to drink alone, you know." Her voice was husky. It was a pretty blatant invitation.

Adam smiled, taking her drink and his from the bartender and leading Valerie away. It wasn't so much that he wanted to be alone with her as he didn't want other people overhearing what they said. There were several FBI agents here, including the boss. He didn't want it getting around somehow that he'd been flirting with the county coroner, even if every man in the office did have a thing for her.

"I enjoyed dinner the other night," Valerie said, taking her glass from him. "Cheers." She touched her glass to his and sipped the straight Scotch.

"Me, too."

She halted, oblivious to the crowd; people walked around them. "I should probably give up, shouldn't I?" She was smiling.

He sipped his soda, wondering where M.K. had gone. He'd lost sight of her as she approached the bar almost an hour ago. "What do you mean?"

"You know what I mean." She glanced over the rim of her glass, her smile playful. "I've practically invited you to my bed, Agent Thomas, but you're not biting."

He looked down. "I told you—"

"I know. Your partner. I guess what I was saying was that

I didn't care." She swirled her glass and the ice cubes clinked together. "I'm not looking for a *relationship*, Adam." She seemed to almost scoff at the idea. "Just a roll in the hay. Maybe a dinner once in a while before the roll."

Adam sipped his soda. "I'm flattered, but—"

"Please, spare me. She's a lucky woman." Valerie walked away. "Have a good evening, Special Agent Thomas."

"You, too." He raised his glass and then turned away, searching the crowd for M.K. He still didn't see her. He hadn't seen Sophie or Liza Jane in a while, either. As he scanned the crowd, he spotted Mark standing alone against a wall, empty-handed.

Good for you, Adam thought as he walked toward him.

Liza Jane finished the last of the champagne and left the glass on a tray on a stand near the entrance to the hallway that led to the bathrooms. She'd left Jesse talking to some FBI agents her grandfather had introduced her to. Apparently one of them was married to a doctor or something. She slipped away to sneak a glass of champagne because Jesse had made it obvious he'd have no part of drinking, not even a drop, and he didn't want her drinking, either. It wasn't like Liza Jane wanted to get drunk or anything. She had a paper due in English Lit Monday morning, so she'd have to work on it all day tomorrow if she was going to get it done. She just liked champagne.

Glancing over her shoulder to see if Jesse was looking for her, she went down the hallway. She knew the bathrooms were down this way somewhere. Her parents had never belonged to this club but her grandfather was like a founding member or something.

Liza Jane spotted one of the bartenders, a guy she knew from English Lit class. He was standing in an open doorway, grabbing a smoke. "Hey, Del."

He whipped around, looking like he was afraid he'd gotten caught taking a break, then relaxed when he recognized her. "Hey, how's my favorite reporter?"

"I'll be fine once I find the bathroom."

He laughed, blowing smoke out the door. "Keep going. You're headed the right way."

She walked backwards down the hall in the direction he pointed, facing him. "Nice hat."

He tipped the sailor hat. "Pays for the education. Buys the beer."

"I hear you." She waggled her finger. "But you better give up those cancer sticks or you won't live long enough to reap the benefits of either."

He just waved her off and she laughed, turning around to continue down the hall. She spotted a door and just as she was about to turn the corner and push her way in, it opened, startling her. Professor Connelly, her biology teacher, was coming out.

"Oops," Liza Jane said, coming to a halt. "Now wouldn't that have been embarrassing, walking into the men's room?"

The professor glanced past her, then back. "What a pleasant surprise, Liza." He looked her up and down the way guys did in the student center. "You're looking quite fresh and lovely tonight."

"Thanks." He wasn't his usual proper self. He'd been drinking. She could smell the gin on his breath. She knew the smell of gin because it was what Mark drank. "My grandfather is kind of in charge of this thing." She hooked her thumb in the direction of the ballroom. "So I come every year. It makes him happy."

"Well, I must say." He rested one hand on the wall next to her head, sort of trapping her. "You clean up awfully nicely."

Liza Jane could have sworn he was staring at her boobs. Not like there was a lot there to stare at. "Well, thanks." She gave him a quick smile, grabbed the skirt of her dress, and ducked under his arm. "'Scuse me, Professor. Ladies' room." She pushed into the next door, relieved it was the right one.

"Freaky," she murmured under her breath as she hurried for one of the stalls.

I stand against the wall, hoping I am inconspicuous, cool glass in my hand. The music is playing, handsome gentlemen, lovely ladies dance. The crowd is beginning to thin. The fund-raiser has been a success, I presume. Money has been donated to the hospital and graciously accepted. Those who wish to drink too much and make fools of themselves in public, have.

I have enjoyed myself this evening. Enjoyed being a part of the world, of accepted society, if only for a short time. But my pleasure has been short-lived. I saw Dr. Fisher earlier, talking with this person and that, and as I watched him I began to wonder what he was speaking of. And who.

At first, I told myself it was irrational, but now, I wonder if it is not. He admitted to speaking to his wife about me. What if he has told others? Mentioned me, if only in passing?

I shift my gaze to the bar. Students were hired this evening to serve as waiters and additional bartenders. There was one who was very attractive. One who I thought found me attractive.

Dr. Fisher has warned me that I can control my desires. My needs. I do not have to go out and fulfill every fantasy.

As if by magic . . . or destiny, said young man looks at me at that very moment. He has a cocky smile beneath the sailor hat and rather attractive buttocks in the too-tight white pants he has been forced to wear as part of the silly costume. He reminds me of a young man I had a fling with years ago; it turned out badly. Billy broke my heart, leaving me for a mutual friend, Kyle.

I watch as this Billy incarnate picks up a tray of empty glasses and moves toward me. He stops in front of me and I catch my breath. He is so beautiful.

He does not look at me. No one else would even know he spoke to me.

"Would you like me to take that for you?" His voice is sexy. Breathy.

"I'm not quite finished," I manage to say.

"I could use one myself, but we can't drink while we're clocked in," he says, picking up dirty glasses from a table beside me. "I was thinking about going out for a drink after. Would you care to join me?"

He is a bold young man, and smart, too. He understands my need for secrecy, my newfound Billy. I again find myself gazing at his hard buttocks.

Imagining . . .

It has been too long since I've had sex. Dr. Fisher would never come out and say so but I think that might be precisely what the doctor would order, if he had the balls.

"It would be more than an hour before I could meet you," I hear myself say.

"No problem. I've got to clean up here first." He dares a quick, cocky smile.

The best part about Billy is not his personality, it is his anatomy. His huge—

"Say, one-thirty or so?" The waiter in the sailor hat named a bar on the edge of town away from the college bars. It is a place that has a reputation for attracting the gay population.

I lift my cool glass to my warm forehead and nod.

Chapter Twenty-four

M.K. closed her eyes, holding the cold glass of water to her forehead. "I feel silly. I'm sorry."

Adam chuckled, sitting down on the edge of the mattress. "I've been fantasizing about getting you into bed for weeks, but this isn't quite what I had in mind."

"Don't make me laugh if you want to keep those shiny shoes shiny, buster." She closed her eyes to keep the bed from spinning too fast. "I can't believe this. I didn't have that much to drink."

"I know." He smoothed the sheet he'd pulled over her.

She'd let him help her get her dress and panty hose off, but that was as far as it had gone. She'd just sleep in her bra and panties or take them off after he was gone. After the bed stopped spinning.

"You've been under a lot of stress and you were unwinding a little. Letting your hair down," he teased, toying with a curl on her cheek.

"Please tell me Crackhow didn't see me."

"He didn't see you. And even if he had, what would he have seen? You coming out of the ladies' room, me taking your arm and walking you to the car."

M.K. groaned. "I should have had something to eat, but I was afraid the darned dress would be tight across the butt and you'd think I was a cow."

He laughed. "You a cow? Martha Karen, you're an itty-bitty thing. How could I ever think you were a cow? Besides, what makes you think I'm interested in the size of your rump?"

"Go away and let me die in peace," she moaned.

"Yeah." He glanced at the digital clock beside her bed. "I do need to go. If you don't think you need anything else."

"Go." She took another sip of the water and held the glass out to him.

"You took the aspirin?"

She nodded, eyes closed.

"And you promise that tomorrow you'll eat, you won't drink chardonnay on an empty stomach, and you will do something other than work all alone in front of the TV all day."

She raised her palm to solemnly swear.

"Okay. I'll call you tomorrow." He leaned over and kissed her on her forehead and then got up from the bed.

M.K. heard him flick off the light switch, leaving her in the blessed darkness. The truth was, she didn't know what had made her sick, the wine on the empty stomach or what Sophie had told her.

I sit in my car, trembling all over. It is almost four in the morning and I know that I must get home, but I cannot bring myself to start the engine. I know that the police are suspicious of drivers at this time of the morning. It is this time of the morning that the cops find the drunks, the thieves, the criminals. I stand a much better chance of being pulled over than usual. If my car is searched, my career is over . . . my life is over.

I glance over at the seat beside me and even though it is still dark, I can see the form of the object I stole.

I do not know what made me meet that young man in the bar. Delbert. His name was Delbert, and he was an economics major at Chesapeake Bay. I do not know what made me agree to go home with him. To park my car on another block and walk with him to his apartment over his grandmother's garage where he had the nice dog named Maxwell.

It was purely sexual, at first. The lure of the forbidden. Then . . . then . . .

A sob rises in my throat.

I see Billy. I see myself crying. I remember the pain of my heartbreak. My first true love. Superimposed over these memories are flashes of Del's face. Del laughing. Billy saying I'll find someone else. Del . . . Billy . . . Del . . .

I did not realize until I slowly began to undress him how much he had hurt me. How much I had loved him and how little he had cared. I had not realized how long I had been angry with Billy. Not until I saw his lovely flesh, felt the silk of his skin, the heat of it in my hand . . . my mouth.

It was the most beautiful object I had ever seen. The most perfect. I had wanted it for my own and I had taken it and now it is mine.

That thought brings me out of my daze.

I know that I must get home and clean myself up. Rid myself of my clothes that could carry potential evidence in the form of body fluids. If any DNA is detected, it could make my life more complicated.

Finally feeling calm enough to drive safely, I start the car and pull out. I drive home, taking care to obey all traffic signals and speed limits. I take my trophy home.

"Ah, Jesus," Adam said. He took one look at the body on the bed and then turned away, wiping his mouth with the back of his hand.

M.K. stood between the bed and window, scribbling in

her notepad. She didn't say anything about his inappropriate language. It was all she could do not to puke right now.

She was still wearing her coat, though she'd been here more than an hour. A person just couldn't shake this kind of chill.

"You all right?" she asked after a moment. She didn't look at him, afraid to. She'd barely been up, head pounding, mouth dry, when the office had called, saying she and Adam were being called to a crime scene in Ashview.

Fortunately, she'd been able to get her act together before she arrived at the crime scene. A hot shower and a big cup of coffee had helped. On the way over, she'd worked on compartmentalizing. It was the best way for her to deal with things. She placed everything in neat little boxes in her head, keeping everything separate: her family in Philadelphia and how she felt about them, her attraction to Adam, what Sophie had told her last night about him, and the heinous crime scene unfolding in front of her right now.

The dead young man sprawled on the bloody sheets was keeping her mind off everything but the crime scene.

"I'm fine," Adam said, still looking away. "How about you?" He looked up, lowering his voice. "Your head okay? I felt bad after I left. I should have stayed with you."

"I told you to go home, and I'm fine. I took about a hundred ibuprofen this morning." She looked down at her notes. "Grandmother found him at noon. Said he usually sleeps in after working Saturday nights as a freelance bartender, but he always brings her the Sunday paper before noon. When he didn't show up, she got concerned, came over and knocked. Got her key when he didn't answer."

Adam slipped one hand into his coat pocket. They were wearing practically identical three-quarter raincoats only hers was navy blue and his was khaki. "And he's a student at the college?"

"Yup."

"And no one saw anything, of course. Not coming or going?"

She shook her head.

"Girlfriend?"

"Yes, but she's gone to Jersey for the weekend. Parents' anniversary or something." M.K. circled the girl's name the grandmother had provided. She'd want to interview her as soon as possible. "Name's Delbert Pardee. Twenty-two. Senior." She looked up. "You recognize him?"

"No. Should I?"

M.K. studied the area around the bed, trying to see if anything caught her eye, if anything appeared out of place in the studio apartment. "You didn't even look."

"I looked." Adam's tone was sharp.

She let it go. "He was at the hospital ball last night. I got a drink at the bar from him. You don't remember him?"

"No."

"He was at the bar to the left of the orchestra. The one that looked like a boat or something. He was wearing a—"

"M.K.," Adam snapped. "I don't remember him."

She drew back, not giving herself the option of being hurt by his gruffness. "You're cranky."

His eyes narrowed. "This kind of thing makes me a little cranky, okay?" He glanced in the direction of the kitchenette area where several male Ashview police officers were standing. They were trying to get as far away from the bed as possible while they waited for the deputy coroner and the FBI forensic evidence team to arrive. "It makes all men cranky."

She didn't say anything. Instead, she went back to her notes. Detailed notes she could later copy onto a legal pad to add to the pile of legal pads back at the office.

"I have to ask," Adam said after a minute. He was calmer now. "Is it here?"

"No. I looked. Cops looked. EMTs looked. In the sheets. On the floor. Even outside in the driveway."

"He took it?"

"He took it," she said quietly. "Delbert Pardee died from blood loss when someone cut his penis off and took it as a souvenir."

"No evidence? What do you mean, no evidence?" Adam demanded, leaning over the table where she'd spread out her notes.

"What do I mean? I mean the same thing I've been telling you for weeks."

"There was blood all over the place." He threw one hand up, accidentally spilling coffee on the cuff of his shirt. "Shit," he muttered, taking a step back, rubbing at the stain.

"There *was* blood. I managed to get the lab to put a rush on the results. It was all the victim's, every sample."

"The semen stains?"

"Victim's."

"And no fingerprints? No other body fluids?"

"No additional body fluids. If the killer ejaculated, somehow he kept it to himself."

"This just can't be." Adam sipped his coffee. He looked tired, like he hadn't slept in the three days since they'd been called to Del Pardee's apartment. "Maybe you missed something."

"I didn't *miss* anything, Adam," she snapped. "*We* didn't miss anything. Whoever killed Del Pardee knew what he was doing. He knew how to keep the crime scene clean." She stood up, pressing her hands into the boardroom table stacked with files and her notepads. "I told you my theory."

"A cop?"

"You discounted it. You practically laughed at me."

He put his coffee cup on the edge of the table. "I did not laugh at you," he scoffed.

"You laughed at me and you told me my idea was way off base, but I think it's time we at least consider it's a possibility."

"M.K., I put you off because I thought you were headed in the wrong direction."

"No," she shouted. She'd had it with him. He'd been difficult to work with all week. He'd barely said two words to her and neither had been personal in any way. He hadn't mentioned the kiss they had shared at the ball or the discussion they had had about their feelings for each other. It was like it had never happened. "You put me off because you can't stand the thought that I might be right." She tapped his chest. "That my intuition might be better than yours."

"That's the most ridiculous damned thing I've ever heard," he shouted back, swinging his hand. He hit his coffee cup and with one swipe, sent it and two legal pads flying across the room in a trail of black coffee.

The cup hit the wall, splattered the last of the coffee on it, and fell to the carpet with a clunk.

M.K. crossed her arms over her chest, but she never flinched. She'd spent too many years in her father's house to be intimidated by one thrown cup of coffee. Adam Thomas wasn't even in James Shaughnessy's league.

He stared at the coffee stain on the wall for a second and then looked away. "I'm sorry."

Suddenly, he was the easygoing, wraparound-sunglasses surfer guy again. All he needed was the Hawaiian flowered shirt. "I'm really sorry, M.K. That was way out of line."

"You need to get some help," she said.

"What are you talking about?" He looked up.

She hesitated. "I talked to Sophie the other night. She told me about Mark's wife. About Laura."

He swore softly under his breath. "She had no right."

"Adam, I could have looked in your file or in Mark's file."

"She had no right," he repeated.

"No, maybe she didn't." M.K. came around the table and picked up her two notepads, wiping at the wet coffee splotches. She left the cup where it lay. "But s' e told me anyway, and

I'm concerned." She dared a quick glance at him. "I'm worried about you."

"I'm fine. Sophie needs to worry about Mark. That's who she needs to worry about."

"Adam." M.K. grabbed his hand. "Please?"

He looked at her for a minute and then down at the carpet. "I . . . I'm seeing someone, a psychiatrist. I'm fine, though, really. A hell of a lot better than Mark." He ran his fingers through his hair, but he held tightly to her hand. "If I can just get through the next month. Just get past it."

She nodded. "I can help. I want to."

"M.K., you have no idea how devastating . . . You don't know what it's like to . . ." He looked away, his eyes glistening. "What it's like to trust your instincts and be completely off base. So far off base that you—" He halted in midsentence. Took a breath. "Can we maybe talk about this some other time? I mean, I want to talk to you about it. I think you would understand better why I am the way I am. Why . . . why I'm having a hard time going with your gut feelings on things when—"

"Adam, we can talk about it another time." She squeezed his hand and let go, returning to her chair. "I won't bring it up again. Not to you. Not to anyone. You tell me when you're ready to talk." She reached for one of her notepads and flipped up the top sheet of paper. "You want to get back to work?"

He nodded.

"Now, because a trophy was taken, we can assume this is our guy again." She reached for her pen. "Let's split up this list of friends and family and both start calling. We need to know who his friends were, at work, at school. We need to see what his connection is to the other victims."

"M.K., we've been over this." He picked up his coffee cup. "I don't think we're going to find a connection to the other victims."

"There's got to be a reason why he's choosing these kids." She thumped the pad with her pen.

"No, there doesn't. He's psycho. Crazy people are crazy because they do crazy things."

"But don't you see, Adam?" She looked up at him. "It's not crazy to the killer. To the killer, it makes sense." She looked down at her notes again. "Which means the clues have to be here. The answer has to be here, I can feel it. I can feel *him*. We're just missing it."

Jerome exhaled in exasperation and crossed his legs in the opposite direction. He needed to seriously consider taking some time off. Time to be with Sela, time to adjust to the inevitable. He didn't feel as if he was doing his patients justice. He wasn't doing Blue justice.

This was the second appointment this week and Jerome felt as if he was making no progress whatsoever. Blue would barely speak, and when Jerome spoke, the patient didn't seem to be listening. It was as if Blue no longer wanted treatment, or worse, had lost hope.

Jerome glanced at the clock on the coffee table. Fifteen more minutes. Fifteen more painful minutes.

"Blue," he said, returning his attention to the person in front of him, trying to focus. "I sense you're frustrated, and I have to confess I am as well. You're obviously unhappy with who you are. You have behaviors you want to change, but—"

"Have you seen that show, Doctor? The one about the college students?"

Jerome smiled, pleased his patient was actually initiating conversation. Sometimes, treatment could seem to drag for weeks, months, while a psychiatrist prodded and questioned, but when the patient brought up a subject, it was often very close to an issue that needed to be addressed.

"The reality show," Blue said, hands tented, gaze firmly fixed on Jerome.

"You mean *Fraternity Row*?"

A nod.

"I have to confess, I have." Jerome chuckled. "My wife adores it. She never misses an episode. I tape the show so she can watch it again later."

"What do you think of Axel?"

"What do I *think* of him?" It was an odd question.

"Do you find him sincere?"

"I . . . I suppose I do." Jerome lifted his shoulder. "As sincere as any twenty-one-year-old can be."

"That's a good point, Doctor. No one that age is sincere. I wonder how everyone is so easily fooled by him. By all the fraternity brothers and their shallow problems. Their lies. Their lascivious lifestyles."

The tone of Blue's voice made the hair rise on the back of Jerome's neck. The patient was no longer looking at him. No longer seeing him, at least.

"You . . . you don't care for them, then?"

"I think we are easily deceived. We want to be a part of the group, we want friends, lovers," Blue said. "But we can never be a part, can we?"

"Is that how you feel, Blue?" Jerome shifted forward in his chair, unable to resist his feelings of empathy. "Is that how your medical condition makes you feel? As if you can belong nowhere?"

"Did you hear the big announcement concerning the show? Did you see that part? Liza Jane reported that one of the major networks has purchased it. They will be in the new fall lineup next year." Blue looked at Jerome. "Can you believe that? That someone would pay millions of dollars for that kind of bullshit? Those lies? Those deceptions?"

Jerome slid back in his chair, studying his patient closely. "I find it interesting that you feel so strongly about this show, Blue. Can you tell me why?"

"I was only speaking in generalities," Blue snapped. "What do I care what those kids do? What they think? If they invite me to their damned parties!"

The patient's last word was almost shouted.

Blue expected to be invited to college students' parties?

Jerome looked up at the clock again. Time was up, yet he was tempted to allow the session to go over.

He couldn't, though. He had to stop at the pharmacy on the way home. Sela needed another vial of her painkiller. She couldn't be without it all night.

Blue saw Jerome look at the clock and rose suddenly. "Time's up, isn't it?"

"Do you feel you need to stay longer?" Jerome followed the patient to the door. "If we need to spend some more time together—"

"Certainly not, Dr. Fisher." Blue smiled. "I'll see you next week. And please, give my best wishes to Mrs. Fisher."

Chapter Twenty-five

"Yes, good afternoon, this is Dr. Jerome Fisher. Two weeks ago I had a patient's records transferred to me and I'd like to speak with the physician who treated this patient." He adjusted his glasses to read the name in his notes. "A Dr. Bartholomew Cooper." He paused.

"Yes, of course." He gave the patient's name and social security number and then his own social security number. "I understand. We follow the same procedures in my office. Patient confidentiality must always be protected. I'll hold."

He tapped his pen on his desk in his den. He'd taken the day off because Sela had been feeling poorly this morning, worse than she had all week. She was still sleeping after being heavily sedated. While she was sleeping, he thought he might as well get a little work done. It was a good time to call California, anyway.

Jerome scribbled Blue's psychiatrist's name on a notepad while he waited. "Yes, I'm here," he said after a moment. "I was actually hoping to speak with Dr. Cooper, if that would be possible. I'd be happy to have him return my call when it's convenient."

Jerome lifted his pen off the notepad. "Passed away? I'm

sorry." It wasn't what he was expecting. "I'm sorry," he repeated, taken off guard. "Was he elderly?" Again, he paused to listen. "No? I see. An accident? How tragic. Was Dr. Cooper the only psychiatrist who treated this patient in your office?"

He drew a circle around the doctor's name and a line through it. He was just so shocked, though why, he didn't know. People certainly died in accidents, not just in cars, but at home, too.

"I see. Well, thank you very much. I appreciate your assistance. Have a good day."

He hung up the phone and stared at the patient records file that was growing thicker by the week. What bad luck. He really would have liked to have spoken to Dr. Cooper.

He wondered with whom else he might be able to speak, then remembered that the physician who did the surgery was mentioned in the patient's records. He flipped open the file, turning pages until he found the name. There was no phone number provided, but he knew what hospital the physician had performed the surgery in. He called operator assistance, and a minute later was being put through to the surgery group the doctor belonged to.

Jerome gave the receptionist a brief explanation of why he wanted to speak with Dr. Abbott and then asked if he could have the doctor return his call.

"Excuse me?" he said. "Dead? Heavens, I'm so sorry."

For a moment he didn't know what to say. "Nine years ago?" Blue's psychiatrist had also been dead nine years. "A home invasion?" Jerome said into the phone. "How tragic." He paused. "Yes, yes, I suppose I would like to have a copy of the records sent. I . . . I'll have my secretary call you next week to make the appropriate arrangements."

Jerome hung up the phone, rose from his chair, and walked out of his den office, a bit stupefied. Both doctors who had treated Blue for years were dead. Dead nine years.

He walked into the family room, where he'd left the big Sony TV on just for noise. Just for company. He was doing that a lot these days. Coming out to watch it at night, too, when he couldn't sleep. He didn't want to disturb Sela.

He wandered into the bedroom. He was pleasantly surprised to find his wife awake. "Hello, sweetheart." He immediately put on a smile for her. "Had a nice nap?"

"Nap?" She turned slowly to look at the clock beside her bed. "You've let me sleep all day."

He sat down on the edge of the bed and took her hand in his. "You were tired."

She struggled to sit up, grimacing in pain. "You're making me sleep my life away." She pulled her hand from his.

"I am not."

They were silent for a moment. She adjusted her bright purple scarf. It was her favorite these days. She said it made her complexion look less sallow.

"Tell me what you've been doing today," she said. Both of them knew they didn't have time for petty arguments.

"I don't know. Puttering around. I fixed the leaky faucet in the powder room. I read a little. Watched TV. You know, TV is a wasteland in the middle of the day."

She smiled. "You get any work done? I thought you were going to take the day to catch up on some of your files. You keep saying you're so far behind."

He glanced away, not sure if he wanted to tell her about the phone calls he'd just made.

"Jerome Fisher," she said. "Look at me."

He hesitated. Turned.

"What's wrong?" she demanded.

He started to shake his head but saw that look in her dark eyes. He knew he was no match for her. "I don't know. Probably nothing." He fiddled with the flowered sheet tucked around her waist. "I thought I would call Blue's psychiatrist in California. Speak directly with him, see if he could give me some insight."

"And?"

"He's dead, Sela."

"Oh, that's too bad."

"Yes. An accident, apparently. He . . . electrocuted himself in his garage. Years ago. Nine."

"How awful for his family. I know you're disappointed." It was her turn to take his hand. "But you can do this, Jerome. On your own."

"I called the physician who did the surgery, as well. Just on impulse. It was a long time ago, of course, things happen, but . . ."

"But what?"

Jerome looked at her. "Sela, he's dead as well. He's been dead nine years. But he didn't die of natural causes, either. There was a home invasion and he and his wife were both murdered. The killer was never found."

"Oh, heavens." She brought her hand to her sunken chest. Then she looked up at Jerome. "Surely you don't think . . ."

"I don't know what to think," Jerome said. He rose to pace at the end of their bed.

She thought for a moment. "Well, have you seen any indication that the patient might have ever been in the state of mind to harm anyone?"

"No." He ran his hand over his closely shorn hair. It was getting fuzzy, beginning to look a little unkempt. He needed a haircut, but there just didn't seem to be time to do things like that these days. He needed to go to the dry cleaners, too. Yesterday morning he'd had to pull a shirt from the dry-cleaning bag and iron it to wear.

"Then why—"

"I don't know, Sela. I just have this bad feeling about this patient all of a sudden. Something is happening. Something is changing in Blue's life, and I can't seem to find out what it is. I'm worried."

"And you say Blue hasn't indicated any desire to kill?"

Again, he shook his head. "No. But I've witnessed outbursts of anger in the last two sessions that I've never seen before. It's almost as if the patient becomes another person."

"Do you suspect a multiple personality disorder?"

He halted at the end of the bed. "No. I don't think so." He looked at her. "It could be possible, though, I suppose." He hesitated. "In all these years I've only treated the one multiple-personality, but her diagnosis was quite clear from the beginning. Remember? She was just a teenager when I began seeing her."

Jerome reached the closet doors and turned around to go the other way, going over in his head his most recent conversations with Blue. "You know, we had a very odd dialogue the other day, concerning that show you like, of all things. You know, *Fraternity Row*. There was an unbridled hostility there that . . ." He shook his head, unsure how to express to his wife what he had sensed that day. "I just don't know. The patient's anger seemed directed, not necessarily to the show, but to the students that attend the college."

"Oh, heavens, Jerome," Sela breathed, wide-eyed. "You don't suppose your patient could be—"

"The campus killer?" He met her gaze. "That hadn't occurred to me, Sela."

"But it's a possibility?"

He nodded slowly, thinking the idea was too far-fetched to believe. But was it too far-fetched to be considered?

I stare at Liza Jane's lovely face, listening to her campus update. She tells her viewing audience that there have been no breakthroughs in the case of the killer who is preying on campus students. According to the FBI, the case has stalled. Parents are up in arms; more students are transferring out or simply dropping out for the semester. She reminds us that students, both male and female, must be careful, taking extra precautions, not going home with someone they do not know well. Del learned that the hard way, didn't he?

I chuckle at my sick sense of humor.

She goes on to give us an update on the purchase of

Fraternity Row. Because it has been sold to the network, the week before Christmas the campus station will air its last show. The next time it's broadcast, it will be for the entire nation on prime-time TV.

I know all this, so I am not paying a great deal of attention to what she says. I am too busy looking for a picture of a sailor hat in a magazine. I have already found Billy, in a *Vogue.* A men's cologne model. They look remarkably similar, really. The model, Billy, Del. Interchangeable.

"In celebration of the network sale and the notoriety it will bring to our small-town campus," Liza Jane is saying, "the college will be throwing a party, one the likes of which Ashview has never seen, I'm told."

I look up from my magazine. Liza Jane suddenly has my full attention. The slick magazine slides off my lap to the floor. I grab the remote. Turn up the volume.

"Tentatively planned for December fifteenth," she tells me, "the entire campus will be invited. I'm told it will be held in the Theresa Cromwell building."

The Cromwell building is the campus's athletic center. It is state of the art, with multiple gymnasiums, an indoor pool and track, and a large amphitheater used for concerts and such. Last year I saw Bob Dylan there. It was quite nice. What is interesting is that it's all under one roof. The college could certainly throw a hell of a party there. Not only everyone on campus, but everyone in Ashview would show up for such a celebration. There is no way of telling how important *Fraternity Row* will become to the town, once the show puts it on the map before the eyes of America.

"It's not been confirmed yet," Liza Jane continues, "but there have been reports that the network will help foot the bill." The camera angle changes, and suddenly Liza Jane is looking right at me.

"That's all for now." She nods her head, her tiny blond dreadlocks framing her beautiful face. Beauty and brains, I muse.

"This is Liza Thomas at WCBC. Good night and keep safe."

Music comes up and the credits begin to roll. I can tell money has already begun to trickle into the little local-access cable station. The camera shots are greatly improved, as are the graphics.

I switch channels to a documentary on Ancient Egypt and pick up the magazine I have dropped on the floor. I am excited about the idea of Chesapeake Bay College's grand party in celebration of going big-time on network TV. I am excited because I've just gotten the most brilliant idea.

If Chesapeake is going to have a party, I can have a party of my own. It all comes to me in a moment of brilliance. I imagine flames shooting up the walls of the gymnasiums. I imagine doors locked that should have been unlocked. I imagine the screaming.

All those tragic deaths. Those so-called innocent students.

I imagine myself watching from the parking lot.

I imagine myself smiling.

Jerome shifted in his chair, trying not to look at the clock. He was very uncomfortable today, uncomfortable with himself as well as his patient. Though there have been gaps of silence in their conversation, the session has been going surprisingly well. Jerome hasn't mentioned his phone calls to Blue's physicians. He saw no need to. He has tried not to think about what he and Sela discussed—the possibility that Blue could be somehow connected to the student deaths at Chesapeake Bay College.

He focused on his patient's face, trying to listen to what was being said. He thought they might actually be making a little progress. Blue had just stated feelings of disjointedness.

"Is this something you've recently become aware of?" Jerome questioned.

"No. No, I believe it's been with me a long time. Since childhood."

"And you believe this . . . *feeling* is a result of your condition?"

"Dr. Fisher, have you any idea what it is like to know you are different from others from the day you first take a breath? No one says anything for years, but they look at you. They whisper. You know that they know something awful about you."

"But these people who knew—I assume you mean your family, perhaps those medical personnel who treated you—surely you must realize they cared for you? That your family loved you? They probably thought they were protecting you by not telling you before you were old enough to comprehend the diagnosis."

"You're not listening, Doctor. You're not listening." There was a thread of anger in Blue's voice.

"I'm listening. I'm trying to understand, but you must help me." Jerome slid forward in his chair. "You have to help me so that I can help you."

"I spent my entire childhood trying to make up for what I feared was wrong with me. Once I knew, once my father, ironically a physician, explained to me why I looked different than other people, I made it my life's work *not* to be different. To fit in. To blend in."

"And were you successful?" Jerome asked quietly, sensing they were on the verge of something very important that Blue needed to say.

The patient turned to him. "At first. When I was in high school. As I said before, I just stayed under the radar, tried to be as unnoticeable as possible."

"But what about when you went to college? You told me that by the time you went to college, you knew you wanted the surgery. You knew who you wanted to be. You had chosen a sex. How did those around you take that?"

"How do you think they took it?" Blue exploded, coming

out of the chair. "They found out and they treated me like a freak!"

Jerome instinctively pulled back. "Please sit down," he said quietly. In all these years he had only once been forced to call the police. He hoped today would not be the second time.

The patient, now trembling all over, sat down. "I'm sorry."

"It's all right," Jerome said quietly, keeping a professional tone. "There are Kleenex there if you need them." He pointed to the wooden box Mrs. Elright always made certain was full.

"I'm fine."

"No, Blue," Jerome said, "you're not fine. What happened in college? You said they found out. If you were already living the life of the sex you had chosen, how did anyone know you were a hermaphrodite?" He hesitated. "Did you confide in someone? Is that what happened?"

The patient's head shook.

"No?"

"No. I . . . I didn't tell." It was a gasp.

"Tell me what happened," Jerome pled.

"I can't. It's too horrible."

"Did someone hurt you?"

"They pretended to be my friends. They invited me. They made me think I could be a part of their world!" Blue spat.

The way the patient spoke made the hair bristle on the back of Jerome's neck. The pain, the anger was so intense, so directed toward these people from Blue's past. And the mention of breasts was odd. Eerie. The cheerleader killed at the college had had her breast sliced off.

Jerome was suddenly afraid.

Blue looked at him.

Jerome looked down. Cleared his throat.

"I'm sorry," Blue said, quickly growing calm. Too quickly. "I apologize for my behavior. My outburst was totally inappropriate."

Jerome kept his gaze focused on his notes. He pretended to write something down. "Blue, would you consider checking yourself into an overnight facility?"

"A *psychiatric ward*?" The patient chuckled. "Certainly not. How would that appear? Surely you don't think the powers that be would allow me to continue to work if they discovered I was mentally unstable. Which I am not."

"I . . . I didn't say you were mentally unstable. I only . . . wondered if an extensive workup might—"

"I don't think that will be necessary, Dr. Fisher." The patient rose. "You and I, we're doing just fine. I am utterly confident in your ability to help me work this through. It's really not as bad as it appears." Blue chuckled. "It's not as bad as that must have seemed. You understand, it's only that I don't have anyone with whom I can talk about this. No one here knows about me, about what I am. It's been years since I've been able to talk this through with anyone."

Yes, Jerome thought. *And that person is now dead, isn't he?*

"I'll see you next week, Doctor. Thank you."

Jerome sat in his chair for a moment after the door closed. He was scared.

What if Blue was the campus killer? What could he do to prevent another death? Obviously he couldn't go to the police. He had absolutely no proof, nothing beyond this bad feeling and a word here and there. Even if he was willing to risk his practice to break the patient/doctor confidentiality laws, what would the police have to go on? He heard on the news only the other night that they were baffled because there was no evidence, forensic or otherwise.

Jerome rose from his chair, staggering a little. He needed to get home. Needed Sela. She would know what he should do.

* * *

"Sign here and here." The skinny, scar-faced man behind the pawnshop counter points. He does not look at me to check to see if my face matches the picture ID I have gone to the trouble to purchase over the Internet. I pick up his pen, thinking I should wash my hands thoroughly when I get back to work. I sign the forms with a careless scrawl. Jerome Fisher, M.D.

"And is that it?" I ask. I am amazed how easy it is in this country to purchase a handgun. A simple three day waiting period. A fake ID. Clothing and an altered voice to hide my true identity.

The man behind the counter sweeps up the official documents. The purchase of the gun with its serial number will be recorded in some state computer bank. Possibly federal. Not that I care.

"Thank you very much," I say, looking down at the Ruger .45. "Could you possibly put it in a bag?" I push the box of bullets I have also purchased toward him.

The clerk stares at me, blank-faced. I wonder what his problem is. Too much alcohol and drugs? Poor gene pool? I guess both.

"It's not something I want to walk down the sidewalk carrying in plain view," I explain to the knucklehead.

He grunts something and digs under the counter, coming up with one of those thin white plastic bags used in grocery stores. *Thank you* is printed in a banner across the bottom. He places the pistol and the box of ammunition inside.

"Could you double bag it?" I ask.

He exhales in exasperation, but complies with my request.

"Thank you," I say, heading for the door. "Have a nice day."

The bell over the door jingles as I step out into the chilly afternoon. The air smells like snow. The weatherman this morning on the TV was predicting the first snow of the winter. I hope he is right. I love snow.

* * *

Jerome nodded on and off in the reclining chair he had dragged into the bedroom from the den. He kept opening his eyes to check on Sela, then drifting off again. They were getting close to the end; they both knew it.

A few hours ago, he'd almost called for an ambulance, but she had convinced him, through tears streaming down her cheeks, that she really didn't want to go. All she needed, she said, was another injection of painkiller. Just an hour earlier than scheduled. No harm could come of it. What was he afraid of, she had somehow managed to tease. Was he afraid she might die?

Tonight Jerome felt as if he was dying. He wished desperately that he could somehow bear the pain for his wife. For them both.

A sound awakened him. Unsure of what he had heard, he glanced at Sela, who was asleep, breathing shallowly, then at the clock. It was after eleven. He had slept longer than he thought.

He heard the sound again. This time he was fully awake. It was the doorbell.

Who on earth would be ringing the doorbell at this time of night?

He climbed out of the chair, still feeling a little disoriented from his nap. Maybe it was Patricia. The nurse had wanted to stay tonight but Jerome had insisted he could take care of his wife. He told Patricia that Sela would want her to go home to her family. Maybe Patricia had come back to check on them.

He walked out of the bedroom, down the hall, toward the foyer, shuffling in his old slippers. But wouldn't she have just called if she was concerned?

The doorbell rang again and he unlatched the dead bolt and opened the door. Standing there was Blue.

"Dr. Fisher, good evening," the patient said.

Jerome instinctively took a step back. In all his years of

treating patients, not one had ever come to his home. "Good evening, Blue. What are you—"

"I was wondering how your wife was."

"Blue, I'm sorry, but you mustn't be here. I'm going to have to ask you to leave." Jerome rested his hand on the door-knob. "If you need to talk to me, you have to call the number I've given you."

"I just wanted to see how she was. See if there's anything I can do." The patient took a step closer.

"I'm sorry, but that's impossible," Jerome said sternly. "If you don't go now, I'll have to call the police."

Blue shoved Jerome backward so hard that he fell to the carpet. One of his slippers flew off and his glasses shifted on his face so that he could only see out of one eye.

The patient closed the door. Locked it. "Now, Dr. Fisher, I certainly can't have you do that, can I?"

Jerome, still seated on the foyer floor, adjusted his glasses. That was when he saw the gun.

Chapter Twenty-six

I take pity on Dr. Fisher and offer my hand to help him to his feet. "I'm sorry," I say. "I didn't hurt you, did I?"

"What . . . what are you doing here?" he asks.

I can tell that he has been asleep. He is wearing pajamas with one of those old-fashioned cardigan sweaters over them. He is afraid.

I lean over and push the lost slipper toward him so that he can slide his foot into it. "I've come to see your wife."

"No," he says stubbornly. "She's very ill. She can't have visitors."

"But I feel like I know her." I take his arm, forcing him to walk through the foyer into the hall that I suspect will lead me to the master bedroom. The house, a 1940s Cape Cod with a large addition in the back, is nice inside. The furniture is cheery. The paint and wallpaper and artwork is in very good taste. I suspect that it is Sela who has done the interior decorating. She is a very classy woman, I can tell.

"Please," Jerome says.

I know that he is truly afraid now and I feel sorry for him. All he has tried to do is help me. I wish that I did not have to do this. I know that I must, though, so I set aside my feelings. "Take me to Sela," I say.

"What do you want? If you want me to help you, Blue, this is not the way."

"We're past that," I say.

We emerge from the dark hallway into the bedroom that is lit by two bedside lamps. It is a large room; the walls are painted a deep purple and the draperies and bedcoverings are a lovely African batik print. Sela, a tiny, frail black woman with a purple scarf on her head, is asleep in the bed. She looks half dead to me.

I will be doing her a favor.

"Will she wake up?" I say, still holding tightly to his arm. He has ceased struggling.

He stares at the gun in my hand. "No. No, she's sedated."

"Excellent." I study the drugs and medical equipment on the table beside the bed. Blood pressure cuff, digital thermometer, a red box for disposing of contaminated items. Syringes. Vials of medication. Diamorphine. A strong painkiller.

"When was her last dose of painkiller?"

"Um." He glances at the clock.

I loosen my grip on his arm a little. He adjusts his glasses. Stares at the clock. "T . . . two hours ago." He gazes into my face. "Please, Blue. Let's sit down and talk."

"You know it's me, don't you?"

He stares at me for a moment. The look on his face changes as he comprehends what I speak of. As he realizes that I know he knows.

"No," he says. He shakes his head. "I . . . I don't know what you're talking about."

I make a clicking sound between my teeth. I'm beginning to grow impatient. I need to get home, get something to eat, and get to bed. It's been a long day. "You know," I whisper. "I killed those students."

"Blue, listen to me. I . . . I can't disclose what you tell me. You don't have to—"

"Yes, you can. It's not like TV. If I confess to killing someone, if I tell you I am going to kill again, then you're obligated to turn me in to the authorities."

"I . . . I wouldn't do that."

He is shaking all over now. Swaying and weak-kneed. I fear he's going to fall and won't that be a mess, if he falls and injures himself? Knocks himself out?

"Sit down," I say. I help him to sit in the easy chair beside Sela's bed. She is still sleeping. Keeping one eye on the doctor, I check her pulse.

"Don't touch her," he shouts.

"Shhh," I warn. Her pulse is thready. She is dying. I know it. She knows it. Dr. Fisher knows it.

"I need you to give her another injection," I say, pointing with the loaded pistol to the vial of diamorphine on the table.

"No," he cries. "She's already had nearly double what was prescribed."

"I'm sorry," I say softly. "Is she in a great deal of pain?"

Tears fill his eyes now. "Yes," he whispers.

"Then really," I say, looking down at the doctor, "we'll be helping her, won't we?"

He shakes his head. "No." Tears trickle down his cheeks. "I won't do it," he says in a moment of obstinacy. "I won't kill her."

I sigh. I rub my eyes with my gloved hands, taking care to keep the pistol aimed at Dr. Fisher. "If you don't," I say, "then don't you see, I'll have to." I smile down at him. "Only I won't do it with that." I nod toward the table with the syringes and medication. "I'll do it with this." I give the pistol in my hand a nod.

"Why?" He is crying full-out now. "Why would you kill my Sela? What has she done to you?"

I glance away, amazed that such a smart man is so slow to

comprehend. "Jerome . . . may I call you that?" When he doesn't answer, I go on. "Jerome, I have to kill *you* because you know what I've done. Surely you don't want Sela left behind? If you die and she doesn't have anyone to care for her, she'll have to go to a hospital. I know you don't want her to live out her last days in a hospital, cared for by strangers, mourning her loss of you."

Dr. Fisher looks at his wife. At me. "You want me to kill her with an overdose?"

I nod.

"And then what?"

"Then you'll have to take this gun and shoot yourself. A murder-suicide. Very tragic."

He gasps.

"Now, now, Jerome, it's really not as bad as it sounds. There's no pain. Not if you do it right. In one burst of light, you'll be gone. You'll be walking through the pearly gates with your Sela."

"No. No." He just keeps saying it.

"Don't you see?" I say, trying to persuade him. "Really, this is the perfect ending. You know you'll be lost without her. I could tell that, even back in your office when you spoke of her."

He just sits there. I check the clock. "Come now, Jerome," I say sternly. "Let's get moving here. You give her the injection, or I'll shoot her. Only it won't be in the head. Do you catch my drift?"

He stares at me. I can see in his dark eyes that he knows there is no other way.

"Come, come." I waggle the pistol to hurry him along. I am amazed how good it feels in my hand. How much I like the feel of it. It's a pity I'll have to leave it here with Dr. Fisher. Of course it is, after all, his, isn't it?

"Do it now," I whisper.

Jerome reaches out with a shaky hand and picks up a syringe. He lays it on his lap and slowly reaches for the vial of painkiller. It is funny how he suddenly appears to me to be an old man.

"Give her a full syringe," I suggest gently. "It will happen quickly this way. Her breathing will be suppressed. Her heart will just stop."

Hands shaking, he fills the syringe.

"That's it. Now give it to her."

I watch as he shifts forward in the chair, adjusts his glasses, and pulls back the blanket. He lifts her pajama top and gives her the injection in her hip. She is nothing but skin and bones.

"Good-bye, Sela," he whispers. "I'm sorry. So sorry. I love you."

I wonder if Jerome will give me a hard time now about killing himself. I am pleasantly surprised when he reaches out for the gun.

"Thanks for dinner, Dad," Liza Jane said, cramming another bite of cheeseburger into her mouth.

Adam sat back in the booth at College Park and sipped his beer. "I just thought it had been a while since we did this. Whenever I call, you're always too busy for your old man."

"Ignore him," M.K. said, reaching for the salt. "It's supposed to be this way when you go to college." She shook the shaker over her basket of fries. "It's how young women are supposed to separate from their parents. Find their own way in the world."

Adam frowned. "Look who's talking. You went to a community college and stayed home."

She slid the saltshaker across the table at him. "Because I thought, at the time, that I had a responsibility to my siblings. I made a mistake. A mistake my parents shouldn't have allowed me to make."

Liza Jane chewed on a fry. "I can't imagine living at home

again now that I've been gone a few months. I love you, Dad," she looked up at him, "but I sure don't want to live with you. I like coming and going when I please. Eating what I want to when I want to."

He set down his beer. "That's fine, just so long as you don't completely abandon me. I moved here so we could be closer." He reached for his chicken sandwich.

"So, M.K.," Liza Jane said, "what's happening with the investigation? Seems like things have been pretty quiet. It's almost scarier now."

"You win." M.K. looked up at Adam after checking her wristwatch. "I said it would take at least half an hour before she asked. You said less than half an hour. Twenty-seven minutes. I pay the bill."

Liza Jane laughed. "Come on. You couldn't expect me *not* to ask. I think half the kids in my classes have left or are skipping, saying there's no way the college can flunk them this semester."

"Of course we couldn't expect you not to ask. No more than you could expect us to answer," Adam smirked. His cell phone went off and he reached into the leg pocket of his cargo pants. He glanced at the screen that had lit up. "Hmm," he said. "It's my dad. Hello? Hey, Dad. What's—"

Adam's dad didn't let him go on. "Excuse me, ladies," he said to M.K. and Liza Jane as he slid out of the booth and walked away. *Be right back*, he mouthed.

"That's weird," Liza Jane said, watching her dad walk across the pub toward the hallway, where it was probably quieter. "Gramps never calls Dad on the cell phone. You know what that's about?"

M.K. watched him walk away, curious now, too. She and Adam were in a strange place right now in their relationship. In some ways they were becoming very close. They spent a lot of time talking about a lot of things painful to both of them. In the last week, M.K. had told him more about her family life, and the pain her father still caused her, than she'd ever told anyone. Adam talked a lot about the job, about his failed marriage. They hadn't discussed the Lombardi case, but they skirted the issue time after time, and M.K. had a feeling that once the anniversary passed, he'd be able to talk about it. The strange thing about this relationship was that though they held hands sometimes, kissed, it hadn't gone beyond that. In a way, that was okay with M.K. She felt like they were really getting to know each other.

"Okay, while he's gone," Liza Jane said, scooting over closer to M.K., "tell me what's going on with the case. The papers say it's stalled. What the heck does that mean?"

M.K. took her time answering. She certainly wasn't giving Liza Jane any information she shouldn't, but there was no reason why the young woman shouldn't have a better understanding of police investigative terms and procedures. If she really was interested in some kind of career in the reporting field, the more she comprehended, the better she would be at her job.

"It basically means that the case is open, but we're not moving forward."

"You've given up?"

M.K. reached for her diet soda. Since the night at the ball, she was staying away from alcohol. Adam was intoxicating enough for her right now. "No, we haven't given up. We've just exhausted all of our leads. We have some suspects we're watching—"

"Like Buddy and Professor Connelly."

M.K. frowned. "You think maybe you need to spend a little more time on your biology homework and less time jumping to conclusions?"

"I know you questioned them," she accused.

"I questioned you, too." M.K. glanced up. She could see Adam still talking on the phone. Something was wrong. She could tell by the look on his face. She hoped no one was seriously ill.

Liza Jane scrunched up her face. "Oh, please. That's so

lame. You asked me about who I saw near Wooten Hall that night. That's not the same thing."

"Liza Jane." She shook her head. "I'm not giving you anything."

"There was sex involved in the last case, wasn't there?" Liza Jane pressed. "Homosexual sex. But that doesn't really fit in, does it? Except for the part about the killer taking his dick." She munched on another fry. "What do you think he's doing with all those body parts? Building a Frankenstein or something?"

To M.K.'s relief, Adam returned to the table.

"M.K. was just updating me on the campus killer case," Liza Jane said as her father slid back into the booth.

"I was not." M.K. sank an elbow into the teen's side. She liked Liza Jane and she thought the young woman liked her. Theirs wasn't quite the kind of friendship adults shared, but it was definitely a friendship apart from what M.K. had with Adam. She liked the idea of that, of having friends . . . of any age.

"My dad," Adam said, setting his cell on the table. "He's really upset."

"What's wrong?" M.K. asked.

"You remember Jerome Fisher, the psychiatrist? He and Dad were friends."

"Sure." M.K. wiped her mouth with her napkin and laid it down, giving him her full attention. "Distinguished black gentleman."

"He . . . he killed his wife and then himself. Dad just heard."

"Oh, my God," Liza Jane exclaimed. "You're kidding." She grabbed her messenger bag from beside her on the bench and dug into it, pulling out a notebook.

"Put that away," her father snapped. "This is a person, Liza Jane. He was your grandfather's friend."

"What happened?" M.K. asked.

Adam lifted his hand. "Apparently Dr. Fisher, Sela, was

doing very badly. She wasn't expected to live much longer. She was in a great deal of pain." He paused. "Apparently he . . . Jerome gave her an overdose of some kind of morphine. Killed her and then killed himself."

"He had enough medication to overdose, too?" she asked.

"No." He shook his head, looking down and then up at M.K. "That's the weird thing. He probably did have enough to overdose as well, according to my father, but he shot himself."

"Oh, heavens," M.K. breathed. "Is your father all right?"

"Yeah. I mean, he's shook up, but he's all right."

Liza Jane reached for her burger again. "Poor Gramps."

M.K. hadn't finished her meal but she wasn't hungry anymore. She was finding the job did that to her. In the last three months, she'd lost the ten pounds she'd been wanting to lose for ages without even trying.

"I think I'm going to go over and see my parents."

"Sure," M.K said. "Of course."

"You have your car here?" he asked Liza Jane.

"Yeah. It was so cold I chickened out and drove over from my dorm," she answered. "I couldn't get anyone to walk over with me anyway."

"You mind giving M.K. a ride home? I'll give you money for gas." He slid out of the booth. "I think I should go now. Dad's really upset. Says he's known Jerome for years. Says he can't believe he would do such a thing."

"I don't need gas money, Dad. I'm fine. You go see Gramps. Tell him I love him."

M.K. slid out of the booth. "You want me to go with you?" she asked quietly, looking up at him.

He shook his head, reaching out to rest his hands on her hips. "Nah. Thanks, though. You mind me not taking you home?"

"Of course not. It's your father. He called you because he needed you. You should go."

"Okay, well, I'll see you at the office tomorrow?" He looked into her eyes.

She smiled. "Sure."

He brushed his lips against hers and she couldn't resist closing her eyes. She couldn't wait for December fifteenth to pass. She couldn't wait to see what was going to become of her Adam. She was getting more cautiously optimistic with each day.

"See you, kiddo," he called to Liza Jane as he released M.K.

"See you, Dad. Don't worry," his daughter called after him as M.K. slid into his seat. "She won't tell me any FBI secrets. At least not any big ones!"

"What the hell is this?" Crackhow demanded, practically throwing the morning paper across his desk.

M.K. glanced at Adam standing beside her, and then stepped forward to pick up the paper. It was open to page two of the *Baltimore Sun*.

LOCAL STUDENT CRACKING CASE, the headline read.

M.K. didn't have to read on to know who it was about. A snapshot of Liza Jane in her signature pink bandana and blond dreadlocks was featured with the article. Her name ran just before the article.

"I'm going to ask you two again," Crackhow shouted across his desk. "What the hell is going on here?"

"I don't know." Adam grabbed the paper out of M.K.'s hands. "Maybe I could read it first so I would know what you were talking about."

"She's telling people that this killer is someone on the inside, that it's a law-enforcement agent," Crackhow said. "Possibly even someone from the Bureau. Where the hell did she get that? Where's she getting the information?" He slammed his fist on the desk.

M.K. felt so bad for Adam. She knew very well that he didn't know anything about the news article. "I can assure you, Captain, neither Special Agent Thomas nor I have provided this student—"

"His daughter—" Crackhow interrupted, pointing a bony finger.

"Neither Special Agent Thomas nor I have provided *his daughter* with any information about these cases."

"He's right. She says it right here," Adam grunted. "She says it's a law-enforcement agent, someone with an educated understanding of police procedure." He slapped the paper with the back of one hand. "She provides evidence that suggests her theory." He looked up at M.K., accusation in his eyes. "All circumstantial, but readers aren't going to see that, are they?"

She stared back at him. He thought she had told Liza Jane her theory. The jerk thought—M.K. looked back at Captain Crackhow. "We'll speak with her, sir. Find out where she got her information."

"Little late now, isn't it?" he demanded. "I'll have the governor calling me again."

"We'll let you know what we find out, sir." M.K. walked past Adam and out the door.

He followed her, still carrying the newspaper. "You told her your damned lame-ass theory, didn't you?" he demanded. "You told her about the weird *feeling* you had."

She kept walking. "I did not."

Other agents were rising out of their chairs to see what the commotion was about. They were used to her and Adam arguing by now, but this was obviously bigger, better than usual.

"Adam—"

"You wanted her to like you. You wanted to be friends with her, to get to me, so you—"

"You—" M.K. wanted so badly to curse at him. With one hand she shoved opened the door to the ladies' room; with the other, she grabbed his arm and dragged him in behind her.

"Will you please lower your voice?" she demanded.

"Do you have any idea what this could do to our case?" he exploded, shaking the paper at her. "Any idea what it could do to our careers? You don't take your *weird feelings*, your *unsubstantiated theories*, and pass them on to a reporter. Not even if she is only nineteen years old!"

M.K. stood with her arms crossed over her chest, staring at the tiled floor. Adam's voice echoed all around her. "You done?" she asked quietly when he was at last silent.

"That's all you're going to say?"

She looked at him, so angry she could have slapped him. "How dare you question my integrity," she whispered harshly. "How dare you suggest I would allow my personal feelings for you—" She cut herself off, looking away, too angry even to express what she was thinking. "I'll call her," she said, walking past him. "I'll find out where she got the idea from."

"No. You stay away from her. I'll call her."

M.K. threw up her hands, close to tears, refusing to let him see them. "Fine," she said, walking away. "You talk to Liza Jane. I'll go back to trying to find out who's killing these kids."

"What's that supposed to mean?" he called after her. "You saying I'm not doing my part in this investigation?"

M.K. grabbed the bathroom door and jerked it open. "What I'm saying, Adam, is that you can just . . . just go to . . . Hades," she said. And she let the door swing shut behind her, leaving him in the women's bathroom.

Chapter Twenty-seven

"Come on, come on, pick up," Adam muttered. After the fourth ring, the phone clicked and her voice mail picked up.

"It's Liza. Leave a message, and I might call you back."

This time, Adam didn't bother. He'd been trying to call Liza Jane all weekend. He dropped the phone on the messy kitchen counter and walked to the sink to gaze out at the autumn woods behind his town house. He'd rented the place, though it was a little pricey, considering what he voluntarily paid in child support, because he liked this view. From the kitchen, the small dining area, or the master bedroom he could see the undeveloped forest with its towering pine trees and hardwoods and dense thicket of briars indigenous to the area. The leaves had all fallen from the pin oak trees weeks ago and the greenbriers had died back. It looked so bare now. Lifeless.

Like the way he felt.

He closed his eyes. He'd really screwed up with M.K. at the office Friday. He didn't know where his daughter had gotten her information. Hell, she might have come up with the conclusion on her own. What he did know was that M.K. hadn't told her. He'd probably known it when he'd stood in the bathroom and accused her.

It was just that it made him so angry to hear her saying things she based on a hunch rather than hard evidence. He was just trying to protect her. Spare her. If only someone had done the same for him. That day he went to the little Italian restaurant with Mark and Laura and he spotted Lombardi, his cop intuition had told him everything was cool. The guy knew the feds were on him, knew Adam and Mark were on him. The minute he spotted Adam and Mark at the table, Adam had known he would beat feet.

He closed his eyes, clutching the edge of the sink. He thanked God every day that Liza Jane had been sick that day, running a fever. Sophie had cancelled at the last second. Adam remembered how pissed he'd been. Their marriage was already on the rocks by then. Had been for awhile.

He squeezed his eyes tighter, fighting the wave of memories washing over him. Even when Lombardi had started to approach the table, Adam still believed they were safe. That Mark and Laura were safe.

Adam flinched suddenly at the sound of the gunfire in his head.

What had Lombardi been thinking? If he was going to be indicted, going to be forced to rat on his co-workers, he'd rather be dead? And why not take a couple of federal agents with him?

Adam flinched again at the sound of the second shot. By the time he realized what was happening, saw Mark fly back under the impact of the bullet, Lombardi was already pulling the trigger again.

He saw the look on Laura's face as her head exploded. Saw the blood and brain matter fly through the air, splatter against the wall.

By then, Adam had pulled his service weapon, was firing. It was too late. Lombardi got off one more shot. Shattered the glass window behind Adam. Missed him.

Adam unloaded all seven shots into him. One after another. But it was too late. Laura was already dead. His instinct had been wrong and it had cost Laura her life, Mark his marriage. Sophie and him their marriage.

Adam opened his eyes, shaking. It was the first time in years and years he'd allowed himself to replay the entire incident in his mind.

He reached for the phone, gave himself a moment to recover, and punched in the numbers.

"'Lo."

"Hey, Sophie, it's me." He leaned his back against the counter, feeling better. Amazingly better.

"Hey, me."

She sounded tired. Even more so than usual.

"You okay?" he asked.

"Great, actually. Savannah's at a friend's, Mark's in the spare room putting the crib together, and I'm lying down."

"Sorry, I didn't mean to bother you."

"You're not bothering me, Adam. I need to get up and start supper, anyway. I'll have to pick up Savannah soon. What's up?"

"I was wondering if you'd talked to Liza Jane this weekend."

She didn't answer.

"That a no or a yes?"

Sophie sighed. "I talked to her briefly after her article came out in the paper. She was afraid you were going to be pretty pissed."

"She's got good reason to think that. She lets that paper print that bullshit, and then she doesn't even have the guts to return my phone calls!"

"Adam," Sophie said calmly, "our daughter is many things, but a coward is not one of them. It took a lot of those so-called guts for her to send that article to the *Sun*. You know they paid her for it."

"Great. She going to start paying her own tuition?"

"I think," Sophie said pointedly, "that she's avoiding you because she's tired of *your* bullshit."

"What's that supposed to mean?" He started loading dirty

dishes into the dishwasher. Had he really made this big a mess in two days? He couldn't even remember having canned ravioli, and yet here was the evidence, smeared all over the countertop.

"It means she understands that there are certain things the two of you are simply not going to agree upon. She thinks you should agree to disagree and move on. She's tired of fighting the same fights." She was quiet for a second. "Kind of the way I began to feel."

He flipped on the faucet to drown a fork covered in dried tomato sauce. "That's a pretty low blow, Sophie."

"Sorry, dear. It's the truth."

He dropped the fork in the sink and let the water run. "I'm not calling her to fight with her."

"Yes, you are," Sophie said. "You're calling to tell her why she shouldn't have sent that article to the *Sun*. Why she shouldn't have said the suspect might be a law-enforcement officer."

"You read it?" He lowered his foot to the lever on the trash can and dropped two empty cans in.

"Of course I read it. And I have to say, she made some good points. Her evidence bears thought. Maybe it is some kind of cop."

"Her evidence is circumstantial. It's inconclusive."

"So? She's nineteen. She's not a veteran FBI agent. She stated what she believed to be true from the information she had."

He put two dirty plates and three glasses into the sink. "She shouldn't be saying these things, damn it!"

"If I didn't know better, I'd think you were jealous."

"Jealous?" Adam cradled the phone on his shoulder, squirting dish detergent into the sink. He submerged both hands in the soapy water. "That's ridiculous."

"Is it? I understand the case is stalled. What if the FBI agent's daughter is closer to figuring out who's killing these kids than he is?"

Adam shut off the water and began to viciously scrub a plate with a Teflon sponge. "Jesus, now you sound like M.K."

"She say the same thing?"

"No." He groaned. "But she's just got better manners than you do. Crackhow was really pissed about the article. I said things I shouldn't have said. M.K. got pissed. You see how this is going for me."

Sophie laughed. "So call your girlfriend, tell her you're sorry."

"She's not my girlfriend." He hit the faucet and rinsed off the plate.

"Okay, so apologize and make her your girlfriend. The two of you are good together. She's cute and she's smart. A hell of a lot smarter than you are."

"Thanks." Finding another spot of hardened tomato sauce, he dipped the plate in the hot water again. "Okay. So what do I do about your daughter? I'm upset because I'm concerned for her safety. This guy is crazy, Sophie."

"No duh."

He had to smile. She sounded like Liza Jane. Or did Liza Jane just sound like her mother? "I'm serious. This is the worst I've ever seen. The scariest."

"So tell your daughter that," Sophie said. "Tell her what your concerns are, without going off on her."

"I don't—" He took a breath. "Okay. But first I have to be able to talk to her. I even went by her dorm this afternoon. Car was gone."

"Keep calling her. Eventually she'll pick up."

"Okay." He rinsed the plate again and, satisfied it was finally clean, he put it on the drain board. "Thanks."

"Sure."

He could hear her smiling.

"And when you do talk to Liza Jane . . ."

"Yes?"

"Tell her to call me. I saw the doctor Friday. I'm dilating. I should go anytime now."

"Sophie, that's great. I'm so excited for you guys." And he meant it. He really was.

"About time, wouldn't you say? I'm a week overdue."

"I'll tell her. Now, you take care. Let Mark make dinner and go for Savannah."

"'Bye, Adam."

He hung up the phone and dropped both hands into the sudsy dishwater. When he was done here, he'd try Liza Jane again. By then, maybe he'd have the guts to call M.K., too.

Liza Jane sat on a bar stool between Muriel and one of the girls from the TV station, Sam. Sam was having a beer because she was legal. Jerry was just letting Liza Jane and Muriel sit at the bar instead of one of the tables or booths at O'Shea's because it was a slow Sunday night. Weather was crap. There weren't even too many guys there watching the football game, which was a good thing because Liza Jane wasn't a fan of professional football.

"Aha! Got you again," Muriel cried in triumph.

Liza Jane pushed the little answer key to the video trivia game across the bar top. "Fine, you win."

"But you always beat me." Muriel leaned back on her stool to talk to Sam, who was busy flirting with the bartender. "She always beats me. Especially in the English poetry category."

"So I'm an English poetry geek." Liza Jane sat back on the bar stool and crossed her arms.

"You're sure cranky tonight." Muriel threw a piece of popcorn from the basket on the bar at her. "You'd think you'd be celebrating. Your first paid job."

Liza Jane deflected the popcorn kernel with her arm. "I think I'm going to head back to the dorm. Catch up on some reading for English Lit."

"Party pooper," Muriel accused. She turned back again, blocking Liza Jane's escape. "Sam, Liza's a party pooper."

Sam didn't answer. She was too busy flirting with Jerry.

Liza Jane jumped down off the bar stool.

"You can't go alone. Call security to escort you."

"Sure," Liza Jane answered.

"Hey, that your cell ringing?"

She plucked her pink knit beanie out of her messenger bag and pulled it down over her dreads. It was playing the tune from *Inspector Gadget*. "Yeah."

"You're not going to answer it?"

"Nope."

"Why not?"

Liza Jane slipped into the wool pea coat she'd gotten at the same shop where she'd bought her gown. Eleven bucks. "Because it's my dad," she sang.

"That's right. You can set your new phone for a different ring for every caller. I told my mom I wanted the same phone but she says I should get a job. Call security."

"I will. See you back at the room."

"Okay. Sure," Muriel called.

Liza Jane wrapped her scarf around her neck and stepped out into the dark. She had no intention of calling for a security escort. It would take them twenty minutes to get there and she was ready to go home now. The quickest way was to cut through the parking lot, through the hole in the fence behind O'Shea's. The same way Jessica Lawson had probably been going the night she died. But Liza Jane couldn't go that way. Not in the dark. Not when she'd seen Jessica lying there, dead.

Instead, she turned left and headed up the sidewalk. The weatherman had predicted snow flurries tonight, but it felt like rain to her. Sleet, maybe. She lowered her head, walking down the sidewalk. There weren't many cars parked along the street. A lot of the businesses, like her mom's store, were closed on Sundays. It was a real drag for college kids.

She continued along the lonely street, wishing someone

from the city would come out and fix the damned street lights that were out. She glanced behind her, thinking it was even a darker night than usual. She still had her editorial to turn in for the paper this week. Maybe it would be about the unsafe streets of Ashview. It was no wonder kids were being killed. A dark street like this had to be a haven for axe murderers and people like that.

Looking behind her, she crossed the street. She saw a flash of headlights from behind her reflect off a garbage can. She almost ran into the can. Another safety issue the mayor and the town police needed to look into.

The headlights got brighter as the car got closer. It slowed, and Liza Jane looked nervously over her shoulder wondering if maybe she should have called for that escort. She couldn't tell who it was. She lifted her hand over her brow, squinting.

"What are you looking at, buster?" she muttered, turning around, walking faster.

The car pulled up beside her. The window on the passenger side went down.

"Liza?"

She thought she heard her name, but it was windy out and she'd pulled her beanie down over her ears. She couldn't see into the car. She walked faster.

"Liza. Wait."

She looked again. It was so dark on the street, the headlights were so bright . . . Who was calling her?

Suddenly the car made a loud bleep and it flashed a circle of bright blue lights.

Liza Jane threw on her brakes, almost slipping on the icy sidewalk, even though she was wearing her fake rubber-soled Doc Martens. "Jeez! You scared the crap out of me, Jesse." She walked up to the cop car, leaned in, and slapped the inside of the door. "How was I supposed to know you weren't the killer?"

"What are you doing walking home alone this time of night?" he asked. "Get in."

She opened the door. "You're on duty. You're not supposed to be giving girls rides home."

"You walk here alone, too?"

"No. With Muriel and this other girl, Sam." She got in and closed the door, dropping her bag on the seat and thrusting her hands forward toward the heater.

"Put your seat belt on."

She rolled her eyes.

Once she was properly belted in, he pulled away from the curb. "I'm serious, Liza Jane. You can't be walking around alone in the dark on campus. Why can't you students get this through your thick heads? You're not immune to this guy. No one is."

A little warmer, she sat back on the seat. She'd decided, now that she'd gotten used to it, that Jesse was actually kind of cute in his uniform. He was so clean-cut, so all-American looking. So far out there, that he was kind of in. "You read my article in the *Baltimore Sun*?" she asked.

He signaled, turning off Main Street. "Yeah. You pissed a lot of guys off at the station."

"Why?" She pulled off her beanie and unwound her scarf.

"Because you're saying it's one of them."

"I said no such thing." She patted the seat between them. "So you did read it." She grinned. "What did you think?"

"I thought it was very good. I also thought it was dangerous."

Liza Jane looked out the window. They were on a street that ran along the west side of the campus. On a Sunday night, all the academic halls were closed and dark; the street was empty. Kids were staying in at night. "Dangerous how?"

He surprised her by hitting the brakes and pulling off the street. He threw the big car into neutral and turned to look at her, placing his arm on the back of the seat.

"What are you doing?" she asked. "I thought you were taking me home."

"It's dangerous, Liza Jane, because if the killer reads that article in the *Sun*, he might be worried. What if you lead the police to him?"

"That's ridiculous," she scoffed.

He looked her right in the eye, unsmiling. "Is it?"

She looked straight ahead, crossing her arms over her chest. "You surprise me, Jesse. You of all people. I thought you'd be supportive. I thought you liked me."

"I am supportive. I do like you." He shifted the car into gear again. "Which is exactly why I'm telling you that you need to be careful what you say in print."

"I know my dad's probably saying exactly the same thing."

"Probably saying?" Jesse asked, pulling back onto the street. "What do you mean? You haven't talked to him?"

"No." She frowned, looking out the window. "He keeps calling me. It's just that I know he's pissed."

"That's certainly a mature response."

She glared at him. "He doesn't understand what I'm doing. Why I'm doing it."

"I bet he probably understands better than you think. You're driven. Where'd you think you got that from?" He pulled into the parking lot beside her dorm, into the emergency-vehicle reserved space right next to the door.

She made a face. "You're probably right."

"So talk to him."

"I will." She nodded. "I just wanted to give him a couple of days to cool his jets, that's all." She turned to him. "I want to ask you something and I want you to be honest with me. Do you think my idea that the killer is a law enforcement agent or something like that is completely off the wall?"

He sat back in his seat. "No, I don't."

"Because I've been thinking about trying to get an interview with someone who might be able to tell me some things from a different perspective. What do you think?"

"I don't think there's anything wrong with looking at a case from a different perspective," Jesse said. "I just think you need to be careful about how you present your information to the public."

"Yeah. My last broadcast is probably the week after next. Without *Fraternity Row*, no one's going to tune in to the college station anymore. I'd really like to have some breaking news to finish with."

"Just promise me you'll be careful." He reached out to cover her hand with his.

She smiled. "Can you kiss me in that getup?"

"No. It would be unprofessional."

She got up on her knees. "Fine, so I'll be the one who's unprofessional." She covered his mouth with hers, giving him a big kiss, and then threw open the door, backing out, laughing. "'Night, Jesse. Thanks for the ride."

He just sat there, looking stunned.

I sit in front of the TV, cozy in my pajamas, with a cup of hot tea on the end table beside me. The volume is down on the TV so I can concentrate.

On the floor, at my feet, is my collage. It's quite lovely, really, such an expression of my feelings. Far more expressive than the silly journal Dr. Fisher wanted me to keep. "Silly Dr. Fisher," I say, waggling my finger at him pasted on the posterboard now. Sela is there, too. She is smiling back at me. I like to think that she actually appreciates what I did for her. God knows if I was ever that ill, in that much pain, I would hope someone would kill me.

I look back at the newspaper article on my lap. It is from the second page of the *Baltimore Sun*. Friday edition. Liza Jane stares back at me, smiling. She is so beautiful, but it is not her beauty I envy the most. It is her mind. The Ashview police, the state police, the FBI—she is smarter than all of them. Smarter because she has come the closest to me.

I pick up the scissors. Her article is bold and insightful and I am very proud of her.

Of course, I cannot allow her to continue her investigation.

I carefully cut her smiling face from the newspaper and reach for the glue. I am not sure how I will have her, but I have a feeling she will come to me.

Chapter Twenty-eight

Monday morning, M.K. was on a tear. All weekend she'd stewed over what had happened between her and Adam on Friday. She was upset with him. Upset with herself. This was why it was never going to work between them. Not that there really *was* anything between them. She couldn't let personal stuff get in the way of the professional, and with Adam . . . he just made that impossible.

She marched to his desk to tell him so, only to find that he'd gone to Philadelphia for the day to interview witnesses from an old case. Without telling her. He wouldn't be in the office until the next day, coward that he was. She thought about calling him on his cell, but she didn't want to have this conversation on the phone. That was why she hadn't picked up when he'd called her five times yesterday afternoon and evening.

M.K. returned to her own cubicle, madder than fire. Last night she'd decided to start going back over all the evidence she'd collected in the last three months on the campus-killer case, specifically looking at the victims and the body parts that had been removed. That had to be the trail to the killer.

She didn't care what Adam, the senior agent, had to say

about intuition having no place in crime investigations. The
hard evidence he harped on wasn't pointing her in any direction, mainly because there just wasn't any. The case was stalled.
But she wasn't going to let it stall. She was going to jump-
start it by any means she had available to her, and if that
meant trusting her intuition, following leads discovered by a
nineteen-year-old college student, or walking the campus alone
at night looking for the son of a gun, she was going to do it.

M.K. marched down the hall and into the conference
room she'd been using for the last two months. She sat down
in her chair and glanced at the list she'd made Friday of com-
parisons she wanted to make, directions she wanted to go.
Second on her list, highlighted with yellow marker, was to
compare the official autopsy reports. She knew what they all
said, at least what the preliminary reports had said, but she
wanted to put them in front of her all at once. Maybe something would stand out that she'd missed. Like all the other
ideas she'd jotted down, it was a long shot, but at this point a
long shot might be the only thing between the killer and his
next victim.

Of course, comparing the autopsy reports would mean
actually *having* them. Something Adam had been promising
to take care of for weeks . . . longer than that. She'd never
gotten copies of the audio tapes, either. She didn't blame Dr.
Wood. It wasn't her fault, really; it wasn't her responsibility.
She did blame Adam. It wasn't that she didn't have empathy
for him concerning what had happened to him and Mark, but
it wasn't an excuse for not doing his job.

She got out of her chair and marched out of the conference room and down the hall, past her cubicle, grabbing her
coat from her chair as she went by. Enough was enough. If
Adam couldn't get those reports, she'd get them herself.

Traffic on 695 was a mess. Thanksgiving was Thursday.
Travelers were already on the roads, headed for grandmother's

house, Martha Stewart's, somewhere. Personally, M.K. was thinking about skipping the trip home to Philly, and the holiday torture that would involve, and having a frozen turkey dinner in front of the TV while she worked.

It took her an hour and twenty minutes to get to the county building in Annapolis. She parked the car and strode through the reception area, flashing her ID as she walked past the receptionist behind the glass wall. She took the stairs to the basement. She was definitely not in the mood for the elevator.

She walked right into the morgue, not caring whether she walked in on an autopsy or not. She just wanted the reports due her. To her surprise, Dr. Wood wasn't even there, nor was her part-time assistant. She did find a gum-popping twenty-year-old on her hands and knees, filing papers in a tall cabinet behind the doctor's desk.

"Hello," M.K. said, knocking on the doorjamb.

The young woman, dressed in a short denim skirt, jumped up. "Ah, jeez, you scared me." She laughed. "I thought you were maybe one of those dead people in those drawers come back to life or one of those creepy body parts come looking for a body." She pressed her hand to her chest, glancing up at the specimen jars that lined the shelves of the M.E.'s office.

For once, the eyes and ears and livers didn't bother M.K. These days, only living things scared her. "I'm Special Agent M.K. Shaughnessy," she said, showing her ID. She tried to sound friendly, appear easygoing. It seemed to work for Adam. "I was looking for Dr. Wood."

"Um, she's not here. Court or something. I'm new. Tracy Stump." She laughed nervously and hooked a thumb with a long, fake nail on it in the direction of the file cabinet. "I'm supposed to file. Do paperwork. Help her get caught up and stay caught up." She popped her gum. "Not sure I'm going to like working down here, though." She grimaced. "With dead people, I mean. But I've got a little boy, and his daddy took off. And the county does pay benefits."

M.K. nodded, thinking this turn of events might just work out to her advantage. "I didn't need to see Dr. Wood, actually." She smiled. "I just wanted to pick up some autopsy reports and some tapes. Maybe she left them for me in an envelope or something?" She moved into the office, glancing around the desk as if looking for them.

Tracy scrunched up her face. "She didn't say nothing about it when she left." She glanced at the clock on the wall out in the autopsy room. "She'll be back in maybe an hour. You want to wait?"

"I'd like to, Tracy, but I can't. Important case," she said solemnly.

Tracy's eyes widened. "Ohhhh. Yeah. I bet." She eyed M.K.'s waist. "And even though you're a girl, they let you carry a gun and everything?"

M.K opened her arms with another smile. "They let me carry a gun and everything."

"Hmmm." Tracy turned away, scratching her chin with a fake nail. "Well, why don't we see if we can find those things ourselves?"

"Excellent idea. I could give you the last names of the victims. Would that help?"

"Yeah, that would help. She told me to put all these other autopsy reports in alphabetical order in these blue files here." She studied the metal file cabinet. "And I saw a whole bunch of tapes in a drawer over there." She pointed to another. "I just thought maybe Dr. Wood liked to listen to a cassette player when she worked down here but those aren't music, are they?" She pulled open a drawer in a file cabinet.

M.K. took a step closer. "No, Tracy, I'm afraid that's not music."

It was almost eight by the time M.K. got home. She had to stop at a Big Mart to pick up one of those little cassette tape players. Then, on impulse, she stopped for a bottle of wine, too. She hadn't spoken to Adam all day. He hadn't even tried to call.

Not bothering to take the time to change, M.K. left her service-revolver holster on the end of her bed and pulled her robe over her clothes. Her apartment was chilly. She kicked off her shoes and settled in her chair in the living room to listen to the autopsy tapes, leaving the TV off. She'd already gone over the reports she'd pilfered from Dr. Wood's office after she'd gotten back to her office. To her disappointment, but not surprise, nothing stood out. There was nothing unusual about them. Nothing Dr. Wood hadn't told them in her preliminary reports.

M.K. popped the double A batteries out of their package and placed them in her new cassette player. She then poured herself a glass of merlot; she was skipping her dinner in anticipation of what she knew she would have to listen to. She put the earphones on and slipped the tape Dr. Wood had recorded while doing Jessica Lawson's autopsy into the cassette player. M.K. didn't care what Adam said; she knew that was where she had to begin, because she knew that was where the killing began.

"Liza Jane, this is Dad," Adam said into his cell phone. There was so much static, he hoped she would be able to make out his message. "Honey. I need to talk to you. I'm over being angry. Now I'm just worried."

He kept one hand steady on the steering wheel. It was raining again. Sleeting in some stretches of I-95 and the roads were slick. He'd passed three accidents in the last ten miles.

He had left the Philadelphia field office later than he'd hoped to and the drive home was taking longer than usual. The beginning of holiday traffic, he supposed. He wanted to get back into town in time to go by M.K.'s. Of course, now it was getting late. Maybe he'd just call her when he got there.

He felt like he should apologize to her in person, but a phone call was better than letting it go another day, wasn't it?

"I'm serious, Liza Jane," he said into his phone. "This is my stern-father voice."

The phone beeped.

"Ah, hell," he groaned. "Phone's running out of juice and the charger's not working," he said quickly, wanting to get everything in he wanted to say before it cut off. "Look, you need to call me back. On my house phone if you can't get through to me on my cell."

It beeped again. Any minute it would go dead. It had happened twice last week. He just hadn't had time to get a new car charger.

"And call your mom," he added. "She's about ready to have the baby, you know. Doctor said—"

The phone went dead and Adam threw it down on the seat beside him, using every curse word he could think of, M.K. Shaughnessy be damned.

Liza Jane heard the *Inspector Gadget* tune when her phone rang and she was tempted to pick it up. It was childish to keep ignoring her dad, but she didn't want to get into an argument with him right now. She needed to keep her head clear for this interview.

She gripped the wheel of her VW bug, trying to keep it on the road in the sleet. Route 301/50 headed east toward the Bay Bridge was jam-packed, and she'd already passed several accidents where people had slid into the guardrails or hit the car in front of them. She didn't like driving in this kind of stuff, but when she'd called Dr. Wood, the M.E. had been nice enough to agree to see her. She'd said she was working late tonight and would be happy to tell her what she could about the process she went through to examine bodies, without, of course, releasing any information on the campus killer that she wasn't permitted to release.

Liza Jane had told the coroner she understood, explaining that her father had already given her a lecture on the very same subject. Dr. Wood knew her father, so they had both laughed. She seemed nice. Friendly. Liza Jane wondered what a nice doctor was doing working on a Monday at eight o'clock at night Thanksgiving week, but she guessed she was just like her father and M.K. and even Jesse. Always giving the job a hundred percent. Liza Jane hoped she was doing the same thing.

She spotted the exit sign for downtown Annapolis and put on her signal, thankful she was almost there. Maybe by the time she got done with the interview, the rain and sleet would have stopped.

M.K. swallowed a sip of wine, listening closely to the audio-tape Dr. Wood had made during Peter Wright's autopsy. The words she had just heard sent a shiver down her spine.

Nothing had really seemed out of place in the Jessica Lawson tape. Or in the Bart Johnson tape. But by the third recording, by the time she reached Peter Wright's autopsy, something did stand out. Just a single phrase—a single word, really—out of place

It was probably nothing, she told herself. She knew she couldn't jump to conclusions. She had to listen to all the tapes first. Be sure. And even then, *could* she be sure?

Sweat broke out on her forehead and she stood up to peel off her bathrobe. She popped the Wright tape out of the cassette player, letting it fall to the floor, and reached for the tape labeled in the M.E.'s neat handwriting, *Tiffany Faulk*.

She inserted the tape, hit "play" on the player, and then began to fast-forward it, stopping to listen, then skipping forward again. After listening to the gruesome procedure three times, she knew the process a medical examiner followed when doing an autopsy on a homicide. And she knew now what she was looking for.

* * *

Liza Jane walked down the stairs, her footsteps echoing all around her. She hoped she was going the right way because this was pretty creepy, going into the basement of the county building in the dark. As Dr. Wood had promised, the one door out front had been unlocked, but the lobby had been dark. She just followed the doctor's directions and went down the hall, down the stairs.

At the bottom of the stairwell, she pulled off her pink beanie and gave her head a shake. She was soaking wet from the run across the parking lot. Dr. Wood had told her she needed to park in the back; otherwise, when security came, her car might get spotted and then Dr. Wood would get called on the carpet for having civilians in the morgue after hours. Crazy regulations, she'd told Liza Jane on the phone.

Liza Jane peered down the hallway lit only by those emergency lights on the ceiling that were required in public buildings. She unwound her wet scarf and crept down the hall, beginning to wonder if this was such a good idea. Her father was going to kill her. Especially if she got something good out of Dr. Wood. Especially if it was a lead her father hadn't found yet.

Ahead, she spotted the door with MORGUE written across it in big, black, creepy letters. Liza Jane gulped. Well, here she was. She wondered if she should knock. Dropping her beanie and her scarf into the side pocket of her messenger bag, she tapped lightly on the door. There was a small window, too high on the door for her to see through, but she could see there were lights on inside. The doctor said she would wait for her. Liza Jane tapped again, and when there was still no answer, she opened the door.

It was one of those big, heavy metal doors. It squeaked like crazy. Actually, it groaned. "H . . . hello?"

Her voice echoed again. The room looked kind of like a big operating room in a hospital, all tiled, with a stainless steel table and big lights overhead that were out right now.

"Come on in," a woman's cheery voice called. "I'm back here, in my office."

Liza Jane let the door clunk shut behind her. On the other side of the tiled room, she saw a glass wall. It was an office. A pretty blond woman in a white coat sat behind a desk, waving to her.

"Dr. Wood," Liza Jane said. She walked through the dark tiled room into the brightly lit office, trying to look as professional as she could, knowing she probably looked like a drowned rat.

By the time she got there, Dr. Wood had risen and walked around the desk. She offered her hand and Liza Jane shook it. She was a lot taller than Liza Jane. Really tall. At least six feet. She was dressed in black wool pants and a gray silk blouse under the doctor's coat. Nice clothes. Not Liza Jane's style, but expensive.

"You must be Liza Jane Thomas," she said warmly. "You look like your father."

"Everyone says so." She nodded, smiling. She was used to it. Most people didn't realize she was adopted. She didn't usually go into it, though. Not that it was a big secret, but she just got tired of telling the story. Yes, she did look just like her mom and dad; no, it was not their sperm and egg she was conceived from.

"Hey, that's a compliment." The doctor laughed. "Your dad's hot. I keep trying to get him to go out with me."

Liza Jane laughed as she looked up at the jars that lined the shelves on the back wall of this office. They had human organs floating in some kind of liquid. "Wow," she said. "Are those real?"

Dr. Wood smiled. "Sure are."

Liza Jane stared at the jars in fascination. Hearts, livers, eyeballs. She took a step closer. "Oh, my gosh," she said, squinting, then drawing back a little. "Is that some poor guy's dick?"

Dr. Wood came up behind her. "From the beginning, I

knew you were a bright young lady, Liza. You're the first person to notice."

She raised her hand behind Liza Jane like she was going to put her arm around her, but instead, she clamped a cloth over her mouth and nose that smelled awful.

"What—" Liza Jane tried to get away, but she couldn't breathe. The doctor was holding the cloth too tight on her face. Suddenly she was nauseous. The room spun. The livers and lungs and . . . a finger in the jars spun around her. She felt herself falling, and then everything went black.

Chapter Twenty-nine

When Adam finally made it to Ashview, he decided to run by Liza Jane's dorm. When she headed off to college, he'd promised never to show up at her room unannounced, but she'd just have to get over it. His cell phone battery was dead and he needed to talk to her whether she wanted to talk to him or not.

He banged on the locked dorm door for a full five minutes before a girl in sweatpants and pink bunny slippers let him in. "You're supposed to swipe your ID card to get in," she said, walking away.

Adam chuckled. Apparently she hadn't noticed he was old enough to be her father.

He walked through the lobby, where there was a big communal TV. A bunch of girls and guys, the girls in PJs, were watching something on Comedy Central. He shook his head. Co-ed dorms. What a life.

He went down the hallway he hadn't been down since the last week of August when he helped Liza Jane move in. Her door was open, her roommate Muriel sitting at her desk. Adam knocked on the door frame.

Muriel looked up and, seeing him, popped out of her chair. "Hi, Liza's dad."

"Hey, Muriel."

She was dressed in PJs, too. Cotton pants with poodles wearing skirts all over them, and a matching top. White bunny slippers. Apparently they were in with eighteen- and nineteen-year-old girls. He'd have to remember that and get Liza Jane a pair for Christmas.

"She's not here."

"I didn't see her car in the front lot, but I know she parks in different places," he said.

Muriel rolled her eyes. She was cute, but not beautiful like Liza Jane. "I keep telling her that all she has to do is go to security and get a sticker. She's already got, like, ten parking tickets."

"I'm sure she'll appreciate you sharing that with me." Adam shook his wet raincoat. "You know where she went?"

She wrinkled her nose. "I'm probably not supposed to tell you."

"And I'm probably not supposed to handcuff you and haul you off to jail, either, but it can be done."

Muriel laughed, but she was obviously not entirely sure he was joking. "Liza Jane says you're funny. You really *are* funny."

"Cough it up, Muriel, or spend the night in the clink."

"You can't tell her I told." She waggled her finger. Blue sparkly nail polish.

"Cross my heart and hope to die," Adam said, going through the motions across his hibiscus-patterned polo. It was damp, too.

She dropped her hand to her hip, thrusting it out in a typical teen pose. "She had a big interview."

"With whom?"

"That medical examiner in Annapolis." She wrinkled her freckled nose again. "I can't remember her name. Dr. somebody."

"Dr. Wood?"

"That's it." She pointed.

"Tonight?"

"The doctor was working late or something. Liza seemed really excited that she was willing to talk to her."

"About what?"

Muriel rolled her eyes. "The campus serial killer, of course."

Adam groaned. His daughter was going to get him transferred to Tulsa yet. "Okay. Thanks." He walked away. He didn't know what was wrong with Liza Jane. Surely she realized the M.E. couldn't tell her anything about the case. Surely, Valerie realized it.

"You want me to tell her you came by?" Muriel called down the hallway.

"Just tell her to call me or die," he hollered back.

Adam walked out of the dorm lobby into the driving rain. He ran across the parking lot but was totally soaked again by the time he got his Jeep unlocked and climbed in. He was cold and hungry. He just wanted to get home and take a hot shower and maybe open up another delicious can of ravioli. This thing with Liza Jane could wait until tomorrow.

He rested his hand on the steering wheel—wet, too.

All of a sudden he had the strangest feeling. He could have sworn he heard Liza Jane call his name. He glanced out the window, out the windshield. There wasn't a soul there. No sign of her lime green VW.

He shuddered, started the engine, and turned the heater on full blast, rubbing his hands together for warmth. He considered driving to Annapolis.

His daughter would be furious with him if he showed up at her interview. He should just go home. Wait for her to call him, or try her again later. But he still had that weird feeling.

He threw the Jeep into reverse, pulled to the exit of the dorm lot, and contemplated which direction to go: left toward home, right toward Annapolis?

* * *

Perfect.

M.K. stared at the word she'd scribbled on her notepad. Five times. Five autopsies, and five times the same word. It was the only word out of place on every tape. In examining each victim, the doctor had made a reference to the body part as being *perfect*. Even Jessica's lock of hair, which she had told M.K. and Adam she hadn't noticed was missing.

M.K. stood in her dark living room for a moment. Could it be possible . . .

It couldn't, and yet . . .

She was suddenly so overwhelmed by a sense of foreboding that she was shaking all over. She grabbed the phone as she walked back to her bedroom to get her shoes. She dialed Adam's house and got his answering machine. "Call me," was all she said.

Sitting on the edge of her bed, she pulled on her boots, unsure even where she was going yet. She tried his cell. All she got was his voice mail there, too. "Adam," she said. "I need you to call me the minute you get this. On my cell. I don't care how late it is."

She tied up her boots, grabbed her coat and service weapon off the bed, and ran for the door, on pure intuition.

M.K. cruised through the front parking lot of the county building in Annapolis. There wasn't a single car there. The lights were all out in the lobby. The place had to be locked up for the night. Dr. Wood wasn't here.

She braked in front of the building, staring at the dark glass. She still couldn't shake the feeling that she had to be here. It didn't make any sense, she knew. It made so little sense that she was glad that Adam hadn't called her back. He'd just make fun of her.

She lifted her foot off the brake, gliding toward the exit. Then, on impulse, she turned right instead of left, going behind the building where there was additional parking. Of course that made sense. That had to be staff parking.

As she came around the corner, she spotted two cars parked side by side. A nice Toyota sedan . . . and a lime green VW bug.

Her breath caught in her throat. She slammed on the brakes, sliding on the icy pavement sideways into a parking space. She jumped out of her car, closing one hand over her service revolver, the other on the cell phone in her coat pocket. She dialed Adam's number again. Still nothing.

As she checked the two back doors, she contemplated calling 911 or at least the office. What was she going to say, though? She had this weird hunch, she needed to see Dr. Wood and when she got here she thought she recognized her partner's daughter's VW and she was afraid the college-age woman might be in danger? If she called with that information, she'd be back in Quantico crunching statistics before her coat dried out.

Both rear doors of the building were locked. How did Liza Jane get in . . . if she was here at all? If that was her car. But how many lime green VW bugs with a *Sublime* bumper-sticker could there be?

She walked around the building to the front, trying each glass door. The farthest one clicked and opened. M.K.'s heart seemed to skip a beat.

She had no idea what to do. Should she draw her weapon? What for? It was just a dark building. An empty, dark building—so far.

To satisfy the weird intuition that was still pumping adrenaline through her veins, she unsnapped the leather strap that prevented her Glock from being drawn.

She walked through the empty, cavernous lobby, down the hall to the stairs. Her footsteps echoed so loudly in the stairwell that it was almost deafening. Nothing like warning people you're coming. She tried to walk carefully, making less sound.

At the bottom of the steps, she crept down the dark hallway illuminated by the red emergency evacuation lights. She knew her way to the morgue.

A light in the window.

Someone was there. Dr. Wood? Liza Jane?

M.K. had no idea what she was going to say when she walked in, what she was going to do. But she was the one with the gun, right?

She rested her hand on the doorknob and tried to stand on her tiptoes to see through the window. She wasn't tall enough. All she could see was the green tile wall and the doorway that led to the drawers where the bodies were stored.

She took a deep breath, turned the knob, and walked in.

"Oh, sweet God," she heard herself murmur.

On the autopsy table was a body. A body with white-blond dreadlocks.

Tears welled in M.K.'s eyes. Was this why Adam hadn't returned her calls?

She took a step toward the table.

What had happened to Liza Jane? Sweet, bright Liza Jane?

"Good evening, Agent Shaughnessy," a female voice said from behind her.

M.K. had no idea where Dr. Wood came from. Suddenly she was just standing there in scrubs with a cap on her head, a scalpel in her hand.

M.K. was shaking all over. Cold. Wet. In shock. "She . . . she's dead?" she gasped, taking another step toward the autopsy table, reaching for her crucifix and Miraculous Medal around her neck.

M.K couldn't see any wounds, any blood. Liza Jane's eyes were closed. She just looked like she was sleeping.

"Not yet."

It took a heartbeat for Dr. Wood's reply to sink in.

M.K. grabbed for her service revolver, spinning around. Dr. Wood lunged forward, hitting M.K. full force in the chest, knocking her to the hard, tiled floor.

M.K. screamed. Grunted as she hit. She'd almost had her weapon drawn. She rolled onto her back.

Dr. Wood lashed out, striking M.K.'s right arm with the scalpel. It burned like fire. Blood blossomed on her wet raincoat sleeve. M.K. watched in horror; everything seeming to move in slow motion, as her gun flew out of her hand and slid across the tiled floor.

M.K. tried to sit up, tried to shove the doctor off, but the M.E. was so much bigger than M.K. So much heavier.

M.K. felt the blade of the scalpel pierce her skin again. This time deep. Her chest. It burned.

Bright lights exploded in her head. In front of her eyes.

Dr. Wood plunged the knife into her chest again. M.K. coughed. Choked. She looked down to see her new blouse covered in blood. None of it seemed real.

She felt herself fall back onto the tile floor again. Her head hit hard and bounced. She coughed again and droplets of blood flew from her mouth with her spittle. "I'm sorry, Adam," she whispered as the blackness enveloped her. "Adam."

"Ah, I see you're awake," Liza Jane heard a voice say.

She blinked, confused as to where she was. She was lying on her back in a narrow bed. Green tile walls. A hospital? She remembered driving on 50. Had she had an accident?

There were big, bright lights overhead like in an operating room. Her arms were secured at her sides. Had she been hurt? Did she need surgery?

She turned her head in the direction of the kind voice. She saw the face, and then it all came back to her in a rush of terrifying flashes, like images in an old eight-millimeter film.

"What are you doing to me?" Liza Jane demanded, fighting not to become hysterical.

"Are you feeling all right?" The doctor approached, dressed now in green scrubs as if she were about to perform a procedure. "A little nauseous, probably. The chloroform does that."

Liza Jane cringed as the doctor moved closer, but there was no way for her to get away. She was tied down . . . tied down to an autopsy table.

Liza Jane wanted to scream, but something in her gut told her not to. Besides, who would hear her in the basement morgue? No one was here. "I don't understand," she said softly.

"Few people do," the M.E. answered matter-of-factly as she rolled a cart with a tray of surgical instruments toward the autopsy table.

Liza Jane was shaking all over. Scared to death. But she was angry, too. She remembered the penis in the jar and she knew it was Del's penis. And if she looked closely, she knew she would find Peter's ear and Tiffany's breast, too. "It was you," she accused loudly.

Dr. Wood smiled. She wore a mask, but it was still down around her throat. "I knew from the start that you were bright. A law-enforcement agent who knew police procedure?" She ran her hand over the instruments as if making a mental checklist. "You were almost right."

"You killed them," Liza Jane whispered.

"They deserved what they got for what they did to me," she snapped.

Liza Jane stared at her, her anger stronger than her fear now. "What do you mean, they *deserved* it? What could those kids have ever done to you? Did you even know any of them?" she demanded.

"Heavens." The doctor drew back her head. "You're feisty, aren't you? Even in the face of death. What an excellent heroine. You almost saved the day, you know. Somehow Special Agent Shaughnessy was right behind you."

"Right behind me?"

Dr. Wood walked around the table and Liza had to turn her head to follow her with her gaze. "What are you talking about? M.K came here? Looking for me?"

Dr. Wood gave a sympathetic smile. "Walked right in not fifteen minutes ago. You were still unconscious." She walked over to a countertop and opened a cupboard in search of something. "I didn't get a chance to ask her why she'd come."

Liza Jane could feel her brave front waning. "Where . . . where is M.K. now?"

"Dead, I'm afraid." Dr. Wood had returned to the far counter; she glanced over her shoulder, frowning. "Tucked away until I can figure out what to do with her. You know, you've really made a mess of things for me." She turned back to the cupboard. "Aha, here it is." She turned to face Liza Jane, some kind of weird saw in her hand.

"What . . . what's that?" Liza Jane breathed.

Dr. Wood looked down at the menacing piece of electrical equipment in her hand. "Cranial saw, dear."

Liza Jane wanted to scream. She wanted to cry. She wanted her daddy. She tried to jerk her arms and legs free but gave up after a moment, knowing she couldn't escape. "Wh . . . why?" she whispered. "You said they did something to you. What did they do? What did *I* do?"

Dr. Wood glanced away and to Liza Jane's surprise, the doctor's eyes welled with tears. "You know, my psychiatrist asked me the same question. I just couldn't tell him. Not a man. It . . . it was too embarrassing. Too shameful."

Liza Jane's thoughts were flying in a hundred directions at once. M.K. was dead. Dr. Wood was going to kill her, too. But she didn't want to die. She didn't want to miss the birth of her new baby sister or brother. She wanted to finish college. Be a newscaster. Surf with her dad again next summer. "I'm a girl," Liza Jane heard herself whisper. "You can tell me."

Dr. Wood slowly approached the autopsy table. She set the saw down on the tray, gazing off into the distance as she folded her arms over her chest. "I'm not what I appear, Liza Jane. I'm not the beautiful woman you see."

Liza Jane held her breath. She had no idea how she was going to get away. Maybe she could convince the doctor to let her go. All she knew right now was that she needed to listen. "You're not?" she said, taking care to sound nothing but sympathetic.

Dr. Wood shook her head. "No." She paused. "Liza Jane, do you know what a hermaphrodite is?"

She thought hard. "A . . . a person born with male and female genitalia?"

Dr. Wood nodded. "But it's not just the body parts, sweetie. It's what's inside." She tapped her left breast. "What's inside that can't be altered."

"I don't understand." Then Liza Jane realized she had to be talking about herself. "You're a hermaphrodite?" she whispered, trying not to sound as shocked as she was.

"Yes, I'm a man and a woman," the doctor said. "Only I look like a woman because I had surgery. I take hormone injections."

"You said they hurt you," Liza Jane probed. She felt sick to her stomach. Like she was going to throw up. But she knew by the look on Dr. Wood's face that this had to do with the killing. Killing her. Killing the others. "How did they hurt you?"

The doctor turned away, and for a moment Liza Jane was afraid she wasn't going to tell her. Then, thankfully, she started to speak again.

"I was in college. I had already made the decision that I would become a woman. Have the surgery to have my penis removed, a vagina formed. I was already taking the hormone treatments. Blossoming."

Liza Jane couldn't see her face but she sounded like she was smiling. Reminiscing.

"I tried really hard to fit in. To be a part of the group. There were little defeats. Little jibes from fellow students who must have sensed I was different."

"Little jibes don't make you kill people."

Dr. Wood spun around, startling Liza Jane, and for a moment she feared she'd pushed her too far.

"They invited me to a party," the doctor continued in an

eerie voice. "There at the frat house. Phi Kappa, right on Fraternity Row."

"Here?" Liza Jane asked in shock. "You went to college at Chesapeake Bay?"

The doctor turned toward her. Nodded. "I went to the party. I had too much to drink. I danced. I thought the boys liked me." Tears filled her eyes again. "They did like me, but then . . ." She wiped at her eyes, smearing black mascara. "Then the fun got out of hand. I . . . I was too drunk. I told them I didn't want to go to the bedroom with them." A sob escaped her lips. "They . . . they dragged me into the back. They pulled off my blouse. Then . . . then . . ."

"They tried to rape you, didn't they?" Liza Jane asked. Against her will, her heart went out to the woman . . . to the man . . . to whatever Dr. Wood was.

"They . . . were going to rape me, but . . ."

Liza Jane's eyes widened. "You hadn't had the surgery yet."

"I hadn't had the surgery yet."

"They saw . . ."

"They found that I had a penis. Breasts and a penis." Another sob. "They called me a *freak.*"

Liza Jane was crying now, too. For the doctor. For herself. "They shouldn't have done that. They had no right." She fought to stay in control of her emotions. "But Dr. Wood, that doesn't give you the right to kill kids now. It doesn't give you the right to kill *me.*"

"They thought they were all so *perfect,*" she said, wiping at her eyes again, her tone changing. She reached for the plug on the saw and inserted it under the table. "But they weren't perfect. Just a little bit of them was."

"I still don't understand." Liza Jane was on the edge of hysteria. She couldn't stop looking at the saw. It was a cranial saw, one used to cut open your head. Get to your brain. "You . . . you cut off their body parts to—"

"Separately, they are imperfect," Dr. Wood interrupted,

seemingly in a daze now. "Cruel. Ugly. But together, they could be perfect. Not male. Not female. A perfect person," she said, reaching for the cranial saw. "And in you, my dear," she smiled sadly, "I see the perfect mind."

There was a sound on the far side of the room. Dr. Wood looked up. Liza Jane turned her head.

The door flew open.

"Daddy!" Liza Jane screamed.

Chapter Thirty

Adam saw Liza Jane on the autopsy table and for a moment his cognitive thought processes abandoned him. She was dead. His baby girl was dead. But then his years of experience on the job forced his brain to take over.

No. She wasn't dead. He had heard her scream.

Adam reached for his weapon in his shoulder holster under his coat. At the same instant, Valerie Wood passed the saw to her left hand and pulled something from the waistband of her scrubs.

A gun.

It didn't make any sense. Nothing here made any sense.

She pointed it at him.

Adam knew, as a trained FBI agent, what he had to do. He squeezed the trigger, but it was an instant too late. The guns exploded. Liza Jane screamed. Something hit him hard in the chest and knocked him backward. His weapon fell from his hand and skittered out of reach.

He hit the tile floor hard and looked down in disbelief at the left side of his chest. His new shirt was bright with blood. He'd been shot.

His head hit the tile floor hard, bounced, then hit again and everything went black and silent.

A sound startled M.K. awake in her bed. No ... not in her bed.

Panic fluttered in her chest. She was somewhere dark and cold. In a box.

A nightmare.

Except that she was awake. Awake, but she couldn't breathe. She felt like an elephant was sitting on her chest.

It was so dark. So close.

She panted, fighting the panic that radiated through her body, threatening to shut down her ability to think. To reason.

Where am I? Where am I? her mind screamed. *Get me out!*

But she couldn't get out. There were walls around her. Cold walls.

Suddenly, she remembered Liza Jane on the autopsy table. Dr. Wood with a scalpel. A terrible nightmare.

No. It was real. It had happened.

M.K. tried to move her arms, forcing herself to breathe as normally as possible. There was no room around her to move, wherever she was. Where the doctor had put her. Put her after she'd stabbed her and left her for dead.

It was Dr. Wood. Dr. Wood had been killing the students on the campus. Dr. Wood had killed Liza Jane. Tried to kill her.

But M.K. wasn't dead.

Somehow she managed to get her hand up to her neck. She gripped her crucifix and Miraculous Medal. Prayed to God to help her, and then she reached up and began to press her fingers to the cold metal overhead. It was all around her; she was trapped.

Think, think, M.K. told herself. Her chest hurt so badly. And she couldn't breathe. It was worse than any elevator. Dark. Cold. Close.

Where had Dr. Wood left her? She tried to make her brain function, tried to think. They had been in the morgue. She remembered the tile floor. The autopsy table. Liza Jane's blond dreadlocks.

At that moment, M.K. realized where she was, and she was so overwhelmed with terror that for a minute she was paralyzed. She couldn't reason, she couldn't react.

She was in one of those cold-storage drawers. The kind medical examiners used to keep the dead bodies cold.

"Heavenly Father," she whispered. "Heavenly Father."

But she didn't expect God to sweep down and save her. God had given her a brain to save herself, hadn't He?

Think!

A drawer. A gruesome drawer, but a drawer, nonetheless. Drawers slide out.

M.K. tried to catch her breath. She felt like she was suffocating. Buried alive.

Drawers slide out. Couldn't she just slide the drawer out and climb out?

But what if there was a latch?

Why would there be a latch? To lock dead people in?

M.K. almost laughed aloud in relief.

"Okay, okay," she whispered. "Drawers slide out."

But which way? She pressed her hands to the freezing cold metal overhead again and tried to push toward her feet. It didn't budge.

It wasn't going to work! She was trapped. Dead.

No.

M.K. gritted her teeth and pushed again. This time she felt her body move. She heard the sound of metal gliding on metal and a band of light appeared inside the box from overhead, behind her. She pushed again, harder this time, frantic to get out now.

Slowly the drawer glided open and M.K. caught a glimpse of the white ceiling. She panted hard, trying to catch her breath. She had to get out. She had to.

But what if Dr. Wood was still here? How would she get away?

A sound came from the other room. Like a power tool. A drill or something.

Sweet heaven. Dr. Wood was about to do Liza Jane's autopsy! M.K. pushed as hard as she could on the drawer above her and she slid out to her waist. She tried to sit up and her head spun, but she kept moving, ignoring the blood, the elephant still on her chest.

She had to be quiet. Couldn't let the good doctor know she had escaped. She had to get help.

Taking a deep, hopefully calming breath, M.K. rolled out of the drawer, onto the tile floor. She was so winded from that little bit of exertion that she had to lie there for a minute and catch her breath again.

She heard Dr. Wood's voice in the other room.

Who was she talking to? M.K. wondered now what the sound she heard earlier had been. The one that had awakened her.

She sat up, waited for the room to stop spinning, and then rolled over onto her hands and knees. She had blood everywhere. Even her hands now. It was sticky. Warm. She crawled forward a few inches and reached for her Glock in her shoulder holster.

Gone.

She remembered now seeing it glide across the tile floor when Dr. Wood knocked her down.

She had to get out of here.

She crawled forward, inch by inch, leaving bloody, smeared handprints in her wake. At the doorway she stopped, tried to catch another strangled breath, and peered around the corner.

The doctor's back was to her. She was standing at the autopsy table, close to Liza Jane's head, the saw poised.

M.K. squeezed her eyes shut for a moment. She didn't want to see this. Couldn't watch. But something at that instant made her open her eyes.

Liza Jane moved. She moved!

M.K. was so startled that she had to close her eyes, grip the door frame. Liza Jane was still alive!

M.K. made herself open her eyes. Ignore the spinning room. The nausea. Liza Jane was still alive but Dr. Wood intended to do something with that saw.

Not as long as M.K. still drew breath.

She pulled herself to her feet, leaving blood smeared down the pale green door frame. She had to get her Glock. Where was her Glock?

She tried to crane her neck to see farther into the morgue's main room. Her vision blurred. Swam. She was close to passing out again.

There was something on the floor on the far side of the room. Someone. She saw blond hair, a pool of blood, a flowered shirt . . .

At that moment, M.K. almost lost it. She almost screamed.

But then, out of the corner of her eye, she saw the little blond dreadlocks move. Over the sound of the saw in Dr. Wood's hand, she heard Liza Jane shouting. Cursing.

M.K. glanced around frantically, looking for something to use as a weapon. Anything.

Why not use the pistol in the holster on your back? a little voice in her head said.

She almost laughed aloud in relief. Of course. The backup. Her Kel-Tec .32.

Leaning against the wall to hold herself upright, she reached around her back, and felt the lump. Thank God Dr. Wood hadn't found it. M.K. unsnapped the little leather strap that held the tiny pistol secure and freed it. She closed her hand around the handle, her finger on the trigger, and took a staggered step forward, refusing to allow herself to think about Adam and the pool of blood. What mattered right now was the living. What mattered was Liza Jane.

"Dr. Wood," M.K. said, taking another step closer. She was in firing range now.

The doctor didn't respond. Hadn't heard her above the deafening whine of the saw.

"Dr. Wood!" M.K. shouted, using every bit of strength she had left to take another staggering step.

The doctor spun around, her eyes widening in astonishment. Then she smiled, shutting off the saw with a quick flick of her finger. "Well, isn't this a surprise," she said.

"M.K.," Liza Jane cried.

"Shh," M.K. soothed.

"My dad!"

"One thing at a time." M.K. kept her gaze fixed on the M.E., her arm stretched out, finger on the trigger, just as she had been taught at the academy. "Put that thing down and step away, Dr. Wood. *Now.*"

"Of course. No need to shout, Special Agent Shaughnessy."

She was so cool. So calm. She had to be a psychotic killer. No one else could act this way under such circumstances.

Dr. Wood lowered the saw to the table.

"She's got your gun!" Liza Jane warned.

As Dr. Wood dropped the saw onto the metal tray with her left hand, she picked up something in her right and whipped around to face M.K. again.

M.K. kept her gaze fixed on the target. "You're not going to shoot me with my own gun," she whispered, her voice surprisingly strong.

The doctor raised the Glock, pointing it at M.K. "You're not going to shoot me at all."

"Want to bet, bitch?" M.K. ignored the gun barrel pointed at her and squeezed the trigger.

The gun exploded. Liza Jane turned her head away. The doctor went down on her knees and tried to lift the Glock again.

M.K. squeezed off a second round.

The doctor fell face first on the green tile floor and didn't move again.

"You got her! You got her," Liza Jane shouted, laughing, crying hysterically. "She shot my dad. He's bleeding a lot. You have to help him."

M.K. felt herself sway. The room was tilting again. She took a step back, grabbed for the wall to support herself.

"You're hurt," Liza Jane said through her tears. "If you can get to me, untie me, I can help. I can call for an ambulance."

"Not sure I can walk," M.K. whispered. She pressed her back to the wall as her knees buckled and she slowly began to sink. Her hand went to her coat pocket, still wet with rain . . . with her blood. "Have a phone," she heard herself mumble. Trying to keep her focus just another moment longer, she pushed her pistol into her pocket and punched 911.

"This is the 911 operator," a voice said. "What is the nature of your emergency?"

"This . . . this is FBI Special Agent Shaughnessy," she said. "I . . . I need an ambulance. Maybe two."

She thought she gave the address of the building. Hoped she did. The last thing she saw as her eyes drifted shut was Liza Jane's brave smile and Adam's bloody shirt.

There was a knock at M.K.'s hospital room door and she opened her eyes to see Adam standing there, grinning. His left arm was in a sling but he wore his trademark Hawaiian shirt and a pair of khakis. All that was missing were the sunglasses. "So, you're finally awake. Can I come in?" he asked, already on his way in the door.

Even though a nurse had told her in the emergency room, just before she went into the operating room, that her partner was going to be okay, she was relieved to see him in the flesh. She fought the tears that stung the backs of her eye-lids.

"I would have brought you flowers," he told her, approaching the bed. "But they just released me, and I couldn't find anything that wasn't already dead in the gift shop downstairs."

She laughed, then gripped her chest with both arms. "Ouch. Don't do that. Don't make me laugh."

He sat down on the edge of her hospital bed. For a moment there was an awkward silence. She had a feeling they both had a lot to say to each other—it was just going to take some time.

"Hey, how'd you get released so quickly?" she asked.

"Good looks. Charm." He grinned. "That and the fact that I had a clean shot through the shoulder and you had a punctured lung and some other gooey stuff I didn't want to hear about."

She grabbed her chest again.

"Easy, there." He took her hand and lifted it to his lips. "I don't know how to thank you for saving Liza Jane's life, M.K.," he said, his voice cracking with emotion.

She didn't fight the tears this time. It was all the medications she was taking—the painkillers, she told herself—that were preventing her from controlling her sentiments. "I'm just so glad you're both all right. I was afraid . . ."

"I know." He kissed her hand again and then pressed it between his two larger hands. "So how'd you know it was her? The M.E."

"I tried to call you," she said quickly. "There was no answer, not at home or on your cell."

"My cell was dead. When I got back from Philadelphia, I went looking for Liza Jane."

"I knew Dr. Wood had something to do with the killings when I heard her audio recordings of the autopsies." She looked down at the white sheets sheepishly. "I sort of borrowed them from her office that day while she was in court."

"These were the same tapes she conveniently kept forgetting to send over," he said, obviously upset with himself.

"When I heard her talking about the body parts that were missing, how perfect they were, I could just feel something in her voice." She looked up at him. "But how did you know to go to the morgue?"

He shook his head as if it was a mystery. "I went to the dorm, looking for Liza Jane. Her roommate told me she had an interview with Dr. Wood."

"That made you suspicious?"

"Not at all. I was ready to go home. Chew Liza Jane out the next day. Then I got this strange feeling." He hesitated. "After what happened with Mark and Laura, I haven't been able to trust my instincts. I was so far off base that night . . ." He glanced away, taking a moment to get hold of himself. "M.K., I knew I needed to get to Annapolis. I actually heard Liza Jane call my name *in Ashview*, and I still almost—"

"That doesn't matter," she assured him, looking up into those killer blue eyes. "What matters is that you did listen to your intuition, your instinct, whatever you want to call it."

He smiled grimly. Nodded. "Yeah, I guess you're right."

"I guess I am." He didn't let go of her hand, so she didn't let go of his. "So, is this the strangest case you've ever heard of in your life?" She lay back on her pillow, feeling a little dizzy all of a sudden. "It still doesn't make complete sense to me."

"Well, she . . . he . . . it *was* crazy. I guess it's not ever going to make complete sense to us. You're not going to believe what we found in her apartment. But, from what we've pieced together from what Dr. Wood told Liza Jane and the psychiatric records we were able to obtain, she'd had an identity problem since birth. As what they call a *true hermaphrodite*, she really was both sexes."

"Even after she had the surgery," M.K. said softly. "Crackhow told me medical records have been located. She actually had surgery to have her—"

"Please." He pulled his hand from hers and held it up. "Don't say it."

M.K. chuckled. Gingerly. Even breathing still hurt. "I guess she was never able to recover from those frat boys trying to rape her. Finding out and telling everyone." She looked at him. "So I can see killing college students. They hurt her. She wanted to hurt them back." She frowned. "But why cut parts of their bodies off? Why take them?"

"I guess it had something to do with what you heard her say on those autopsy recordings. Something about perfect body parts."

"Male and female," she said softly. "Parts of a whole."

"A whole, perfect person that she would never be, I guess."

"Incredible," M.K. breathed. "Sick."

"And a little pathetic," he mused. "Well, I guess I better get going." He rose from the bed. "I promised Liza Jane I'd come by and see the new baby."

"A little girl. I heard." M.K. could feel the tears welling again. *What was with this medication?*

"Yup, another little girl. Best thing is, it was apparently enough to snap Mark out of whatever funk he was in. He's vowed to stop drinking. He's been an alcoholic his whole life, you know. Just fell off the wagon. But he started going to AA again. I think he's going to be okay."

"That's good to hear."

He reached out to brush her hand with his fingertips. "Hey, Liza Jane is supposedly going to get to name the new baby. She asked me to ask you what M.K. stood for."

She closed her eyes for a minute. It was almost time for her pain medication again. Her head was beginning to swim. "I know very well you know. You looked it up in my service records."

"First day."

She smiled. Opened her eyes.

"So I'm thinking they'll name her Mary Katherine. Call her Katie."

"*Katie.*" M.K. smiled. "I like that. My mother would like it."

"You get some sleep."

"Will you come back later?"

"If you want me to."

She met his gaze. "I want you to."

"Then I'll be here." He leaned over and brushed his lips against hers. It was a lingering kiss, one that held promise. "Hey, by the way," he said, looking into her eyes. "What's this I heard from my daughter about you calling someone a bitch?"

M.K. burst into laughter. She was still holding her chest when he walked out the door.